"Once in a very great while, an author does everything right—as Koontz has in this marvelous novel [which] features electrifying tension and suspense, plus a few walloping surprises.... This thriller also stands out for its brilliant tightrope walk between the amusing and the macabre.... Above all ... Koontz has created a hero whose honest, humble voice will resonate with many.... This is Koontz working at his pinnacle, providing terrific entertainment that deals seriously with some of the deepest themes of human existence: the nature of evil, the grip of fate and the power of love."
—*Publishers Weekly* (starred review)

"If Stephen King is the Rolling Stones of novels ... Koontz is the Beatles." —*Playboy*

"One of Koontz's best novels ... a darkly humorous literary pastiche ... Packed with plenty of original surprises, and at least one lump-in-your-throat moment." —*The Denver Post*

"Koontz merrily takes bizarre situations and makes them completely believable. For a chiller, the book is surprisingly warm, set among charming eccentrics.... Odd Thomas describes himself as merely a fry cook who leads an unusual life; Koontz ... serves this one up tasty and hot." —*People* (critic's choice)

"While still sustaining the requisite level of creepiness, Mr. Koontz manages to tell a breezy, overtly inspirational story that should attract a few fans of its own.... Vonnegut-style fancifulness."
—*The New York Times*

"Chilling and moving. *Odd Thomas* is a brilliantly observed chronicle of good and evil."
—*Norwich Evening News*

"*Odd Thomas* is one of Koontz's finest books, and Odd himself is a superb character. A hit."
—*The Independent on Sunday* (London)

"Dean Koontz straddles the genres. . . . *Odd Thomas* is certainly a page-turner. . . . A read-at-a-sitting novel—with a terrific final twist." —*The Observer* (London)

"Odd Thomas becomes exactly the kind of hero that's needed. . . . Koontz keeps the tension high, the suspense long, and the humor on the wry side as *Odd Thomas* builds to an explosive and heart-wrenching end." —*South Florida Sun-Sentinel*

"What makes *Odd Thomas* a remarkable read is the author's masterful characterization. . . . These characters become a part of the reader's life."
—*Rocky Mountain News*

"*Odd Thomas* is one of Koontz's most beguiling novels. Strange, eerie, packed with characters who steal your heart, and events that could happen in your own hometown. The author's own philosophy slips into this tale of ordinary people in extraordinary circumstances as gently as a dream touches your heart. . . . Little life lessons light as air, yet deep as the ocean."
—*Tulsa World*

"The plot simmers and boils as Koontz builds his signature level of suspense [which] reaches an unbearable level. Uplifting . . . Odd Thomas is another name for courage, truth, and devotion to your fellow man, and I liked him a lot." —Baton Rouge *Advocate*

## FOREVER ODD

"Odd's strange gifts, coupled with his intelligence and self-effacing humor, make him one of the most quietly authoritative characters in recent popular fiction."
—*Publishers Weekly* (starred review)

"The nice young fry cook with the occult powers is [Koontz's] most likable creation. . . . Candid, upright, amusing and sometimes withering."
—*The New York Times*

"A marvelously narrated cat-and-mouse game."
—New York *Daily News*

"Good-to-the-last-page enthralling . . . stranglehold suspense." —*Booklist*

"An inventive . . . mix of suspense, whimsy and up-lift . . . It's refreshing to come across a character as good-hearted as Odd. [Koontz] is an interesting writer with a voice all his own." —*The Washington Post*

"Heartfelt and provocative . . . a wonderfully rich and entertaining story." —*Chicago Sun-Times*

"Concise, addictive . . . chills, action and suspense . . . signature Koontz . . . He has been delivering uplifting messages in the context of a fictional genre better known for cheap thrills. . . . Odd is one of Koontz's most compelling heroes. . . . A worthwhile and highly entertaining read." —*The Flint Journal*

# BROTHER ODD

"Poignant . . . quick-moving . . . Koontz deftly mixes [in] humor . . . as he tackles the big questions: Can humans prove that God exists? And why is Elvis scared to go to Heaven?" —*People* (4 stars)

"Koontz gives his character wit, good humor, a familiarity with the dark side of humanity—and moral outrage." —*USA Today*

"Supernatural thrills with a side of laughs . . . Odd Thomas's latest adventure will make a believer out of even the hardest-nosed soul." —*The Denver Post*

"An irresistibly offbeat mix of [the] supernatural . . . and laugh-out-loud humor." —*Publishers Weekly*

"Thrilling, rather poignant . . . heart-stopping . . . Terrific characterization and patient plotting mark Koontz's work, and this novel about the triumph of modesty over hubris proves exemplary on both counts. A work both exciting and engaging—and with its heart in the right place." —*Kirkus Reviews* (starred review)

"An unforgettable character in another unforgettable book!" —*Romantic Times* (top pick)

# ODD HOURS

"One of the most remarkable and appealing characters in current fiction . . . The other characters are nearly as colorful. . . . Beautifully written, with frequent literary allusions . . . and nuggets of homespun wisdom . . . another literary home run."
　　　　　　　—*The Virginian-Pilot*

"Koontz's writing in the Odd Thomas novels is among his most crisp as he imbues these novels with bits of philosophy about identity and destiny. There also is a stunningly accurate and heartfelt passage about love."
—*South Florida Sun-Sentinel*

"Another spellbinder . . . Odd Thomas stands on the brink of his greatest adventure. . . . The person we all aspire to be." —Binghamton *Press & Sun-Bulletin*

## ODD APOCALYPSE

"Wry, offbeat . . . This supernatural thriller surely ranks as one of the series' funniest."
—*Publishers Weekly*

"Odd Thomas is the greatest character Dean Koontz has ever created. He's funny, humble, immensely likable, courageous, and just a joy to read about. . . . *Odd Apocalypse* [has] really got everything a great book needs. The characters are complicated and interesting. The story is very unique and provides a great deal of suspense. The ending is open enough that you crave more, but aren't left on a cliffhanger. . . . There's a lot to love about every Odd book. . . . This brilliant series . . . has stayed strong." —*Seattle Post-Intelligencer*

"[An] astonishing series . . . spooktacular!"
—*RT Book Reviews* (4½ stars)

"This is the most fanciful . . . Odd Thomas escapade. . . . An sf-tinged tale seemingly indebted to H. G. Wells (*The Time Machine*, *The Island of Dr. Moreau*), H. P. Lovecraft (the Herbert West stories), and Orson Welles (*Citizen Kane*). Koontz makes Odd's narrative voice as winning as ever." —*Booklist*

"A fast and frightening tale . . . Koontz blends steam-punk machines, time travel and Shakespearean wisdom [and] play[s] with descriptive language and humor in the face of danger." —*Bookreporter*

"With this offering Odd's fanbase . . . is certain to grow." —*Library Journal*

## DEEPLY ODD

"There's never anything predictable about an Odd Thomas adventure. Another satisfying entry in this wildly popular series. It's Koontz, and it's Odd. Class dismissed." —*Booklist*

"Koontz's unique hero Odd Thomas' life takes another wild turn in the newest installment of this mind-bending series. . . . Koontz is a true master of blending the macabre and fantastical and somehow making it feel grounded in reality."
—*RT Book Reviews* (4½ stars)

# By Dean Koontz

*Innocence* • *77 Shadow Street* • *What the Night Knows*
*Breathless* • *Relentless* • *Your Heart Belongs to Me*
*The Darkest Evening of the Year* • *The Good Guy*
*The Husband* • *Velocity* • *Life Expectancy*
*The Taking* • *The Face* • *By the Light of the Moon*
*One Door Away From Heaven* • *From the Corner of His Eye*
*False Memory* • *Seize the Night* • *Fear Nothing*
*Mr. Murder* • *Dragon Tears* • *Hideaway* • *Cold Fire*
*The Bad Place* • *Midnight* • *Lightning* • *Watchers*
*Strangers* • *Twilight Eyes* • *Darkfall* • *Phantoms*
*Whispers* • *The Mask* • *The Vision* • *The Face of Fear*
*Night Chills* • *Shattered* • *The Voice of the Night*
*The Servants of Twilight* • *The House of Thunder*
*The Key to Midnight* • *The Eyes of Darkness*
*Shadowfires* • *Winter Moon* • *The Door to December*
*Dark Rivers of the Heart* • *Icebound* • *Strange Highways*
*Intensity* • *Sole Survivor* • *Ticktock*
*The Funhouse* • *Demon Seed*

ODD THOMAS
*Odd Thomas* • *Forever Odd* • *Brother Odd* • *Odd Hours*
*Odd Interlude* • *Odd Apocalypse* • *Deeply Odd*

FRANKENSTEIN
*Prodigal Son* • *City of Night* • *Dead and Alive*
*Lost Souls* • *The Dead Town*

*A Big Little Life: A Memoir of a Joyful Dog Named Trixie*

# Dean Koontz

# Deeply
# Odd

*An Odd Thomas Novel*

Bantam Books  New York

2014 Bantam Books Mass Market Edition

Copyright © 2013 by Dean Koontz
Excerpt from *The City* by Dean Koontz copyright © 2014 by Dean Koontz

Published in the United States by Bantam Books, an imprint of Random House, a division of Random House LLC, a Penguin Random House Company, New York.

Title page art from an original photograph by Benjamin Earwicker

A signed, limited edition has been previously printed by Charnel House. Charnelhouse.com

BANTAM BOOKS and the HOUSE colophon are registered trademarks of Random House LLC.

Originally published in hardcover in the United States by Bantam Books, an imprint of Random House, a division of Random House LLC, in 2013.

This book contains an excerpt from the forthcoming book *The City* by Dean Koontz. This excerpt has been set for this edition only and may not reflect the final content of the forthcoming edition.

ISBN 978-0-553-59308-2
eBook ISBN 978-0-345-53569-6

Cover art and design: Scott Biel
Cover images: (man's face) Florence Caplain; (truck) Allan Davey/ Masterfile

Printed in the United States of America

www.bantamdell.com

9 8 7 6 5 4 3 2 1

Bantam Books mass market edition: June 2014

*This book is dedicated to Stephen Sommers,*
*who kept his promises*
*in a world where almost no one does.*
*With admiration and affection*
*from the Odd author.*

They followed the light and the shadow,
and the light led them forward to light
and the shadow led them to darkness.

—T. S. ELIOT,
Choruses from *The Rock,* VII

# Deeply Odd

# One

BEFORE DAWN, I WOKE IN DARKNESS TO the ringing of a tiny bell, the thimble-size bell that I wore on a chain around my neck: three bursts of silvery sound, a brief silence after each. I was lying on my back in bed, utterly motionless, yet the bell rang three times again. The vibrations that shivered through my bare chest seemed much too strong to have been produced by such a tiny clapper. A third set of three rings followed, and then only silence. I waited and wondered until dawn crept down the sky and across the bedroom windows.

Later that morning in early March, when I walked downtown to buy blue jeans and a few pairs of socks, I met a guy who had a .45 pistol and a desire to commit a few murders. From that encounter, the day grew uglier as surely as the sun moved from east to west.

My name is Odd Thomas. I have accepted my oddness. And I am no longer surprised that I am drawn to trouble as reliably as iron to a magnet.

Nineteen months ago, when I was twenty, I should have been riddled with bullets in that big-news shopping-mall shoot-out in Pico Mundo, a desert town in California. They say that I saved a lot of people in my hometown. Yet many died. I didn't. I have to live with that.

Stormy Llewellyn, the girl I loved more than life itself, was one of those who died that day. I saved others, but I couldn't save her. I have to live with that, too. Living is the price I pay for failing her, a high price that must be paid every morning that I wake.

In the nineteen months since that day of death, I have traveled in search of the meaning of my life. I learn by going where I have to go.

Currently I rented a quaint, furnished three-bedroom cottage in a quiet coastal town a couple of hundred miles from Pico Mundo. The front porch faced the sea, and yellow bougainvillea cascaded across half the roof.

Annamaria, whom I had known only since late January, occupied one of the bedrooms. She appeared to be ready to give birth in about a month, but she claimed that she had been pregnant for a long time and insisted that she would be pregnant longer still.

Although she said many things that I failed to understand, I believed that she always spoke the truth. She was mysterious but not deceptive.

We were friends, never paramours. A lover who is enigmatic will most likely prove to be a cataclysm waiting to happen. But a charming friend whose usual warmth is raveled through with moments of cool inscrutability can be an intriguing companion.

The morning when I set out on a shopping expedition, Annamaria followed me as far as the porch. She said, "Daylight savings time doesn't start for another five days."

At the bottom of the steps, I turned to look at her. She wasn't a beauty, but she wasn't plain, either. Her clear pale skin appeared to be as smooth as soap, and her large dark eyes, which reflected the sparkling sea, seemed as deep as galaxies. In sneakers, gray-khaki pants, and a baggy sweater, she was so petite that she might have been a child dressed in her father's clothes.

Not sure why she had mentioned daylight savings time, I said, "I won't be long. I'll be back hours before sunset."

"Darkness doesn't fall to a predictable schedule. Darkness can overwhelm you any time of the day, as you know too well."

She once told me that there are people who want to kill her. Although she had said no more and had not identified her would-be murderers, I believed that she was as truthful about this as about all other things.

"I'll stay here if you're in danger."

"You're the one in danger, young man. Here or

there, anywhere, you're the one perpetually on the cliff's edge."

She was eighteen, and I was nearly twenty-two, but when she called me *young man,* it always felt right. She possessed an air of timelessness, as if she might have lived in any century of recorded history, or in all of them.

"Do what you must," she said, "but come back to us."

*Do what you must* sounded ominously significant, not the language one might use to send a friend off to buy socks.

From behind Annamaria and beyond a window, Tim watched solemnly. Crowding close to him on the left and right, paws on the windowsill, gazing out at me, were our two dogs, a golden retriever named Raphael and a white German shepherd named Boo. Only nine years old, Tim had been with us for over one month, after we rescued him from an estate called Roseland, in the sleepy town of Montecito. I've written about that ordeal in a previous volume of these memoirs. We were his only family now. Because of his unique history, we would soon need to fabricate an identity into which he could grow in the years to come.

My life is as odd as my name.

Tim waved at me. I waved at Tim.

Just before stepping out of the house, I had asked the boy if he wanted to accompany me. But with a benign smile, Annamaria had said that neither Xerxes nor Leonidas had invited small children to accompany them to Thermopylae.

In 480 B.C., three hundred Spartans under the command of Leonidas had for a while held at bay two hundred thousand Persians under Xerxes in the battle of Thermopylae, before being slaughtered. I failed to see the similarity between my modest shopping expedition and one of the fiercest military engagements in history.

Even though it is always fruitless to seek an explanation from Annamaria when she makes such baffling statements, I considered asking for amplification. But she had opened the door for me, had waved me out of the kitchen, followed me onto the porch, and stood smiling at me as I looked back at her from the bottom of the steps. The moment to press her for elucidation seemed to have passed.

Annamaria's smile is so comforting that, in its radiance, you can almost believe that this world offers nothing more threatening than what you'd find in Pooh Corner—in spite of her references to the slaughter of the Spartans.

I said, "The bell rang last night."

"Yes, I know."

I didn't think she could have heard it from her room, through two closed doors.

Previously she had told me that if the bell rang in the night, we would soon thereafter move on to a new place.

She said, "I'll see you again when the wind blows

the water white and black," and she turned away, retreating into the cottage.

Beyond the beach, the sea spread blue to the horizon. The day remained still and mild, and the sky was so clear that it seemed I should be able to discern the stars in spite of the sunshine that concealed them.

Not mystified but certainly bewildered, I walked north half a mile to the heart of the village, with a wariness that I hadn't felt minutes earlier. Shaded by ancient California live oaks, the downtown shopping area was a three-lane street flanked by just six blocks of stores, restaurants, and quaint inns. If you wanted a real town, you had to go up the coast to Santa Barbara.

I didn't know that a guy would soon offer to neuter me or that he would be carrying a pistol fitted with a sound suppressor. I have a psychic gift that occasionally includes a prophetic dream, but when awake, I do not see moments of the future.

When I first noticed the truck that pricked my curiosity, I did not realize that a formidable enemy was behind the steering wheel. I didn't even get a glimpse of the driver.

My unrelenting curiosity has gotten me in big trouble. It has also saved my butt a lot of times. On balance, it's a plus. And it isn't true that curiosity killed the cat. Usually, cats are done in by coyotes or Peterbilts.

Anyway, my curiosity is part of my gift, my sixth sense. I am compelled to indulge it.

The truck was an eighteen-wheel ProStar+. The cool-looking, aerodynamic tractor with the massive grille and lizard-eye headlights was painted red and black with sparkly silver striping. The black trailer bore no corporate logo or advertising.

As I reached the shopping district, the eighteen-wheeler cruised past me, into the heart of the village, heading north. Without realizing what I was doing, I picked up my pace to a racewalk. When the ProStar+ braked at a stop sign, I almost caught up with it.

As the behemoth accelerated across the intersection, I began to run, which was when I realized that I knew intuitively something about the truck must be evil.

Well, not the ProStar+ itself. I'm not one who believes that a vehicle can be possessed by a demonic spirit and, driverless, speed around town to run down people for the thrill of tasting blood with its tires, any more than I believe that Herbie, the Volkswagen in that series of Disney movies, had a mind of its own with a desire to bring lovers together and to thwart villains. If you believe the former, you have to believe the latter, and the next thing you know, you'll be taking your Ford, with its sexy GPS voice, to the car wash just to see her naked and soapy.

I fell rapidly behind the truck, but then, near the northern end of the village, it turned left off the street, toward a supermarket. If the driver had been making a delivery, he would have gone behind the building to the loading dock. Instead, he pulled to a stop across several parking spaces at the end of the lot nearest to the street.

By the time I reached the eighteen-wheeler, where it stood in the trembling shade of a row of breeze-stirred eucalyptuses, it was unattended. Catching my breath, I walked slowly around the vehicle, looking it over.

My intuition bristled like the hackles on a dog. Heightened intuition is part of my sixth sense.

The day was mild, the breeze mellow, but the area immediately around the truck was colder than could be explained by eucalyptus shade alone. When I put the palm of one hand against the sidewall of the trailer, it felt as though the driver had pulled off the road to wait out a blinding snow squall at high elevation.

This wasn't what truckers called a reefer, which hauled frozen food. No refrigeration unit was mounted on the front wall of the trailer, behind the tractor.

I stood on the step beside the fuel tank to peer through a side window of the cab. Leather seats, wood panels and trim, an angled middle console with CD player and GPS, and a roomy sleeping box behind the cockpit provided a cozy environment.

From the overhead citizens-band radio with the drop-down microphone hung a string of red beads onto which were threaded five white skulls the size of plums. They appeared to have been carved by hand, perhaps from bone.

People decorated the driver's compartments of their vehicles with all manner of items. Miniature

skulls no more proved this driver dangerous than a
dangling figurine of the Little Mermaid would have
proved him to be an innocent dreamer.

Nevertheless, I went around to the back of the rig
to study the rear doors of the trailer. Maybe I needed
a key, maybe not.

Before I could ascertain how the long latch bolts
worked, a low silky voice asked, "Do you like my
truck, dirtbag?"

He stood about six feet two, which gave him a few
inches on me. Although he looked perhaps thirty-
five, his spiky hair was white, as were his eyebrows.
He had Nordic features and a melanoma-doesn't-
scare-me tanning-booth glow. His eyes were the precise blue of the water in a toilet bowl equipped with
one of those sanitizers—and just as appealing.

Ever hopeful that even a situation that seemed
fraught with the potential for violence might turn
out to be an occasion for mutual understanding and
camaraderie, I pretended not to have heard the *dirtbag* part.

I said, "Yes, sir, she's a beauty."

"You want to know what I'm hauling? Curious,
are you?"

"No, sir. Not me. Just an admirer of trucks."

His teeth were so unnaturally white that I felt in
danger of sustaining a radiation burn from his smile.

"Are you a believer?" he asked.

In the circumstances, the question seemed so
loaded that any too-specific answer might offend.

"Well, sir, I guess we all believe in one thing or another."

He looked as though he believed in rhinestone-cowboy clothing. His custom, pointy-toed black boots were inlaid with patterns of white snakeskin. Black jeans with scarlet stitching along the hems, inseams, and pockets. Red silk shirt with black stitching. A black bolo tie with what might have been a carved-bone slide in the form of a serpent's head and matching bone aglets. His black sports coat featured scarlet lapels and collar peppered with sequins.

"If you're a believer," he said, "how many steps are there in the stairway to Heaven?"

"Well, sir, I'm no theologian. Just a fry cook out of work."

"There are just *two* steps in the stairway to Heaven, dirtbag. The first step is touching my truck. The second is not explaining yourself to my satisfaction."

"Sir, the truth is, she's a beauty and I've always wanted to be a long-haul trucker."

"You never wanted to be a long-haul trucker."

"I will admit that's a stretch, but she *is* a beauty."

The .45 Sig Sauer with silencer appeared in his hand the way a dove appears in the hand of a good magician, as if it materialized out of thin air. Worse, the pistol was aimed point-blank at my crotch, which wouldn't have worried me so much if it had been a dove.

"How would you like to be a eunuch, never be troubled again by performance anxiety?"

He fried me with his bright smile, and I was like an over-easy egg on the griddle, waiting for the spatula.

"I wouldn't much like that, sir."

The line of eucalyptus trees largely screened us from passing traffic in the street. People came and went from the supermarket parking lot, but they were all much closer to the building than to us. They weren't interested in a couple of truckers, and the cowboy's body prevented them from seeing the gun.

"You think I won't do it right here in the open. But you'd be surprised what people don't see. They won't hear the shot. You'll drop before you get the breath to scream. The instant you drop, I'll stomp your throat, crush your windpipe. Then I'll handle you like you were a drunk, prop you against one of those trees, like you're a hobo sleeping off a bender. Nobody wants to check out a piss-drunk hobo. And I guarantee, no one will remember me. No one will have seen me."

I recognized sincerity in his toilet-water eyes, and I knew that, as crazy as it sounded, he might flush me out of this world.

Being as I'm a low-key guy and as ordinary-looking as any other unemployed fry cook, considering also how genuinely terrified I must have looked, he didn't expect me to seize his wrist in both of my hands. I forced the muzzle of the Sig Sauer away from my dangly things, farther down between my legs.

He squeezed off a shot, which made less noise

than did the slug ricocheting off the pavement near my left foot.

Maybe I couldn't have twisted his wrist hard enough to make him drop the weapon, but something extraordinary happened. When I touched him, even as the bullet left the sound suppressor with a soft *thup,* the parking lot went away, and for a few seconds a vision in my mind's eye swelled outward to encircle me.

I seemed to be standing in a moonless night, before a stainless-steel platform on steel legs, a round stage, lit by the leaping flames of four torches fixed to tall poles. On the stage, in straight-backed chairs, sat three children: a boy of about eight, a girl of perhaps six, and an older girl who might have been ten. Something was wrong with them. They sat wide-eyed but slack-mouthed, their hands limp in their laps. Emotionless. Drugged. A white-haired man in a blood-red suit, black shirt, and black mask ascended to the stage on steel steps. He was carrying a flamethrower. He torched the children.

The vision burst like a bubble, reality returned, and the cowboy and I staggered backward from each other, the pistol on the pavement between us. His stunned expression and a wildness in his eyes told me two things: First, he'd seen the same vision that I had seen; second, he was the masked man in the red suit, and he already intended at some future date to set helpless children afire in an insane act of homicidal performance art.

I had just experienced my first portent of the future that did not come in the form of a prophetic dream.

He went for the dropped pistol, but I was able to kick it under the eighteen-wheeler even as his fingers were an inch from the prize.

As if from a forearm sheath, a knife slid into his right hand, and a thin six-inch blade sprang out of the yellow handle.

I dislike guns, but I'm no fan of knives, and I carry neither. I turned away from him and ran across the parking lot, toward the market, where he wouldn't dare slash at me in front of witnesses.

Suddenly the entire world seemed to have turned hostile, as if the spirit of ultimate darkness had arrived to rule, his hour come round at last. Even my morning shadow, following as I ran westward, seemed to have ill intentions, as if it would catch me, drag me down.

When I glanced back, the cowboy trucker wasn't coming after me. I couldn't see him anywhere. I slowed to a fast walk, so as not to draw attention to myself, and when the automatic door slid aside, I went into the coolness of the market.

If I had been in Pico Mundo, my hometown, I would have known what to do. The chief of police there, Wyatt Porter, understood me and believed in me. On my say-so, he would have detained the cowboy and searched the truck.

But I had been on the road for some time now,

going where my unusual talents were most needed, drawn by siren songs that I could not hear but to which my blood responded. Nobody in this place knew me, and I would sound like just another drug-addled paranoid, another piece of sad human wreckage of the kind that littered the landscape of an America that seemed to be rapidly fading out of history in a world growing darker by the day.

In the market, I stood at a closed checkout station, pretending to be searching for a particular magazine among the many offered, but in fact watching the customer doors at the north and south ends of the building.

Little more than a month earlier, in a town called Magic Beach, I had for the first time, by touch, recognized a potential murderer. On that occasion, into my mind's eye—and into his—had erupted a scene from a nightmare of nuclear Armageddon that I'd dreamed the previous night, and I had known that he must be part of a conspiracy to atomize American cities. But I had not dreamed of these children set afire upon a stage.

I didn't expect the cowboy to follow me. I expected him instead to board his big rig and head for whatever highway to Hell might be programmed into his GPS. The vision surely rattled him as much as it did me. But as I long ago learned, expectations are fragile and easily shattered.

The cowboy came through the north doors, spotted me at once, and approached purposefully. He looked like a star in some parallel-world version of Nashville's Grand Ole Opry, one that featured *maniac* country singers.

I hurried down the cereal aisle, turned right, and crossed the big store to the produce section, buying time to think.

Even if I could find a sympathetic shopper or a credulous clerk, or an off-duty police officer picking through the McIntosh apples, I couldn't seek help from anyone because of the aftermath of my few weeks in Magic Beach. Bad people were in jail in that town, and other bad people were dead. Homeland Security and the FBI had been brought in at the end of those events by an anonymous phone call that I placed; and now they were seeking someone fitting my description, though they had no name. I dared not attract the attention of the police in this smaller town, which was little more than a hundred miles farther along the coast from Magic Beach.

In this big, complex, often mysterious world, I don't pretend to know much. How to make fluffy pancakes might be the most important knowledge that I possess. In spite of my ignorance, I know without a doubt that if federal officers of any agency were to suspect that I possess paranormal abilities, I would spend the rest of my life in custody, being used for their purposes.

I would also be studied and might be the subject of unpleasant experiments. I have a perhaps irrational but nonetheless genuine fear of scientists sawing open my skull while I'm awake and sticking pins in various parts of my brain to determine if they can make me cluck like a chicken or bark like a dog, or sing the lead role in *The Phantom of the Opera*.

A spectacle in black and red, the cowboy arrived in the produce department. His pistol and his knife were tucked out of sight, but his face announced his madness as obviously as if he had been shouting gibberish and capering like a monkey.

At that moment, I realized something more striking about this man than just his wardrobe and his taste for psychotic violence. In spite of his flamboyance, he seemed to elicit no special interest from the shoppers or the market staff around us. They appeared all but oblivious of him.

Of course, a lot of people these days have developed a kind of radar to spot the numerous lunatics among us, and when that little alarm of recognition goes off in their minds, they keep their heads down and avert their eyes. They go about their business as if they are tuned out of here and now, instead tuned in to their private realities: *Look at that weird dude with blue fire shooting out of his eyes. And look at these peaches! These are lovely peaches! I have never seen finer peaches than these superb peaches! And look at those grapes. I'm going to buy some peaches and grapes. Or maybe I should mosey over to the baked goods and browse there until I have thought over this . . . this scary peaches-and-grapes thing for a while.*

But I suspected that he drew no attention for some other reason, which eluded me.

The cowboy approached me and stopped on the other side of the wide display bin, which offered four varieties of apples on my side, potatoes and sweet potatoes and leeks on his side. His fixed smile reminded me of a hyena, if a hyena had an excellent oral-health plan and a first-rate dentist.

He said, "You come with me and answer some questions about what happened back there, and I'll kill you easy. You don't come, I'll blow away a couple of these innocent women shopping for groceries, and *then* I'll kill you. Want that on your conscience?"

I didn't think this was a guy who ever bluffed. He did what he wanted to do and moved on.

As crazy as he might be, however, he didn't want to go to prison or to be shot down by police responding to the outrage that he had just now proposed.

When I didn't answer him, he drew the silencer-equipped pistol from under his sports coat and shot a cantaloupe on the pile that an elderly woman was examining. Chunks of rind and orange melon flesh flew into the air and spattered the shopper.

She startled backward. "Oh! Oh, goodness!"

Although the cowboy still held the Sig Sauer, when the woman looked around in perplexity, her gaze rested longer on me than on him, and the pistol didn't seem to register with her. She was bewildered, not afraid.

Apologizing as if from time to time these darn

cantaloupes just blew up on people, a produce-department clerk hurried to the elderly woman, showing no interest in the cowboy. The other customers focused on the clerk and the melon-soiled lady.

The trucker's hyena smile grew wider.

I remembered something that he had said when he threatened to make a eunuch of me in the parking lot: *You think I won't do it right here in the open. But you'd be surprised what people don't see.*

He expected me to run, whereupon he would have to shoot me in the back and forget about the interrogation that he wanted to conduct. But as he might have remembered from our recent encounter in the parking lot, expectations often don't pan out, and what he did *not* expect was an assault with high-velocity fruit.

Without taking time for a windup, I snatched a Red Delicious apple off the display in front of me and put a spin on the pitch. It hit him dead-center in the face, he staggered backward, and a second Red Delicious bounced off his forehead as blood streamed from his nose, stunning him so that he reflexively dropped his gun. I had been a pitcher on our high-school baseball team; and I could still put the ball where I wanted it, with wicked speed. Moving fast along the display bin, I plucked up a couple of Granny Smiths, which are hard little green numbers used for baking. The first hit his mouth maybe two seconds after he took the Red Delicious to the head, and the second caught him in the throat, dropping him to the floor, overwhelmed by apples.

Shoppers cried out, staring at me as if *I* were the deranged man and as though the costumed cowboy with the silencer-equipped pistol were as innocent as a lamb set upon by a rabid wolf.

The produce-department clerk shouted at me, I threw a Granny Smith with no intention of hitting him, he ducked, he popped up, and I threw another Granny Smith. He turned and fled, crying out for help, and all the terrified customers fled after him.

Around the other side of the display bins, the apple-stunned cowboy, bleeding from his nose and from a split lip, was on his hands and knees, reaching for the pistol that he had dropped. He would retrieve it before I could kick it away from him.

I ran from the produce department. Past displays of exotic imported crackers, cookies, and candies. Left into the long back aisle. Past coolers offering cheeses and a bewildering variety of pickles.

Before I got to the fresh-meat display, I slammed through a pair of swinging doors, into an immense stockroom with tall metal shelving units to the left and right.

A couple of stock boys in white aprons looked up from their work as I sprinted through their domain, but they wisely did not pursue me. Now I was the beneficiary of that lunatic-identifying radar that I mentioned earlier. As if desperately fleeing men raced wild-eyed through this place a few times every day, the stock boys continued preparing huge carts full of bagged potato chips and Cheez Doodles for delivery to the selling floor.

Passing a cart on which were stacked open cases of canned goods, I borrowed a two-pound can of baked beans, and then another.

At the back of the stockroom, in line with the door by which I had entered, another metal door led to a loading dock and the service alley. I left it ajar, to indicate where I'd gone, and stood with my back against the building wall, a can of beans in each hand.

Such is the absurd and violent nature of my life, that I am not infrequently reduced to battles involving highly bizarre bad guys and unconventional weapons that Mr. Matt Damon and Mr. Daniel Craig *never* have to deal with when, always solemn and dignified, they save the world in their movies.

I expected the cowboy to follow me as quickly as he was able. He didn't seem to be a guy who quit easily, nor did he seem to be one who would proceed with caution. When he plunged through the door, eager not to lose track of me, I would bean him with one can and try to smack the gun out of his hand with the other.

After a minute or so, I began to wonder if I had disabled him more than I'd realized. At about the minute-and-a-half mark, the door opened slowly. One of the stock boys warily peeked out, reeled back in pale-faced fright, as if I were Dr. Hannibal

Lecter holding two severed heads, and hurriedly returned to his Cheez Doodles.

I put down the cans, jumped off the loading dock,
and sprinted toward the north end of the building.

If the cowboy decided to disengage, I needed to
get the license number of his truck. I could make an
anonymous call to the highway patrol, accuse him
of hauling contraband of one kind or another, and
give them an excuse to look in that black trailer.

Although my special intuition told me that he had
not yet abducted the children, there would almost
certainly be *something* incriminating in his trailer.

I turned the corner, ran along the north wall, and
burst into the parking lot, where sunlight dazzled
off a hundred windshields. The truck was gone.

I hurried among the parked cars, slipped between two trees in the row of tall eucalyptuses at the
end of the lot, halted on the sidewalk, and looked
both ways along the street. No red, black, and sparkly silver ProStar+.

From a distance came a siren.

After crossing the street, I headed south, glancing
in shop windows, just a young guy off work, with a
day to kill, not at all the kind of hooligan who would
terrorize innocent grocery shoppers with a ferocious
barrage of fruit.

I made a mental note to mail five dollars to the supermarket to pay for the damaged apples when this
business with the cowboy was concluded. I wouldn't

pay for the cantaloupe. I hadn't shot it. The maniac had shot it.

Yes, I had fled into the market, drawing the maniac after me; therefore, an argument could be made that part of the cost of the cantaloupe might be my responsibility. But the line between moral behavior and narcissistic self-righteousness is thin and difficult to discern. The man who stands before a crowd and proclaims his intention to save the seas is convinced that he is superior to a man who merely picks up his own and other people's litter on the beach, when in fact the latter is in some small way sure to make the world a better place, while the former is likely to be a monster of vanity whose crusade will lead to unintended destruction.

Not a penny for the damn cantaloupe. If I was wrong and woke up in a chamber in Hell, eternally drowning in the slime and seeds found at a cantaloupe's core, I would just have to deal with that.

As I followed the sidewalk south, the bright image of the three torched children plagued me. I didn't know when or where the cowboy trucker intended to burn them, or why. My sixth sense has limits and often frustrates more than serves me.

*Do what you must,* Annamaria had said. Her words seemed to be not merely advice meant for this moment but also a recognition of the likelihood that, after all, I would *not* be back long before sunset.

I really needed socks and a new pair of jeans. But given a choice between replenishing wardrobe items and trying my best to prevent children from being cooked alive, the correct course seemed obvious. Hurrying through the village, along a sidewalk dappled with sunshine and oak shadows, I intended to do the right thing. Ironically, in order to do the right thing, I needed to steal a car, and quickly.

# Two

THE COWBOY TRUCKER HAD WHEELS, AND I didn't. He was getting farther away by the minute.

As the siren swelled louder, rotating emergency beacons flashed far to the south, approaching.

Immediately ahead of me, a muscular man with tattooed arms and a pit-bull face sprang out of a Ford Explorer parked at the curb. Leaving the driver's door open and the engine running, making an urgent keening sound, he ran past the bank in front of which he had left the SUV, raced past two other buildings, and disappeared around the corner, as if perhaps he had a prostate as big as a grapefruit and an urge to pee that sent him rushing pell-mell toward the nearest restroom.

The bank was a sleek contemporary building with big windows. In spite of the tinted glass, I could see two men inside. They were wearing identical President-of-the-United-States masks. They held what appeared to be short-barreled pistol-grip shotguns. I figured the employees and customers must be lying on the floor. Evidently, none of them in there could hear the siren yet.

At once I climbed behind the wheel of the Explorer and closed the door. I put the SUV in gear, pulled into the street, and drove perhaps seventy or eighty yards before the racing police car swept past me on its way to the supermarket.

I have never owned a motor vehicle. If you own one, you must purchase insurance for it, repair it, wash it, wax it, fill the tank with gasoline, scrub bug remains off the windshield, periodically rotate the tires. . . . The demands of a motor vehicle never stop.

Because my sixth sense is a massive complication, I simplify my life every way that I can. I own little, and I have no desire to possess any more than I already do. I would no more buy a car than I would acquire a performing elephant.

In the past, when I had needed wheels, I'd borrowed vehicles from various friends, and I'd always returned them without damage. But I had lived in this town only a month. And because I had been pretty much hiding out and waiting for the call to action that would send me traveling once more, I had not joined a book group or claimed a personal stool in a favorite pub where everybody knew my name.

In this emergency, the only way that I could obtain a suitable vehicle was to steal one. Stealing from thieves seemed less of a crime than taking from honest people. I wouldn't go so far as to say that Providence put this Explorer before me precisely when I needed it, because I wouldn't want to imply that God collaborated with me in auto theft. But if it wasn't Providence, it was *something*.

I circled a block, returned to the main drag, and headed south this time. When I passed the bank, two well-armed presidents were standing on the sidewalk, frantically looking north and south for their getaway wheels. I felt that I should do something to alert the police to the robbery, but running these guys down seemed extreme.

They recognized the Explorer and started into the street. I waved, tramped the accelerator, and was out of shotgun range in about three seconds.

A couple of blocks south of the bank, a decapitated woman was crossing the street. In black high heels and a slinky blue dress, she appeared to be attired for a party, and she held her severed head in the crook of her left arm.

Ordinarily, I would have stopped to comfort her and see if I could do anything to help her move on from this world. But she was already dead, just a spirit now, and those three imperiled children were still alive, so the kids came first.

Rare prophetic dreams and keen intuition are not the primary aspects of my paranormal ability. If those were the only unnatural talents I possessed, I might lead a relatively ordinary life and be able to hold a job more taxing than that of a short-order cook. Say a furniture-store manager or a home-appliances repairman.

Most important and exhausting is my ability to see the spirits of the lingering dead. They are reluctant to leave this world either because they are afraid of what awaits them on the Other Side or because they remain determined to see their murderers brought to justice, or because they love this beautiful world and refuse to let go of it.

The dead don't talk. At best, they lead me to their killers or, if they weren't murdered, react to me in ways that allow me to make accurate deductions about them based on what their behavior implies. At worst, they resort to an insistent pantomime that is as annoying as the least-talented street mime who has ever pretended to walk against a nonexistent hurricane wind. In the case of a mime who won't get out of my face until I give him a dollar, I might respond to his performance with a pantomime of violent vomiting; but that seems disrespectful and even cruel when dealing with the dead.

Generally speaking, these spirits aren't threatening, but now and then one of them goes poltergeist in anger or frustration. The results can play havoc with your household budget. Trust me, no insurance company on Earth will pay on a claim that an infuriated spirit tore apart your plasma-screen TV and wrecked your family room.

In this instance, the decapitated woman did not

turn toward me beseechingly. Usually the lingering dead know that I can see them, and they are drawn to me. This one seemed oblivious of me, and I drove straight through her with no more effect than driving through a swirl of mist.

Suspended on a chain around my neck, under my sweatshirt, the tiny bell began to ring itself again, three silvery bursts of sound like those it had produced shortly before dawn.

The bell had been given to me on the night when Annamaria told me that certain unnamed people wanted to kill her. She had taken the pendant from around her neck, offered it to me, and asked, *Will you die for me?*

Amazing myself, I had at once said yes.

Now the inexplicable ringing of the bell apparently signified that my next challenge was at hand, that the time had come to move forward in my quest for meaning and purpose.

To the east, several residential streets ran parallel to the village's main artery, and to the west were Coast Highway underpasses that led to shoreside neighborhoods, but I was compelled to ignore them. I drove directly to the access road that carried me onto the southbound lanes of the Coast Highway, past the town line, with the ocean to my right, the crazier part of California a few hundred miles behind me, the somewhat less crazy part of it still about seventy miles ahead.

The final aspect of my paranormal ability is psychic magnetism. If I need to find someone and don't know where he is at the moment, I concentrate on his name or picture his face in my mind's eye, and then I walk or bicycle or drive around at random, until psychic magnetism draws me to him. Usually I find him within half an hour.

Ahead, flanked by parched meadows of pale grass stippled with widely separated live oaks, the highway rose gradually toward a crest. In this sparsely populated stretch of coast, traffic remained light. If the cowboy in the ProStar+ was ahead of me, as intuition insisted, he must be cruising beyond this hill.

The Ford Explorer was a fine machine. Sturdy, easy to handle, it rode almost as smoothly at seventy miles per hour as at sixty, only minimally less well at eighty. I looked forward to seeing how it handled at ninety.

Someone starting my memoirs with this volume might think that I'm a lawless youth, an itinerant fry-cook rebel. But I didn't steal the car to profit from it, only to get on the trail of the homicidal cowboy trucker before he receded beyond the range of my paranormal perception.

For the same reason, I broke the posted speed limit, which otherwise I would not have done. *Probably* would not have done. *Might* not have done. I must admit, the older I get, the more I like speed almost as much as I like hash browns. There's something mystical about perfect hash browns, something that stirs the soul, and the same is true of speed.

Now, ahead of me, a Honda maintained such a leisurely pace that the guy behind the wheel might have been a Zen Buddhist for whom the act of driving was a disciplined meditation more concerned with enlightenment than with progress.

Intending to pass, I glanced at my side mirror to be sure that the left lane was clear, and I discovered an eighteen-wheeler looming alarmingly close. I hadn't heard the truck, but now I did, and when I glanced at my rearview mirror, the snarling-shark grille of the ProStar+ seemed to be gnashing its chrome teeth in anticipation of a satisfying bite.

One thing I failed to disclose about psychic magnetism: Once in a while, not often but often enough to make me wonder when I will be sufficiently frazzled to require a Prozac prescription, this strange gift draws my target to me instead of drawing me to my target. This might seem to be a fine distinction of little importance, but it can be a life-or-death issue when a big rig, weighing seventy thousand pounds or more if loaded, driven by a maniac, hurtles into the rear bumper of your stolen Ford Explorer.

Before I could stomp the accelerator to the floor and try to outrun the cowboy, he rammed me hard enough to bounce the Ford off its back tires, tipping it forward for an instant. The steering wheel spun through my hands, I struggled for control, the tailgate window imploded, plastic cracked, metal tore with a banshee shriek, and I could no more regain control than I could vaporize the big rig with a well-chosen magic word.

I spat out a number of well-chosen words, but none of them was magic.

I'm not quite sure of the subsequent physics of the encounter, but somehow the Explorer turned its starboard flank to the ProStar+ and briefly stuttered violently sideways. More windows burst and the SUV noisily cast off pieces of itself, like one of those lizards that can escape by shedding at will the tail that is in the teeth of its attacker. Then, with the indifferent majesty of a freight train rolling on its rails, the big rig rumbled past, and the Ford was forced off the road, across the graveled shoulder. It plunged bow-first down a long, grassy embankment. It ricocheted off a boulder, off an ancient ficus tree, tipped, rolled, and slid on its roof about fifty feet until it came to rest where the shore grass transitioned to sand.

I wondered why the air bag hadn't deployed. But then I realized that a vehicle belonging to professional criminals might have been modified to make it not only faster and easier to handle but perhaps also to remove from it any features that might hamper them in a slam-bang pursuit with police hot behind them. Besides, they weren't the type to worry about collision injuries, any more than they would employ a BABY ON BOARD bumper sticker even if they turned from bank robbery to kidnapping.

Happily, the safety harness kept me from harm,

although now I hung upside down in the inverted vehicle, with the ocean vista above my head and the blue sky under my blown tires. I might have taken a little while to savor this unusual perspective if I hadn't smelled gasoline.

# Three

AS I CLIMBED THE MEADOWY SLOPE TOWARD the Coast Highway, I expected the Explorer to burst into flames behind me, but it merely lay in ruin, belly exposed as if it were some sad beast soon to be a meal for carrion crows.

By the time I arrived at the summit and stood on the shoulder of the road, the ProStar+ was long gone, as were the other cars and trucks that had been in the northbound and southbound lanes when the cowboy had attempted to murder me with an eighteen-wheeler. Blacktop receded into sun-baked silence, still and lonely, as if the rest of humanity had vanished from the planet while I'd ridden the runaway Ford to the shore.

Some of the people in those vehicles must have seen what happened, yet none stopped to ascertain my condition or to offer assistance. The world howls for social justice, but when it comes to social responsibility, you sometimes can't even hear crickets chirruping.

Engine noise drew my attention to the north. A car appeared in the distance, and the closer it came, the longer it grew. When it stopped on the side of the highway, in front of me, it proved to be a black superstretch Mercedes limousine.

The front tinted window on the passenger side powered down, and when I bent to peer into the limo, I discovered that the driver was a pixie. Standing, she might have been an inch short of five feet. She could see over the steering wheel only because she was perched on a firm pillow. Elderly, slight but not frail, she wore her white hair in a Peter Pan cut.

"Child," she said, "you look in need of something. Are you in need of something?"

I could see nothing to be gained and all kinds of complications that might arise if I mentioned the thoroughly wrecked Ford Explorer on the beach below.

"Well, ma'am, I need to get south in a hurry."

"South where?"

"I'm not quite sure."

"You don't know where you need to go?"

"I'll know it when I get there, ma'am."

She cocked her head and regarded me in silence for a moment, and I thought of a cockatoo, perhaps because of her white hair and the birdlike brightness of her stare.

"Are you a cutthroat murderer?" she asked.

"No, ma'am."

I chose not to say that I had sometimes killed in self-defense and to protect the innocent. Killing is different from murder, though most people tend to get nervous when you try to explain why one might be acceptable but never the other.

"Are you a rapist?"

"No, ma'am."

"You don't look like a rapist."

"Thank you."

"You don't look drug-crazed, either."

"People often tell me that, ma'am."

She squinted at me but then smiled, apparently having decided that I wasn't *trying* to be a wiseass.

"Do you have a job, child?"

"I'm a fry cook, currently unemployed."

"I don't need a fry cook."

"I think everyone does, ma'am, they just don't know it."

A Peterbilt, a motor home, and a Cadillac Escalade roared past, and we waited for silence.

She said, "What I need is a chauffeur."

"I thought you were the chauffeur."

"Isn't anybody in this big old boat but me. Four days ago, up in Moonlight Bay, Oscar Dunningham, my best friend and my driver for twenty-two years, dropped dead of a massive heart attack."

"That's terrible, ma'am. I'm sorry."

"Maybe it would be a tragedy if Oscar wasn't

ninety-two years old. He had a good life. Now he's ashes in an urn, flying back to Georgia where the truly sad thing is his mother will see him buried."

"His mother is still alive?"

"She's not some walking-dead zombie, child. Of course she's alive. Or was this morning. You never know. None of us does. If it matters at all, I'm eighty-six."

"You don't look it, ma'am."

"The hell I don't. When I see myself in a mirror, I scream."

In fact, she had one of those fine-boned, perfectly symmetrical faces that time could little distort, and her soft skin was not so much wrinkled as precisely pleated to sweet effect.

She said, "Can you drive?"

"Yes. But I can't take a job right now."

"You don't look like a shiftless good-for-nothing."

"That's kind of you to say. But the problem is, I have this thing I've got to do."

"Somewhere south of here, you don't know where, but you'll know the place when you get there."

"That's right, ma'am."

Her blue eyes were neither clouded nor sorrowed by age, but were alert, quick, and clear. "This thing you've got to do—have you any idea what it is?"

"More or less," I said. "But I'd rather not talk about it."

"Okay, then," she said, putting the limo in park

and applying the emergency brake, but leaving the engine running, "you be my chauffeur and just drive us where you need to go."

"You can't mean that, ma'am. What kind of chauffeur would that be?"

"The kind I can live with. A lot of the time, I don't much care where I go, just so I go somewhere."

She got out of the limousine and came around to the passenger side. She was wearing a yellow pantsuit with a white blouse that featured frilly lace-trimmed collar and cuffs, and a gold brooch with little diamonds and rubies arranged to form a glittering exclamation point.

When she looked up at me, I felt extraordinarily tall, like Alice after consuming a piece of cake labeled EAT ME.

"As my chauffeur," she said, "you need to open the door for me."

"I can't be your chauffeur, ma'am."

"I'll ride up front with you to get to know you better."

"I'm sorry, but I really can't be your—"

"I'm Edie Fischer. I don't hold with formalities, so you can just call me Edie."

"Thank you, ma'am. But—"

"I was named after St. Eadgyth. She was a virgin and martyr. I can't claim to be a virgin, but the way the world is sliding into darkness, I might yet be a martyr, even though I don't aspire to it. What's your name, child—or are you as unsure of that as you are of where you're going?"

I have in the past used aliases. Using one now made sense, if only to avoid having to explain the origin of my first name for the ten thousandth time. Instead, I said, "My name's Odd Thomas."

"Of course, it is," Mrs. Fischer said. "And if you need to be paid in cash, I am entirely comfortable with that arrangement. Please open the door for me, Oddie."

Oddie and Edie. I had seen and enjoyed *Driving Miss Daisy,* but I was neither as reliable nor as noble as Morgan Freeman's character, Hoke. "Ma'am—"

"Call me Edie."

"Yes, ma'am. The problem is, I'm looking for a dangerous man, this trucker who dresses like a rhinestone cowboy, and maybe he's looking for me."

Without hesitation, she zippered open her large purse to show me the pistol nestled among all the lady things. "I can take care of myself, Oddie. Don't you worry about me."

"But, ma'am, in all good conscience—"

"Now that you've gotten me intrigued," she said, "there's no way you're going to shake loose of me. Child, I need a little danger to keep the blood creeping through my veins. Last time I had some major fun was Elko, Nevada, four months ago, when Oscar and I outfoxed those government fools and helped that poor creature get home again."

"Poor creature?" I asked.

"Never you mind." She zippered shut her purse. "Let's find your rhinestone cowboy if that's what you want."

I opened the door. She got into the limousine.

# Four

THE MERCEDES LIMO HAD A TWELVE-CYLINDER engine and two fuel tanks, providing both speed and range.

Not a single cloud sailed the sea of sky above, and the coastal land rolled in gentle waves.

Riding shotgun with panache, voluminous black purse on her lap, Mrs. Fischer pointed to the radar detector that was fixed to the dashboard and then to something that she called a laser foiler, which she assured me meant that, regarding velocity, we were at little risk of being caught when we broke the law. I had never heard of a laser foiler; but she claimed that it was reliable, "as cutting-edge as any technology on the planet."

She said her previous chauffeur, Oscar, had driven her across the United States, Maine to Texas, Washington State to Florida, again and again, often with the speedometer needle past the one-hundred mark, and they had never gotten a single speeding ticket. They had explored a hundred cities and a thousand small towns, mountains high and lush, deserts low and arid, anywhere a superstretch limousine could be piloted.

The current car was an impressive machine. So little vibration translated from the pavement into the frame that we seemed to be floating swiftly southward, as if the highway were a racing river.

"Oscar was a good employee and a perfect friend," Mrs. Fischer said. "And he was as restless as I am, wanted always to be going somewhere. I knew him better than I ever knew either of my brothers. I would like to know you as well as I knew him, Odd Thomas. Even if I just live to be as old as Oscar, you and I will travel many thousands of miles together, and the journey will be so much more fun if we're friends and understand each other. So . . . are you gay?"

"Gay? No. Why would you think I'm gay?"

"You're chasing after this rhinestone cowboy. That's all right with me, child. I have nothing against gays. I've always liked men a lot, so I understand why you would."

"I don't like men. I mean, I like them, I'm not a man-hater, but I don't love them. Except, you know, in the sense that we should all love our fellow man. But that means man and woman. In general. You know, like the whole human species."

She favored me with a grandmotherly smile, nodded knowingly, and said, "So you're bisexual."

"What? Good heavens, no. I'm not bisexual. Who would have the time or energy for that? I'm just saying, I'm fine with loving all mankind in theory, which is different from dating them."

She winked and said, "So you mean, you're gay in theory but not in practice."

"No. I'm not gay in theory or practice."

"Maybe you're in denial."

"No, not at all. I love a girl. My girl, Stormy Llewellyn—she's the only one for me and always will be. We're destined to be together forever."

My contention is that I'm not a total conversational idiot, although the foregoing exchanges might indicate otherwise. Engaged once more in psychic magnetism, concerned that I might again draw the cowboy to me instead of being drawn to him, getting accustomed to handling the massive limo, I was distracted.

Mrs. Fischer said, "'Destined to be together forever.' That's sweet. You're a sweet child."

"We once got a card from a carnival fortune-telling machine, and that's what it said."

As the speedometer needle crept past ninety, the highway might have been a runway. I felt as if we were on the brink of being airborne.

Mrs. Fischer said, "I hope you're not one of these moderns who thinks marriage isn't necessary. You're going to marry the girl, aren't you?"

"Yes, ma'am. It's all I want."

"You wouldn't be saying that just to please an old woman and keep your new job, would you?"

"No, ma'am. I haven't accepted the job. I'm not your chauffeur."

"Call me Edie."

"Yes, ma'am."

"Seems that you're driving my car, like you *are* a chauffeur. Of course, maybe I'm senile and imagining all this. *When* are you going to marry this Stormy?"

"I don't know an exact date, ma'am. I have to die first. Wait. I'll need to explain that. Stormy . . . well, she died, and we can't ever be together in this world now, only in the next."

"This is true? Yes, I see it is. You believe in an afterlife?"

"Yes, ma'am. Stormy believed in two afterlives. She said this world was boot camp, to test and toughen us, to prepare us for the next life of service in some great adventure. Our third and eternal life comes after that."

"What a unique concept."

"Not so much. You've heard of Purgatory, like Catholics believe. Well, maybe the next life is Purgatory—except with lots of running, jumping, chasing, and fighting with demons or something."

"That makes sense," she said.

Surprised by her quick acceptance, I said, "It does?"

"In eighty-six years, child, I've learned the world is a far more mysterious place than most people realize and that every moment of life is woven through with meaning. In fact, I learned that much by the time I was twenty-six, one oven-hot night in the little town of Lonely Possum."

"Lonely Possum? I never heard of it."

"Lonely Possum, Arizona. Not many people have heard of it. But one day, maybe soon, everyone in the world will know its name."

The thought of Lonely Possum becoming world famous seemed to please her, because she smiled widely, dimpling both cheeks, and let out a sigh akin to those that diner patrons once made when they finished a plate of my roast-beef hash.

I said, "What happened sixty years ago, that oven-hot night in Lonely Possum?"

She winked. "Never you mind."

"Why will everyone in the world know the name one day?"

"When you've been my chauffeur for a month or two, when we know each other better, I'll share that with you."

"I'm not your chauffeur, ma'am."

"Call me Edie."

"Yes, ma'am."

Southbound, we topped a rise and started down a long easy hill, and in one of the northbound lanes, a California Highway Patrol car passed us. Too late, I let up on the accelerator. The officer braked, switched on his rooftop beacons, drove across the median strip, and soon fell in behind us.

Mrs. Fischer said, "He didn't zap you with radar or anything. He doesn't have a smidgen of proof. It's just his word against yours."

"But I *was* speeding."

"Admit nothing, child."

"I can't lie to a policeman, ma'am. Well, not unless maybe he's corrupt or a maniac or something. It's okay to lie to evil."

As I pulled to a stop along the side of the road, Mrs. Fischer said, "Then you better let me do all the talking."

"I'm the driver. He'll expect answers from me."

"Not if you're a deaf-mute."

"That would be another lie. Besides, they might let a mute drive, but I'm not so sure about a deaf person."

"So then you're just mute. And you don't have to lie. I'll say you're a mute, and then you just don't say anything."

Putting down the power window, watching the side mirror as the patrol car pulled in behind us, I said, "This is a bad idea."

"Nobody's going to the slammer, child. Unless you're wanted by the law."

"I'm wanted, but they don't know my name and don't have a photo, just a description."

Her expression was one of dismay, but not because I was a wanted man. "Oddie, you are too truthful for your own good. I didn't *ask* if you were wanted. There was no reason whatsoever to volunteer the information."

"Sorry, ma'am. I thought you should know."

Behind us, the driver's door of the patrol car opened.

"Child, you said it was okay to lie to evil. Maybe I'm evil."

"You're not evil, ma'am."

"Appearances can be deceiving. Maybe I'm the most evil person you've ever met. Maybe I'm *demonic*."

"No, ma'am. I've met some *way* evil people. You're a cream puff."

In the side mirror, the man who got out of the patrol car looked like Hercules' bigger brother, a guy who, at every breakfast, with his dozen eggs and pound of ham, drank a steaming mug of steroids.

Mrs. Fischer seemed miffed that I had called her a cream puff. "I'm about to lie to a policeman, child. Doesn't that make me just a little bit evil?"

"It's wrong," I said, trying to soothe her hurt feelings, "it's bad, no doubt about that, but it's not evil."

"You shush now," she said, "and leave this to me."

A moment later, the massive cop loomed at my window, blocking the morning sun as effectively as an eclipse. He bent down and looked into the car, mouth puckered in a frown and gray eyes squinted, as if the Mercedes were an aquarium and I were the strangest fish that he had ever seen.

He was a handsome bull, I'll give him that, even though his head was as big as a butcher's block. Those singular eyes were not the shade of ashes, not dull but bright, almost silver, steel that flensed away the skin of deception and saw the guilt beneath.

"Do you know how fast you were going?" he asked, which I've heard is what they always ask, giving you the option of telling the truth and convicting yourself or lying to a cop and thereby further incriminating yourself.

I forgot that I was a mute, but before I could speak, Mrs. Fischer said, "Andy Shephorn, is that you?"

His dissecting stare cut from me to her—and softened from blade steel to velveteen rabbit. "Edie Fischer, as I live and breathe." His smile seemed to be too full of teeth, all as large and white as piano keys. "What is it—four years?—and you don't look a day older."

"Because I look a *decade* older. How many children do you and Penny have now? Last I recall, it was five."

"Seven," he said, "but we intend to stop at eight."

"Worried about your family's carbon footprint?" she asked, and they both laughed.

Although the cop was leaning in my window, his face inches from mine, I seemed to have become invisible to him.

To Mrs. Fischer, he said, "Since the boomers

didn't bother to have enough kids to pay their Social Security for them, someone's got to do it."

"I'd love to see your children again—and the two new ones."

"Come around anytime for dinner."

"I'll do that when this current little adventure is over."

"Where's Oscar—sleeping in back?"

"Dear, I'm afraid Oscar passed away four days ago."

Tears welled in Andy Shephorn's eyes. Proportioned to match his features, the tears seemed as large as grapes, and he was striving not to spill them.

Mrs. Fischer saw his distress and said, "Oh, dear, it wasn't a grisly ending, not at all. Oscar and I were in a lovely restaurant. We'd had a divine dinner. He finished the last of his dessert, as good a crème brûlée as ever we'd tasted. As he put down the spoon, his eyes widened, and he said to me, 'Oh, I think the time has come to say good-bye,' and he slumped dead in his chair."

Knuckling the tears out of his eyes, Shephorn said, "He was a fine man. Except for him, I'd never have met Penny."

"He knew she was the perfect wife for you."

I could smell the salt in his tears, I swear I could, and the spray starch in his uniform shirt, the scent of which was liberated by his body heat. The limo felt humid, a laundry on wheels.

"By the way," Mrs. Fischer said, "this young man is my new chauffeur, Thomas."

Officer Shephorn didn't extend his grief-wet hand, which was almost twice the size of one of my hands. "I'm pleased to meet you, Tom."

Pressed back in my seat to give his formidable head as much room as possible, I said, "Likewise, sir," my voice miraculously restored to me, a mute no more.

"You've got big shoes to fill, Oscar's shoes."

"I'm aware, sir."

"And you never will have a stroke of good fortune better than to find yourself under the wing of Edie Fischer." Before I could reply, Shephorn said to my passenger, "Is Tom here smoothed out yet?"

"Not yet," she said. "He's only been with me less than an hour. And he's not fully blue yet, either. But he's far more blue and a lot smoother than anyone his age I've ever met. He'll be fully blue and smooth in no time."

"Good. That's good. With the Oscar news, I'm almost afraid to ask—how's Heathcliff?"

"Heath is still dead, dear."

"But otherwise all right?"

"Oh, yes, he's perfect. Listen, Andy dear, I'd love to chat all day, but we're in something of a hurry."

"Where do you need to be?" the cop asked.

She said, "Somewhere south of here, we don't know where, but we'll know the place when we get there."

"Would you like a police escort? I can clear the way ahead of you, no problem."

"You're a sweetie," Mrs. Fischer told him, "but this is a thing we have to do ourselves."

"You always have been independent. But I guess that's the way."

"That's the way," Mrs. Fischer agreed.

When Andy Shephorn extracted his head from the driver's window, fresh air rushed in as if a cork had been popped from a bottle. As he stepped aside, sunshine found me, and it felt good on my face.

I didn't power up the window until we were on the highway once more, accelerating.

In the rearview mirror, Andy Shephorn stood where we had left him, looking after us. He didn't actually raise his hand to his brow, but he seemed to be in the posture that accompanied a salute, as if my elderly passenger were a senior officer.

My psychic magnetism was engaged but not in high gear, the rhinestone cowboy lurking in the back of my mind, mostly a shadow, except for blue eyes that seemed to whirlpool like flushed water. While Mrs. Fischer and Officer Shephorn had been schmoozing, the trucker, would-be burner of helpless children, had opened a wider lead on us. Even at ninety miles an hour, we wouldn't find him in the next few minutes. When we were closer to him, then I would need to focus more intently on the memory of his face.

I said, "How long have you known Officer Shephorn?"

"About eighteen years. We had a flat tire. That was another limousine. Oscar was seventy-four and entirely fit, but when Andy came along and saw the situation, he insisted that Oscar step aside and let him change the tire."

"So in return, Oscar introduced him to his ideal mate?"

"Penny. She's smart, pretty, ambitious, and loves kids. She has a degree in viniculture."

"I'm ignorant."

Mrs. Fischer patted my shoulder. "Child, you're no such thing. No one can know every word in the language. Viniculture is the study of winemaking. Penny already had some land, some vines, when she met Andy Shephorn. Every year she—they—grow the place a little more, sell another hundred cases above what they sold last year. Soon it'll be another four hundred, then another seven hundred. State police can retire after thirty years. Then he'll work with her in the winery. By the time they turn the place over to their kids—nine, not the eight they're planning—the brand will be famous. They'll have to build an entire trophy room at the winery just to display all their awards, and it'll be their family business for generations."

"That's really specific, ma'am. For a prediction, I mean."

"It's not a prediction."

"It's not? Then what is it?"

"It's what is."

I thought about that, but I wasn't enlightened. "You remind me of a girl I know named Annamaria."

"About forty years ago, I knew an Annamaria Youdel. She was a gifted clothes designer and seamstress. She made all her own clothes. I guess she had to, considering she stood five feet two and weighed three hundred sixty pounds. She had two gold teeth right in front. She shaved her head every day and kept her eyebrows plucked. Her face was as smooth and pink and sweet as the face of a baby, though babies don't have three chins."

"Different Annamaria," I said.

Theologians tell us that this is a fallen world, that Adam and Eve broke it when they fell from grace. Maybe you're not a believer, but if you're honest, you'll have to agree that *something* is wrong with this place. Senseless violence, corrupting envy, greed, blind hatred, and willful ignorance seem to be proof that Earth has gone haywire, but so is the absurdity that we see everywhere. The people of a broken world, off the rails and wobbling trackless on their journeys to oblivion or meaning, are frequently going to be foolish, sometimes in entertaining ways. When amusing, their foolishness—and mine—can be a lamp that brightens my spirit in spite of all threats and suffering. I suspected that by the time this was done, Mrs. Fischer would leave me glowing.

I said, "So I guess you even know how many grandchildren Mr. and Mrs. Shephorn will have."

"Thirty-two."

"How many will be girls?"

"Eighteen."

I glanced away from the road. Mrs. Fischer's smile was impish. Passing an eighteen-wheeler emblazoned with the Pepsi logo, recalling her answers to the peculiar questions that the policeman had asked, I said, "So I'll be smoothed out and fully blue in no time."

"That's right, child. You're already remarkably advanced."

"What does that mean—to be smoothed out and fully blue?"

"You'll understand when you're smooth and blue."

When I glanced at her, she winked at me again.

I asked, "Who's Heathcliff?"

"Heath. My late husband. The one true love of my life. He died twenty-eight years ago this April."

"Officer Shephorn knew your husband was dead."

"Of course."

"But he asked if Heathcliff was 'otherwise all right.'"

"You're an excellent listener. I like that."

"But then you said your husband was perfect."

"And he is."

"Dead but perfect."

Instead of explaining that apparent paradox,

Mrs. Fischer extracted a roll of chocolate candies from her huge black purse. She said, "Treat?"

Suddenly I felt *pulled* southward, not merely carried by the momentum of the hurtling Mercedes, but drawn by psychic magnetism. The rhinestone cowboy was no longer far ahead, and we were swiftly closing on him.

# Five

NO TRUCK STOP WILL EVER BE MISTAKEN for a far-future spaceport, but this one—Star Truck— had such a science-fiction feel that I would not have been much surprised if Captain Kirk and Mr. Spock had beamed down from an orbiting Starfleet retirement home in their bunny slippers, jammies, and walkers. The canopies over the many gas-pump islands were sleek stainless-steel ovals trimmed with neon tubing that, at night, would lend them a flying-saucer feel, and the pumps looked like platoons of robots at parade rest. The facade of the huge building was clad in stainless steel—probably a convincing plastic imitation of stainless—with the lines and the details of a classic Art Deco diner, but that didn't give it the appeal its architect most likely intended; because of its size, the place had an ominous military quality, as if it must be the headquarters of the extraterrestrial overlord of an invading force from another planet.

The large property was fenced for security, an important feature for truckers in an increasingly lawless time that required many of them to pack guns, legally or not. Two extra-wide lanes led into the facility, two out, and they passed through the same gate, between barriers of chain-link, monitored by a pair of pole-mounted cameras. A banner above the entrance promised PARKING LOTS PATROLLED 24/7.

According to an enormous sign bordered by stars that most likely twinkled colorfully at night, Star Truck offered a smorgasbord of road-warrior services: ALL FUELS, 24-HOUR GARAGE SERVICE, RESTAURANT, SNACK BAR, MEN'S AND WOMEN'S SHOWERS, MOTEL ROOMS, LAUNDROMAT, BARBERSHOP, TV LOUNGE, GAME ARCADE, TRAVEL STORE, GIFT SHOP, CHAPEL.

In recent years, to save fuel, the tractors of most eighteen-wheelers had gotten more aerodynamic. If you could tune out the roar of the big engines, you might imagine that those sleek Peterbilts, Volvos, Freightliners, Macks, Fords, and Cats were gliding across the blacktop without effort, like antigravity craft in a *Star Wars* movie. Even the classic, boxy, battering-ram designs of Kenworth and Intercontinental had made some concessions to diminish wind resistance.

The flashy and sinister ProStar+ with the red-and-black tractor and the black trailer was parked among forty or fifty other rigs at the north end of the property. As I cruised slowly past, memorizing the license-plate number, I could see that no one was in the cab of the tractor, and I had no sense that the rhinestone cowboy might be with his vehicle.

Moments earlier, I had told Mrs. Fischer that the flamboyant trucker was planning three murders, but I hadn't told her how I'd come across this information.

"That's his rig," I said, braking to a stop.

"Let's set the cops on him."

"No, see, I have some negative history with the police in Magic Beach, which isn't that far from here. And the FBI might be looking for someone who fits my description. I haven't been a bad boy, ma'am, but some exceedingly treacherous people got themselves shot to death and a whole lot of property got pretty much busted up. And I wouldn't like to have to explain to the authorities how just a simple fry cook uncovered a plot to nuke four cities, took down several terrorists, and got out of that town with all his skin."

"You aren't a simple fry cook."

"That's my point, ma'am."

She cocked her snow-capped head and gave me that cockatoo stare again. "You're quite a riddle."

"Look who's talking."

"So what you're doing is like in those Agatha Christie novels—Miss Jane Marple, amateur detective?"

"I'm not much like Miss Jane Marple."

"You've got a sweet face," Mrs. Fischer said, and pinched my cheek. "I suspect your mind is as sharp as Miss Marple's, although you haven't given me much evidence of that yet."

Edie Fischer didn't look anything like my idea of Jane Marple, but if some network ever brought back *The X-Files* with Agents Mulder and Scully as eighty-somethings, she could pass for a geriatric Gillian Anderson, who had played Scully.

The rhinestone cowboy and his custom-painted eighteen-wheeler were as mysterious as Cigarette Smoking Man and everything else in that old and perpetually enigmatic TV show.

I said, "I'd give anything to know what he's hauling."

"Don't say such a reckless thing, child. If I were the devil, I'd ask what you mean by 'anything,' and you'd probably convey the intensity of your curiosity by repeating *'anything'* with emphasis, and just like that—*zap!*—you'd be inside that trailer, you'd see what it's loaded with, but you'd have sold your immortal soul for next to nothing."

"It can't be that easy to sell your soul."

"So now you're a PhD in demonic negotiation? Where did you get your degree, sweetie, from an Internet university run by some fifty-year-old guy who lives in his parents' basement and has nothing in his wardrobe but sweat suits?"

"It's funny, ma'am, how sometimes you're so sarcastic but it doesn't sting."

"Because of my dimples. Dimples are a get-out-of-jail-free card."

"Anyway, you're not the devil, Mrs. Fischer."

"Call me Edie. Listen, child—if you're at a party with a hundred people and one of them is the devil, he'll be the last one you'd suspect."

Piloting the limousine away from the trucks and past the pump islands, I said, "I'm not much for parties. Sometimes you have to wear a funny hat, sometimes they expect you to eat sushi, which is like eating bait. And there's always some totally drunk girl who thinks you're smitten by her, when what you're wondering is if she'll vomit on your shirt or instead on your shoes."

"My point wasn't parties, as you well know."

At the south end of the sprawling complex, I parked the limo in a lot reserved for cars, pickups, and SUVs.

More or less thinking out loud, I said, "If he sees me before I see him, I'm probably toast."

"Some amateur detectives are masters of disguise," Mrs. Fischer said.

"Yeah, but Inspector Clouseau borrowed my master-of-disguise kit and never returned it."

"Arm candy can be an effective disguise."

"Arm candy?"

"An adorable grandmother clinging to your arm for support."

"I'm not involving you in this, ma'am. You don't

know me, how dangerous it is to be around me. I'm grateful for the ride, but we part company here."

From the glove box, she extracted a poofy black-and-green-plaid cap with a short bill and a plump upholstered button on top, the kind of thing sixty-year-old men wear when they buy a convertible sports car to impress women half their age.

"It belonged to Oscar. He had real style."

"I hope his chauffeur's uniform wasn't a kilt. Ma'am, a hat isn't much of a disguise."

"Put it on. Put, put," she insisted. From the glove compartment she withdrew a pair of sunglasses and handed them to me. "You can wear them, they aren't prescription."

Although the cap fit, I felt silly in it, as if I were trying to pass for a Scottish golfer circa 1910.

Zippering open a small leather case that she also took from the glove box, producing a two-ounce bottle containing a golden liquid, Mrs. Fischer said, "Let me paint some of this on your upper lip."

"What's that?"

"Spirit gum." From the case, she plucked three or four little plastic bags. "Mustaches," she said. "Different styles. A handlebar wouldn't be right for your face. Something more modest. But not a pencil mustache, either. Too affected. Oh, I also have a chin beard!"

"Why would you carry a mustache-and-beard kit in your car?"

She seemed genuinely perplexed by my question. "Whyever *wouldn't* I carry one?"

Gently but firmly I insisted, "I won't wear a fake mustache."

"Then a chin beard. You'll be a whole new person."

"I'll look ridiculous."

"Nonsense, Oddie. You'll look impressively literary. With that cap and sunglasses and a chin beard, everyone will think you're a famous poet."

"What poet ever looked like that?"

"Virtually every beatnik poet, back in the day."

"There are no beatniks anymore."

"Because most of their poetry stank. You'll write better," she declared, unscrewing the cap from the bottle. "Stick out your chin."

"I'm sorry, ma'am. No. I respect my elders and all that, and you've been especially kind, but I won't glue a beard on my chin. I don't want to look like Maynard G. Krebs."

"Who is Maynard G. Krebs?"

"He was Dobie Gillis's friend on that old TV series maybe fifty years ago, they're always rerunning it somewhere."

"You don't look like a lard-ass couch potato."

"Thank you, ma'am. I'm not. It's just that everything sticks with me, like even the name of Dobie Gillis's friend."

She beamed with obvious delight as she screwed

the cap back onto the bottle. "You're such a nice boy—and a genius, too."

"Not a genius. Far from it. I just have a sticky mind." I reached out to shake her hand. "Good-bye, good luck, God bless."

Patting my hand instead of shaking it, Mrs. Fischer said, "Take your time. I've got a good book to read."

"I don't know what's going to happen next, but I know I'm not coming back to you."

"Of course you are. You're my chauffeur."

"I don't want to put your life at risk."

"Don't be so hard on yourself, child. You're a *good* driver."

"I mean, I have dangerous enemies."

"Everyone does, dear. Now, go have fun playing Miss Marple, and I'll be here when you're finished."

# Six

IN PLAID CAP AND SUNGLASSES, LOOKING LIKE a pretend Scottish poet golfer who left his chin beard at home, I approached the front doors of Star Truck. They slid open automatically with a pneumatic hiss, which seemed to be an expression of disdain at my appearance.

I was in a kind of lobby, a spotless space, about twenty feet wide and thirty long. As outside, the walls were clad in stainless steel, but up close, I could confirm that it was plastic, excellent fake steel but fake nonetheless.

To the left were glass doors under a red plastic sign that announced TRAVEL STORE in white letters. They sold everything from wrench sets to cushioned insoles, racy postcards to Bibles, audiobooks to zinc ointment. My psychic magnetism gave no indication that the rhinestone cowboy could be found in there.

The restaurant, to my left, would be divided into one area for ordinary motorists and another for professional drivers, who received quicker service. In this strange age of eager victims, no doubt there is always a legal action grinding through the courts, seeking to prohibit the partitioning of customers at truck stops, to forbid the serving of such high-cholesterol fare as cheese meatloaf, to require other choices besides country music on the jukebox, and to disallow trucker slang that can't be understood by nontrucker customers.

In the center of the lobby stood a square kiosk, on each side of which a map revealed where to find the many services offered by Star Truck. The map wouldn't help me locate the rhinestone cowboy, since it didn't have a moving, blinking indicator light labeled PSYCHOPATH.

Beyond the lobby lay a wide corridor flanked by a large video-game arcade, a barbershop, a combination bakery and ice-cream store, a gift shop. . . . Except for the store windows and glass doors, almost every surface, from floor to ceiling, was either plastic or vinyl, almost seamless, bright and smooth and clean. These days, whether part of a chain or a family operation, most truck stops looked as if they had been extruded on-site in a single continuous piece from a machine of fantastic proportions and capabilities.

Nevertheless, the place had a welcoming air, partly because everything was clean and bright, but also because so many of the truckers I passed looked like everybody's favorite uncle or buddy in one movie or another. They tended to be beefy men with ruddy faces and work-worn hands. Most wore jeans or khakis, T-shirts or polos. Some had more John Wayne style than others, but most of them boasted at least one cowboy touch: a Stetson instead of the widely preferred baseball cap with trucking-related logo, a bronze bucking-horse belt buckle, cowboy boots instead of engineer boots or athletic shoes. Large bellies, where they overhung belts, somehow did not appear sloppy but seemed instead to be armor against a hostile world, and whether thin or heavy, these men looked as though they could take care of business, no matter what the business might be.

A few glanced at me, some nodded, and a couple of them smiled thinly. Most ignored me, perhaps because the stupid cap and the sunglasses indoors suggested that I might be problematic.

Of course, after a half decade of economic chaos and societal decay, the once robust fellowship of truckers had been tattered by competition for routes and loads, by the high cost of fuel, by the deteriorating condition of highways, and by an avalanche of new laws governing their jobs that made the freedom of the open road less free. Camaraderie had once been encouraged by CB radios, by a shared Americanism, and by simple faith. These days, their faith was everywhere mocked, their America seemed to be rusting away, and they turned inward more than they had once done.

Women truckers had been in the mix for quite a few years: Some were the wives of their co-drivers, some partnered with another woman, and a few were brave and alone. Like people everywhere, they came in all kinds of packages, but they tended to be prettier than most people supposed women truckers would be. All those I encountered on my ramblings through Star Truck smiled at me, every single one.

I figured I looked amusingly idiotic. But even after I took off the cap and turned the sunglasses to the top of my head, the ladies still smiled at me. I don't know why. Nothing was hanging out of my nose. My traveling tongue didn't discover a shred of breakfast ham or anything else wedged between my teeth.

Seeking my quarry, I roamed all over the public areas of the main building, from the tucked-away chapel on the ground floor to the upper floor, where I found the laundry room, the chiropractor's office, the big TV lounge, and the showers. The showers were in a long corridor, behind a series of numbered and locked doors.

The attendant, a cheerful woman in a blue uniform, wore a name badge that identified her as ZILLA, like Godzilla without God. She was petite and appeared incapable of destroying a city.

After I paid the fee, Zilla gave me a fluffy towel with a washcloth and a clear plastic bag containing a miniature bar of soap, a tiny bottle of shampoo, and an equally tiny bottle of conditioner. When she reached for the key to Shower 7 that hung on the Peg-Board behind her, I asked if I could have Shower 5 instead. Zilla said they were all identical, and I explained that five was my lucky number. If she thought I was a geek for having a lucky-shower number, she didn't show it.

Shower 5 was actually a complete no-frills bathroom with a toilet, a sink with a mirror above it, and a shower with a frosted-glass door fitted with a towel bar. The floors and walls were covered with glossy-white ceramic tile, including a built-in bench just outside of the large shower stall. Everything sparkled and appeared to be not just clean but sanitized. You would have been willing to stand barefoot on the floor, but you wouldn't have been willing to eat off it.

Trucker teams often had sleeper tractors with a double bed, an under-counter refrigerator, and a microwave behind the cockpit, but they didn't have a bathroom. On long hauls, they didn't want to pay for a motel room just to take a quick shower.

After hanging the towel and the washcloth on the shower door and setting everything else on the counter beside the sink, I glanced in the mirror, decided I looked only slightly more buffoonish with the sunglasses atop my head, as if I had a second pair of eyes nestled in my hair, and then turned in place, studying the room.

Five isn't my lucky number. I don't actually have a lucky number any more than I have an official Odd Thomas tree or flower, or bird. Claiming to have a lucky number wasn't a lie, at least not a serious one, because no one could possibly be harmed in any way by such a statement. It was instead a finesse. I finesse a lot.

I was drawn to Shower 5 by psychic magnetism. Considering that I was searching for the rhinestone cowboy and considering that this room was unoccupied, I'm not sure what I expected to find.

If he had been here earlier, perhaps I detected a residue of psychic energy much the way that a bloodhound can track an escaped convict by the scent of the man's shed skin cells, drops of sweat, and other spoor.

Although the shower room smelled of a lemon-scented disinfectant and seemed to have been thoroughly cleaned between users, I sought paranormal evidence of my quarry by touching the chrome spigots on the sink, the flush handle on the toilet, and the pull on the shower door. None of them inspired a frisson of weirdness reminiscent of the trucker in the supermarket parking lot.

As I considered whether I should turn on the water and pretend to take a shower for the benefit of Zilla at the attendant's desk or just leave without explanation, movement at the periphery of vision caused me to turn to my left in alarm. I remained alone. The activity seemed to be in the mirror, to which I stood at such a severe angle that I could not see what moved impossibly in the reflection of this stilled chamber.

When I stepped to the sink, the shower room in the mirror was not lined with white tiles. The walls were bare concrete. Instead of several flush-mounted lights in the ceiling, a single fixture with a cone-shaped metal shade dangled on a chain. Although I felt no draft, the hanging lamp swung lazily, its swooning circle of light causing phantoms of shadow to glide around like dancers in a slow waltz.

Something spattered wetly against my right cheek, and I turned to find myself no longer in the Star Truck shower room but in a drab chamber, as grim as a dungeon, with concrete walls like those in the mirror. Maybe not concrete. It was more like . . . the *idea* of concrete. I don't know what I mean by that. And now I felt the draft that swayed the hanging lamp. More startling than the sudden change of venue was the presence of the rhinestone cowboy, whose spittle slid down my face.

His materialization, like a summoned demon manifesting inside a pentagram, caused my breath to catch in my throat, and the big .45 Sig Sauer pistol with the silencer, aimed at my face, fully paralyzed me.

My only weapon was my wit, and though it could wound, it could not kill. In fact, at that moment, I couldn't think of a cutting line and, disgusted by the gob of spit, I said only, "Yuck."

In the gloom, the spiky white hair made him look like one of those troll dolls that, to me, have always appeared less cute than psychotic. His cyanide-blue eyes, which seemed to glow from within, matched the poisonous character of his words: "Are you all out of Granny Smiths and Red Delicious, Johnny Appleseed? I'd like it if you explained to me who and what you are, but I'd like it even better if you were just dead."

Without giving me the courtesy of a brief reprieve to tell him what *I* would like, he pulled the trigger, and the flesh of my throat dissolved like glass, a thousand shards of pain shattering through me as blood fountained up my throat and drowning darkness pulled me down.

# Seven

DEATH PROVED TO BE DREAMLESS, IF DEATH IT was, and then I woke, lying on the white-tile floor.

The sunglasses had been flung off my head and broken at the bridge. They lay directly under the fluffy white towel and washcloth that hung from the bar on the door to the roomy shower stall.

I was on my side, in the fetal position, and I might have been crying for my mommy if Mother hadn't been a deeply disturbed woman who, during my childhood, had often threatened me with a gun. I was raised not with the principles of Dr. Benjamin Spock in mind, but according to the even darker theories of Dr. Jekyll.

I felt no pain, but I was reluctant to raise a hand to my throat, for fear of finding torn flesh, a gaping wound. When I dared to swallow, however, I was able to do so, and I realized both that I could breathe and that the taste of blood didn't foul my mouth.

Having lost my reason for existence when I lost Stormy Llewellyn nineteen months earlier, I lived a life I didn't need. Although I had no fear of death, I hoped to avoid excruciating pain, long suffering, and concussion-induced blackouts from which I would awake with embarrassing tattoos. Now I was relieved to find myself mysteriously alive, relieved largely because I had pledged to protect Annamaria from those who would kill her, because I felt compelled to save the three innocent children that the cowboy trucker intended to set afire, and because suddenly I had a fierce appetite for a platter of cheese meatloaf, steak fries, and coleslaw, which I hoped to satisfy before I died again and stayed dead.

One good thing about a condemned man's last meal is that he doesn't have to worry about acid reflux.

Getting to my feet, I realized that I wasn't alone. I spun toward the other with less than balletic grace, as Baryshnikov might have moved if he had ever performed *Swan Lake* while drunk, my hands out in front of me as if to catch any bullets that might shortly be in flight.

On the tiled and built-in bench adjacent to the shower sat a famous portly man in a three-piece black suit, white shirt, black tie, and black wingtips polished to a high shine. His round face, full cheeks, and two chins had been less pronounced but evident even in photographs of him as a young child. Then as now, his lower lip protruded far past the upper;

however, as both a boy and a man, he never appeared to be pouting, but seemed instead to be pondering some profound idea.

"Mr. Hitchcock," I said, and he smiled.

So soon after being shot dead and finding myself miraculously alive again, I wasn't ready for Alfred Hitchcock. Bewildered, I went to the sink, leaned toward the mirror, searched the reflection for the concrete walls and the single hanging light—for the dungeon or abattoir, or whatever the place had been—but saw only the clean, bright shower room.

I have never liked looking at myself in a mirror. I don't know why exactly. I'm not movie-star handsome, but I'm not the Creature from the Black Lagoon, either. I'm pretty much a face in the crowd, which is a blessing when, like me, you have a reason not to draw attention to yourself. There's just something unsettling about studying your reflection. It's not a matter of being dissatisfied with your face or of being embarrassed by your vanity. Maybe it's that when you gaze into your own eyes, you don't see what you wish to see—or glimpse something that you wish weren't there.

At least my face was not splashed with blood, and my eyes were not dead-flat yet fevered like those of a zombie. I didn't know what it felt like to be a lingering spirit unwilling to pass over to the Other Side, but I was certain that it didn't feel like this. If the encounter with the rhinestone cowboy had not been a hallucination or a vision of a future confrontation, if I had in fact been shot in the throat and killed, I was nevertheless alive again by virtue of a miracle.

I didn't try to puzzle through how such a thing could be. The world is filled with mysteries; and I have learned that every mystery will either explain itself—or it won't. I can't force Nature to draw back her curtains and reveal the hidden machinery that constitutes the true workings of the world.

When I turned once more to Mr. Hitchcock, the great director gave me two thumbs up.

I sat beside him on the bench. My hands were shaking. I clutched my knees to still the tremors.

"I saw you the other day," I said, "walking on the shore, past the cottage we've been renting. You waved at me."

He thrust out his lower lip even farther and nodded. Although his face was perhaps best suited for a dour expression, he smiled and seemed almost merry. Judging by the wry look in his eyes, I thought that he had something to say that would have made me laugh. Having died in 1980, however, he was a spirit, and spirits never speak.

In previous volumes of these memoirs, I have written of other famous souls who have sought me out, hoping that I could help them find the courage to cross over. Mr. Elvis Presley was with me for a few years before I understood why he lingered in this world and could convince him to leave it. Mr. Frank Sinatra kept me company for a much shorter time, a more volatile spirit than the King of Rock 'n' Roll, always exciting and perhaps more helpful to me than I was to him, though Old Blue Eyes eventually did cross over.

From those experiences, I wrongly concluded that if another famous person among the lingering dead came to me for counseling, he or she would be a legendary singer. Perhaps Bing Crosby or Bobby Darin, or John Lennon. On some bad days, I worried that it might be Sid Vicious or Kurt Cobain.

Instead, Mr. Alfred Hitchcock, surely one of the five greatest directors in the history of Hollywood—maker of *Psycho* but also of the sparkling comedy *Mr. and Mrs. Smith* and numerous masterpieces in between—had come to me for help, decades after his death. I already knew much about him. Later I would learn much more. But at that moment in the Star Truck shower room, I felt intellectually inadequate to counsel a man of such accomplishment.

Still shocked from being murdered and resurrected, if in fact such a thing had happened, I found myself speechless. I stared at him for a long moment, and then looked around the white room as if what I ought to say to him might be printed boldly on the walls. It wasn't. Consequently, more embarrassed by my loss for words than by any stupid thing that I might say, I babbled in search of substance.

"Sorry, I'm a little shaken. The walls were concrete. The cowboy was just suddenly there. Or maybe he wasn't. He shot me point-blank in the throat. Or maybe he didn't. I'm sorry. You don't know about the cowboy. He's not a cowboy, really. He drives a big truck, not a horse. Nobody *drives* a horse, of course, it doesn't have wheels, but you know what I mean. The creep called me Johnny Appleseed. Not that the name Johnny Appleseed is an insult. Johnny was really a great guy. It was the way he said it. Scornfully. With contempt. He's a nasty piece of work. I mean the cowboy guy, not Johnny Appleseed. I don't have anything against Johnny Appleseed. If he hadn't planted all those trees a couple hundred years ago, I wouldn't have had any ammunition in that supermarket and I'd probably be dead now in the produce section."

Mr. Hitchcock raised one hand to rest his chin on it, and he regarded me with keen interest, as if I were Sherlock to his Watson, although I was more likely Larry-Curly-Moe to his Einstein.

After several deep breaths, I regained my composure. "Sir, I'll do what I can for you. I'm honored that you've come to me. But since you weren't murdered, then you must be reluctant to cross over for personal reasons. Psychological reasons. Maybe a sense of guilt. Maybe remorse for something done in life."

He raised one eyebrow.

"Mr. Presley and Mr. Sinatra," I said, "were almost as public about their private lives as they were about their careers, so I was able to puzzle out the reasons why their spirits lingered here. I think you kept your family and your personal life private, and since you can't talk, this is probably going to be a difficult case for me, so I just hope you'll be patient."

He removed his hand from under his chin and used it to pat me on the shoulder in a kindly manner, as if to reassure me that, having lingered in this world so many years, he did not expect to be led directly to a celestial escalator.

The spirits of the lingering dead feel as warm and solid to me as does any living person. They could comfort me with a pat, as Mr. Hitchcock had just done, or accept comfort from me, but they could not punch, claw, strangle, or otherwise mutilate me. If they struck out in anger, their fists passed through me without effect.

The only human spirit that can be dangerous to the living is one that goes poltergeist. This condition results from frustration and rage. The furious ghost draws energy from some dark place and pumps it into this world, flinging everything from books to furniture, to storms of cutlery.

Generally speaking, spirits capable of going poltergeist were unredeemed if not malevolent. If they ever finally departed this world, they would most likely wind up in the Dark Side of the Other Side, where you never get cookies or hot chocolate. There were exceptions, poltergeists of good intent, of which Mr. Sinatra had been one, when he came to my rescue in a desperate moment in Magic Beach, little more than a month earlier.

I am aware that this part of my experience has

started to sound like shameless name-dropping and calls into question my veracity. In my defense, I can only say that the spirits of famous people are a tiny fraction of the lingering dead whom I have helped to cross over. And if you think I've imagined them in order to sell more copies of my books, you are proved wrong by the fact that these memoirs will not be published while I'm alive, to ensure that I will never be imprisoned in a secret government facility and studied like a lab rat.

Besides, regardless of where I might be going on the Other Side, whether into the Light or the Dark, I won't have a use for royalties after I'm dead. If I've got my theology right: In the Light, all that I could ever need or want will be free; and in the Dark, no currency ever minted can buy my way out.

Mr. Hitchcock stopped patting my shoulder, rose from the tiled bench, and crossed the room. He beckoned with one finger, and as I rose to my feet, he walked through the closed door, into the hallway.

Apparently, travel is much easier when you're dead. No need to concern yourself with doors, toll-booths, or airport security agents who want to probe your butt.

When I opened the door and stepped into the hall, Zilla was at her workstation, folding freshly laundered towels.

Mr. Hitchcock stood a hundred feet away, at the intersection of this corridor with one serving the TV lounge and the chiropractor's office. He raised his right arm high and waved, as if we were in a crowded train station and he needed to attract my attention through the bustling throng.

The attendant couldn't see him, of course. She said to me, "Is something wrong?"

"I decided I didn't need a shower, after all, ma'am. The *idea* of a shower was refreshing enough."

"I can only give you a partial refund," she said apologetically.

Eager to follow Mr. Hitchcock, who seemed to intend to lead me somewhere, I said, "That's all right. I don't need a refund."

As I turned away, she stepped out from behind her station and approached me. "Wait a minute, sir, please. It's just, you see, whether you used the towel or not, we still have to wash it, and clean the room."

She was earnest and clearly wanted to treat me fairly.

"I understand," I assured her. "No problem."

"But I *can* return half your money."

"No, ma'am, really, it's fine. It was only the idea of a shower, but I paid for it with paper money, which is only the *idea* of money, so it was a totally fair exchange."

My attitude perplexed her into silence as I hurried toward Mr. Hitchcock.

He led me along the intersecting hallway to the very back of the building, where he phased through a fire door labeled STAIRS. I opened the door and entered the stairwell in a more traditional manner, in time to see him floating down the first flight, his feet a few inches above the treads.

As I followed, looking down on him, I decided he had manifested not as he had been late in life but as he had been in his early fifties, hair still dark but receding, the beginning of a bald spot at the crown of his head. He was born in 1899, so his fifties were the 1950s, a decade in which he made *Rear Window, Dial M for Murder, Strangers on a Train, North by Northwest, To Catch a Thief, The Wrong Man,* and *Vertigo,* more classic films than most directors produce in a lifetime. *Rebecca,* the first version of *The Man Who Knew Too Much, Notorious, Spellbound, Suspicion, Shadow of a Doubt,* and so many other great works were already in his past. *Psycho, The Birds,* and others were in his future.

We descended four flights, which put us in the basement. With the aplomb that he exhibited routinely in life, the director floated through another closed door, and I discovered that beyond it lay the mechanical heart of the truck stop, a chamber that perhaps seemed more vast than it was, housing huge boilers, chillers, a maze of big PVC pipes serving the heating-cooling system, and banks of circuit breakers. There was also much equipment that I could not identify, in fact so much that I might very well have been in the engine room of a starship.

Cold harsh light fell from the fluorescent fixtures. Shadows had sharp edges, and the stainless-steel housings of the various machines glistened as if crusted in ice.

Mr. Hitchcock cast no shadow at any time, of course, and my own shrank under my feet as we came to a halt beneath a large array of fluorescents in what seemed to be the center of the room. He put one finger to his lips, suggesting silence, and then tilted his head to the right, cupping a hand around that ear in a theatrical gesture, which reminded me that he had begun his long career in silent films.

I cocked my head, too, and we stood there in a comic posture, as if we were Laurel and Hardy puzzling over the source of a peculiar sound that would prove to be a block-and-tackle failing in the moment before a piano dropped on our heads. The humming and purring of the machinery had no menace, however, and I heard nothing else, certainly nothing that would put the hairs up on the nape of my neck.

But then I *did* hear something, two men arguing, their words muffled and not quite decipherable— yet close. Surprised, I turned, but no one shared the open center of the room with us, and between the banks of machinery, the aisle by which we had arrived here was also deserted. Other passageways serving additional rows of machines waited to be explored, but I didn't think I'd find the two men in any of them. That angry pair seemed near but not quite real, their voices sonorous and distorted like those of malevolent presences in a dream.

Their conversation faded, then returned, louder

and closer than before, though still indecipherable, as if they were just a few feet away but on the farther side of a wall that I couldn't see. I turned again, and an infuriated man in jeans and a black-leather jacket stalked past close enough to touch, oblivious of me.

His face was hard and seemed subtly broken, the countenance of a stubborn but inept boxer who had taken too many devastating punches. Fierce under heavy lids, his eyes shifted here, there, here with the desperation of a beast born to be free but caged from an early age.

And he was semitransparent.

The lingering dead look as real to me as they would have appeared in life. If they don't manifest with mortal wounds—as did the decapitated woman crossing the street—and if they don't pass through walls or float inches above the ground, I am not often able to recognize them as spirits.

This stocky, thick-necked man with the fractured-stone face was not a spirit. His voice, though seeming to be filtered through a foot or two of cotton batting and distorted like a recording played at too slow a speed, was nonetheless far different from the silence imposed upon the deceased.

He changed course abruptly, passed *through* me, and I shuddered as a chill marked the moment when we occupied the same space. As I turned, he stopped one step away, swung back to me, and we were face-to-face. He had abruptly ceased talking. He looked left, right, up, down, and I suspected that he'd felt a chill, as well, but he didn't otherwise react to me. From my perspective, he was a see-through ghost, as in a movie, but I was invisible to him.

For a moment I perceived—without quite seeing— that the room he occupied had the same dimensions as the chamber in which I stood, but that it was an empty and desolate space. Cold concrete and ashen light.

The second man in that other basement now spoke again, stepping into view: the rhinestone cowboy. He was as semitransparent as the guy with whom he argued.

Turning from me, the first man joined the would-be murderer of children, and they walked away, swiftly fading from sight as their voices slid into silence.

I no longer sensed that alternate basement. But then came a sound like two metal fire doors falling shut, one a fraction of a second after the other, the former softer than the latter.

When I turned to Mr. Hitchcock, I found that he was watching me. As though soliciting my reaction to what had just happened, he raised his eyebrows.

Although I am not an important person by any definition, at that moment I almost felt like one. In spite of my paranormal ability, I am just a hapless out-of-work short-order cook who struggles to fry well when he has a job and, if possible, at all times to do the right thing. But now I suddenly thought of all those male leads in Mr. Hitchcock's films, and I felt obligated to fulfill his directorial expectations, to answer his raised eyebrows with a remark witty enough to be delivered by Cary Grant.

Instead, I said, "Uh . . . wow . . . see . . . you know . . . the thing is . . . I don't understand. Where were those two men? Where are they now? Was their argument something that happened here earlier? Or something that'll happen in the future?"

He shook his head and then tapped the face of his wristwatch with one finger, perhaps to indicate that the time in both basements was the same, that what I'd seen had happened just now. Or maybe he had done a Rolex commercial during his life and felt a duty to sell the brand even after death.

"Sir, I'm confused."

With fingers widely spread, hands framing his face, with an expression of amazement, Mr. Hitchcock mocked me, as if to say, *You? Confused? Who knew? Astonishing! Impossible! It beggars belief!*

If he'd been Quentin Tarantino or Oliver Stone, I might have been a bit offended—or even alarmed by the possibility of mindless violence—but in his day he'd been known for his unexpected clowning and practical jokes. His friend, the actor Gerald du Maurier, had been appearing in a play at St. James Theater, in London, when during a performance Mr. Hitchcock somehow had gotten a full-grown horse into the star's dressing room without anyone seeing it happen. When du Maurier returned at the end of the play, he found the huge animal content-edly eating grain from a feed bag.

Now the director turned from me and glided across the basement as if he wore ice skates and the floor were a frozen pond, and I had to hurry to keep up with him. He passed through a heavy fire door, which I yanked open in his wake, wondering if this might be the door that I had heard crash shut twice in quick succession when the see-through cowboy had de-parted the other basement or this basement, or both.

With my confusion growing more profound, I rushed along a drab corridor to a pair of elevators—the smaller for people, the larger for freight—where Mr. Hitchcock stood. As I arrived, a bell sounded, the first set of doors slid open, he stepped into the waiting car, and I followed him.

Even if I'd been able by then to come up with a line worthy of Cary Grant, before I could have de-livered it, the director soared through the roof of the elevator and disappeared. I had never known a ghost to be this exuberant, this frolicsome, and his apparent delight in his supernatural abilities flum-moxed me.

Stepping out of the elevator into the hallway lined with shops on the main floor of Star Truck, I spotted Mr. Hitchcock to my right, standing by the service-map kiosk in the lobby. He raised his right arm high and waved at me, as though I might not recognize him among the dozen or so truck drivers currently entering and leaving the building.

As I approached, he winked out of existence—and then reappeared on the far side of the glass doors of the main entrance.

Exiting the building, joining Mr. Hitchcock, I sensed the cowboy nearby, although he was nowhere in sight. Then I saw the ProStar+ receding along the exit lanes from Star Truck, speeding toward the Coast Highway.

The roar of a nearer engine followed by the shrill squealing of brakes startled me backward. The super-stretch Mercedes limo ran down Mr. Hitchcock and slid to a smoking-rubber stop in front of me.

He couldn't have been roadkill, of course, because he lacked material substance. He was just *gone*.

Through the open window in the driver's door, Mrs. Edie Fischer said, "Hurry, child, or we might lose him."

In the distance, the red-and-black rig disappeared into the underpass beneath the highway.

I darted around the car, climbed in the front passenger seat, pulled my door shut, and glanced through the open privacy panel into the passenger compartment. "Where is he?"

Of course Mrs. Fischer didn't know that I was looking for Mr. Hitchcock, who I thought must have entered the limousine through the undercarriage.

Perched on her booster pillow, barely able to see over the steering wheel, piloting the immense car around the service islands, she said, "You called him a flamboyant rhinestone cowboy, but I saw him, and there's no honest honky-tonk in that man. He's flam with none of the buoyant. All deceit, lies, trickery. Planning murder, is he? Child, you need to take him down."

"I knocked him flat with apples—Red Delicious, Granny Smiths—but even as much as I hate guns, I probably need one."

Indicating the purse on the seat between us, she said, "Take the pistol I showed you earlier."

"I don't want to get you in trouble."

"Sweetie, that gun's even harder to trace than apples."

I didn't feel that it was proper to open her purse, even though she invited me to do so. Besides, I didn't have an immediate use for the weapon. For the time being, we were only following my enemy. I wasn't going to shoot out his tires or leap from the speeding limo to the driver's door of the truck. I'm not Tom Cruise. I'm not even Angelina Jolie.

Entering one of the exit lanes, Mrs. Fischer accelerated toward the underpass. "Belt up," she advised.

By this point, I knew her well enough to take such advice without hesitation.

Coming out of the underpass, ascending the curved on-ramp to the Coast Highway, she rapidly accelerated, as if the laws of physics did not apply to her. If we'd been in an SUV or an ordinary car, we might have demonstrated the power of centrifugal force, might have rolled off the roadway at the apex of the arc. The limo was heavy, however, with a low center of gravity, and we rocketed to the top of the ramp at launch speed.

Contemptuous of the yield sign, Mrs. Fischer pressed great blasts of sound from the car horn as a warning to any motorists who might be approaching from behind her in the right-hand lane. The limo shot onto the highway, whistling south toward the targeted ProStar+.

"Take it easy," I warned. "We don't want to catch him."

"But you said he's going to murder three people. He has to be stopped."

"We'll stop him, but not yet. We need to see where he's going, what he's up to. He's not in this alone. That reminds me, did you see another guy come out of the truck stop with him?"

"No. He was alone. So this is a *conspiracy*?" She lingered on the last word, as though the sound of it enchanted her.

"I don't know what it is. This other guy—he's wearing jeans and a black-leather jacket. Lizard-lid eyes, stocky, looks like he was into one of those martial arts where he broke cement blocks with his face but sometimes the block won."

"This is more delicious by the moment." She grinned broadly, and her adorable dimples were so deep that faeries might have lived in them. Having eased up on the accelerator, she said, "So we'll just stay far back and keep the truck in sight—is that it?"

Relying on my psychic magnetism, we wouldn't even have to keep the ProStar+ in sight, but I didn't want to explain to her that I was like Miss Jane Marple *with paranormal abilities*.

"Yes, ma'am. Just keep it in sight. Nothing bad is going to happen right away. He doesn't have the children yet."

I realized my mistake even as I spoke.

She understood the significance of what I said. Her smile faded, her dimples withered. Her voice grew so tough that she sounded as if she might be Clint Eastwood's hard-bitten sister. "That's who he's going to kill—three *children*?"

Reluctantly, I said, "Yes, ma'am, I believe so. Two girls—one maybe six years old, the other ten. And a boy of about eight."

"Evil is always drawn to the innocent," she declared with the precise note of contempt and disgust that, if she were Mr. Eastwood and if this were a Western, would have been punctuated with a stream of tobacco juice well aimed at a spittoon. "How do you know he's going to kill children?"

"I'd rather not say, ma'am."

"Call me Edie."

"Yes, ma'am."

"I'd rather that you *did* say."

"What if first you tell me what it means to be smoothed out and fully blue?"

After a silence, she said, "I'll tell you when I tell you, but this isn't the when."

"That works for me, too, ma'am."

Squinting at the distant eighteen-wheeler as though she might vaporize it with her stare, Mrs. Fischer said, "If I catch the freak laying a hand on a child, I'll feed his testicles to coyotes while he watches."

She didn't look quite so adorable at the moment. She looked like a mean Muppet hot for vengeance.

# Eight

IN THE TIGHTLY CLUSTERED SUBURBS JUST north of Los Angeles, the ProStar+ turned away from any hope of the sea, and we followed. Soon Highway 101 became State Route 134, the widest river of concrete that I had yet seen, which offered passage through the metropolitan sprawl to stark and lonely mountains in the east.

I was born in quiet Pico Mundo, where prairie surrendered to desert long before my time, and I lived there for more than twenty years. But the memory of my loss was too much with me in Pico Mundo. Although I knew that Stormy Llewellyn would not have hesitated to cross over to the Other Side, I woke many mornings with the hope that her lingering spirit would come to me, that I might see her again, and I went to bed at night to dream of the reunion that the day had not produced.

When at last I ventured out into the world, seek-

ing peace that I could no longer find in my hometown, I went only as far as St. Bartholomew's Abbey,
on the California side of the Sierra Nevada, high in
the mountains, where I stayed as a lay resident in the
monks' guesthouse for half a year. My adventures
since leaving the monastery had taken me to the town
of Magic Beach, to a roadside enterprise called Harmony Corner, to a strange private estate in Montecito, but only now, for the first time in my life, into the
outer precincts of a major city.

Maybe I am by nature too lacking in sophistication
to appreciate or adapt to life among teeming multitudes. The sight of one community after another flowing together without discernible borders, the vast
valley and the serried hillsides encrusted with miles
upon miles of houses and low-rise buildings, here
and there clusters of high-rises: It oppressed me, and
though we were traveling through it all at great
speed—past exits for Burbank and Glendale and
Eagle Rock—I felt enchained, claustrophobic.

The volume of traffic increased by the minute.
Afraid of losing our quarry, Mrs. Fischer wanted to
close the gap between us and the truck.

I insisted that we remain at such a distance that
we could just barely see the eighteen-wheeler. "You
said he's all deceit, lies, and trickery, and that's true.
But he's also . . . I don't know. Intuitive. Strangely
intuitive. If we aren't extremely careful, he'll become aware of us."

She glanced at me, her face that of a wizened

pixie but her eyes as analytic as the lasers of some facial-recognition scanner that could read volumes of information even in the blandest expression that I might turn upon her. "And if we lose him, Oddie?"

"We'll find him again."

"How can you be so sure of that?"

Rather than meet that blue stare a moment longer, I shifted my gaze to the habitations of humanity that, in their plenitude, raised an inexplicable but nonetheless terrible foreboding in my heart.

When I didn't reply to her question, she answered it for me. "Maybe you're so sure of finding him again because you're 'strangely intuitive' yourself."

I didn't respond because her words were not just words; they were also bait. She had her secrets and I had mine, and for the time being, we would keep them to ourselves.

The clear sky, under which I had left Annamaria back at the cottage, remained clear here to the north of the city. But ominous palisades of dark clouds rose in the south and appeared to be falling toward us in a slow-motion avalanche. A wind had come out of the south, as well, shuddering the trees. The high-soaring, graceful flocks of birds seen previously were gone, replaced by quick pairs and lone individuals that flew fast and low, darting as if from one temporary roost to another in search of the safest haven in which to ride out a coming storm.

"What happened to your disguise?" Mrs. Fischer asked.

"Disguise?"

"Oscar's lovely plaid cap."

"I don't know. I must have left it somewhere. I'm sorry."

"And the sunglasses?"

"They broke when—" I almost said *when the cowboy shot me in the throat,* but caught myself. "They just broke."

She clucked her tongue. "Not good. Now there's just the chin beard and the choice of mustaches."

"I'm done with disguises, ma'am. They won't fool this guy."

Across the wide highway, through the valley, over the tiered foothills, and up the rough slopes of the San Gabriel Mountains, vast ragged shadows suddenly flew northward, although the clear sky revealed no cause for them. In all my troubled life, I had never seen anything like these swift shades, as if aircraft as large as football fields—and larger—passed low overhead in jet-speed squadrons.

I almost exclaimed about them, but then I realized that Mrs. Fischer was unaware of this spectacle. She leaned forward over the steering wheel, squinting to keep the distant ProStar+ in sight among other eighteen-wheelers that might at any moment change lanes and screen her from it. Even if focused intently on the truck, she would have been aware of the racing shadows if she had been capable of seeing them. Evidently, they weren't real shadows but perhaps were instead portents of some threat, visible only to me.

The many densely populated communities encircling us were more oppressive than ever, huddled, hivelike. In the stroboscopic flicker of light, the impossible shadows seemed not only to race over the landscape but also to flail at it, and the buildings and all the artifacts of mankind appeared to twitch and shiver much as the trees shuddered in the rising wind.

For me and for a moment, present and future became one, the latter floating on the former, sensed more than seen, presenting itself as feelings and metaphors rather than as a detailed vision of what was to come in the days and years ahead. Claustrophobia wound around me, tighter and tighter, as if it were grave cloth and I were being mummified. For all that great cities had to offer, they were nonetheless mazes of streets. Mazes could thwart and trap. Broad, open freeways offered freedom only until clogged with traffic—or barricaded. Any neighborhood, rich or poor, was potentially a ghetto, every ghetto easily converted to a prison, every prison a potential death camp. To both sides of the highway, the residences and offices and retail outlets seemed at one moment to be burnt-out and boarded-up, but an instant later they appeared to be bunkers and battlements arrayed not against a common enemy but each against the other in a war of all versus all. Now I *felt* the shadows that flailed the land, as though they were accompanied by shock waves, and the flickers of sun-light were almost bright enough to blind. In addition to the broad freeway along which vehicles raced at high speed, I was also aware of these same concrete arteries in a state of sclerosis, perhaps hours or weeks or years from now, commuters halted bumper-to-bumper. As insubstantial as figments of a dream yet terrifying, an angry mob invaded my vague premonition, a faceless horde bringing grim detail to the vision, metastasizing along the lanes of stalled cars and trucks, smashing windows, tearing open doors, dragging motorists and passengers onto the pavement, blades glinting, guns firing, boots stomping terrified faces. Blood.

I might have lost consciousness for a few seconds, because when I opened my eyes, the landscape was no longer darkened by fast-moving and inexplicable shadows. The surrounding communities were neither in ruins nor fortified against conflict, traffic sped along the freeway, and Mrs. Fischer sounded worried when she said, "Oddie, what's wrong? Do you hear me? Oddie?"

"Yes, ma'am, I hear you."

The images from the premonition faded, but I still had a sense of being in the path of malevolent, implacable forces. That wasn't an unusual feeling for me, but this time the threat felt imminent.

"Are you all right?" Mrs. Fischer asked.

"Sort of. Yeah. I'm fine. Just a little thing there for a moment. What's up?"

"I think we've lost him." She drove as fast as ever, switching lanes with bravado, passing between a pair of eighteen-wheelers that bracketed us like cliffs, searching for the one that got away. "There were suddenly so many trucks and I *thought* I still had a lock on him, but then I realized it was a different rig."

State Route 134 had become Interstate 210. The highway signs promised exits for Azusa and Covina.

The dark clouds massed in the south were dramatically closer than before, and I suspected that I had been unconscious for minutes rather than seconds.

"Ma'am, you better get all the way over to the right. Take the next exit."

"Do you know where he's gone? How can you know where he's gone?"

"I have a hunch."

Working the car toward the right lane, Mrs. Fischer said, "A hunch? A hunch isn't worth spit."

"Well, this one is, ma'am. It's worth spit and then some."

"Your hunches usually pay off, do they?"

"I learn by going where I have to go," I said, determined not to explain psychic magnetism.

She didn't slow down much for the exit ramp.

I said, "Left at the bottom."

Because no traffic approached on the intersecting surface street, she didn't obey the stop sign.

"Come to think of it," she said, "how did you know he would be at that truck stop earlier?"

As we went through an underpass beneath the freeway, we politely pretended not to see the obscene spray-painted graffiti, which was colorful but, as usual, unimaginative. I suspect that those who see equal merit in graffiti and the work of Rembrandt might be wrong.

I said, "Trucker at a truck stop. It seemed logical."

"That's all it was? Just logic?"

"Yes, ma'am."

"You're dancing around the truth, child. You told me it was only all right to lie to evil."

"And you said you might be evil."

"Might be. I didn't say I was."

"Please turn left in two blocks, ma'am."

"Fact is, I'm not evil."

The effect of the premonition had diminished enough to allow me to smile. "First you said you might be evil, now you say you're not. I better tread carefully with you."

We passed through a once prosperous retail area where a third of the businesses were gone, many of them restaurants, and the remaining shops and services had a tattered look that suggested they were week-to-week enterprises. Some days lately, it seemed that *everything* was a week-to-week enterprise, including the country and the world.

A traffic signal turned green to accommodate us, and I said, "After the intersection, pull to the curb."

Mrs. Fischer braked to a stop in front of a thrift shop operated by the Salvation Army.

I said, "I'll be going the rest of the way alone, on foot."

"Is that really wise?"

"I'm not sure anything I do is wise, ma'am, but I've stayed alive a lot longer than I ever expected."

"What do you want me to do?"

"I'm grateful that you came along, and I'm thankful for your help. But I don't want you to be hurt because of me. You need to get on with your life while I get on with trying to understand mine."

After her many years of living, perhaps even from her childhood, Mrs. Fischer's eyes were the sky reflected in the sea, eternity mirrored in the everlasting waters. Even if she had not given voice to the next thing that she said, meeting her gaze, I would have known that the secrets to which she often alluded were real and profound and no less strange than my own. She said, "Something big is coming, Oddie. Something so very big that the world will change. I know you feel it, too."

"Yes, ma'am."

"How long have you felt it?"

"Almost all my life. But more so lately."

"Much more so lately," she agreed. "Child, do you know where truly great courage comes from, the kind of courage that will never back down?"

I said, "Faith."

"And love," she said. "Faith is a kind of love, you know. Love of what is unseen but certain. Love makes us strong and brave."

I thought of Stormy and how the loss of her had tempered my steel. "Yes."

"Heath and I never had children. I believe that I wasn't given any children because I needed to save all that love for a time late in my life when I would need it to give me courage."

Suddenly the rising wind rose faster, buffeted the limousine, and conjured a dust devil full of leaves and litter that whirled up from the gutter and followed a drunkard's path down the center of the street.

She said, "You see, many years ago, three times I had the same vivid dream about a motherless, fatherless boy who was nevertheless not an orphan. Are you without a mother and father, Oddie?"

"They're still alive, ma'am, but they were never a mother and father to me. I've been on my own since I was sixteen."

"When I saw you standing beside the Coast Highway, I recognized you from the dream, though you are not a boy any longer."

Several pages of a newspaper flocked along the street, faux birds of ill omen, flapping ungainly wings of words.

"What's the story of your dream?" I asked. "What happens in it?"

"A true and lovely thing. That's all I'll say for

now. But I will never, as you suggest, get on with my life by leaving you here and driving away. If you must go by foot now and alone, so be it. But I'll get on with my life by waiting right here until you come back."

"I wish you wouldn't."

She opened her voluminous purse. "Take the gun."

I thought of the premonition: universal war, all against all. If such a conflict was coming, it wouldn't happen in the next day or the next week, probably not even in the next year. Maybe it wouldn't ever happen. The future isn't set. Our free will creates our future.

Mrs. Fischer plucked the weapon from her purse and pressed it into my hands. "Take, take. I've got others."

As I tucked the pistol in my waistband and under my sweatshirt, I said, "You seem to be prepared for anything."

"We all better be prepared, child." Her eyes remained solemn even when she smiled. She reached out and gently pinched my cheek. "Be safe, Oddie. Come home."

# Nine

WHEN I GOT OUT OF THE LIMOUSINE, THE
wind tossed my hair and threw dust in my eyes, as if
it were a malicious spirit. The day was chilly for
Southern California in early March, especially considering that the storm front had come in from the
southwest. The sea, which this gruff wind would
have bullied into whitecaps, must have been unusually cold. I could faintly smell the distant shore,
mostly the astringent scent of iodine given off by certain seaweeds when they are tossed onto the beach to
decompose above the tide line.

I walked past the thrift shop to the nearby corner
and turned left. The two- and three-story buildings
were old, mostly of painted brick with cast-stone
Art Deco details in their parapeted roofs and pedi-
mented windows. Phoenix palms lined the street,
more stately than the neighborhood in which they
flourished.

Instead of consciously choosing a route, I went where psychic magnetism drew me, never sure when I might find myself before a door and know that my quarry waited beyond it, or round a corner and come face-to-face with him, or hear the word *dirtbag* spoken behind me and turn to discover that my talent for attraction had drawn him to me instead of me to him, his silencer-equipped Sig Sauer in my face—or crotch.

Ahead of me, from high in a wind-tossed phoenix palm, four rats that were remarkably fat for these lean times descended from their fair-weather nest in the thick dry skirt just below the glorious spray of green fronds. Like a precision drill team, they came one behind the other, nose to tail, legs synchronized. At the bottom of the tree, the quartet spilled over the curb, into the gutter, and disappeared through the bars of a drainage grate, as disciplined as any human family in the vast flat Midwest when the tornado sirens wailed and the house had to be abandoned for the storm cellar in the backyard.

Although I know the world is an intricately more complex place than it appears to most people, although I understand in my blood and bones that humanity is a turbulent family aboard an endless train, on an infinite journey to shores that can only dimly be imagined by the living, I don't see signs and portents everywhere I look. Most often, a haloed moon means nothing more than that reflective volcanic ash has made its way into the stratosphere, and a two-headed goat is only a genetic curiosity. The mommy-porn genre currently sweeping the book industry and the Babylonian excess of most television shows probably fall within the historical norm in our culture's sleaze index and are not omens of the imminent collapse of civilization, though if I were not so busy, I might start building an ark.

Those four brown rats, however, descending at precisely that moment instead of any other, impressed me as being more than merely rodents on the run from threatening weather. For one thing, at the curb, before slinking into the gutter, each turned its head toward me, its whiteless eyes as glossy as black glass, its scaly tail lashing back and forth twice before it continued out of sight into the drain.

I found myself drawn to the curb, where I stood staring at the large rectangular grate, shivering with recognition. It was made in an age when public works were elegant and well crafted instead of slipshod. The parallel iron bars met a four-inch iron ring in the center of the design. Within the ring, a stylized iron lightning bolt angled from right to left. On a fogbound night in Magic Beach, more than a month previously, on a street deserted but for me, I had been drawn to such a grating, below which grotesque shadows capered in pulses of eerie light.

On that occasion, in the grip of curiosity, I had knelt to peer between the bars, into the culvert, seeking an explanation for this unusual display. I had been by some means induced into a half trance, so that I lowered my face ever closer to the drain, over-come not only by a compulsion to learn what might lie below but also by the intense expectation that, whatever it proved to be, I needed it as surely as I needed air and water and food to sustain life.

The sudden arrival of an unexpected ally on that lonely street in Magic Beach had broken the spell and had brought me to my feet. Later, I felt that I had been close to discovering something that might have been the end of me—not merely death but a more terrible and enduring end.

Now, I did not follow the rats to the grate, but turned away and walked swiftly, not quite running. I went four blocks, the battalions of incoming storm clouds forgotten, oblivious of the wind, the rats banished from my mind. Rather, I succumbed to one of those fugues that sometimes strike us when, below the age of ten, we chance upon a truth meant only for adults, a sharp truth that stabs darkness into the light of innocence, that makes us at once rebel against this assault on wonder, that sends us away to games and bicycles and all manner of distractions, from which we rise in a few hours, like a sleeper from a dream, having spun a cocoon of denial to protect us from that piercing truth, although it is a fragile cocoon that in time will dissolve.

Halting at a street corner, looking back the way I'd come, I had no memory of the buildings I had passed, only of the lightning-bolt grate that lay four blocks to the south. For that distance, I'd even forgotten why I'd come here. Now I remembered the rhinestone cowboy, his spiky white hair, his pitiless stare, his vacation-in-Hell tan.

My heart lagged my brain, beating hard and fast, as if I were still within a step of the ominous drain grating. Giving it time to settle into a rhythm less suggestive of a crisis in an ER, I studied my surroundings.

I had arrived in a district of old industrial buildings, mostly constructed of dark-red or pale-yellow brick with slate or tile or corrugated-metal roofs, others of stucco cracked and stigmatized with stains of such disturbing shapes that they might have depicted Armageddon reflected in a fun-house mirror. Some structures appeared still to be in use. Others were untenanted or abandoned, diminished by missing windowpanes, months of debris compacted by wind and rain in their doorways, and weeds bristling from cracks in the pavement of the adjacent parking yards, around which chain-link fencing sagged.

As the last blue sky shrank northward, thunderheads towered as if they were mountains thrusting violently from the earth's crust in a fierce seismic and volcanic age millions of years before any living thing yet crawled the planet.

I walked south, into the wind, retracing my route for a block and a half—noticing that other street drains lacked the lightning bolt—until I arrived at the mouth of a wide alleyway similarly lined with industrial buildings and warehouses. In some other pockets of this neighborhood, workers labored, deliveries were being made and shipments loaded. But here, in spite of wind-stirred power-company lines that softly whistled overhead, there lay a stillness more suited to a ghost town than to any place in a living city.

As I entered the alley, the sun abruptly submerged in clouds, and the bleak, black shadows of utility poles melted into the potholed pavement. On both sides were elevated loading docks, man-size doors, big roll-ups, and latticed windows of many small panes so filthy that they were all but opaque.

Past the middle of the block, I was drawn to a building narrower than the others, with a man door and three roll-ups large enough to admit trucks of any size. The windows were as blinded with dust as all the others, but lights inside lent the glass a silvery sheen.

Beyond doubt, the cowboy trucker was nearby. The image of him in my mind's eye grew brighter and more colorful and so fearsome that, to prevent him from fulfilling his threat, I wished fervently that I had bought a Kevlar jockstrap.

At the man-size door, I stood with my head cocked, listening. When I heard nothing, I drew the pistol from my waistband. I tried the lever handle, and the unlocked door opened a crack. Emboldened by the enduring silence, I eased inside and closed the door quietly behind me.

I stood in a brick-walled garage brightened by overhead banks of fluorescent tubes. Only the middle of the three bays contained a vehicle, a white Ford van, one of those small delivery vans used by florists and caterers, although this one had no company name or logo emblazoned on it.

When I opened the van, the cargo area contained nothing, though perhaps soon it would imprison three bound, gagged, and terrified children meant for burning. For the sake of silence, I left the vehicle open.

In the back wall of the garage, opposite the roll-ups, two doors flanked a freight elevator. There is a classic short story in which a man must open one of two doors, aware that a beautiful lady waits behind one and a hungry tiger behind the other, but he doesn't know which door is which. Given my luck, I expected to find tigers to the left *and* right. The freight route didn't appeal, either.

Compelled to the door on the right, I found ascending stairs. They were concrete with glued-on rubber treads for safety, which also served to mute my footsteps. I eased the door shut behind me.

I had climbed halfway to the first landing when I heard two male voices above me in the stairwell. The words bounced between the brick wall on my right and the easy-clean glossy-yellow fiberboard on my left, and were distorted so that I couldn't be certain that either speaker was the cowboy trucker.

With the pistol, I could intimidate them. But if

my quarry was not one of the two, I would have no
way of knowing whether or not I might be threatening innocent men.

I hurriedly descended the stairs, entered the
garage—and found it changed. Instead of overhead
fluorescents, three single-bulb lamps with cone-shaped
shades hung on chains. The poor light shone just
bright enough for me to see that the brick walls were
gone and that bare concrete replaced them.

More startling than any of that was the red-and-
black ProStar+ with sparkly silver striping and its
long black trailer, which stood in the center bay
where the white van had been only seconds earlier. In
this enclosed space, the eighteen-wheeler looked even
bigger than it had appeared to be on the open road,
and although an inanimate object of any size, lacking
consciousness and intention, cannot be malevolent,
this truck seemed as malign as the Death Star with
which Darth Vader atomized entire planets.

# Ten

THE PROSTAR+ STOOD IN THE TRANSFORMED garage as though it had eaten the Ford van. I wondered if I should reconsider my disdain for possessed-vehicle movies like *The Car, Maximum Overdrive,* and *The Love Bug.*

After a life of supernatural engagement, I was not paralyzed by this seeming impossibility. I scurried around the eighteen-wheeler to the side farther from the door that I left open behind me, sheltering there until I could get a glimpse, at an angle through the driver's window and the windshield, of who followed me out of the stairwell. If one of them was the rhinestone cowboy, I might still get the drop on him. If that proved to be impossible—if, say, he appeared with the flamethrower that he intended to use on the children—I could retreat through the outer door by which I'd entered the building and hide elsewhere along the alley, at a position from which I could monitor events.

No one came out of the stairwell, but I heard two men talking. They seemed to be nearby, yet their voices were veiled. The words were distorted beyond understanding, as when the cowboy and the man with the battered-boxer face—semitransparent and unaware of me—had been in urgent angry conversation in the basement machine room at the truck stop.

This time, they did not appear even in phantom form. I had only their voices, by which I could not precisely place them. And then they fell silent.

I was concerned that they had become aware of me, as I had been aware of them in the machine room. Perhaps our circumstances had been reversed and I was semitransparent to them while they were invisible to me.

The next twenty or thirty seconds were as sharp as saw teeth, working on my taut-wire nerves, as I waited to feel the singular chill of one of these men passing through the space that I occupied.

Instead, I heard an engine turn over, not that of the ProStar+, but that of a much smaller truck, though it was muffled and hollow, filtered through some barrier just as the voices had been filtered. I could only assume that it was the white Ford van, which had become invisible to me.

A moment later, a rattling and low rumbling perplexed me for a moment. But then I realized that this was the distorted sound of a big segmented door rolling on its tracks.

I turned toward the alleyway, but none of the three roll-ups was in motion, all snugged down tight.

I listened to the unseen van reverse away from me, out of the garage. Following its departure came the rumble of the huge segmented door descending, although the door behind the ProStar+ and the two flanking it were already down and locked.

In high school, the spirit world frequently distracted me from science studies, and my interest in higher mathematics was no greater than my interest in self-immolation, but I scored well in English. I possessed the ability and the skills to write about the coexistent garages. But I sadly lacked the knowledge to intelligently express a theory explaining how such a thing could be—or, for that matter, why fire makes water boil.

If two garages existed in the same place, in different worlds or dimensions or whatever, I seemed to be, for the moment, in the world/dimension/whatever that was different from mine. And the two men whose voices I heard had evidently driven the Ford van away into the world from which I had come.

In Shower 5 at Star Truck, in the basement machine room of that same facility, and now in the garage of this industrial building, two realities crossed. Shower 5 Elsewhere had not been a shower room at all but a barren place, just as Basement Machine Room Elsewhere had been devoid of machinery, and this garage in Elsewhere was likewise a stark concrete box. I had been shot to death in the Elsewhere shower but remained alive in the real Shower 5. Now the rhinestone cowboy parked his truck in Elsewhere and, with some associate, drove away into my reality, perhaps fearing that authorities were looking for the ProStar+ because he had run me off the road with it—or for a reason I couldn't fathom. This guy was able to do things that people failed to see, like shoot an innocent cantaloupe to bits, and he could step out of reality into Elsewhere when it suited him.

My skull hurt. My brain felt abused. I needed a plate of my own überfluffy pancakes to restore my full cognitive function.

The cowboy might have as many paranormal talents as I possessed, or even more. Maybe. Except . . . Well, it seemed to me that anyone with such astonishing abilities would not dress so ridiculously. Not that I'm saying that every superhumanly gifted person ought to wear jeans and sweatshirts or T-shirts, as I do, or all Ralph Lauren. But boots of carved leather with fancy snakeskin inlays? A black sports coat with red lapels and collar crusted with sequins, as if he was a Grand Ole Opry wannabe? The Joker, Bane, Lex Luthor, the Green Goblin: They all had better taste in clothing than this guy.

Besides, in the real world, as opposed to the worlds of comic books, a guy with paranormal powers would not want to draw attention to himself. Trust me.

Alone with the eighteen-wheeler, I decided to check it out. He had left a set of keys in the ignition, evidently certain that there were no thieves in Elsewhere. The driver's compartment contained nothing of interest other than the string of red beads and little carved-bone skulls, which hung from the overhead CB radio.

On closer inspection than I had been able to do previously, I found that the long vertical latch bolts on the back of the trailer were secured by custom shackles. One of the keys released them.

When I opened the tall doors, a row of LED bulbs brightened along the center of the trailer ceiling, front to back. Immediately inside the doors, a two-panel stainless-steel gate blocked entrance. Into a series of vertical one-inch bars, a talented metalworker had incorporated three pentagrams, a Celtic cross, a Maltese cross, a Latin cross, an ankh, two swastikas, and perhaps a dozen symbols that I couldn't name. Work by an artisan this masterful—not a weld showing, the steel regrained after construction, the dazzling design harmonious in spite of its disparate elements— would have cost many thousands of dollars.

Beyond the gate, the three walls, the floor, and the ceiling of the trailer were painted with the same symbols, sun-yellow forms on a black background. The lighting revealed no cargo.

In fact, it looked like a trailer that *never* carried freight, and if that should be the case, I wondered what purpose it served for the cowboy. Evidently, he wasn't a true trucker after all, just a man who drove a truck. He must earn his living in some other way, though I doubted that, even in this transgressive age, anyone could sustain a paying career as a burner of defenseless children.

Although no lock was apparent, the halves of this gate were firmly secured to each other. I could neither pull nor push them apart.

Only as I began to close the doors did I suspect the trailer might not be as vacant as it appeared. Through the steel filigree issued a disturbing scent as sweet as incense and yet suggestive of decomposition, like nothing I'd ever smelled before. Perhaps it was an odor lingering from a previous cargo, but I had not detected it initially. With the malodor came a sudden chill, not internal to me, less than a draft, a mere breath, an icy effluence that, like spicules of sleet, prickled my face.

Convinced that whatever the cowboy hauled, he didn't merely deal in loads of consumer electronics or goods for the Pottery Barn, I closed the trailer doors. Shot the long bolts. Engaged the shackles.

Although I can't explain why, following exposure to the stink and the chill, I wanted to spend a couple of hours in a bathtub filled with Purell sanitizing gel, maybe take a few turns being irradiated on the carousel of a human-size microwave oven, spend an hour inhaling steam made with water from the shrine at Lourdes, and have my blood drained from my left arm, processed through a state-of-the-art filtration machine, and returned into my right arm free of all contaminants. Afterward, a lollipop would be nice.

I found myself backing away from the trailer and realized that my skittish heart was cantering again, as it had when I'd seen the drainage grate with the lightning bolt.

Suddenly the black-and-red eighteen-wheeler, with its sparkly silver striping, seemed as if it might be some kind of carnival truck, which had unpleasant associations for me. I know that most carnival folks are nothing like their public image. The majority are good people who just don't fit in anywhere else, and they have a complex, charming social structure of their own. I read this book, *Twilight Eyes*, all about them. But I once had a bad experience with two carnies.

This guy named Pecker—I don't think it was his baptismal name—operated a ring-toss concession. His woolly hair was teased precisely as high as the long beard that depended from his chin, so he almost looked like Siamese twins joined at the tops of their heads. He and his joyfully wicked friend Bucket, the owner-operator of cotton-candy and snow-cone machines, had hoped to establish an after-hours carnival concession, at 3:00 one summer morning, in which I would be gagged and lashed to a tree to serve as the target. The two of them intended to take turns throwing hatchets at me. I had done something that annoyed them. Fortunately, I am quick on my feet, tougher than I look (which I would have to be), and I was in the company of a friendly poltergeist that left them bewildered by beating them senseless with a hundred baseballs from the milk-bottle-pyramid concession.

Anyway, having at last gotten the peek into the trailer that I long had wanted, reasonably sure that my quarry had driven away in the white Ford van, I decided to leave this garage in Elsewhere. I intended to depart through the door by which I had entered, expecting that I would step back into my world as magically as I had previously stepped out of it.

Approaching that exit, however, I noticed for the first time that the only light came from the three overhead bulbs dangling in cone-shaped shades, none whatsoever from the three-foot-high bank of latticed windows above the man door and the three roll-ups. Only perfect blackness lay beyond those panes. I had arrived in the early afternoon, and no more than five minutes had passed since then. The coming storm couldn't have seethed in so quickly; even if threatening clouds lowered over the city from horizon to horizon, no storm could have banished every last trace of sunlight. At the door, I paused, pistol in my right hand, left hand on the lever handle.

I sensed that opening this door would be as stupid as seeking the source of gas fumes in a dark basement by striking a match.

Intuition is the highest form of knowledge. What we learn from others can be mistaught by those not a fraction as knowledgeable as they pretend or by those who are propagandists with agendas. We are born with intuition, however, which includes the natural law, a sense of right and wrong. A lot of people rebel so continually against natural law that not only does that part of their intuition atrophy but also every other aspect of it. They strike the match, open the door, give their money to an investment adviser named Slick, and trust that if they are really nice to the thug with the switchblade, he'll be nice to them.

Whatever waited outside this garage in Elsewhere would not be as easy to deal with as a psychopath with a knife.

I backed away from the door, glanced again at the high windows, wishing that the darkness would give way to the murky light of an overcast sky. This was as effective as wishing for world peace.

To look through those windows into the alleyway, I would have to climb to the top of the trailer, an easy enough feat. But the odor and the chill that had passed through the ornamental gate were fresh in memory, and I was possessed by the—perhaps irrational—fear that a trap in the trailer roof would open under my feet and drop me into a kind of trouble that I had never known before.

In need of a room with a view, I returned to the open stairwell door to listen. The quiet was profound, a stillness as in a vacuum. If anyone waited on the upper floor, he must be dead or Death.

Previously, the wall on the left had been paneled in easy-to-clean yellow fiberboard, and the wall on the right had been brick. Now they were both con-crete. On the steps, the glued-on rubber treads were missing. The first time I entered this stairwell, before hastily retreating at the sound of voices, it had been in my world. Now it was in some parallel reality.

Some days I wonder about my sanity. A good cheeseburger usually restores my confidence. If that doesn't work, I watch an episode of some reality-TV show like *The Real Housewives of Wherever,* and by comparison with the stars of the program, I feel as solid as a blacksmith's anvil.

The stairwell seemed unnaturally clean. In the be-calmed air and the cold light, no dust motes drifted in suspension. Not one tattered strand of spider silk waited for a draft to flutter. No desiccated flies or shriveled moths or single scrap of lint littered the stairs.

No cracks or water stains marred the surrounding concrete. Stepping across the threshold, onto the bot-tom landing, I felt that I must be somewhere outside of time, the only living creature in a place to which even the spirits of the lingering dead never ventured.

Warily, I climbed the stairs.

# Eleven

HALFWAY TOWARD THE MIDFLOOR LANDING, I was overcome once more by the perception that these concrete walls were not concrete at all, but were instead the *idea* of concrete, a thought that first occurred to me back at Star Truck, when Shower 5 in the real world abruptly became Shower 5 Elsewhere. I didn't know what I meant by that, but my suspicion was evoked by the continuity of color and texture: an unvarying gray without the smallest stain, without a single line or trace of wood grain from the lumber forms into which the concrete would have been poured, no surface voids or exposed aggregate.

When I slid my left hand along the inner wall, the surface felt at first like concrete, but then like fiberboard with a high-gloss finish, although to my lying eyes it remained curiously perfect concrete. When I put my right hand to the outer wall, my questing fingers slid across bricks and recessed mortar joints that

I could not see, although a moment later the texture of a smooth concrete surface returned.

I didn't know what to make of all this, except that my reality and Elsewhere seemed to occupy the same space at the same time. In Elsewhere, my world floated just below the surface of things; and in my world, Elsewhere was submerged and waiting. Whether this was true everywhere that I might go or only in some locations, I could not know for sure, but I suspected that the two realities intersected only rarely, as in some rooms of Star Truck and in this abandoned industrial building.

Wherever and whatever Elsewhere might be, I didn't think that it was a world like ours, that it was either peopled by different versions of ourselves or by another race entirely. The cowboy trucker had parked his rig here, leaving the keys in the ignition, because he knew that in Elsewhere it would remain undiscovered and safe, which suggested that Elsewhere was a dead zone of sorts, populated neither by anyone nor anything.

The midfloor landing had no windows. I paused to listen but heard nothing other than my stomach grumbling about not yet having received the cheese meatloaf, steak fries, and coleslaw that I had all but sworn an oath to consume back at the truck stop. I continued upward and, at the top of the second flight, I came to a landing door on my right, with more stairs on my left leading to the third floor.

I didn't need to seek the highest vantage point.

Any second-floor window would satisfy my curiosity about the untimely darkness that seemed to lie beyond these walls.

In my world, this building was perhaps eighty years old, dirty and battered and unoccupied if not even abandoned; it had not in any recent decade been refurbished. Judging by the design and the details of its construction, the metal door on the landing was as old as the building. It should have been scratched and dimpled, as no doubt it was in my reality, though here it appeared to be as unmarked as it was on the day it had been installed.

The immaculate condition of the door seemed not just improbable but impossible. And when I concentrated closely and entirely upon it, searching its smooth surface for a sign of wear, I was more than half persuaded that it was merely the drawn *image* of a door, like that in a clever trompe l'oeil painting or on the backdrop of a cunningly designed stage setting, convincing not because of elaborate detail but because the artist's use of perspective and light was masterful.

Nevertheless, the knob felt solid in my grasp, and it turned without resistance. The knuckles of the barrel hinges revolved soundlessly around the pivot pins, and the door opened as smoothly as one liquid flowing into another, so that I could almost believe that I was adventuring in my sleep.

Beyond lay a hallway. The ceiling, walls, and floor were as uniformly gray and smooth as in the garage and stairwell. Overhead hung the usual crude lamps. When I stared hard at the nearest one, it produced less light, not because the bulb dimmed but because the bulb, the shade, and the chain all seemed to diminish in substance when studied intently, as if sufficient scrutiny might in time cause them to disappear altogether. I didn't test that hypothesis because I didn't want to be left whimpering in the dark.

On both sides of the corridor were a few doors like the one through which I had just come. America's primary institution of learning—the movies—has taught us that when we find ourselves in a strange and eerily quiet place with lots of doors, waiting behind one of them will be either a psychopathic killer or a monster of supernatural or extraterrestrial origin. Of course, if it's an Adam Sandler comedy, behind the door will lurk a goofy dude waiting to deliver a joke involving poop, pee, or genitals. I wasn't in such a comedy, but that was all right, because I preferred a psychopath or a monster.

When I opened the nearest door on the right, nothing bit off my head. A single lamp hung in the center of the unfurnished gray room.

I crossed to the windows and was stunned to see the sprawling suburbs of the valley cast in darkness, not one streetlamp or building light to be seen. Far beyond the Hollywood hills, to the southwest, no faintest glow rose from the flatlands of Los Angeles and environs, though on an ordinary night, the incandescence of civilization would shimmer in the air and paint the bellies of the clouds a burnt-butter yellow. Above the black land, the blacker sky had been swept clean of moon and stars.

In the middle distance, three widely separated lakes of low flames glimmered and twinkled red-orange-blue, like the baleful campfires of savage and malevolent settlements. They burned without illuminating their surroundings, as if the night air had unnatural weight sufficient to prevent the light from rising.

Although the uncanny gloom flooded the land before, between, and beyond the pooling fires, the realm on the farther side of the windows was not blind-dark. I was able to discern that the street in front of this building had vanished, replaced by barren ground. And suddenly I knew that the suburbs and the city they encircled had not merely gone dark in a power outage but had ceased to exist either as intact structures or as ruins. In my reality, this building stood in an industrial neighborhood, but in Elsewhere, it seemed to loom alone above a blackened wasteland.

I had wanted a window with a view. Now I wanted a quiet corner in which I could curl up in a ball and suck my thumb until my fairy godmother came and took me away from this hostile, empty world.

In this blighted kingdom, however, wishes were answered in such a perverse way that they were far better left unwished. Twenty feet below, where the street should have been, something moved, a verti-

cal shadow in the otherwise still and amorphous
dark. Squinting, I saw what might have been a man,
but he was so little differentiated from the murk
around him that I couldn't make out his face or determine what he wore. One thing about him was
certain: He didn't have fairy wings.

If the weak light in the room around me filtered
through the glass, none of it reached as far as the
figure below, although it revealed me to him. He
halted, I sensed him looking up, but I did not draw
back from the window. I had already been seen. He
would come to me or he wouldn't. After a moment,
he approached the front of the building, disappear-
ing into the recessed entrance.

Pistol in hand, I returned to the second-floor hall.
Moments before, I had climbed the west stairs,
which originated at the garage in back. The door at
the east end of the hallway suggested another stairwell rising from the front of the building, which was
probably the one by which he would come to me.

My keen intuition, which had often been my salvation, was largely a mental faculty, its physical expression limited to an occasional tingle at the nape of
the neck, the hairs bristling on the backs of my hands,
and—unseemly but true—a certain tightening of the
scrotum, although that last reaction was about as
erotic as a spinal tap. In this instance, a swift series of
chills quivered violently through me, as if I were constructed entirely of taut harpstrings that thrummed
with glissandos of foreboding.

At all costs, I needed to avoid a confrontation with that shadowy figure. I didn't know *why* I must keep my distance from the man, if man he was, and I had no one to ask, because intuition is a one-way communication from God, who never seems inclined to satisfy our curiosity, perhaps because, given the chance, every one of us would be like a child on a family road trip, endlessly asking *Are we there yet?* or the equivalent.

I turned away from the east end of the corridor and hurried to the west stairs, by which I had come up from the garage. Going down again seemed foolhardy, in part because leaving the building wasn't an option. If I ventured outside into unknown conditions, I might find it difficult if not impossible to get back inside. I assumed that I would have to be within the envelope of the building to be able to return to my reality when the shift occurred again, which might be hours or mere minutes from now.

After bolting up two flights to the top of the stairs, I pulled on the door, which swung open as silently as those before it, as if its lever handle, latch, and hinges operated with zero friction. For a long moment, I stood on the landing, listening.

When the stairwell door opened on the second floor, I didn't hear a sound. No sudden draft alerted me. I knew the visitor from the wasteland had entered the stairs only when his shadow preceded him, flowing onto the midfloor landing below in such a

sinuous fashion as to suggest that the man yet unseen would prove to be in part a serpent.

I slipped into the hallway and eased the door
shut, although left to gravity, it would most likely
have closed without a click.

The third floor seemed identical to the second. I
doubted that I had time to race all the way to the east
stairs before my pursuer would arrive and see me.

Besides, switching stairwells for hours on end
was not a strategy, hardly even worthy of the word
*tactic*. That gambit was certain to result, sooner or
later, in the two of us coming face-to-face in a doorway, which might not end well for me even though I
had a pistol.

In my experience, sometimes the guy on the other
side of the door possessed something more formidable than a handgun, such as a submachine gun or an
automatic shotgun, or an enraged ferret that he threw
in my face. Or he was clothed head to foot in body
armor and held a surface-to-air missile that, if fired
horizontally, could reduce you to a pile of flaming en-
trails. Or he was wearing a nine-sheath spring-loaded
antique-Chinese automatic-knife breastplate, which
in a split second could skewer you with enough stilettos to kill you and, should you have one, your cat as
well.

Trusting to luck, such as it was, I hurried halfway along the corridor and chose a door to my left.
Beyond, a dimly lighted flight of stairs led up to another door. I was pretty sure the building featured

no more than three stories. Maybe these stairs went to an attic.

I don't like attics any more than I like cellars.

Most people have never found anything in an attic more off-putting than silverfish, dry rot, and faded high-school photographs that remind them of how much promise they once had and of how little it has been fulfilled.

In my case, however, I tend to find things like a collection of shrunken heads hanging by their hair from the rafters or a fighting falcon trained to swoop down and pluck out an intruder's eyes, or a tripwire-activated capture net that drops over any unwanted visitor and cinches ever tighter around him until he's immobilized.

In spite of my experiences of attics, looking back the way I had come, when I saw the door begin to open at the west end of the hallway, I stepped across the threshold onto the landing. I drew the door shut behind me.

Once I was on the roof, I would be outside of the building's envelope, with nowhere to run and with more than a forty-foot drop to the ground below. Nevertheless, I hastily climbed this last flight of stairs because, for one thing, when confronted with the Unknown, of which this man from the wasteland was an embodiment, it was never wise to be confrontational, and because rational optimism is required of anyone who hopes to be a survivor, and finally because there was nowhere else to go.

# Twelve

THE DOOR AT THE HEAD OF THE STAIRS opened not into an attic but instead into a ten-foot-square room as featureless and somehow artificial as all those before it, which soon proved to be a kind of shed on the roof. Directly opposite the entrance door waited an exit, through which I stepped onto the flat and parapeted top of the building, closing that last door behind me.

Without a window between me and this absolute-black sky, the effect of such undetailed heavens was profound, frightening not just because of the uncanny darkness but also for a reason that eluded me. Or perhaps the reason was not elusive. Maybe I dreaded acknowledging and considering it, for fear that contemplation would soon sweep me out of the main currents of sanity, into a tributary of madness.

Indeed, the roof was a lunatic place, disorienting under a moonless and starless vault that seemed at first to be an eternal void, but the next moment might have been the low ceiling of a cavern deep in Earth's crust, and then again a void. In spite of the distant lakes of fire, if they were truly fire, the land around this isolated structure lay nearly as dark as the sky above, providing so little ambient light that I could not see as far as any edge of the roof, which in my reality had been guarded by an Art Deco parapet. Even in the remote reaches of the Mojave, even on a night when two thousand feet of dense ecliptical clouds separated the desert from the glowing wonders of the universe, the land gave off at least a dim light, the product of natural radiation, of minerals in the soil, and of certain vaguely luminous plants. Not here. This outer darkness, so complete, seemed to be capable of a kind of osmosis, gradually penetrating me to blacken my thoughts and eventually extinguish my hope.

I could barely see the pale forms of my hands—one fisted, the other clenching the pistol. As I took a two-hand grip on the weapon, it remained all but invisible, and I almost squeezed off a shot just to see the muzzle flash and know that I wasn't going blind.

Although I wanted to put more distance between me and the door of the shed, wanted to find something behind which I could hide—chimney stacks, air-conditioner housings, anything—my feet seemed to be embedded ankle-deep in long-settled roof tar. But my inability to move was entirely psychological, the blackness above pressing down like deep strata of soil and rock, squeezing upon me from all sides, until it seemed that Fate, in league with Nature, intended that I should become nothing more than a brittle fossil in a thick vein of anthracite.

With effort, I shuffled backward a step, another and another, but then halted as a dizziness overcame me and as I began to think that I must be turning as I retreated, gradually arcing away from the roof shed, where the man from the wasteland might at any moment appear. I needed to keep the pistol trained upon that door, because if the stranger came through it with the obvious intent to attack, he would be back-lighted only briefly. I would have but a second to discern his intent and another second to squeeze off a shot before the door fell shut.

When he was no longer silhouetted by the lighted shed, I might discover that he could see in the light-lessness of this wretched reality as well as I was able to see in the full sun of the day. He could then stalk me at his leisure, while in a growing panic I shot at phantoms until I expended all ten rounds in the pistol's magazine.

Although I am an optimist, my imagination can conjure countless deadly hands from any shuffled deck before the cards are dealt. I am, therefore, perplexed by so many people who, whether they're optimists or pessimists, trust any dealer as long as he claims to share their vision of how all things ought to be, who trust their own vision to the extent that they never question it, and who believe that four of a kind and royal flushes always fall by chance in a world without meaning. To such folks, Hitler was a distant and half-comic figure—until he wasn't; and mad mullahs promising to use nuclear weapons as soon as they obtain them are likewise harmless—until they aren't. I, on the other hand, believe life has profound meaning and that the meaning of Creation itself is benign, but I also know that there are such things as card mechanics who can manipulate any deck to their great advantage. In life, little happens by chance, and most bad hands we're dealt are the consequence of our actions, which are shaped by our wisdom and our ignorance. In my experience, survival depends on hoping for the best while recognizing that disaster is more likely and that it can't be averted if it can't be imagined.

The roof-shed door opened. The man out of the wasteland appeared with the jaundice-yellow light behind him, a silhouette of which I could see no details whatsoever.

Standing five-ten or five-eleven, he seemed to have an athletic physique, though he wasn't the hulking terminator or the sinuous shape-shifter that I might have feared. As far as I could tell, he held no weapon.

No light from the stairs managed to leak out onto the roof, as if some magical barrier contained it, and I couldn't know whether or not he saw me. But he didn't slip quickly out of the shed and dodge to one side; he paused in the doorway instead, blocking the door with his body, giving me plenty of time to kill

him. His confidence seemed to suggest that he didn't
bear me any ill will and therefore assumed I would
not harm him, that he was merely curious about me
and anticipated nothing more than curiosity in return.

The longer he dared to stand there, however, the
more his confidence seemed to be a troubling boldness, even effrontery. His continued silence made little sense if his sole reason for pursuing me was mere
curiosity. Moment by moment, I found his attitude
more arrogant and threatening.

Unless his vision was cat-clear in the dark, he
could not know that I held a pistol. He might be
convinced to explain himself if he was made aware
that, at a distance of perhaps fifteen feet, I could
blow him out of this hostile world into another.

Intuition told me not to speak a word. His stillness might be a taunt, inviting me to ask who he
was and what he intended. If he wanted me to speak
first, then my doing so would in some way surely
disadvantage me.

As much as it is anything else, my life is a series
of pursuits and confrontations. Suddenly I realized
that when this man appeared and came after me, I
fell into my usual habits and routines, allowing the
strangeness of this dark world to recede from my
awareness, as if I were grateful to escape into the
familiar game of cat and mouse. As a result, giving
myself to action, I'd failed to consider that the issues and ideas and needs motivating this man might

be as different from my desires and motives as his world was different from mine.

Whatever his hesitation in the doorway might imply, whatever his silence was meant to convey, my interpretation of his behavior would most likely be wrong. I was in new territory in every sense of the word, standing waist-deep in the surging waters of the unknown, which is the worst place to find oneself, for that riverbed is treacherous underfoot and those currents are as unpredictable as they are deadly.

Intuition *and* reason told me to remain mute and to be prepared that when he spoke, *if* he spoke, what little I thought I knew about this place and this man would be washed away. And then events would rush forward in waves, in drowning cataracts.

My expectation was fulfilled a moment later, when the silhouette declared, "My name is Odd Thomas. I see the spirits of the lingering dead." His voice was mine.

He stepped forward, and the door swung shut behind him, sweeping away the dirty-yellow light in the stairwell.

# Thirteen

THERE CAN BE NO MORE DREAMLIKE MOMENT than to encounter yourself in a dark place and to know in your marrow as surely as in your mind that only one of you will leave this rendezvous alive.

Yet this was not a dream.

In the worst nightmares, a threshold of terror is reached at which your pounding heart achieves a pace that would set off a cardiac-monitor alarm if you were in an ER, hyperventilation and elevated blood pressure lead to an attack of pulmonary hypertension, and you are violently ejected from sleep, heart hammering so loud that your eardrums seem about to split from the concussions, chest aching, unable to draw an adequate breath. For a moment, you are convinced that the malevolent presence from the nightmare, whatever its nature, is still upon you, smothering you, but within seconds, the familiarity of the waking world is an antidote for your panic.

As the man who claimed to be me approached and as the door fell shut behind him, leaving us in an abyssal dark, my heart achieved the requisite pace to trigger an alarm, my breathing became so fast and shallow that a pain rose in my breast, but I did not wake because I was not sleeping.

Intuition urgently insisted that I move quickly to my right and squeeze off three spread shots at where the Other Odd Thomas would be if he continued on a straight line toward my original position. I regret to say that I allowed my intuition to be overruled by instinct—which urged me to *Shoot now, this instant, shoot or run, run!*—but which simultaneously raised in me an existential horror of shooting someone who claimed to be me and who sounded exactly like me. In human beings, low superstition is inevitably entwined with instinct—one struggling for dominance over the other in moments of high risk—a linkage that no doubt dates to our caveman days. And so fright shivered through muscle, sinew, and blood—a dread that if I killed this Other, I would at the same time kill myself.

Instinct is an animal faculty, independent of instruction and reasoning, but far inferior to intuition, which is a grace unique to humanity. Instinct will never mislead a deer that senses a hunter in the woods and bolts for the cover of a thicker stand of trees, because animals are not subject to superstition that can pollute pure instinct, as we are.

Besides, instinct always triggers instant action, the

fight-or-flight impulse. But because modern human beings are accustomed to the comforts of Starbucks and smartphones and aerosol cheese and athletic shoes with air-cushion insoles, we rarely find ourselves in crises that can be resolved as easily as choosing to run or attack, other than in the competitive crowds at an electronics store on the first bargain-price shopping day after Thanksgiving. Intuition, on the other hand, arises from the perpetual calm in the core of the soul, and it requires of us discrimination and adroitness if it is to serve us well.

During that blackout on the roof, I was no more discriminating and adroit than a night-grazing rabbit abruptly paralyzed by a double flash of lightning and a hammerstrike of thunder loud enough to cleave stone. The Other had spoken in my voice, therefore I was him and he was me, and to shoot seemed to be suicide.

In my defense, I was stupidly immobilized only for a moment, but that proved long enough for him to seize me by the throat with both hands. His touch was cold, his grip tight.

Even at less than arm's length, I couldn't discern the barest outlines of his face. If I had been able to see him, to stare into my own face sans mirror, perhaps I would have been further inhibited, but blindness allowed me to squeeze the trigger, and I pumped two rounds into his chest at point-blank range. The hard reports echoed through the darkness, not only out across the vast wasteland but off something overhead, as though the sky might in fact be plated over with a material more substantial than clouds.

Unfortunately, two hollow-point 9-mm slugs seemed to have less effect on him than flea bites. His left hand continued to clutch my throat as if his fingers were the steel digits of a robot, but now he clasped the back of my head with his right hand and pulled my face closer to his.

I fired again, again, and twice again, but four bullets had no greater effect than two. Even if he had been wearing a Kevlar vest, the impact of the rounds would have been like fist blows, staggering him if not dropping him to his knees.

He pulled me closer, and he seemed to be whispering something, but the gunfire had left me temporarily half deaf, and I couldn't understand what he was saying.

Although he wasn't choking me, just holding fast to my throat, I inhaled no less violently than a man trapped in a submerged car as he hungrily sought the last air in the bubble near the ceiling.

Relinquishing my double grip on the pistol, I felt for his face and found his chin, which I tried to force upward with the heel of my left hand. With my right, I thrust the business end of the weapon against his exposed throat. Because my arm was trapped between us and my elbow jammed firmly against my abdomen, the recoil was absorbed so that the muzzle didn't jump off target, and I emptied the magazine of the last four rounds.

Even though the first six shots had had no effect, I steeled myself for gouting blood, a spray of flesh and bone and brains, but these last four rounds were likewise ineffective, as if the pistol had been loaded with blanks.

I dropped the gun or it was wrenched out of my hand, and we were at each other in what should have been evenly matched combat, but he was stronger, uncannily strong. Only a spirit could be impervious to ten bullets, but no spirit could harm me except by going poltergeist, not with its hands, only with inanimate objects hurled in raptures of rage with streams of spiritual power drawn from a malignant well.

With one hand against the back of my head, the other on my throat, unfazed by my punches, he succeeded in drawing me closer, until our foreheads knocked together. Still I was unable to see anything of the Other in this father of all darknesses.

His lips were close to mine, but I couldn't feel the barest exhalation issue with his words when he said urgently, roughly, "I need your breath."

Clutching his throat with both hands, I tried to strangle him, while he seemed to want to force me into an unholy kiss. I found the muscles of his throat flaccid, soft, disgusting, as though in spite of his great strength, no life existed in him. The tissues of his neck compressed under my throttling hands, but I couldn't choke him, as if he had no breath that could be denied him, no blood in his carotid arteries that might be withheld from his brain. And yet he was strong, insistent, an immovable object and at the same time an irresistible force.

"Your breath, piglet," he demanded in a wolfish snarl, "your *breath*."

His flesh felt more gelid than that of a room-temperature corpse before the heat of decomposition begins to warm it again, chill and clammy and reminiscent of a fish pulled from a cold lake. I felt in the presence of something unclean, although no smell whatsoever rose from him, neither pleasant nor offensive, which further suggested that what animated him was not life as we think of it.

As he chanted *your breath,* I somehow knew that I still must not speak, that to say anything would be to concede that he might be worthy of my curses, and in so acknowledging him, I would give him some crucial advantage in our struggle, which was growing more desperate by the moment.

His voice was mine but sinister, suited to the pitch-darkness enveloping us, a voice from the endless night, *of* the endless night. He was so close to administering the kiss of death that, although I could not feel his exhalations, his words vibrated faintly against my lips: "Give me your breath, piglet, your breath, and the sweet fruit at the end of it."

I couldn't shove him away, couldn't pull away, couldn't wound or stagger him. He was as deadly as a tar pit, quicksand personified, and he would draw the life from me as greedily as a henhouse fox draining yolk and egg white out of a bitten shell.

Abruptly, gray light from a storm sky dispelled the darkness, and with the reappearance of the filtered sun fell cool rain in torrents, thousands of silvery droplets performing a fairy dance across the roof. The Other had vanished. The resurrected city of my reality lay round about, blurred by the downpour. The parapet again marked the perimeter of the building. Evidently, I didn't need to be within the envelope of the structure to be returned here, only in contact with it, and it seemed that while I could move between worlds, albeit involuntarily, the Other Odd Thomas—whatever it had been—could not, a creature solely of that wasteland.

Although I have a competent command of language, I cannot string together a beadwork of words sufficient to express the gratitude I felt for being brought out of that dark land into this world of light and hope, this manifest yet mystical world of ours, where sorrowful mysteries are outnumbered two to one by those that are joyful and glorious. Trembling violently, I sank to my knees. In disgust, with one hand and then with the other, I scrubbed my lips, although the thing that would have kissed away my life—and more than my life—had not quite been able to do so.

I didn't mind being soaked to the skin and chilled, because the rain washed from me the feeling that I was unclean where the Other had touched me. With relief but also with some apprehension that the blinding dark might again depose the daylight, I recovered the dropped pistol, crossed the roof to the shed, and opened the door.

The interior of the shed was not as clean and featureless as it had been when I first ascended to it in that other realm. Enough storm light found its way inside to reveal abandoned spiderworks tattering in the corners of the ceiling, a generous layer of dust on the shelves, and a litter of paper scraps and broken glass across the floor. On the shelves stood a few oddly shaped cans so old and rusted that their labels could not be read.

The air was redolent of wood rot and a lacquer-like smell that came from something that for weeks or months had been oozing from one of the rusty containers. I realized that in the other-world version of this building, there had been no odors, either foul or sweet, just as there had been no sounds except those that I made.

When I opened the creaking door at the head of the single flight of narrow stairs, I smelled mold and dust. The shaft was dark except for watery light below, where the lower door hung open and askew on two of three hinges.

In the third-floor hallway, I discovered the source of that vague illumination: three skylights. The hollow rataplan of rain on the slanted panes unnerved me because it masked other sounds that I might need to hear, and I hurried to the west stairwell.

By the time that I made my way down to the garage on the ground floor of this crumbling structure,

I reached the conclusion that the other version of the building, the one without dust or odors or fine details, was not a part of the black wasteland with the distant lakes of fire. It possessed a character different from both this world and that one, as though it must be in some kind of borderland between realities, a sort of way station.

The garage contained no vehicle. The white van once stored there had been driven away earlier by the would-be burner of children or perhaps by his hard-faced stocky friend in the black-leather jacket. The fancy ProStar+ was secreted in the *other* garage, the one in the borderland building, to be retrieved when its owner had need of it.

Evidently, the rhinestone cowboy not only knew of these way stations but also seemed able, unlike me, to come and go from them at will.

I tucked the pistol in my waistband, under my sodden sweatshirt, glanced at the high latticed windows to be sure that the lightless wasteland had not again closed around the building, and left by the man-size door.

I stepped into the storms, the one that is merely weather, and the other that is the story of humanity.

# Fourteen

THE SLIGHTLY CONCAVE PAVEMENT IN THE alleyway channeled a rush of rainwater that carried with it crisp golden ficus leaves like fairy boats, stiff-legged dead beetles, cigarette butts, an empty foil condom packet, tiny purple petals that the wind might have shaken down from the limbs of early-blooming jacarandas, and all manner of flotsam, every scrap of it familiar yet somehow ominous.

I felt a little bit as if I were debris, too, swept along by the cataracts of falling rain. When at the end of the alleyway I turned right on the sidewalk, the runoff swelled deeper in the gutter, and among the trash borne on that tide was the hollow rubber head of a Kewpie doll. Although I hurried, the head kept pace with me, and though it bobbled back and forth in the current, its painted blue eyes seemed always to fix upon me.

As I approached the street drain capped by the

iron grate with the stylized lightning bolt, the flow in the gutter quickened, and the doll's head swept away from me. The cascading water washed the myriad bits of refuse between the bars of the grating—except for the severed pate of the doll, which was too wide to pass and which came to rest upright, its ragged neck in one of the gaps between the lightning bolt and the ring that encircled it, its stare still turned on me.

I halted. Stood there. Waiting, watching.

The rain silvered the day, and for a moment it seemed that the only color was the blue of the doll's eyes.

Not everything that happens during the day is an omen portending a good or evil development in the future, but everything has meaning to one degree or another, for the world is an ever-weaving tapestry from which no thread can be pulled without destroying the integrity of the cloth. The breadth of Creation makes it impossible for us to step back far enough to see the story that the tapestry tells; the intricacy of it, from the macro to the micro to the subatomic, makes it impossible for us to comprehend the megatrillions of connections between the threads in just one small fragment of the whole.

Yet there are uncanny moments when each of us recognizes that the surface of events is just what the word denotes, a *surface* under which lie layers beyond counting, that what's really happening is always more than what appears to be happening, that the apparent meaning of an event is only the smallest part of its fullest meaning. In such moments, most people—wise or foolish, simple or smart—truly *feel* the wonder of the world and perceive poignantly but briefly that at the heart of our existence lie mysteries so supremely grand in character that we cannot comprehend them in this life. The tendency then is to treat this revelation as an aberration, to react with fear or pride, or both, and to attribute the experience to mere confusion, stress, one glass of wine too many, one glass of wine too few, or any of innumerable unlikely causes.

Of this cowardice, I am no less guilty than anyone. Because my life has always been rich in strangeness, I am pretty sure that I choose to see less than I should in the weave of every day. I feel pressed to the limits of my capacity to cope, or at least that is my excuse for sometimes failing to allow an even greater sense of mystery to inspire me.

There in the rain-swept street, however, at the lightning-bolt grating, as the trapped and tilted head of the doll gazed up at me, I could not fail to recognize the mystical in the moment. And as I stood transfixed, as the water with its freight of trash and litter poured between the bars, I glimpsed three fluttery pulses of orange light traveling right to left through the culvert below, followed by three more, the same Halloween light I'd seen in another drain under a similar grating in Magic Beach more than a month earlier.

On that night, in that coastal town, the heavens

had been too dry to wring out any rain, but the sea had given up a thick fog that billowed lazily through the streets. Sound had risen from that drain, at first a susurration like many voices whispering, but then what might have been the shuffling of innumerable feet, as if some lost battalion were compelled by Fate to search wearily for the war in which its every member had been meant to die.

If this drain offered such a sound, it was masked by the sizzle of falling rain, by the *slish-slish-slish* of tires on wet pavement, and by the runoff splashing through the grate. The fluttering light came again in three distinct throbs. Something seized the neck of the Kewpie doll from below, the hollow rubber head deformed, and the face folded in upon itself as it was yanked down and away.

Maybe one other detail that I thought I saw was a product of my ever-active imagination or some kind of psychological projection, but I will always believe that it was real. As the doll's head was pulled between the bars, as its features squinched, its face became my face, and the snatching away of it seemed to be a promise that before long I would be taken, too, not merely by Death but also by a determined collector in some dark power's employ.

I didn't linger at the grating but hurried on through the wind and rain. When I turned the corner and saw the enormous limousine parked where I'd gotten out of it, I was inexpressibly grateful to Mrs. Fischer for ignoring my plea that she get on with her life and leave me to deal with my troubles alone. I didn't want to have to hitch a ride with a stranger, who would most likely turn out to be a psychopathic cannibal, and I wasn't likely to stumble upon a second crop of bank robbers whose getaway vehicle I could steal with a clear conscience.

As I approached the black Mercedes, my attention was drawn to my right, to the pair of glass doors at the entrance of the Salvation Army thrift shop. Standing inside, gazing out, were Mr. Hitchcock, Annamaria, and my dog Boo.

Being the spirit of a man who had not died by any kind of violence, the director wasn't doomed to haunt one location to the exclusion of all others, although as an honest and trenchant critic of his own films, he might have felt obligated to roam forever the sound stage on which he shot most of *The Paradine Case,* one of his few turkeys. Now that he had come to me for help, he was able to materialize wherever I went.

Earlier, when I mentioned our two dogs, the golden retriever Raphael and the white German shepherd Boo, I neglected to say that the former is a living dog and the latter is a ghost, the only spirit dog that I have ever seen, Rin Tin Tin of the afterlife, who had been with me since my stay at St. Bartholomew's Abbey in the California mountains.

Dog and film director could go wherever they chose without need of transportation, but Annamaria, my pregnant traveling companion of recent days, made of flesh and bone like me, was limited to walking or riding some conveyance. That she had gotten here so close on my heels, that she had been able to find me at all, defied belief.

She was aware of my ability to see spirits, but as far as I knew, she could not see them herself and could not know that two ghosts stood with her.

Beyond the glass doors, Mr. Hitchcock waved at me. Boo wagged his tail. Annamaria merely stood there in her sneakers, gray khaki pants, and baggy pale-pink sweater, smiling enigmatically.

She is at all times enigmatic. And though some might say that she has her secrets, I would go so far as to say that perhaps she has no secrets, which require a conscious act of withholding, but instead has her mysteries, which I am invited to understand if I possess the intelligence and the patience and the faith to unravel them.

Skeins of silver rain unspooled ceaselessly around and over me, and after a moment of paralysis, I started toward the doors of the thrift shop.

Lightning ripped the sky, so near that the accompanying crash of thunder shuddered the air even as the flash was at its brightest. After the events of this day, I felt targeted, and I juked as though to dodge that flaming lance, turned, looked up, and saw the black clouds throbbing with inner light, as if another bolt was being fashioned in the factory of the storm.

When I turned back toward the thrift shop, the dog and the director and Annamaria were no longer watching me through the doors. I had not imagined them, and although Boo and Mr. Hitchcock could dematerialize at will, the pregnant lady with eyes as dark as espresso could not evaporate like a spirit.

I stepped out of the rain, into the warmth of the store, seeking Annamaria, and found something I could never have anticipated.

# Fifteen

THE SPACIOUS STORE OFFERED AISLES OF WELL-mended secondhand clothing, paintings and an array of decorative items for the home, costume jewelry, an entertainment aisle with CDs and DVDs, shelves of used books, old toys fully restored, and much more.

Among the expected merchandise were fanciful items that were intriguing or puzzling, and which might have been amusing if I had not been cold, wet, and freaked out by recent events. A pair of five-foot carved-wood hand-painted blue heron had been adapted as lamps and held lightbulbs in their fierce beaks. A pygmy hippopotamus as large as a Shetland pony, preserved by an expert taxidermist, stood on a stone base that bore an engraved silver plaque with the words PEACHES/BELOVED COMPANION/IN MY HEART FOREVER.

Shoes squishing, dripping and splashing, making more of a mess than Peaches had probably ever done,

I prowled the aisles, looking for Mr. Hitchcock and Boo but primarily for Annamaria. The customers, who had arrived under the protection of umbrellas, regarded me mostly with sympathy. But perhaps my eyes were wild and my demeanor fevered, because a few seemed to see in me a waterlogged lout, and they were quick to get out of my way, grimacing with disdain. Others went pale with fear as if I were the equivalent of Jacob Marley, from *A Christmas Carol,* back from the dead, wrapped not in symbolic chains but in the waters of some river in which I had drowned.

Because I had not come here to shop but instead to find two ghosts and a pregnant enigma, my hurried passage from department to department and my befuddled look caught the attention of a clerk in a Salvation Army uniform. She approached me with evident concern and a buoyant manner in excess of what I had seen in employees of other stores. Judging by the look of me, perhaps she might have expected that, in addition to directing me to recycled kitchen utensils or manufacturer's-surplus dental-care products, she would also have a chance to save my soul.

In her early forties, with hair the color of brandied cherries, skin as pale as powdered sugar and as smooth as buttercream, freckles the precise shade of cinnamon, and a smile as winning as that of a ponytailed little girl in a current TV commercial for ice cream, she looked sweet, and she was. "Oh, dear, dear, dear, the day hasn't been good to you, has it? You look chilled to the bone. How can I help?"

There was no point in asking if she'd seen the spirit of Alfred Hitchcock or a ghost dog, and it seemed inappropriate to stagger into a Salvation Army facility and boldly announce that I was looking for a girl.

And so with my usual aplomb, I said, "Well, through the window, I thought I saw an old friend. I don't mean really old like elderly. I have an elderly friend in the car outside. She's eighty-six, but she doesn't look it, though she screams when she looks in a mirror. The friend in the car, I mean, not the friend I thought I saw in here. The friend I thought I saw, Annamaria, she's a girl. Not a little girl. Like eighteen. Dark eyes and hair, petite, with this smile that makes you feel everything will be all right even on the worst day. Don't get the wrong idea, ma'am. I'm not stalking her. She didn't jilt me. She's not my ex-girlfriend or girlfriend or anything. I only have one girlfriend, and she's forever. I don't mean Mrs. Fischer, the elderly lady in the car. Mrs. Fischer's just a friend. She thinks she's my employer. But I'm not a chauffeur. I'm a fry cook. Although not recently, what with one crazy thing after the other."

When I finally wound down, the clerk said, "You must be Thomas."

For a moment, I seemed to have exhausted my supply of words, and then I found a few. "Yes, ma'am. How did you know?"

"Your sister purchased some things for you."

"My sister?"

"She said you'd be along in a while. She's a very

self-possessed young woman. Very impressive. With such a graceful and kind way about her."

"Yes, ma'am, that's her, all right. What did she purchase?"

"Just what she knew you'd need. Come with me."

As she led me toward the back of the store, I said, "Did she purchase Peaches, the stuffed pygmy hippo?"

The clerk's laugh was musical. "You're teasing me."

"Did she?"

"No. Of course not."

"Good. I couldn't fit it in the car. I'd have to put wheels on Peaches and ride her home."

"You have your sister's sense of humor."

"We're a funny family."

"I asked when the baby was due, and she said she'd been pregnant forever and still had a few years to go."

"That's Sis, sure enough."

We arrived at a short hallway with changing rooms on both sides, where customers could try on the secondhand clothes.

The clerk said, "There's a basket in the room. If your new things fit, just put all your wet clothes in the basket. Your sister said you'd want to donate them."

At the last room on the right, an OCCUPIED sign hung on the doorknob.

"It's your room," she said. "I reserved it when your sister said you'd be along shortly."

"Thank you, ma'am. I'm sorry for dripping all over your store."

"Oh, dear, don't you worry. That's why God made mops." She patted me on the shoulder and left me alone.

On a bench in the changing room were a white T-shirt, a pair of briefs, socks, blue jeans, a blue crew-neck sweater, a pair of Nike basketball shoes, and a black raincoat with a hood.

Everything fit perfectly. I left my wet clothes in the plastic laundry basket.

In the right-hand pocket of the raincoat, I found a disposable cell phone. It rang in my hand.

I felt as if I were in a *Mission Impossible* movie. The internals of the phone would probably melt into slag as soon as we finished our conversation.

"Hello?"

As always, her words seemed to float to me on the warm currents of her voice. "Do you remember the promise you made to me when I gave you the pendant with the bell?"

"Yes, ma'am." Because the walls of the changing room were thin, I lowered my voice. "You said some people wanted to kill you. And you asked me if I'd die for you. I said yes, somewhat to my surprise."

"But not to mine. When my hour of need arrives, how will you be able to die for me if you're already dead from pneumonia?"

"I was just a little wet."

"And I'm just a little pregnant. You should wear galoshes, too."

"I'm not a galoshes kind of guy. Where are you right now?"

"Where you left me. At the cottage by the sea, with Tim. We baked cookies, and now we're eating them while we play cards."

"How could you be at the cottage, a couple hundred miles from here, and buy me these clothes?"

"Every place is the same place in the end."

"Another riddle."

"You hear riddles, but I never speak in them."

High in the flooded sky, thunder crashed like great structures falling into ruin, and here below, the building vibrated as if with a premonition of its own destruction.

I said, "The clerk told me you called yourself my sister."

"People hear what they need to hear."

"I wish you *were* my sister."

I swear I could hear her smile when she said, "That's sweet of you, odd one, and I know you don't intend to diminish me."

"Diminish you? What does that mean?"

"It means what it means, as you will understand in time."

In the silent wake of the thunder, more intimate sounds arose from the ductwork behind a ventilation grille, in the back wall of the dressing room, near the ceiling. The soft *ponk* and *bink* of sheet metal dimpling and tweaking under some weight. An intermittent ticking accompanied by a faint slithering noise.

"Now tell me," Annamaria said, "have the events of the day made you afraid?"

"For a while there, yeah. But I'm okay now."

"Acknowledge your fear, odd one. Fearlessness is for the insane and the arrogant. You are neither. Those who rely on you for their lives will be well served only if you fear what you should fear. You are a unique soul, a child of grace, but you can still fail yourself and others."

I thought of the Green Moon Mall in Pico Mundo, nineteen months earlier, when many had been saved but some had died, when among the dead had been she whom I loved more than myself, more than life.

I sat on the bench where I had found my fresh clothes folded and waiting for me. "Truth is, ma'am, I'm more afraid than I have been in a long time. And I'm afraid to be afraid."

"Afraid to be afraid, but why?" she asked, though it seemed to me that she knew me as well as I knew myself and that her question was therefore moot.

"Because I've always gotten by on grit and little more. Or be fancy and call it fortitude. I can endure pain and trial, and not lose hope. Grit and wit— laughter in the dark is my surest defense. I usually hold off fear with a joke, but that only works for a while. What true courage I might have is limited and comes from desperation, brief spurts, just enough to get through a crisis. If the crisis is protracted, as I suspect this one will be, if fear is constant for too long, then courage will for darn sure bleed out of me when I need it most."

Annamaria was silent so long that I thought I had embarrassed her with my confession, but that seemed not to be the case when she spoke. "Young man, there are few people who understand as much about themselves as you understand about yourself, to the depth that you understand it. But your greatest strength is that there are things you *don't* recognize about yourself."

"Which would be what?"

"There's one kind of ignorance that is the very essence of enlightenment, and I won't tell you what it is, because it is an ignorance that makes you so beautiful."

Evidently, I hadn't embarrassed her, but the word *beautiful* embarrassed me because it had no relationship to the mug I see in mirrors. "Another riddle," I said.

"If you want to think it is."

The hardest crack of thunder yet shook the afternoon, as if the sky were stone that had fractured clean through. Either echoes of the thunder rattled the sheet metal or something in the heating duct was agitated by the storm.

I said, "What frightens me is, there's a difference in what's happening today, this time, this situation. . . ."

"Yes," Annamaria said, as if she knew of my recent experiences.

I said, "The spirits who seek me out aren't for the most part malevolent, just lost. The evil that comes my way is mostly stuff we might see in the newspapers and wouldn't find unusual. An old high-school friend turned child-killer, cops gone bad, terrorists with a boatload of nukes . . . But what I've seen today is different in kind and magnitude. Stranger. Darker. More terrifying."

"Anyone who learns the true and hidden nature of the world will be terrified, Oddie, but there's a safe harbor past the terror."

"Is that what I'm learning today—the true and hidden nature of the world?"

"Tim promises he'll save two cookies for you. They're very good, if I say so myself. Listen, because of who you are, it's inevitable that eventually you will peel the onion, so to speak, and see the truth of everything."

"I'd rather just chop the onion, fry it with a dribble of olive oil, and put it on top of a cheeseburger. Sometimes I have a dream in which I'm nothing but a fry cook, with a paycheck every Friday, good books to read, and all my friends in Pico Mundo."

She said, "But that is only a dream. Your life has always been a journey metaphorically. And since you left Pico Mundo, it has become also a literal journey from which you can't turn back."

I watched the grille over the ventilation duct and thought about the quartet of rats abandoning the phoenix palm in formation, but no pointed twitching nose or radiant blood-drop eyes appeared.

She continued: "Every journey has a destination, known or unknown. In a journey of discovery like yours, the pace quickens and the disclosures mount steadily toward the end."

"Am I nearing the end of mine?"

"I'd guess that what's behind you is much more than what lies ahead, though you have a way to go yet. But I'm not a fortune-teller, odd one."

I said, "You're something."

"Be afraid in proportion to the threat," Annamaria said, "but if you trust yourself, we will see each other again—"

"'—when the wind blows the water white and black,'" I finished, quoting her words from earlier in the day. "Whatever that means."

"It means what it means, Oddie. Remember, there are cookies waiting here for you."

She disconnected, and I switched off the disposable cell phone.

When I stood up from the bench and stared at the grille near the ceiling, all grew quiet in the duct beyond.

I tucked the pistol in a deep pocket of the raincoat and opened the changing-room door, prepared— though not eager—to learn the true and hidden nature of the world. But first I stopped in the thrift-shop men's room. Even the most urgent journey of discovery must allow time for the journeyer to pee.

# Sixteen

PERCHED ON HER PILLOW, MRS. EDIE FISCHER piloted the Mercedes limousine northeast on Interstate 15, into a steadily darkening day, leaving the city and its suburbs well behind us, outracing the storm but not yet the sullen clouds that paved the sky in advance of the downpour. Between Victorville and Barstow, meadows made green by the four-month rainy season gave way to fields of wild golden grass on the brink of the Mojave, where that season had been shorter and drier than it had been across the lower lands closer to the coast. Mile by mile, the gilded grass cheapened to silver, soon the silver grayed, and at last plush meadows succumbed to gnarled and bristling desert scrub.

Twelve cylinders of internal combustion powered us, and psychic magnetism guided us as I held the face of the rhinestone cowboy in my mind's eye. I'd taken off the hooded raincoat and dropped it through the open privacy panel between the front seat and the passenger compartment.

The cell phone was tucked in one of the two cup holders in the center console, in case it rang again, though that seemed unlikely. Annamaria's meaning might be as puzzling as a five-thousand-piece jigsaw of one of M. C. Escher's most intricate drawings, but she always said succinctly what she wanted to say. She wasn't given to long, chatty conversations about the weather or celebrities, or the aches and pains of a life in gravity.

In such a short time, Mrs. Fischer and I had achieved a degree of friendship that allowed periods of silence without awkwardness. I felt comfortable with her. I was reasonably sure that she would never shoot me or stab me, or set me on fire, or throw acid in my face, or lock me in a room with a hungry crocodile, or dump me in a lake after chaining me to two dead men. Such confidence in a new acquaintance is more rare these days than it once was.

Twenty-six miles south of Barstow, I said, "Now we've driven out of the rain, we could switch places without you getting wet."

"I'll keep driving. I'm not tired. Haven't been tired since the thingumajig."

"What thingumajig?"

"The implant doohickey with the three little lithium batteries. I shouldn't talk about it."

I frowned. "Implant? Like a heart pacemaker or something?"

"Oh, don't you be concerned, child. It's nothing like that. My ticker's fine."

"Good. I'm glad to hear it."

"They put this gismo in your buttocks. Well, in one buttock, on the right. Used to worry it might be uncomfortable on long rides, but I don't even ever know it's there."

I half suspected that my chain was being pulled. "Whyever would they implant anything *there*?"

"Because that's where it needs to go, of course."

"What does?"

"The doohickey gismo."

"What does it do?"

"Everything they said it would. This is all a little indelicate, dear. I'd rather not discuss it anymore."

Generally speaking, when someone asks me not to inquire further about his or her butt implant, whether it's a little old lady or not, I politely refrain from posing additional questions, but I was sorely tempted to seek more information in this case.

Instead, I said, "Sure. All right. But I still don't think you should do all the driving. We might have a long way to go."

She deployed her legendary dimples to take the sting out of what she had to say. "No offense, sweetie, but you make me a little crazy when you drive."

I was surprised to hear my reply: "But I'm your chauffeur."

"Well, what I think maybe we should do is, we should give you a different job description."

"Such as what?"

"How about—male secretary?"

"I have no secretarial skills, ma'am."

Driving with one hand, Mrs. Fischer reached out to pinch my cheek affectionately. "God love you, child, you don't have the best chauffeuring skills, either."

"Back at the truck stop you said I was a good driver."

"You are a good driver, dear. But you dawdle." Her sudden smile was radiant. "I know! You can be my *fry cook*."

"You said you didn't need a fry cook. But really . . . *dawdle*?"

"Well, I've changed my mind. I need a fry cook. Yes, you dawdle. You're no Steve McQueen, dear. In fact, you're no Matt Damon."

"Matt Damon is no Jason Bourne. He has a stunt driver in those movies."

"Well, it seems silly to hire a full-time stunt driver for my chauffeur, sweetie. Fry cook it is."

"Ma'am, I had this beauty up to ninety back there."

"My point exactly. How do you expect ever to catch this nasty rhinestone cowboy of yours that way?"

"Look, Mrs. Fischer—"

"Call me Edie."

"Yes, ma'am. Anyway, you don't need a fry cook. You said you're always on the road, you eat at restaurants all the time."

"I'll buy some restaurants here and there, so whenever we're near one, we'll stop and you can cook for me."

"You're not serious."

"It makes perfect sense to me."

"Good grief, how much money do you have?"

"Oh, gobs and gobs of it. Don't you worry." She reached across the console to pat me on the shoulder. "My delightful fry cook."

I don't know why I couldn't let go of it, but I said, "You're not even doing ninety now."

"One hundred and four miles an hour, child."

I leaned to my left to look more directly at the speedometer. "Wow. It sure doesn't feel like we're going that fast. I guess that's one of the pluses of a Mercedes."

"It's partly Mercedes, but also the aftermarket work that went into it. This baby is souped."

We rocketed past a guy in a Ferrari, probably on his way to Vegas. I think he was wearing a poofy cap, though it wasn't green and black.

"Hundred and ten," Mrs. Fischer said, "and smooth as butter."

"It really is souped," I acknowledged.

"Radically souped. There's this nice man in Arizona, everybody calls him One-Ear Bob, though his name's Larry. He's such a big handsome bruiser, you hardly notice the ear thing, except you tend to tilt your head to one side when you're talking to him. His front business is a combination real-estate brokerage, insurance agency, souvenir shop, and roadside cafe. But he makes his real money in secret, in the buildings far at the back end of his property, where he can do anything you want done to a vehicle and then some."

"Why secret?"

In a dramatic but unnecessary whisper, she said, "Because a lot of what One-Ear Bob does to cars breaks the law."

"What law?"

"Oh, all kinds of laws, sweetie. Idiot safety laws, bone-headed environmental laws that actually contribute to pollution, the laws of physics, you name it."

"Arizona, huh? Wouldn't be Lonely Possum, Arizona, would it?"

Suddenly coy, she said, "Might be, might not."

"What happened there sixty years ago on that oven-hot night?"

"Never you mind. Now let me tend to my driving. With all this conversation, my speed's fallen to a hundred."

From the console between the front seats, I fetched a box of 9-mm ammunition about which Mrs. Fischer had told me earlier. I had emptied the magazine of the pistol while resisting my assailant on the roof of the building in Elsewhere. Now I pressed ten rounds into it and locked it into the butt of the weapon.

Mile by mile, the desert grew more stark, a vastness of sand and rock, mesquite and sage and with-

ered bunchgrass, with here and there low shapes of
rock that looked like the serrated backs and long,
flat heads of Jurassic-era crocodiles immense in size,
petrified now and half buried in the earth.

The low clouds were gray in the east, darker
overhead, nearly black in the west. Ahead of us, a
wedge of birds flew high across the interstate, wing-
ing southeast.

Pico Mundo, my hometown, lay more than a hundred miles in that direction. Perhaps I might soon be
led back there. If patterns exist in our seemingly patternless lives—and they do—then the law of harmony insists that the most harmonious of all patterns,
circles within circles, will most often assert itself. If
my end was coming, it might find me in those familiar streets that I loved and through which I had been
haunted for so much of my life. But we were racing
away from Pico Mundo at the moment, and I sensed
that the case of the man who would burn children
was not the one that would lead me home.

I put ten rounds of ammunition in each front
pocket of my jeans. For one who dislikes guns as
thoroughly as I do, I strangely find myself resorting
to them more frequently as I make steady progress on
my circular journey from loss to acceptance of loss,
from failure to possible redemption.

A sign announced the interstate exits to Barstow, a
community of military installations, railyards, warehouses, outlet stores, and chain motels. Although I
intuited that I would find my quarry much deeper in

the Mojave than this place, I suddenly said, "Here. Exit here. He's done something in Barstow. Something terrible."

By the grace of Mrs. Fischer's expert driving and One-Ear Bob's improvements to the vehicle, we decelerated as efficiently as if we had reverse rocket thrusters, crossed three lanes in an exquisite arc that brought us to the foot of the exit ramp, and swept into Barstow, home of the Mojave River Valley Museum.

We had come now to one of those times in my life when humor was no longer an armor, when any joke would have been an abomination, the slightest smile a transgression.

"The children," I said. "The two girls and the boy. They lived here."

"You mean *live* here," Mrs. Fischer corrected.

Taken by a sudden chill, I said, "No, I don't believe I do."

# Seventeen

THE RHINESTONE COWBOY ONCE PROWLED the streets of Barstow to what end I thought I knew, but he was gone now, his corrupted and magnetic spirit an attractant that issued from some nest deeper in the barrens.

The superstretch limousine looked out of place in this humble desert burg, eliciting interest when we passed other motorists and pedestrians. As we cruised residential neighborhoods according to my whim, Mrs. Fischer made tight corners with ease.

On a street of neatly maintained stucco houses, behind desert-friendly landscapes reliant on succulents and sage, a residence stood in the shade of immense Indian laurels that massed their surface roots around them like tangles of sleeping pythons. As nowhere else in the vicinity, cars and SUVs and pickups—and one police sedan—were clustered at the curb and in the driveway. Carrying baking pans and casseroles, four women of the neighborhood came along the street to the front walk of the house. On the porch, several grim-faced men were engaged in what appeared to be an earnest and quiet discussion dealing with something more serious than sports, and through the windows I could see what seemed to be a solemn gathering of people.

"This is where they lived," I said, and Mrs. Fischer didn't need to ask to whom I referred. "The cowboy trucker . . . I don't think he was ever at this place. It's the children, my memory of their faces that has . . . drawn me here."

Were I to go inside, seeking information, I would surely become a suspect. I had no authority, no credentials, no reason that I could offer why this stricken family should trust me. If I spoke about my paranormal gifts, I would be considered at best a kook, at worst a charlatan seeking publicity and an easy path to profit. If I inspired suspicion in the police, I might be detained long enough to ensure that I would not find the abducted children in time.

Even lingering in the street a moment too long was inadvisable, and I said, "Ma'am, let's ease away from here. There's another place I feel the need to see . . . if we can find it."

Two blocks later, as I asked her to turn left, Mrs. Fischer said, "What do you call it, child?"

"Call what?"

"This bloodhound ability of yours."

For a moment, I considered answers with which I could continue to stonewall her.

She said, "Was it this that helped you save all those lives in the shooting at that Pico Mundo mall—or do you have other talents, as well?"

"You've been doing some research when I've been out of the car."

"For the longest time, I resisted the Internet, too busy seeing the world to bother with a computer. But a smartphone makes it easy even for an old gypsy like me."

"I call it psychic magnetism, ma'am. It's a way of . . . finding people."

"The newspapers said you were a hero. But there were never any details of how you discovered the plot and foiled it."

"I didn't talk to the press afterward. My friend Wyatt Porter, he's chief of police in Pico Mundo, and he has always helped me keep my secrets. Anyway, I didn't foil any plot like in the movies. People died that day, ma'am."

"Only a fraction as many as those who would have been killed if you hadn't stepped up."

I shifted uncomfortably in my seat, adjusting the shoulder strap on the safety harness, though that wasn't the cause of my discomfort. "Well, if I hadn't intervened, someone else would have."

"Not much reason to think so, considering the kind of world we live in now."

I suggested that she make a right turn, and we rode in silence for two blocks.

She said, "The mall shooting wasn't the last thing you took on yourself, was it?"

"No, ma'am. It wasn't even the first. But I don't take them on so much as they . . . they just come to me. There's no way to avoid any of it."

She braked at a stop sign and looked at me. There was worry in her wizened face and sorrow in her eyes. "I read about your loss that day."

"She isn't lost forever, ma'am. Only until this world finishes with me and I can go where she's gone."

"In respect of that loss," she said, "I'm not going to pry at you anymore, child. I'm curious, of course. Who wouldn't be? But I have no right."

I nodded, not in agreement with her but in gratitude, and she drove through the intersection.

"Here's a thing I think," she said, then paused as if to make sure that she found the most apt words. "Sometimes in life a thing happens, sometimes it's a person, and you know that what happens *next* and for some time, maybe for minutes or hours, will not be common, will not be just life moving on how it usually does. You know that those minutes or hours will be a gift of clarity, that the truth of the world will reveal itself if you care to look. Day after day, everything we see that seems real is only apparition, a ghost reality that we have conjured up in our self-delusion. Then the clarifying thing happens, and what you need to do, what you *must* do, is not question it, not demand more revelation than what is given, be quiet in the face of it, quiet and grateful that it has been given to you to see this, to be for even a short time aware of the extraordinary layered depths and profound beauty of the world to which we mostly blind ourselves."

I pointed right, and Mrs. Fischer wheeled the limo in that direction.

If someone says that she's having a moment of enlightenment, you don't blow dust in her eyes.

I said only this and only the truth: "I'm nothing more than a talented fry cook, ma'am, but that's a worthy enough occupation in a world where so many things are fried so badly."

A mile later, on the edge of town, we came to a tract of land around which an industrial fence had been engaged in a decades-long slow-motion collapse that was half finished. Piles of tumbleweeds pressed here and there against the chain-link, revealing the predominant pathways favored by the local winds, which were at the moment still.

The entry gates hung open, and we drove between them.

The blacktop parking lot was fissured and pot-holed and pierced in places by weeds. On the graveled storage yard to one side of the hulking building, a mammoth stack of a couple hundred wooden pallets had partially collapsed in upon itself, weakened by rot and termites, bleached pale gray by the Mojave sun, so that the remains looked like the ashen ruins of a giant wicker man burned at the conclusion of a pagan festival. I would not have been entirely surprised if under the rubble were the charred bones of a human sacrifice.

The building itself appeared to be nearly as large as a football field, a corrugated-metal structure anchored by a four-foot-high concrete base. The three big roll-up doors and associated tracks and motors evidently had been salvaged, leaving the abandoned factory open to the elements. Above those doors and a couple of man-size entrances, a badly weathered sign identified the former home of BLACK & BUCKLE MANUFACTURING.

Mrs. Fischer mentioned the flashlight in the glove box, and I thanked her for it.

We got out of the limousine, and she said, "I won't let you go alone this time. But I'm afraid of what we might find."

"I'm pretty sure the children aren't here, ma'am. Not them and not . . . their bodies. They're still alive. But I think they might have been held here for a while. And he was here. The cowboy."

"He was here but never at their house?"

"That's how it feels to me. I don't know what it means."

Without my seeing from where she'd taken it, Mrs. Fischer had one of the other guns she had mentioned, a smaller pistol than mine, but deadly enough.

Although she looked nothing like my grandmother—Pearl Sugars, who had been a professional poker player—Mrs. Edie Fischer sort of reminded me of Granny. Pearl Sugars was the kind of lady you'd want to have your back in a tight spot, and I felt the same about Mrs. Fischer. If an eighty-six-year-old woman has been clear-seeing from a young age, she will have gone through a lot of life developing an eye for snares and pitfalls, an ear for deceit, and a good nose for knavery. And by such an age, a smart woman with no illusions is one to whom courage comes far more readily than it does to those young people who don't yet know the world for what it is.

In the cavernous building, the only daylight came through the missing roll-up doors and from rows of high windows just under the ceiling, nearly thirty feet above the floor. Although we had outrun the storm, the sky remained mantled, and the waning afternoon could illumine little. The factory was a storehouse of rust-scented air, stillness, and darkness.

The flashlight beam couldn't reach as far as any wall, but we were able to determine that nothing of value remained from the days when industry occurred here, nor anything that might provide a clue as to what Black & Buckle had manufactured. The concrete floor was irregularly carpeted in thick dust, drifts of dead leaves, scraps of cardboard, crumpled papers, and other trash that had blown in through the missing doors.

Suddenly a prolonged rustling suggested that in the shadows someone moved through the brittle debris. The concrete-and-metal structure reflected the noise in confusing ways, so that it seemed to come from our left, then from the right, from directly ahead of us, but then from the right again, now very near, now more distant. This auditory distortion perplexed the ear much as a maze of fun-house mirrors might bewilder the eye.

I probed every which way with the flashlight, yet I couldn't find the source of the sound. Perhaps a draft slithered along the floor, disturbing what it touched. But the day outside was in the thrall of the eerie tranquility that sometimes settles upon the land in anticipation of an approaching thunderstorm, and the air within this place was as leaden as the air outside.

The rustling ceased, but the ensuing silence was of a kind in which something crouched and waited. That quality of menace didn't diminish as the quiet lengthened.

"Nothing," Mrs. Fischer said, and the word cycled and recycled through the rafters far overhead, though the echo seemed to be in a voice different from hers.

With the flashlight, I found recent tire tracks leading through the dust; and in those tread patterns, dry leaves had been crushed by the weight of the vehicle. We followed the trail toward the back of the building.

In the last ten yards of the structure, across the width of it, side-by-side offices featured windows looking onto the factory floor. The painted hollow-core doors were scarred and stained, and most of the fiberboard panels were buckled, having pulled partway loose of the frames.

In the southwest corner, a pair of sturdy metal doors drew our attention because beside them were two dilapidated aluminum lawn chairs with green-vinyl webbing, between which stood a Styrofoam picnic cooler and a half-empty bottle of Jack Daniel's. Cigarette butts and nine dust-free half-crumpled Heineken cans littered the floor around the chairs.

The faint scent of beer arose from the residue that had not yet evaporated from those containers.

"They must have kept the kids behind these doors," I said. "Some guys sat here to guard them."

My voice ricocheted around the abandoned factory: "... *kids, kids, kids ... doors, doors, doors ... them, them, them ...*"

The fading echoes were followed by that creepy rustling noise again, louder than before. I slashed the air with the flashlight beam, as though fencing with an invisible foe, but as before I discovered no one.

After the rustling subsided into silence, I tried one of the heavy double doors. With some creaking, it opened onto a generous landing. Unusually wide stairs led down into a grave-dark lower room.

Standing with her back against the other door,

Mrs. Fischer whispered so low that her words could not rise far enough to inspire an echo in the rafters: "Can't both go down there and risk being locked in. I mean, if someone's here to lock us."

"Can't leave you here alone in the dark," I said.

Indicating the three big squares of gray light at the farther end of the vast room, where the roll-up doors had once been, she said, "Those will silhouette him, if anyone's here. And probably no one is."

I said, "I don't need to go down there. The children have been taken somewhere else."

"You owe it to them to be sure. Go now. Get it over with."

She was quietly adamant, but she was also right. I left her alone in the gloom.

I didn't have to prop open the door. Its hinges were corroded enough to prevent it from swinging shut on its own.

As I made my way down the first flight of stairs to a landing, I knew that the children had indeed been held here, because their three faces, as they had appeared in the vision in the supermarket parking lot, rose now in my memory, more vivid step by step.

Descending the second flight, picking out the treads with the flashlight, pistol at the ready, I noticed first that the air was cooler here than on the ground floor and, second, that it smelled of blood.

Blood has an odor faint but distinct, of conceit and modesty, of courage and cowardice, of charity and greed, of faith and doubt, in short the fragrance of what we might have been and the smell of what we are, vaguely suggestive of hot copper, having carried life along the arteries like current through a wire. Because the scent is subtle, however, a room can smell of it only if the quantity spilled is significant.

With dread, I continued to the bottom, into a basement that extended under about a quarter of the building. Perhaps this space had once contained a heating system, boilers, and other machines that were stripped out and sold in the distant past. Now it housed the dead.

# Eighteen

THE DEAD EYES APPEARED TO ROLL TOWARD me in the crusted sockets, but in fact only the reflection of the flashlight beam moved across those glassy curves from which tears would never spill again.

Even two bad men who earn a bad end deserve a measure of discretion from such as me when I write about them, at least as regards the horror of their suffering. Besides, if I detailed their many wounds, you might be persuaded to pity them, and I doubt they were worthy of much tender sympathy. Suffice it to say that the coup de grace in each case was a bullet fired point-blank, just above the bridge of the nose. Before that, they had been tortured extensively with razors or stilettos.

The two were naked, stripped before they were murdered. Later their clothing had been removed from the scene, along with any watches or jewelry they might have been wearing, perhaps to ensure that they would be more difficult to identify if they were ever found.

Their wrists were cuffed behind them, and their hands were sheathed in blood-soaked gray cotton gloves. The latter detail at first baffled me until I realized that these must be the two men who had sat in the lawn chairs upstairs, smoking and drinking while they guarded their hostages. They had worn the gloves to ensure that they left no incriminating fingerprints.

Supposing these were the kidnappers, they must have been part of a larger conspiracy. Evidently the plan called for the children to be stashed here for a while, on the outskirts of town, whereafter others— including the rhinestone cowboy—would arrive to take custody of them and move them elsewhere.

If these two dead men had been discovered drunk and asleep in the lawn chairs, or merely drunk, other members of the conspiracy might have decided to execute them rather than to trust them further.

Although that might be the most likely explanation, the torture seemed illogical, especially the extent and cruelty of it. With three hostages to manage and with the need to spirit them out of the area while local and perhaps federal authorities were searching for them, the killers should have opted for quick mob-style executions. Taking time to carve their victims extensively, slowly bleeding them almost to death before administering the killing shot, seemed as reckless as it was savage.

From their perspective, however, torture might make a sort of cockeyed sense if it was ritualistic, part of a ceremony that this fraternity of the demented required of themselves when they murdered one of their own. I didn't want to believe that was true, because it made them crazier, more vicious, and more dangerous than I previously assumed that they were. The quickest review of the bodies suggested there were similar, patterned wounds on each, but I didn't have the stomach to conduct a thorough analytic review of them.

Most of the blood had soaked into the concrete floor, but one pool remained on which a thin film had formed, suggesting that the victims might have been murdered within the past couple of hours. I stooped to touch the shoulder of the nearest corpse, and though the flesh was cool, it still held some body heat.

Two dead men . . . but not one soul beseeching me for justice. I have observed before that lingering spirits are nearly always those of people who led largely good and admirable lives. Rare is the deeply wicked soul that does not cross over after death. I suspect that for their kind, a debt collector—one with a legendary name and no patience for tardy debtors—insists on payment immediately after the heart has struck its last beat and even as the final exhalation withers in the throat.

I climbed the steps two at a time, and as I drew near the top, I called out, "It's only me."

Mrs. Fischer said, "Only you is exactly what I hoped for, dear."

As we made our way through the building toward the daylight at the roll-up doors, I told her what I had found, though I left out the most disturbing details.

Whoever Mrs. Edie Fischer might be and whatever secrets she might be keeping, I could tell by her calm reaction that she had not led a sheltered life defined only by home, hearth, family, church, and bingo on Saturday night.

Halfway toward the doors, we heard the rustling again, but this time I found the source almost at once. Curved dead leaves like an infestation of hard-shelled brown beetles skittering this way and that, twists of foil and scraps of cellophane spraying up as bright as hot sparks in the reflected flashlight, brittle sheets of crumpled notepad paper crackling, rusted bottle caps clicking-clinking: All were lashed into action by the scrabbling feet and the scaly whipping tails of a flurry of rats. There might have been eight, ten, twelve of the foot-long specimens with coarse brown coats and bristling whiskers and long pale toes. Their eyes were black beads that flared red when the white light caught them at a certain angle, and though the pack curved past us, I felt that I was the primary object of their attention, every ratty stare meeting mine before they swarmed away toward the back of the building, perhaps enticed here by the scent of blood, confused about the source until the metal door had stood open long enough to allow the odor of carnage to rise from the basement.

The moment wasn't melodramatic. I didn't expect them to attack. They were rats, not wolves. But the sight of them oppressed me. Death was always terrible, even when the dead were people who had served as agents of pain and ruin all their lives, but death was made worse by the consideration of these omnivores descending upon the murdered pair. Bodies are in a sense sacred, having been the vessels that carried souls through the world, and that they should ever become mere carrion sickens me.

Mrs. Fischer and I hurried out of the abandoned building, into the late-afternoon light, which was too cool to melt away the chill that prickled through me.

She said she'd drive, and that was all right with me because I felt that we weren't yet done in Barstow. I sensed that the cowboy had been somewhere else in town, no doubt before he came here to collect the children. I was hoping psychic magnetism could lead me not yet to where my quarry was this moment, but first to where he had been earlier, which required a concentration that wouldn't be possible if I were driving.

In the limousine once more, I considered using the disposable cell phone to call the police and report the bodies in the factory basement. I hoped to foil the rats before they feasted.

But during the past few years, the government had spent many billions to develop systems that could capture from the ether every one of the hundreds of millions of daily phone calls and e-mails sent in this country, store them, and conduct high-speed analysis of that data with enormous arrays of supercomputers. In addition, every smartphone was now a GPS by which they could track you if they wanted to, even when the phone was switched off.

My phone was far from smart, but I suspected that if I called the police, they would at once have my position. And maybe they could electronically tag even this dumb phone, so that they would know everywhere I went from this point forward.

I didn't dare reveal myself to the police if I were to be free to find the children and rescue them. Although I had not always saved everyone whom I tried to help, I nevertheless felt certain that, even as flawed as I was, I would be more likely to pull those three kids from the pending fire alone than with even well-meaning policemen kibitzing my every move. Besides, they were certain to regard my claims of paranormal talents as delusional. I might be committed to a psychiatric ward on a temporary hold, and the children would be torched days before I was released.

Mrs. Fischer drove, Hoke to my Miss Daisy. Although I needed to concentrate harder than ever to sense out the cowboy's fading trail through Barstow, distractions plucked at me, each of them arousing in me the thought that I was missing something, failing to see something that I must see if I were to survive: thoughts of the swarming rats in the factory and of the rats descending the palm tree, a pack of rangy yellow-eyed coyotes that had behaved strangely when they had stalked me and Annamaria through a fogbound night in Magic Beach more than a month previously, rats and coyotes that were different creatures and yet somehow one and the same, the head of the Kewpie doll wallowing in the storm runoff and trading its face for mine as it was yanked through the bars of the iron grating, the premonition of a demonic mob slaughtering stalled motorists on the traffic-choked freeway, all of that connected in some way that I could feel but could not define, pointing to some inevitable confrontation, and then three lines from T. S. Eliot's "Burnt Norton" remembered for no apparent reason—*Time present and time past / Are both perhaps present in time future / And time future contained in time past*—and now the carnival-bright ProStar+ with the yellow symbols painted throughout the black interior of the trailer, the gate of symbols made of steel, the wasteland with the lakes of fire and the Other Odd who had come out of that ultimate darkness, Mr. Hitchcock giving me two thumbs up when I woke in Shower 5 after being shot in the throat by the cowboy, a gesture that now seemed peculiar to me or perhaps more meaningful than I'd taken it to be at the time, Mr. Hitchcock raising one eyebrow as if amused when I suggested that he must be suffering some guilt and remorse that kept him from crossing over to the Other Side, the lightning-bolt grate and the eerie light in the storm drain, Mr. Hitchcock leading me into the basement of Star Truck and cupping a hand around one ear to suggest that I listen for what soon proved to be the voice of the rhinestone cowboy in a different version of the basement, a version in Elsewhere. . . .

I managed occasionally to give Mrs. Fischer a direction, though I was barely aware of Barstow beyond the windshield, preoccupied with the swift flow of thoughts and memories, the river of puzzling associations that seemed to have two currents, one enticing me into the past, the other sweeping me toward some terrible cataract in the near future.

When I shuddered violently and said, "Here, this place, right now," Mrs. Fischer pulled off the street, into a parking lot, and braked to a stop.

I came out of my half trance, expecting some place more terrible than the house where a family waited heartsick for any news of their abducted son and daughters, more ominous than the abandoned factory. Instead, we were adjacent to an exit from Interstate 15, in front of a large rectangular diner with a ziggurat-style roof stepping back and up in a pyramidal form, each level outlined in parallel tubes of ruby-red and sapphire-blue neon that were not only cheerful but also seemed to be defiant in the dreary half-light of the waning day and the oncoming storm. The playful architecture was fun to look at, even though I felt certain that the cowboy trucker had been here, and not alone, before he'd gone to the ruins of Black & Buckle Manufacturing to carve and kill two men and to collect the children that he intended to set afire. The place was called Ernestine's.

Tucking the loaded pistol under the seat, I said, "There's something here we need to know."

Mrs. Fischer said, "What would that be?"

"Beats me. But I'll know it when I see it or hear it."

"You don't think you'll need the gun?"

"No, ma'am. Not here."

"Just the same, I'll keep mine in my purse. I've needed it before in the most unlikely places."

# Nineteen

I RARELY HAVE SUCH MIXED FEELINGS about a new place when first setting foot in it as I had upon entering Ernestine's.

On the one hand, I felt as if I had come home. From the age of sixteen, when I moved out of my mother's house to live alone, I had worked at the Pico Mundo Grille, the quintessential diner, where I knew some of the happiest times of my life.

The Grille was scrupulously clean, both in the public areas and in the kitchen, and judging by what I could see of Ernestine's, the hygiene standards were equally stringent. The lighting achieved that perfect median—bright enough to read the menu easily, to be assured that the management was proud enough to cast light into every well-scrubbed corner, and to engage in people-watching, but low enough to be cozy, intimate.

On the long serving counter, at which several

customers sat on chrome stools with red-vinyl seats, were several pedestal displays of cakes under glass, each more enticing than the one before it.

Of all the signifiers that Ernestine's was a class act, however, the mouthwatering smells were the most convincing. Sautéing onions and green peppers in an omelette pan waited for the eggs. Ground-sirloin burgers, sizzling on the griddle, were ready for the cheese. The savor of frying bacon, the scent of toast, the aroma of fine coffee—all of it was seductive enough to test the willpower of the most devout monk in the middle of a fast.

But though I felt welcome here and in my element, as a sailor in love with the sea feels most at home on a ship, an albatross hung around the moment. The cowboy had been here, eaten here; and from my perspective, even his brief presence was a curse upon the place.

With the dinner rush not quite yet begun, seven booths were open, and I was drawn to one in particular, as a boarhound to a boar. The cowboy and I were part of an age-old pattern that seemed like chaos but was not, participants in the perpetual struggle that began when time began, that would not end when we two were dead, that would end only when time itself ended.

I sat where he had sat.

Mrs. Fischer sat opposite me, where perhaps the stocky man with the battered face had enjoyed an early dinner.

Nothing remained to attest to the previous presence of those two men in this booth. Evil travels the world in anonymity, its presence revealed only by the periodic consequences of its desires, like the missing children and the dead men in the factory basement. To most people in this age of denial, those consequences always come as a surprise, because they fear not what they should but only straw men, imagined threats, phantom crises.

Neither Mrs. Fischer nor I had taken lunch, and dinnertime was upon us. Intuition told me that the children were not in immediate danger of being murdered and that the worst thing I could do would be to rush into the breach before I better understood what I was up against. Until I discovered what clue was waiting in Ernestine's to be revealed, we might as well eat.

In fact, although it isn't profound, there are worse mottoes to live by than "We might as well eat." Say your neighbor's secret meth lab blows up, destroying your house along with his. We might as well eat. The secretary of defense announces from Sweden that he is having a sex-change operation, is in love with the prime minister of Russia, and has given his lover our nuclear launch codes. We might as well eat.

The gruesome scene in the factory basement had not spoiled my appetite. If every horror I have seen were to leave me so disgusted that I turned away from food for any length of time, I would be a bag of bones subsisting on bottled water and vitamin pills.

Our waitress, Sandy, was a pretty, thirty-something, freckled blonde. She presented herself to the world with appealing directness: no makeup, hair pulled back in a ponytail, her white uniform fresh and neatly pressed, a pendant cross at her throat, a flag pin on the lapel of her blouse, modest engagement and wedding rings on display.

Waitressing can be a hard and thankless job, largely because it requires dealing politely with people regardless of their temperament or mood, even though sometimes you just want to smack them. You can always tell when a waitress likes her work. She lacks the slouch and shuffle that signifies boredom and grievance. Her smile isn't fixed but comes and goes easily, appropriate to the moment. She makes eye contact and notices details because her customers interest her, not as the source of tips, but as people.

Sandy was taken with Mrs. Fischer's gold brooch in which little diamonds and rubies formed a glittering exclamation point. "It looks like it means something more than just being pretty," she said, "but I wonder what. If you don't mind me asking."

"Don't mind at all," said Mrs. Fischer. "It means 'Seize the day!' It means 'Live life to the fullest!' It means 'Sister, what a hoot it is to be me!'"

Sandy laughed, but then seemed to catch herself, as if for some reason laughter might be inappropriate. "You remind me of my mom. She's done every-thing from teaching skydiving to rodeo to stock-car racing."

"Have you ever gone skydiving?" Mrs. Fischer asked.

"I love my mom to pieces, but we're different. Jim, my husband, he's my skydiving, and my four kids . . . they're my rodeo." She looked away from Mrs. Fischer, through the big window, at the street where passing cars already traveled behind headlights as the day faded. Her eyes seemed unfocused, as if she saw something other than what lay beyond the glass, and a note of sorrow in her voice was not suited to her words. "A month from now, when the desert's all covered for a while in flowers, millions of heliotrope and fiddlenecks, poppies and red maids and yellow coreopsis—that's better in my book than winning any stock-car race." If she had for a moment sunk into a tormented place in her mind, she lifted herself out of it and turned a dazzling smile on us. "I'm just a stick-in-the-mud, I guess."

Although these days a good waitress lives in a time when most people feel aggrieved and often for no good reason, she shows no such disposition her-self and lightens your spirit merely by the gratitude with which she faces life.

We ordered, and after we were served coffee, Mrs. Fischer said, "That girl's the right stuff, sweetie. After you deal with that rotten rhinestone-cowboy bastard, I'll have to come back this way and do a thing or two."

"What thing or two?"

"Whatever seems to be the best thing or two to do."

She smiled with satisfaction, as if an array of possibilities had already occurred to her. She looked cute enough to be Yoda's mother.

I said, "You mean like introducing Andy Shephorn to Penny, and now they're married and building a winery that will be legendary one day?"

"Barstow isn't a friendly climate for vineyards. And Sandy is already happily married."

"Then what?"

She blew on her coffee to cool it, took a sip. "Something will occur to me when I've done a little research."

"Is Sandy smoothed out and fully blue?"

"Not nearly to the extent that you are, child. But she's got what it takes to get there."

Because we were waiting for our food and couldn't yet live by the motto of the moment, I was inspired by another motto: *We might as well schmooze.*

"Ma'am, how did you meet Mr. Fischer?"

She cocked her head, studied me for half a minute, and then said, "I guess I can tell you a little. If we're going to spend the next ten years or more driving hundreds of thousands of miles, we'll be best friends, and best friends share. I was twenty-three, being the finest Blanche that I could be, and

Heathcliff told me that I was born for better things than Blanche."

"Ma'am?"

"Please call me Edie."

"Yes, ma'am. Being Blanche?"

"Blanche DuBois in *A Streetcar Named Desire*. It was a road-company production. I've always liked the road, being on the move."

"You were an actress."

"I thought I was. Some smart people agreed. Heath liked my performance, came backstage after the play, but he said I was born for wonder, not for Williams, by which he meant Tennessee Williams, the author of the play. He invited me to dinner, we had a lovely time, and over crème brûlée, he asked me to marry him."

"What—the same night you met him?"

"Well, after the cute little rabbit and the dove and the waiter taking off his pants, I laughed so much that I knew this was the man for me. I mean Heathcliff, not the waiter, though the waiter was perfectly nice."

"You ate rabbit and dove for dinner?"

"Good heavens, no. The rabbit was too cute to eat, and the dove didn't have much meat on its bones. Heath pulled the dove from my purse, which astounded me because I just *knew* I didn't have one in there. And then right before my eyes, mind you, the dove turned into a rabbit, and then the rabbit vanished—*poof!*—when he draped his napkin over it."

"Mr. Fischer was a magician."

"Call him Heath or Heathcliff, dear."

"Yes, ma'am. So Mr. Fischer was a magician."

"Well, he was and he wasn't, dear. He was many things, and one thing he could appear to be was a magician."

Her periwinkle eyes sparkled with merriment or mischief, or both.

"What about the waiter?" I asked.

"Oh, he was a nice man, but I don't know what happened to him, dear. That was a long time ago."

In the spirit of our eccentric conversation, I said, "I thought maybe he was the best man at your wedding, right there at tableside."

"No, no. Heath's best man was Purdy Feltenham, one of the most charming people I've ever known, though he had to go everywhere with a sack over his head, poor thing."

Aware that we might easily lose track of the pantless waiter, determined not to do so, I said, "Ma'am, what I meant was—why did the waiter take off his pants?"

"Of course he had to, child. When that sweet man asked Heath where the rabbit went after it disappeared under the napkin, Heath said, 'It's in your pants,' and then, of course, the waiter felt it there and was eager to return it. He wasn't the least embarrassed about taking off his pants, even though he had unfortunate knees. Heath had a way of putting everyone at ease in any circumstances. And it turned out, as things had a way of doing around Heathcliff, the little girl dining at the next table with her parents had two months earlier lost her pet rabbit to some illness. She was so happy when Heath gave his magic rabbit to her."

If the diner had had a liquor license, I might have spiked my coffee with brandy, which would most likely have helped me to make more sense of Mrs. Fischer's story. Instead, with only the benefit of caffeine, I said, "What happened to the dove?"

"It turned into a rabbit, child. Weren't you listening?"

"But it can't really have turned into a rabbit."

Her blue eyes widened into bright pools. "Then where did it go?"

"You never saw the dove again?"

"No, dear, I did not. And I certainly didn't eat it. I would have remembered."

"What did you mean, Mr. Fischer was and wasn't a magician?"

"Well, he could certainly appear to be one when he wanted to. He could be almost anything he put his mind to. He was very intelligent and wise, two qualities that don't always go together, clever and kind, in awe of the world and full of fun."

"Was Mr. Fischer smoothed out and fully blue?"

"Yes, but he was unusual among the smooth-and-blue because, although he knew the truth of the world and what comes after, he decided he had to have a backup, which is why he's frozen now."

"He's frozen now?"

She looked a little sad and disappointed, but affectionately so, as she shook her white-capped head. "Heath's body is in a container of liquid nitrogen at a cryogenic-preservation center in New Mexico. If they're ever able to bring back the frozen dead, which they never will be able to do, then he thought he might have a chance to live in both this world and the next at the same time. Even the wisest and best of us can be foolish occasionally."

As I have learned, most mysteries yield to patience sooner or later.

"So that's why you told Officer Shephorn that your husband was still dead but otherwise perfect."

Mrs. Fischer shook one finger at me. "Now, don't you go making arrangements to have yourself Popsicled. There's no need for that. When you disappear from this world, you won't wind up in a waiter's pants, you'll go where you've always belonged since you were born, and it's a lot nicer than a tank of liquid nitrogen."

Sandy arrived with our dinner.

We had two cheeseburgers, french fries, a shared order of fried onion rings, a side of fried cheese for Mrs. Fischer, and a dish of pepper slaw for me.

Mrs. Fischer said, "That pepper slaw would probably shock my arteries into full collapse. Are you really sure you should eat that stuff?"

"It's my one dietary foolishness, ma'am. And less

expensive than being perpetually preserved in liquid nitrogen."

"True enough."

After we had been eating awhile, I was only a little surprised to hear myself say, "It worries me that I'm missing something about Mr. Hitchcock."

"Would that be *the* Mr. Hitchcock, dear?"

Our booth was far removed from the nearest other diners, and I felt increasingly comfortable with Mrs. Fischer because she and I seemed to be more alike than not, acutely aware of the strangeness of the world and charmed by its mysteries. I told her that I saw the spirits of the lingering dead, that they came to me for justice, if they were murdered, or for help in crossing over if they were simply afraid of what might await them on the Other Side.

She reacted as if I had said nothing more startling than that I had played baseball in high school, liked English classes, but had no aptitude for math.

"Alfred Hitchcock has been dead more than thirty years, child. Do the lingering ones hang around here that long?"

"Not always. Not usually. Though Elvis Presley lingered even longer."

"You helped Elvis cross over?"

"Eventually, ma'am."

"Good for you. Heath knew his mother."

"Mr. Fischer knew Gladys Presley?"

"He thought she was the sweetest God-fearing

woman. Reasonably smoothed out and partway blue. Elvis's daddy—not so much." She looked around the diner. "Is Alfred Hitchcock here right now?"

"No, ma'am. He comes and goes. He's . . . different from others that have sought my help before."

"How so?"

"For one thing, he's very easygoing, even amused. There's no anxiety in him."

"Are the others anxious?"

"To one extent or another."

"The poor dears. They don't need to be."

"No, ma'am. Another thing, the dead always want *me* to help *them*. But it seems more as if Mr. Hitchcock wants to help *me*."

"Help you what, dear?"

"Maybe . . . find the rhinestone cowboy. I don't know. I'm missing something, and that worries me."

We ate in silence for a couple of minutes.

Beyond the window, under the low gray sky, the desert day came to night through the briefest twilight.

As here in Barstow, for a couple of weeks each spring, the desert around Pico Mundo suddenly bloomed bright with heliotrope and fiddlenecks, poppies and red maids and more. I hoped that I might live to see the land around my hometown thus enraptured one more time.

I said, "You didn't for a moment think I was crazy when I told you that I see the dead."

"Of course not, child. The world now is crazy. You are as sane as the world once was."

Mrs. Fischer insisted that the treat was on her, and she left a 100 percent tip in cash. With the money, she put down a business card that had no name, address, or phone number. The small white rectangle presented only one of those perfectly round iconic cartoon faces with dots for the eyes and nose, and a big arc of a smile. Instead of traditional yellow, the face was blue. And very smooth.

Carrying the check, Mrs. Fischer led me through the diner to the cashier's station. As we arrived, Sandy finished pouring a refill for one of the customers seated at the counter, returned the coffeepot to the warmer, and took time to ring up our bill.

As the waitress and Mrs. Fischer exchanged pleasantries, I spotted the stack of flyers on the counter beside the cash register. MISSING! the headline declared. Under that, a question: HAVE YOU SEEN THESE CHILDREN?

Here they were—the three faces from my vision. Now the flyer gave me names to go with them. The eight-year-old boy was Jessie Payton, the six-year-old was his sister Jasmine, and the ten-year-old girl was Jordan.

Having noticed my interest in the flyer, Sandy said, "Makes me sick to think about it."

When I looked up, unshed tears stood in her sea-green eyes. I said, "When did they disappear?"

"Between seven and eight-thirty yesterday evening. It'll soon be twenty-four hours. That can't be good, no trace of them by now."

"How did police figure the time?"

"A neighbor, Ben Samples, saw the back door open, knew something wasn't right, went to check. Eight-thirty he found poor Agnes."

"Agnes?"

The salt tide in Sandy's eyes overflowed. She couldn't speak. I understood why, earlier, she'd felt that laughter was not appropriate and why her voice had contained a note of sorrow not commensurate to her description of the desert carpeted in bright flowers.

From a nearby stool, a burly man in khakis and a checkered-flannel shirt, whose coffee had been refilled a moment earlier, spoke up. "Agnes Henry. Reverend Henry's widow. Sweet lady. Did babysittin' to stretch her Social Security. Paytons' trash cans are kept to one side of their back porch. Ben Samples, he notices a lid is half off one. Just enough porch light, so when he happens to look down, he sees a face in there. Agnes. Stabbed through the heart, stuffed in the can like garbage."

Wiping her eyes with a Kleenex, Sandy said, "Chet, good Lord, what's the world coming to, helpless children all over snatched away the same day?"

"It's comin' to the bad end it's always been comin' to," Chet said solemnly.

For a beat, I didn't understand them, and then I

did but wished that I had it wrong. "All over? Other children? Where?"

Chet turned more directly toward us on the swiveling stool. "Two in Bakersfield, one up to Visalia."

All those diner smells that had been so appetizing congealed now into a greasy, meaty malodor, as though beneath every shining moment of culinary delight, the repressed knowledge of the slaughterhouse waited to assert the sacrifice that was the source of that pleasure. The aroma of coffee now had the bitter smell of an emetic.

"Two in Winslow, Arizona," Sandy said, "and four from one family in a suburb of Phoenix."

"Four more in Vegas," Chet said. "Kidnappers killed the parents to get at the young'uns. And one from Cedar City, up to Utah."

"Seventeen altogether," I said.

"Maybe even others nobody knows of yet," Chet said. "This smells like terrorism. Don't it to you? Who knows where it ends?"

Mrs. Fischer crossed herself, the first indication of a traditional faith that I had witnessed from her, although I'd never seen anyone make the sign of the cross with jaws clenched tight in anger and eyes as fierce as hers were just then. Maybe she prayed the rosary every night, or maybe this terrible news reminded her of the Catholicism of her childhood and of why she'd once felt a need for it.

"All these things happened in so many jurisdictions," Chet explained, "nobody saw the pattern till late this mornin', early this afternoon. By then those kids they could be anywhere."

"They've got to be connected, don't they?" Sandy asked. "The TV news says they've got to be."

"Not a ransom demand for a one of them," Chet said. "That gives me a bad feelin'. Don't it you?"

"My folks are staying with us till there's some kind of end to this," Sandy revealed. "Dad, Mom, Jim—they all have guns, and we're schooling at home for the time being."

On the road all day, with no interest in the radio, we had not heard the news. Usually I spare myself from the news, because if it's not propaganda, then it's one threat or another exaggerated to the point of absurdity, or it's the tragedy of storm-quake-tsunami, of bigotry and oppression misnamed justice, of hatred passed off as righteousness and honor called dishonorable, all jammed in around advertisements in which a gecko sells insurance, a bear sells toilet tissue, a dog sells cars, a gorilla sells investment advisers, a tiger sells cereal, and an elephant sells a drug that will improve your lung capacity, as if no human being in America any longer believes any other human being, but trusts only the recommendations of animals.

Not having heard the news, I had been drawn to Ernestine's to make an important discovery, and this was it. The Payton kids were not the only souls in peril. Some demented group was trawling the West for children, to bring them together for burning or to kill them otherwise, on a stage before a select audience more perverse than I cared to consider.

With my paranormal abilities, perhaps I might be the only one who could find the abductees in time to save them. This obligation was so heavy that I didn't know if I had the shoulders to carry it. I have had successes but also failures, because whatever else I might be, I am first and foremost human, and the tendency of our fallen kind is to fall again. To fail so many innocent children—or any of them—would leave me in a dark place, perhaps even blacker than the emotional slough through which I suffered in the weeks immediately after I lost Stormy Llewellyn. I had no choice, of course, but to try.

The likelihood of failure seemed greater than usual, however, because I was one against what seemed to be phalanxes of enemies, and singularly brutal enemies, at that. More troubling than their numbers and bloodthirstiness, they were not the usual scapegraces, criminals, psychopaths, and sociopaths. They might be all of those things, yes, but they were also something more dangerous. At least two of them, the rhinestone cowboy and his stone-faced viper-eyed associate, possessed some paranormal abilities—or supernatural knowledge—unique to them.

Sandy gave Mrs. Fischer her change.

Mrs. Fischer deposited a few dollars of it into a clear-plastic collection bucket for the Special Olympics, which stood near the cash register.

Sandy wished us a safe journey.

Mrs. Fischer plucked a couple of complimentary cellophane-wrapped hard-candy mints from a plastic bowl beside the Special Olympics bucket.

I opened the door for Mrs. Fischer.

Mrs. Fischer gave me one of the mints.

Even if there are moments during the day when all seems normal and when every action of your own and of those around you seems to be unremarkable, the appearance of ordinariness is an illusion, and just below the placid surface, the world is seething.

# Twenty

NOT ALL DESERTS ARE HOT ALL THE TIME. The high ones can be as cold in winter as a Canadian plain. We were near the end of winter, but a chill had come with nightfall. The breeze smelled faintly of the rain that we had outrun but that soon would catch us again.

A huge tricked-up Harley-Davidson stood next to the limousine, basic black but, in the light from the diner, bright with intricacies of chrome.

The couple standing by the motorcycle, taking off their helmets, looked nothing like Hells Angels. Perhaps fifty, tall, muscular but lean, clean-shaven, the man had a salt-and-pepper lion's mane of hair. He was character-actor rather than lead-actor handsome, his face subjected less to emollient lotions and toning gels than to wind and sun, and never to Botox. The woman might have been forty, with the high cheekbones, proud but chiseled features, and polished-bronze complexion that suggested she had floated into this world from the headwaters of the Cherokee gene pool. If *Soldier of Fortune* magazine had merged with *Vogue,* these two might have been models in those pages. I would have bet my liver that neither had the smallest tattoo or love handles, that they didn't care what anyone's opinion of them might be, that they didn't give a thought to fashion yet owned not a single unfortunate item of clothing, and that they didn't tweet in any sense of the word.

In a baritone voice as mellow as fifty-year-old port, the man said to Mrs. Fischer, "We heard on the grapevine that Oscar completed his tour of duty and went home."

Mrs. Fischer hugged the woman and said, "He finished his last spoon of the best crème brûlée we ever had, and the maître d' said nobody who ever died in that restaurant before had passed away more discreetly."

As the man hugged Mrs. Fischer, he said, "Oscar was always a class act."

"How's his mom coping?" the woman asked.

"Well, dear, you don't get to be a hundred and nine without having taken the world on your shoulders a time or two."

Offering his right hand to me, the man said, "My name's Gideon. This is my wife, Chandelle. You must be Edie's new chauffeur. You're Thomas, aren't you? May I call you Tom?"

"Yes, sir." I shook his hand. "But I haven't taken the job yet."

Mrs. Fischer said, "He's very independent, self-reliant."

"That's the way, isn't it," Gideon said.

"That's the way," Mrs. Fischer confirmed.

When the motorcyclist smiled, his countenance crinkled in the most appealing way, as if all the good weather he had ever known had been stored up in his face but none of the bad.

From somewhere came a memory that I at once put into words. "*Chandelle* is French for 'candle.'"

Her smile was as warming as her husband's, much more luminous than a single candle.

Mrs. Fischer said, "Tom and his girlfriend, Stormy, once got a card from a carnival fortune-telling machine that said 'You are destined to be together forever.'"

"I would take that very seriously," Chandelle said.

"I do," I told her.

Mrs. Fischer said, "Stormy passed away young, but he's still faithful to her and believes in what the card said."

"Of course you do," Gideon said. "What kind of fool would you be if you didn't believe in it?"

"Several kinds, sir."

"Exactly."

"Well," Mrs. Fischer said, "we've got something of a crisis to deal with, a real life-or-death thing, and

Tom here is eager to get into the thick of it, though I suspect he thinks he'll be dead by morning."

"Exhilarating," Gideon said.

I said, "Yes, sir, to an extent it is."

Chandelle and Gideon kissed Mrs. Fischer's cheek, and Mrs. Fischer kissed their cheeks, and I kissed Chandelle's cheek as she kissed mine, and I shook hands with Gideon again.

Carrying their helmets, like figures more suited to a dream than to Barstow, the couple moved toward Ernestine's. After a few steps, Gideon looked back and said to Mrs. Fischer, "Will we see you in Lonely Possum, come July?"

"Wouldn't miss it for the world," she assured them.

"And it *is* for the world," Chandelle said to me. "I hope we'll see you there, too."

"I'm certainly intrigued, ma'am."

"Call me Chandelle," she said.

"Yes, ma'am. Thank you, ma'am."

They went into the diner.

The Harley-Davidson was an impressive machine. It looked as if it should be quietly purring like a well-fed and contented panther.

Mrs. Fischer got behind the wheel of the limousine.

I, known to the grapevine as her chauffeur, independent and self-reliant, rode shotgun. That's the way.

Mrs. Fischer unwrapped her mint, popped it into her mouth, and started the car.

As we pulled out of the parking lot, I said, "Better stop for gas, ma'am."

"One tank's full and the other nearly so, dear."

"How can that be? We've been on the road a lot today."

"I believe I told you about One-Ear Bob."

"You told me a little bit about him."

"When I finish this mint, maybe I'll tell you more."

As we took the entrance ramp to Interstate 15, heading east, I said, "How do you know Gideon and Chandelle?"

"I introduced them to each other."

"You're a real matchmaker, ma'am."

"I enjoy making people happy."

"Do they live around here?"

"They have a home in Florida, but mostly they're on the road."

"They're always around these parts in March?"

"Oh, no, they don't have a schedule of any kind. They just go where they feel it's necessary for them to go."

"Did you know they were in Barstow?"

"No, dear. It was a pleasant surprise to see them."

"Sort of like Andy Shephorn pulling us over."

"Sort of like," she agreed.

"Gideon has a great voice. Is he a singer? She looks like she might be a dancer."

"Well, they do all kinds of things, child."

"All kinds of things?"

"Many, many things. And you can be sure that those two *always* do the right thing."

"July in Lonely Possum, huh?"

"It can be fiercely hot, but lovely nonetheless."

No sooner were we on the interstate than the sky caught fire, and the entire desert seemed to leap in surprise, repeatedly, as it was revealed by reflection and then cast back into darkness and then revealed again. Thunder so furiously concussed the night that it seemed the Mojave might break under the blows and collapse into some cavernous realm over which it had been a bridge for tens of thousands of years.

Raindrops as plump as chandelier crystals rapped the limo and stymied the windshield wipers until Mrs. Fischer turned them up to their highest speed. Soon the droplets diminished to the size of pearls, but the fireworks continued for several minutes and with uncommon violence.

When at last the heavens went dark and quiet, when the storm seemed content now with merely trying to drown us, Mrs. Fischer said, "Quite a display. I hope it didn't mean anything."

I half knew what she intended to convey with those words. "I hope it didn't mean anything, either, ma'am."

"You still have a fix on him, Oddie?"

"The cowboy. Yes, ma'am. He's out there. We'll find him."

The lightning and thunder had rattled us back

into the bleak mood into which we had fallen while speaking with Sandy and Chet at the cash register in Ernestine's. We rode in silence, brooding.

Mr. Hitchcock kept making cameo appearances in my tangled skeins of thought, the way that he had slyly inserted himself into one scene in each of his movies. I returned, as well, to consideration of rats and coyotes, and to those lines from Eliot. *Time present and time past / Are both perhaps present in time future / And time future contained in time past.* I had read the poet's *Four Quartets* at least a hundred times, and I understood them in spite of their demanding language and concepts. But I suspected that these lines kept running through my mind not because of what they meant within the poem, but because they expressed, with power, a warning about some threat that I intuited but could not consciously define.

Strange how the deepest part of us isn't able to speak more clearly to the part of us that lives only here in the shallows of the world. The body is entirely physical, the mind partly so and partly not, being both the dense computer circuitry of brain tissue and the ghostly software running in it. But the deepest part of us, the soul, is not physical to any extent whatsoever. Yet the material body and the immaterial soul are inextricably linked this side of death and, so theologians tell us, on the Other Side, as well. On the Other Side, body and soul are supposed to function in perfect harmony. So I guess the problem on this side of death is that when we fell from grace back in the day, the body and soul became like two neighboring countries, still connected by highways and bridges and rivers, but each now speaking a different language from the other. To get through life successfully, body and soul must translate each other correctly more often than not. But in the limo, leaving Barstow, I couldn't quite interpret that warning from the deepest part of me.

As we rocketed along the rainswept interstate, miraculously not hydroplaning off the pavement and into a stand of cactuses as the laws of physics would seem to have required, Mrs. Fischer said, "Wherever it is these child-stealers are holed up, you can't go in after them with just that pistol or either of the other two I have with me. You've got to weaponize yourself better than that."

"I don't much like guns, ma'am."

"Does it matter whether you like them or not?"

"I guess it doesn't."

"You do what you have to do. That's who you seem to be to me, anyway. You're one who does what he has to do."

"Maybe that's not always what I *should* do."

"Don't double-think yourself so much, child. You had a good dinner of properly fried food, and if you want to live long enough to have another one, you've got to weaponize properly."

The rain fell so hard that, in the headlights, the entire world seemed to be melting. The vaguely phosphorescent landscape shimmered as though every acre of it must be liquefied and in motion, seeking a drain into which to pour itself.

"Ma'am, the closest town of any size where they might sell guns is back in Barstow. And they don't just let you put your money down and walk out ten minutes later with a bazooka or whatever it is you think I need. There are waiting periods, police checks, all that."

"That's certainly true in Barstow and in Vegas, but there's a lot of territory between the two."

"A lot of mostly really *empty* territory."

"Not as empty as you think, sweetie. And some places out there, nobody bothers much with waiting periods and the like. What we need to do at this particular time in this particular place is take a side trip to Mazie's and get what you need."

"Mazie's? What is Mazie's?" I asked with some doubt and a little suspicion.

"It's not a whorehouse, though it might sound like one," Mrs. Fischer said. "Mazie and her sons, Tracker and Leander, do a bit of this and that, and they do it all well."

"How long a side trip?"

"Not long at all. Once we leave the interstate, the first road is paved but the second is just gravel, and the third is all natural shale. But none of it's bad road, and it all leads up into the hills, not into the flats, so the chances we'll be caught by a flash flood are so small they don't worry me at all."

"How small?" I asked.

"Tiny, really."

"How tiny?"

"Infinitesimal, child."

The desert doesn't get much annual rainfall, but what it does receive tends to come all at once. A lot of terrific Japanese poets have written uncountable haiku about the silvery delicacy of the rain and about how it vanishes so elegantly into the moonlit river or the silver lake or the trembling pond, rain like a maiden's tears, but not a line of any of them was appropriate to this insane storm. This was more of a Russian rain, in particular a mean Soviet rain, coming down like ten thousand hammers on ten thousand anvils in the People's Foundry of the Revolution.

Mrs. Fischer said, "Mazie's exit is about two miles ahead."

When we got there, the highway sign didn't say anything about Mazie. Instead, it warned ABANDONED ROADWAY / NO OUTLET.

When I noted this discrepancy between what Mrs. Fischer had promised and what the reality proved to be, she reached out to pat my shoulder with her right hand, driving only with her left, though in her defense, I must admit that she had slowed to sixty for the exit.

The two-lane paved road had been built in an age when we were still going to war with European nations, and it consisted of more potholes than blacktop. Fortunately, it didn't go far before it gave way to the gravel road, which was more accommodating, although the deluge was so intense that I had to lean forward and squint to see the track, which seemed always about to wither away into sand and sage.

After we had gone no more than a quarter of a mile on the gravel, the headlights flared off a sign with reflective yellow letters that announced DANGER / STAY OUT / ARTILLERY RANGE / MILITARY VEHICLES ONLY.

When I questioned the wisdom of ignoring such a warning, Mrs. Fischer said, "Oh, that's nothing, dear."

"It seems like something," I disagreed.

"It's not official. Mazie and Tracker put that up themselves, years ago, to scare people off."

"What kind of people would want to come out to this godforsaken place anyway?"

"The kind you want to scare off."

By the angle of our ascent, I knew we were driving into low hills, although in this darkness and downpour, I couldn't see well enough to confirm what I felt. Mrs. Fischer told me when the gravel gave way to a trail of broken shale, though I couldn't feel any difference in the ride.

Shale is brittle and over the millennia is laid down in thin strata, so the fragments can be sharp, which is why I said, "Hope we don't have a flat tire out here."

"It isn't possible, child."

"No disrespect, ma'am, but of course it's possible. Why wouldn't it be possible?"

She glanced at me and winked. "One-Ear Bob."

"What—you have some kind of armored tires or something?"

"Some kind of something," Mrs. Fischer confirmed.

Before I could press for details, we had to stop because of all the snakes.

# Twenty-one

IF YOU ARE FOND OF TARANTULAS AND rattlesnakes, this desert will delight you no less than the Metropolitan Opera enchants lovers of Puccini, Donizetti, and Verdi. It is a veritable festival of spiders, a jubilee of snakes with ten times more fangs per square mile than in Transylvania, and with more forked tongues than you would find even in the halls of Congress.

Mrs. Fischer was quicker than I to recognize what surged across the broken-shale track, illuminated by the headlights, and she braked to a full stop before driving over them. I leaned forward, fascinated by the creepy spectacle of at least a double score of six-foot-long rattlesnakes seething through the storm, some of them slithering flat to the ground, others with their heads raised, all moving south to north, as though they were livestock driven by herdsmen. Their sinuous bodies glistened in the rain, wet dark scales re-

flecting the halogen beams as if some magical energy
shimmered through their muscular, continuously flex-
ing bodies.

Perhaps their subterranean nests had flooded, forc-
ing them out into the downpour, but that seemed
unlikely because their instinct, which was really something more like a program, compelled them to choose
their lairs with entrances shaped to direct water safely
away. Besides, rattlers hunt singly, not in packs, and
they don't pursue prey at speed, but for the most part
lie in wait. These snakes seemed unnaturally compelled, neither escaping from flooded dens nor driven
by a need for food, but harried to some mysterious
purpose.

I thought of the rats earlier in the day, of the
yellow-eyed coyotes in Magic Beach more than a
month previously, and I expected these serpents to
turn their flat, wicked-looking heads toward us and
reveal, by their interest, that what they sought was
*us*. But they glided across the road without seeming
to be aware of the limousine.

"They can't do what they're doing on a night like
this," Mrs. Fischer said.

"You mean the rain?"

"No. The chill. They're cold-blooded."

Of course. Unlike mammals, reptiles don't maintain an optimal body temperature, and their blood
warms and cools according to the temperature of
their environment. They hunt when the desert, having banked the heat of the day, pays it out to the

night. In weather as chilly as this, they should be coiled harmlessly in their nests, lethargic, dreaming the dreams of predators, if they dreamed at all.

Had the double score of snakes become hundreds, I wouldn't have been surprised. Logic argued that such a strange scene might easily get even stranger.

Instead, the last of them slithered off the shale and among ragged clumps of mesquite, and Mrs. Fischer said, "All that lightning a while back . . . I think it meant something."

"What do you think it meant?"

"Nothing good."

She took her foot off the brake pedal, and the limousine eased forward.

To my right, at the periphery of vision, a flicker of movement caught my attention, and as I turned my head, an open-mouthed rattler slammed against the window in the passenger door, making a sound like bare sweaty fists smacking hard into a punching bag in a gym, and fell away at once. Two more erupted through the night, whiplike, eyes aglitter, fangs bared, drops of milky venom spattering the glass on impact and diluted at once by the sluicing rain. A coiled snake can strike at prey exactly as far away as the snake is long, maybe more than six feet in this case, because these were big suckers, unusually big, well fed on tortoise eggs, mice, kangaroo rats, grasshoppers, lizards, tarantulas, and a variety of other treats that you won't find in *your* favorite all-you-can-eat buffet.

Mrs. Fischer said, "Goodness gracious," alerting me to the fact that not all the thudding of snake flesh against limo was on my side of the vehicle.

Undulant serpents seemed almost to swim through the dense wind-driven rain, and collided with the driver-door window, four in quick succession.

"Well, I never," Mrs. Fischer declared, sounding displeased with Mother Nature for this rude assault.

As she tramped on the accelerator, a rattler came over the port fender, snout-first into the windshield, where its hypodermic fangs hooked around a wiper blade, squirting venom. The wiper stuttered before lifting, almost broke, but then flicked the lashing reptile into the night before slapping back onto the windshield to resume rhythmically clearing away the rain.

"Good glass," I said.

"Yes, it is," she agreed.

"One-Ear Bob?"

"Absolutely."

We left the snakes behind.

Mrs. Fischer eased up on the accelerator.

I said, "You ever heard of snakes attacking a car?"

"No, never."

"Me neither. I wonder why they would."

"I wonder, too. And I don't believe a snake can spring that far."

"The length of its body, ma'am."

"These came farther than that."

"I sort of thought so, too."

Bullets of rain broke against the armored glass.

"Have you ever eaten rattlesnake, dear?"

"No, ma'am."

"It tastes good if you prepare it right."

"I'm a little bit of a finicky eater."

"I sympathize. The taste of lamb makes me gag."

"Lambs are too cute to eat," I said.

"Exactly. You can't eat too-cute animals. Like kittens."

"Or dogs. Cows are nice, but they're not cute."

"They're not," she agreed. "Neither are chickens."

"Pigs are a little bit cute."

Mrs. Fischer disagreed. "Only in some movies like *Babe* and *Charlotte's Web*. Those are fairy-tale pigs, not real pigs."

Neither of us spoke for a minute, listening to the rain drumming on the limousine, seeming to float through the night, and finally I said, "So when we finish whatever business we're doing at Mazie's, is there another route out or do we have to come back along this track?"

"There's just this one. But not to worry, child. I don't believe snakes have the capacity to strategize. Anyhow, doing what you have to do, always and without complaint—that's the way."

"That's the way, huh?"

"That's the way," she confirmed.

A pair of thirty-foot Joshua trees appeared on

each side of the road, eerie figures in the storm, less suggestive of trees than of blind creatures that might prowl the floor of an ocean, ceaselessly combing scents and tastes and, ultimately, small fish from the deep cold currents. They had been named by Mormon settlers, who thought these strange giants appeared to be warriorlike but also to be raising their arms beseechingly to Heaven, just as Joshua did at the battle of Jericho.

Easing off the accelerator again, Mrs. Fischer gestured toward the trees. "Even in daylight they look real, but they aren't."

"They aren't Joshua trees? Then what are they, ma'am?"

As we coasted forward, she said, "Just try to ram the gate, and you'll find out."

A nine-foot chain-link barrier, topped with coils of concertina wire with razor-sharp projections, loomed out of the rain, and Mrs. Fischer braked to a stop before it.

Fixed to the gate, a large ominous metal sign featured a skull and crossbones in each corner. Red letters warned: EXTREME DANGER / BIOLOGICAL RESEARCH STATION / VIRAL DISEASES / FLESH-EATING BACTERIA / TOXIC SUBSTANCES / DEADLY MOLDS / DISEASE-BEARING TEST ANIMALS / ADMITTANCE ONLY TO PROPERLY INOCULATED PERSONNEL. Those words were repeated at the bottom of the sign in Spanish.

Mrs. Fischer said, "That's just Mazie and Kipp's way of saying 'Private property, keep out.'"

"Probably works. Who's Kipp?"

"Her husband. You'll love him."

"I thought it was just her and her two sons."

"Well, dear, she's a woman, not a paramecium. She didn't just split in two a couple of times to produce Tracker and Leander."

"Ma'am, the way things have been going lately, I take nothing for granted."

From her purse, she retrieved her cell phone and placed a call. "Hi, Mazie. It's Lulu from Tuscaloosa." She waved at the gate, which I took to mean that a concealed camera was trained on the windshield. "Well, he's my new chauffeur." She reached out to pinch my cheek. "Yes, he's adorable."

Because it seemed to be the polite thing to do, I waved at the camera, wondering if it could detect the blush of my embarrassment.

Mrs. Fischer said, "Oh, that's just because he dawdles. And since we've got an emergency we have to get to, I took the wheel." She listened for a moment, said, "Thank you, Mazie, you're a sweetheart," and terminated the call.

I said, "Lulu from Tuscaloosa?"

As the gate began to roll aside, she said, "Oh, that's just sort of my secret password. When you're in the line of work that Mazie and Kipp are in, you need passwords and codes and cryptograms, that kind of thing."

"What *is* their line of work?"

"Being helpful, dear."

"That's a pretty broad job description."

"Being helpful, but only to those who ought to be helped."

She coasted through the open gate, and I said, "How do Mazie and Kipp decide who ought and who ought not?"

"Well, they take new business only by referral from people they trust. And Mazie has the very best bullshit detector ever. And then there's Big Dog."

We came to a halt in a cage, chain-link overhead as well as on all sides, another gate directly in front of us. The gate behind us rolled shut.

As we waited, I said, "Who's Big Dog?"

"When you see him, you'll know. There just couldn't be any other name for him."

Slanting through the chain-link and the concertina wire, some of the raindrops battered and shaved themselves into a fine mist. Chaotic gusts of wind spun those ravelings of fog into half-formed dancers with featureless faces, as ragged as anything that had been long in grave clothes, and waltzed them across the cage, out into the open night.

"Ma'am, I hate being all questions, but—what are we waiting here for?"

"They're checking out the car to be sure no one else is in it, because maybe we came here under duress."

"How are they checking it out?"

"Beats me. Techie stuff. They're probably scan-ning for insect spy drones, too, though I'm sure there isn't one in the car."

The gate in front of us rolled open, and Mrs. Fischer drove into a large compound that must have had a reliable water source, like an artesian well, because a forest of phoenix and queen palms tossed in the wind. Mazie had made an oasis for herself.

Mrs. Fischer followed a gravel driveway, which appeared to be bordered by beds of succulents. She parked under a portico that, on blistering Mojave days, would shade the front of the house.

Neither the portico nor the residence was elegant. From what I could see, the single-story structure sprawled over as much as ten thousand square feet, but it was built of poured-in-place steel-reinforced concrete left in its "natural" finish, with a flat roof. It looked more like a bunker than like a home, with narrow deep-set windows that featured small French panes within stainless-steel frames and muntins that flashed silver in the headlights.

When we got out of the Mercedes, lights came on in the ceiling of the portico.

"Way out here, they must have their own generator," I said, raising my voice to be heard above the keening wind that thrashed the palm fronds.

"Lots and lots of solar panels," Mrs. Fischer said as she took my arm and pretended that I was helping her to the front entrance. "Plus two gasoline-powered generators, one to back up the other."

"What are they—survivalists?"

"No, dear. They just like their privacy."

More suitable to a vault than to a home, the stainless-steel door opened, and before us stood a fifty-something guy with a shock of red hair and lively green eyes. He had a face as sweetly appealing as that of Bill Cosby, a face of such likability that he would have been perfect to play the father in a TV-sitcom family, not in any contemporary show but in one made back in the day when sitcom dads were more real and less grotesque than they are now, when everyone still knew that families matter, when the word *values* meant something more important than the sales prices at the currently cool clothing store where you buy your gear.

He wore white tennis shoes, khakis, a white T-shirt, and a full-length yellow apron on which were printed the words KITCHEN SLAVE, and he was wiping his hands on a dishtowel. At the sight of Mrs. Fischer, he broke into a killer smile that would have been hard to match even by Tom Cruise or a golden retriever. "Come in, get out of that nasty night." As he ushered us across the threshold, he tucked the towel in an apron pocket. He took Mrs. Fischer's hands, brought them to his lips, kissed them, not as a courtly Frenchman might have done, but as a son might have kissed the worn and aged hands of a beloved mother.

He said, "We were so happy when we heard about Oscar."

"Kipp, dear, you're as kind as ever. Oscar waited

a long time for his big moment, and I'm sure he found the wait worthwhile."

"No suffering?" Kipp asked.

"Not for someone who'd so completely gotten back his innocence. Oscar had been smooth and blue for years."

"It's just great news."

"When the people at the funeral home gave me the ashes in an urn, we all drank some Dom Perignon. You know how much Oscar liked Dom Perignon."

Turning to me, Kipp said, "You must be Edie's new chauffeur."

"Yes, sir. Thomas is the name."

We shook hands, and he said, "May I call you Tom?"

"That's as good as anything, sir."

"Please call me Kipp."

"Yes, sir."

He would never need a knife to spread a pat of butter on his toast. That smile would quickly melt it.

"Have you had dinner?" he asked.

"Yes, sir. Back in Barstow."

"We ran into Chandelle and Gideon outside the restaurant," Mrs. Fischer told him.

Our host said, "That was an amazing thing they did last December in Pennsylvania."

"Wasn't it, dear? And for ever so long, poor Pennsylvania has needed something amazing to happen there."

"We might be outnumbered, Edie, but we're going to win this thing."

"I've never doubted it," Mrs. Fischer said.

"What thing?" I asked.

"The whole amazing thing!" Kipp declared with childlike delight. "Anyway, we were just about to have dinner when you showed up, but I hear you're in a hurry."

Mrs. Fischer said, "We're in a terrible hurry, Kipp. Could you put dinner in stasis and help us first?"

"That's exactly what we've done, we've put it in stasis."

I knew what the word *stasis* meant: the state of equilibrium or inactivity caused by opposing equal forces. I suspected that Kipp didn't simply mean that they had stowed dinner in a warming drawer.

Something huge and black burst into the foyer, and I let out a squeal of alarm that was no doubt identical to the sound that Little Miss Muffet made when a spider sat down beside her on that stupid tuffet.

# Twenty-two

THE CREATURE SURPRISED ME, COMING from my right side, but when I reeled back, I realized this was none other than Big Dog, because he was a really big dog, a black Great Dane with soulful brown eyes. He was the most humongous specimen of his breed that I'd ever seen, his head so large that you might have been able to do a handstand on it if you could have trained him for a circus act. His ears hadn't been cropped when he was a puppy, which is a common practice among breeders; therefore, they didn't stand up but folded forward as if they were the flaps on two velvet purses.

Kipp said, "Don't be afraid, Tom. Big Dog is as gentle as a lamb—unless you mean to harm anyone in this house, which you don't."

"I definitely don't, sir."

"Just call him Big or Biggy, and let him smell you."

I said, "Hey there, Biggy. Big Biggy. Good dog."

The Dane snuffled at my jeans and sweater with such enthusiasm that I half thought he might vacuum them off my body.

Mrs. Fischer cooed to the dog: "Sweet Biggy Wiggy, him such a pretty, pretty boy."

Suddenly done with me, whimpering with extreme doggy pleasure, Biggy collapsed at Mrs. Fischer's feet. He rolled onto his back and bared his belly, tail swishing and thumping on the polished-mahogany floor in recognition of his old friend.

Mrs. Fischer knelt to rub the dog's tummy, and Kipp said, "What do you need, Edie? Birth certificates, driver's licenses, passports, somebody's computer system hacked? Oh, and we've just got some of those insect spy drones the government doesn't want the public to know about, complete with control stations."

Biggy's mouth had fallen open, revealing two curved archipelagos of white teeth in a sea of black gums. In his throat he made a deep purring sound, as though he had swallowed a house cat whole.

As always, Mrs. Fischer knew what she wanted. "Kipp, dear, we need one bulletproof vest for Tom. Then a police gun belt hung with four spare magazine pouches, two Mace holders, one snap pouch to hold a Talkabout, one stretch sheath with a little flashlight, no swivel holster. We need a double shoulder rig so the child can carry a pistol under each arm. We'll need two Talkabouts, one for the gun belt, one for me. We don't want Mace for the Mace holders, but two ten-shot units of pressure-stream sedative. For the pistols, we'll need whatever you can match with sound suppressors. This job falls apart as soon as anyone hears a gunshot. Can you do all that?"

"What do you think?"

Getting up from the Great Dane, she said, "I think you can. Oh, and plenty of copper-jacketed hollow-point ammunition."

Kipp grinned at me, clapped me on the shoulder, and said, "Tom, you must be planning a trip straight to Hell City."

"I'm hoping it's just a suburb, sir."

"Come along. I want you to meet Mazie and the family. Then we'll outfit you pronto."

The sprawling house was furnished differently from what I had imagined and was much warmer and more welcoming than I expected. Intricate and beautifully worn Persian carpets on the hardwood floors. Antique Japanese cabinets. Pictorial Japanese screens on the walls. Shanghai Art Deco chairs and sofas upholstered in rich silks. Stained-glass and amber blown-glass lamps. And scattered here and there, large plush squeaky toys for a ginormous dog.

Later, Mrs. Fischer would tell me who Kipp and his family were and how they came to be in this place. As this is *my* memoir, however, I will use authorial license and insert that information throughout my account of events in Casa Bolthole, which is what they called their desert home.

Kipp had been a hugely successful equities trader in a major investment firm with a sterling reputation. The company had installed a new CEO, a man with deep investment-management background, who had also previously been a senator from a major Eastern-seaboard state before losing his re-election bid. In two years, the senator managed to bankrupt the firm with large reckless bets on foreign bonds and currencies. Even worse, a billion dollars of investors' money had gone missing, not lost in the bond or currency debacles—just gone. Because we live in a brave new world of financial buccaneering in which properly connected politicians, current and former, can steal from the public or private purse with little chance of punishment, the senator was not indicted, but Kipp was. The evidence, as well-concocted as any martini that might please James Bond, persuaded a jury to convict.

Before he had been an equities trader, Kipp had served as an intelligence officer in the marines. He knew a thing or two about surveillance, electronic eavesdropping, and cleverly structured entrapments of the enemy, as did a number of his former marine buddies, who came to his assistance. In a seemingly private venue, when the ex-senator thought he was in the company of a like-minded public servant with equally sticky fingers, after a couple of drinks too many, he gloated about the cleverness with which he had framed Kipp for the charge of embezzlement. A recording made without the knowledge of the subject cannot be easily entered into evidence in a court of law. But between Kipp's conviction and his sentencing, the ex-senator's gloating, with accompanying video, was put on YouTube by an anonymous and untraceable truth teller.

The judge declared a mistrial. The prosecutor dropped all charges. Then something else happened, something far worse, and at his wife's suggestion, Kipp agreed that henceforth they should live off the grid. Through false identities and clandestine means, they constructed Casa Bolthole with a purpose in mind. To this day, the senator remains a free man, so lawyered-up that every time he goes to court, the tramping of attorneys' feet sounds like a Memorial Day parade from a lost time when uniformed servicemen and ribboned veterans marched by the thousands to honor their country and to be honored in return by crowds lining the parade route.

The kitchen in Casa Bolthole was large, with Santos mahogany flooring, golden bird's-eye-maple cabinetry that featured rounded corners as in a ship's galley, and black-granite countertops, all clean flowing lines that soothed the eye. At the round dining table, six places were set for dinner, and the flames of candles fluttered in crystal containers. The overhead lights had been dialed low, and more candles stood on the center island.

At that island, as we entered, Mazie finished pouring Dom Perignon into four champagne flutes. "None for you," she told Biggy as he hurried to her side, nostrils flaring, a potential four-legged alcoholic.

Tall, willowy, beautiful, her glossy black hair worn long, Mazie was wrapped in an elegant black-silk kimono patterned with white koi mottled red and red koi mottled gold. Her large almond-shaped eyes were so dark that, reflecting several points of candlelight, they might have been portals offering two views of a night sky and stars ever receding into eternity.

After more warm greetings and another introduction, we stood at the island and raised the slender glasses, and Mazie said, "To Oscar, in whom the fire and the rose are now one."

Mrs. Fischer and Kipp said, "To Oscar." I didn't have any idea what the toast meant, but I don't have any idea what a lot of things mean, so I said, "To Oscar," as well, and we sipped the champagne, which was icy cold and delicious.

Biggy padded to the corner of the kitchen in which his water bowl stood on a mat, and he noisily lapped at the contents, perhaps joining in a nonalcoholic toast, as if he were the designated driver.

After a second sip of Dom Perignon, Mazie turned to me and spoke as if she already knew what we'd come here to acquire and what task I had set out upon that would require those acquisitions. "Tom, if Tom is your truest name, are you afraid of the battle that lies ahead of you?"

Remembering what Annamaria had told me, I

said, "Yes, ma'am, I'm afraid, but I hope only in proportion to the threat."

"I sense a terrible longing in you, a deep yearning. I hope you don't yearn for death."

"No, ma'am. I yearn for what comes after it. But I'm not keen on suffering."

"None of us are. But we suffer nonetheless. Until we reach that condition Oscar reached a few years ago."

"You mean . . . fully blue and smooth?"

Mazie's smile was beatific, a curve of pure grace. She had an aura of perfect calm and great strength. Her uncommonly direct gaze suggested that she had once stared down Death himself and no longer feared what she might see in other eyes.

Later, I would learn from Mrs. Fischer that Mazie had been an attorney in a major Manhattan law firm when Kipp had been an equities trader. After the video of the senator had been posted on YouTube, clearing Kipp and implicating the former politician in the theft of investors' money, their wobbling world seemed to have been returned to its proper angle of rotation.

But then the worse thing happened. A senior partner in Mazie's firm introduced her to two new clients, Mr. Reasoner and Mr. Power, businessmen who had a complaint against a major competitor, involving patent infringement, which seemed an easy case for a litigator of her talents. Because the clients were wary to the point of paranoia, the first meeting with them took place in a soundproof conference room. After introductions but before the meeting began, the senior partner excused himself "for just a moment," without explanation. As Mr. Reasoner took a seat at the table and opened his briefcase, Mr. Power crossed the room to have a closer look at a bronze sculpture with which he professed to be quite taken, and as he passed behind Mazie, she felt something sting the back of her neck.

When she regained consciousness, her wrists were bound to the arms of a chair. A rubber ball had been placed in her mouth, and her lips had been firmly sealed with duct tape. For a grueling hour, the two men discussed in loving detail their favorite methods of torture, and while they talked, they took turns pinching shut her nose, inducing suffocation panic before letting her breathe again. They made certain she understood that if she wasn't safe in the luxurious offices of this prestigious law firm, she would be safe nowhere. If she couldn't trust a senior partner—or perhaps *any* senior partner, or anyone at all—in the firm where she had worked for eleven years, she could trust no one anywhere.

This was payback, they said, for what Kipp did to the senator, who still had more loyal and powerful friends than could be easily counted. Kipp was innocent, yes, but that didn't matter. The only purpose of the innocent was to be used, like cattle, by those who despised innocence. Oh, maybe the meek will inherit the earth, but not now, not until the end of time. *Now* the meek, the innocent, had to learn to take what was dealt to them and endure it.

Reasoner and Power, obviously not their names, said they would not mark her this time, because the punishment that she and Kipp had earned wasn't to be administered in a single visit. Days or weeks, perhaps even months from now, they would surprise her again, four of them instead of two, and they would brutally rape her until they were satiated. After that, they might give her several months, maybe a full year, in which to anticipate their third visit. No one can be vigilant 24/7 for an extended period of time, and no bodyguards she might hire could be trusted, because the majority of people were easily corrupted. On their third visit, they would torture her, blind her, visit upon her a measure of brain damage that would ensure her permanent disability, but they would not kill her. *Kipp's* punishment was to bear the guilt that would only grow as he saw her emotionally, physically, and intellectually degraded.

Finished with her, they took the duct tape off her mouth, untied her wrists from the arms of the chair, and allowed her to remove the rubber ball from her mouth. Reasoner placed the ball, the tape, and the cord in his briefcase. The two men said, "Have a nice day," and left the conference room. Mazie remained seated for several minutes, telling herself that she was waiting for the senior partner to return and babble out some excuse, perhaps tearfully, about why he had been unable to warn or to protect her. The truth was, she felt too weak to stand. She would never be given an excuse. She was done here. They would already have some reason for firing her, supported by reams of forged documentation. The firm occupied Floors 34 through 37, and when at last Mazie left that conference room, she found the entire thirty-sixth floor deserted. The hush was so eerie that it would not have been hard to believe that the city in all its boroughs had been depopulated. But when the elevator doors opened at the lobby, the bustle and bark of humanity returned, and she had to pass through it. In the street, the braying of car horns and engines and brakes and people overwhelmed her, oppressed her.

For a while, she leaned on a lamppost, head hung, expecting to vomit in the gutter. When she didn't, she went home to Kipp. They had significant financial resources, in fact millions, and the expertise to move them around often enough and cleverly enough to leave a trail that eventually withered away. They made plans that very afternoon, not merely plans to vanish into new identities and hide, although that was part of it, but also to fight back, and not merely against the senator and Mazie's former law firm but, wherever an opportunity presented itself, against any aspect of the vigorously metastasizing corruption that was a terminal cancer in this ever more dangerous postmodern world.

While waiting to vomit in the gutter, Mazie had recalled lines from her favorite poet, T. S. Eliot, who wrote that although the world ceaselessly turned and changed, one thing and one alone never changed. *However you disguise it, this thing does not change: / The perpetual struggle of Good and Evil.* Their plan seemed grandiose, foolish, hopeless, but step by step, as they worked to fulfill it, they found the surest footing they'd ever known. If they had elected merely to change identities and hide, they would have had no hope of full and meaningful lives, because those who cower forget how to stand and, in time, can only crawl. By choosing the path of resistance, they had discovered people like Mrs. Fischer and Oscar, like Gideon and Chandelle, and they had learned the true and hidden nature of the world.

In the candlelit kitchen, Mazie topped off the four glasses of champagne, and we carried them downstairs to the basement, Big Dog in the lead.

This subterranean level, as large as the main floor, was the heart of their campaign of principled resistance. A wide corridor offered rooms to the front of the house on the left, to the back of the house on the right. We were headed to the armory, but first we stopped at a chamber on the left that was occupied by four computer workstations, racks of servers, and all manner of other electronics that I didn't recognize. For all I knew, the young couple currently laboring there might be hacking the CIA or in communication with extraterrestrials in an orbiting mother ship, or playing video games.

The man, in his late twenties, was Leander, Kipp

and Mazie's son. He had one of his father's green eyes, having lost the other one during a tour of duty, as a marine, in Afghanistan, a year before his father crossed the senator. Leander had two-thirds of his dad's winning smile, the last third having been twisted by the scar tissue that disfigured the left side of his face. His wife, Harmony, was as cute as Goldie Hawn in her prime, looked fit and tough enough to win an iron-man contest, and spoke with a Georgia drawl.

As we shook hands, Harmony asked, "Where do I know you from?"

"I'm sure we've never met, ma'am."

"Maybe, but I've seen you. I have an honest-to-God spooky memory for faces," she declared.

"Well, I *do* have a spooky face."

"Yeah, right. About as spooky as any guy in a crazy-popular boy band. I'll remember you before you leave, pilgrim."

"Boy band?" I grimaced. "That's a low blow."

The next big room on the left contained an impressive array of printing presses, scanners, laminators, engraving machines, and other equipment used to forge documents. This appeared to be the domain of Tracker and his second wife, Justine. Leander's identical twin, Tracker had served in Iraq but had returned without wounds. On his first day back, however, he walked in on his wife, Karen, in bed with two men, and twenty-four hours later, he filed for divorce. He had struck gold the second time, not just because of how Justine looked, which was really fine, but also because she radiated intelligence as surely as a lamp gave off light.

Farther along the hall and on the right, we came to the largest chamber in the basement, the armory, which contained more weapons and ammunition than the average gun shop, even more than the average rap star's recreation room. Kipp and Mazie set to work fulfilling our order, and Mrs. Fischer assisted, seemingly as familiar with their stock as they were.

Big Dog padded up and down the aisles between tall metal shelves of inventory, sniffing with apparent approval. After all, in addition to being a pet, he was also a guard dog, and he appreciated the need for a strong defense.

At one point, as he was showing me the pair of Glock pistols he thought best for relatively in-close work, Kipp must have detected my antipathy to guns. He said, "We have no choice, Tom. The world is going mad, overseas *and* here. Year by year, the government ever more aggressively militarizes state and local police forces and even its most seemingly benign agencies. In August of last year, the Social Security Administration purchased one hundred seventy-four thousand rounds of hollow-point ammunition for distribution to forty-one of its offices around the country. They must expect Grandpa and Granny to get really pissed about something the SSA intends to do. The Environmental Protection Agency, too. And Homeland Security ordered seven hundred and fifty *million* rounds in various calibers last August. Now, either they expect a hell of a lot of terrorist attacks or a civil war, and no matter whether the enemy is shouting '*Allahu Akbar*' or 'God bless America,' they must figure they'll have to kill a lot of people."

I stared at him, speechless. His grin was as winning as ever. Finally, I said, "You're a scary guy."

"Good. It's a scary world. You do know guns, don't you?"

"I have some experience of them, sir."

Leander appeared in the doorway to the hall and said, "Mom, Harmony wants to talk to you about something."

After Mazie left, Kipp finished putting everything together and stuffed it into a gunnysack with a drawstring top. Mrs. Fischer paid him, and all of us followed Biggy into the hallway.

Mazie and Harmony were waiting for me. They had a printout of a newspaper story about the mall shootings in Pico Mundo nineteen months earlier. My high-school yearbook picture was featured under a headline that claimed too much credit for me.

"I knew I'd seen your face," Harmony said. "I'm sorry I said the boy-band thing. You're no boy-band phony."

"I'm not what that paper calls me, either."

"Once a decade or so," she said, "the newspaper gets something right, and I think they did this time."

Mazie said, "If you understand the true and hidden nature of the world, you know that even the smallest details are of profound importance. Like a silly nickname. You're not Thomas as in Tom. Odd Thomas. Odd doesn't mean curious or peculiar or eccentric. Something is odd when it can't be matched, when it's singular, alone of its kind."

"Please, ma'am," I objected. "My name is nothing but my name. In a drawer of mismatched socks, every one of them is odd. Nothing glorious about that. A mistake on the birth certificate left the *T* off *Todd*."

Here came again that smile of pure grace. "Nothing so mundane as that. At your birth it was known what name best suited you, and if your parents had wished to name you Bob, the certificate would nevertheless have shown you to be Odd."

Her eyes were night sky again, so dark but full of the infinite possibilities to which the stars bear witness, and I didn't know what to say to her.

She said, "May I touch your heart, Odd Thomas?"

Uncertain of her meaning, I said, "Ma'am?"

She put her right hand flat to my breast. Nothing in her gesture was forward or improper, but tender and loving to such an extent that she almost brought tears to my eyes.

"Women are drawn to you, Odd, not as they may be drawn to other men. I'm sure that your life is full of women who are drawn to you. Because they know or sense that you take a vow seriously, that you're faithful forever, that you recognize and cherish in good women what qualities you loved in the one you lost, that you respect them, that you care deeply about their dignity perhaps even when they don't, that you will never walk away from one in need."

I couldn't let her think of me in such elevated terms, for the truth was not so defined by chivalry as she imagined. I could barely summon enough power of voice to reveal that truth in a whisper: "Ma'am, I've killed two women. Shot them to death."

Perhaps she was by nature a romantic, or more sentimental than she seemed, because my words had no effect on her smile. "If you killed them, they were murderers who had murdered before and would have murdered you."

"I shot them, ma'am. The circumstances don't change that fact. I shot them."

Mazie took one of my hands in both of hers. "Believe me, when your time comes, it will be women who hold you and comfort you during your last moments in this world, who carry you into the next, and who greet you there."

Mazie kissed me on the forehead, as if bestowing a benediction, and I said, "I have done terrible things." Harmony took my hand that her mother-in-law relinquished, her touch another tender benediction, and I said, "I'll do terrible things again." Justine put one hand on my shoulder and kissed me on the cheek in what I at once recognized as the way that I had sometimes kissed the urn containing my Stormy's ashes.

Their reverence was too much for me, to be mistaken for the man that I might want to be but am not, to be thought brave for only going where I have to go and doing what I have to do. I was no less uncertain and unsteady than anyone else in this broken world, often a fumbler and a fool, with more failures than successes. These were good women, good people, and their kindness consoled me. I could never fulfill such lofty expectations, however, and a quiet yet compelling embarrassment drove me to leave as politely and as quickly as possible.

The limousine waited under the portico.

With Big Dog scowling at the surrounding night to ward off any man or animal with ill intentions, Kipp stowed our purchases in the passenger compartment.

Beyond the overhang, rain chased past the house at an extreme angle in an escalating wind.

Mrs. Fischer drove, and I rode in the front passenger seat, the face of the rhinestone cowboy in my mind's eye.

# Twenty-three

WE RODE IN SILENCE ALONG THE SHALE—
and snake-less—track, the length of the gravel lane, and across the potholed blacktop to the interstate, where Mrs. Fischer turned east once more, continuing our interrupted pursuit of the missing children and the men who had taken them.

A sense of duty was as real to me as the pounding rain, and I felt that I might drown in it as easily as in a flash flood. Duty is a good thing, a calling without which no civilization can survive, but it is also a weight and chain that sometimes seems sure to sink you to the airless bottom of a dark pool. I wasn't burdened by a fear of death but instead by a fear of failure. If there were seventeen hostages and I rescued even sixteen, the one lost would be too sharp a reminder of another loss, nineteen months earlier, in the mall in Pico Mundo. I wished—and more than wished—that this responsibility might be lifted from me, but I knew that it would not be lifted.

I believe that Mrs. Fischer gave me the gift of silence because she knew that I had left Casa Bolthole in a state of embarrassment, that I felt inadequate to the challenges of my strange life, and that the more anyone told me that I was equal to those challenges, the more I would feel that I was not. The greatest danger, of course, was to believe that I *was* equal to them, because assurance can morph into arrogance that Death loves to prove unfounded.

The broad highway led east-northeast, and mile by mile, I felt more strongly the black-hole gravity of the cowboy.

Associating with bad men, even for the purpose of defeating them, can make you vulnerable to the allure of evil. A sense of duty can be corrupted into self-righteousness, which can inspire a self-exemption from all laws, an embrace of power and the will to use it ruthlessly. Power is the central promise of evil, the dark light of that lamp, because nothing extinguishes the soul more quickly than pride in power.

Mazie's approval had seemed close to veneration. To endure such extreme praise was dangerous enough. If I came to believe that I had earned it, I would lose everything that mattered.

I was only a fry cook with paranormal abilities that were not a blessing but a weight to carry. And considering that I had no job, I couldn't claim to be even a fry cook, but simply a man with a burden, which was one of the most common creatures on the earth.

The rain fell in torrents sufficient to float an ark. The world condensed into a highway that, for all I could see beyond it, might have ribboned through a void as deep as interstellar space.

We were racing so fast that the cataracts of rain crashing into the windshield were all but blinding, and yet Mrs. Fischer appeared confident about her ability to control the limo under these or any conditions. Humming one tune or another, each of them cheery, my elderly guide, the spiritual daughter of Hawkeye from *The Last of the Mohicans* and the bride of Tonto, was clearly unconcerned about the poor visibility, as though she—or the vehicle itself—could see for miles ahead in these or even worse conditions. I decided not to look at the speedometer.

Finally I said, "What amazing thing did Gideon and Chandelle do in Pennsylvania last December?"

After a hesitation, she said, "You're only just coming into an awareness that you're not alone, Oddie. It's best to ease into a full understanding of the resistance."

"Resistance? Sounds too political for me."

"It's not political in the least, child. It's been going on through all the ages and all the countries of the world, no matter who the ruler is—prime minister, king, emperor, dictator, mullah. Our adversaries exist in every profession, every race, every ethnicity, every class, every political faction—but our friends abide also in all those places."

She looked away from the interstate and smiled. Her brooch, the jeweled exclamation point, sparkled in the dashboard glow.

I asked, "Why is it best to *ease* into an understanding?"

Returning her attention to the highway, she said, "It's best because you need to be able to cope with your fear, which will be perhaps too great to bear if you're abruptly plunged into the full truth. In the thrall of absolute terror, you're less likely to survive what's coming in the hours ahead. Trust me, dear. Take this discovery moment by moment, event by event, allowing fear to increase at the same pace as your understanding. Then you'll grow into your fear and be able to function with it."

Earlier, I had thought that she seemed like the mother of Yoda, the pint-size sage from the *Star Wars* movies. Now she almost sounded like him, except that her syntax was correct.

The rain began to relent somewhat, and I suspected that we might be outrunning the storm once more.

Although the downpour still obscured much of the night here in the emptiness of the Mojave, I saw the sign welcoming us to Nevada, which we flew past as if we were degenerate gamblers desperate for the games of Las Vegas.

We drove steadily farther away from Pico Mundo,

and yet I sensed that somehow I was coming full circle to it, that when I stood before the cowboy, I would discover some unfinished business with which I thought I had dealt in my hometown long before I'd left there. The adventures of which I'd written in multiple volumes of memoirs were in fact a single adventure, during which my understanding of reality evolved until now I seemed to be drawing steadily closer to what Annamaria—and later Mazie—called "the true and hidden nature of the world," which Mrs. Fischer warned would give new meaning to the word *terror*.

Miles later, when again we had driven out of the rain, the glow of Vegas was a sullen fan-shaped beacon on the horizon, a scene like you might see on a poster for a science-fiction movie: lonely highway dwindling toward the eerie light of some interstellar vessel come down to Earth and waiting just beyond the next hill to fill your soul with wonder. But this glow was only Las Vegas, about which there was nothing transcendent, unless your idea of transcendence was topless dancers, a show by Blue Man Group, a run of luck at the blackjack tables, an abundance of free drinks culminating in a system-purging puke, unconsciousness, and a hangover in the brain-searing morning light of the desert.

Suddenly, in my mind's eye, the image of the rhinestone cowboy grew brighter, more detailed.

"Next exit, ma'am," I said. "North."

The ramp led to a two-lane blacktop state route

that took us past an array of unidentified large buildings that might have been warehouses, considering that many national companies distributed their products out of Nevada because it had no inventory tax. We passed a few modest clustered houses, then a few more assorted isolated structures, and a roadside business whose owner called it JEB'S TRADING POST, which included gasoline pumps.

Soon the road rose through rolling hills of desert brush and colonies of pampas grass with tall pale plumes, and then climbed at a steeper angle than before. The spectacle of Las Vegas lights, still miles away and not directly visible, refracting through the moisture-laden low clouds, fading with the distance from the source, paled the sky just enough to silhouette the mountains ahead of us.

As we drew nearer to the cowboy and as the incline increased, my gut tightened, much as it does when you're ten years old and aboard a roller coaster, though what I felt was pure apprehension, with none of the pleasant anticipation of a thrill ride.

Stunted scrub pines appeared, rising twisted and misshapen from the dry, sandy soil. Increasing altitude meant a lower average annual temperature, some slow-release snowpack higher than we would go, and richer soil, where now full-scale pines towered over the roadway.

We arrived at a plateau of deep woods and small meadows. On the right, a blacktop lane that led away among the trees was secured by a low wooden ranch-style gate between two stacked-stone columns. I knew at once that it would lead me to the rhinestone cowboy, but I urged Mrs. Fischer to keep driving.

The plateau was broad. On both sides of the state route, a few more gated lanes led to private properties far back in the forest. Just when the pavement began to rise again, the headlights caught a sign on the left that announced FIRE ROAD / FORESTRY DEPT ONLY.

In the absence of a fire, no one would be using that rough dirt track. Mrs. Fischer parked on it, facing out toward the state route, but in far enough among the trees to avoid being seen by passing traffic, of which we had encountered none since turning off the interstate. She damped the headlights, cut the engine.

When I got out of the limousine, the flanking woods were quiet except for the metallic tick-and-ping of the cooling engine. The air smelled of pines and of something I couldn't name.

On all sides, the night seemed to watch me as if the columnar trees were elements of a coliseum, as if I were the martyr of the hour, as if the darkness were full of lions.

In the passenger compartment of the limo, through the open privacy panel, I said, "Ma'am, I hope this boat is big enough to take all those kids."

"It can comfortably seat ten adults in back, dear. I'm confident we can accommodate at least seventeen wee children."

I opened the gunnysack, withdrew everything that we had gotten from Kipp and Mazie, and began to prepare myself by the frosty glow of the small LED flashlight.

"Ma'am, one thing I didn't ask, and I'm curious."

"What is that, dear?"

"Purdy Feltenham."

"Heath's best man at our wedding. He was such a charmer."

"Why did he have to go everywhere with a sack over his head?"

"He was considerate, dear."

"What did he look like?"

"Purdy was born with terrible facial deformations. Far worse than the Elephant Man. People tended to faint when they saw him."

"I'm sorry to hear that."

"Well, they learned a valuable lesson."

"What lesson?"

"Not to pull the sack off the head of someone who wears one. And not to tease and torment people. A lot of nasty teenagers soiled their pants because they pulled that sack off Purdy."

"A memorable lesson."

"On the plus side, Purdy's looks made him rich."

"How so?"

"He bought his own ten-in-one and was the star of it."

"Ten-in-one?"

"A freak show in a carnival, a tent with ten attractions in it. They're outlawed now, but Purdy became a millionaire back when."

"Still, he had to go everywhere with a sack over his head."

"Don't fret, child. The sack had eye holes."

"That's good to know."

"And he didn't wear the sack in the carnival world, where he spent ninety-nine percent of his time. Carnies accept everyone."

"Not everyone. I had a problem with two carnies once, these guys, Bucket and Pecker. Excuse me, ma'am, but that was his name."

"What was your problem with them, dear?"

"I annoyed them, so they tried to kill me."

"Please tell me you didn't pull a sack off one of their heads."

"No, ma'am. I never would."

"Good. If they were bad men, they weren't friends of Purdy."

"No, I'm sure they weren't. But it's sad."

"What's sad?"

"Purdy must have lived a lonely life."

"He married a beautiful girl, Darnelle, who worked the kootch show. Hootchy-kootchy. That doesn't mean she was a stripper. Kootch dancers didn't strip nude."

"So his face didn't bother her?"

"His face didn't bother anyone, dear, once you got to know him. Purdy was all heart, not all face."

I said, "That's a nicer story than I expected."

"Child, your story will turn out nicer than you expect, too."

"I wouldn't bet everything you own on that, ma'am."

"Neither would I."

"Good for you."

"But only because I'm not a betting woman."

Wearing two shoulder holsters, a Glock under each arm, and a police utility belt hung with all manner of stuff other than a gun, I got out of the car, and Mrs. Fischer got out, too, because the bulletproof vest buckled from behind, and I needed her to cinch it tight so that I could do a final adjustment to the shoulder rigs.

When I was geared-up and ready to go, she said, "Now let me look at you, child."

She couldn't have seen me all that clearly in the dark of the woods, under an overcast sky, but she checked the four spare-magazine pouches on the utility belt, to be sure the flaps were snapped shut. She asked if I had my Talkabout, which is a walkie-talkie, and I said that I had it. Cell-phone service would either be poor or nonexistent in this remote place, so if we needed to scheme together, Talkabouts were the best bet, as long as we were within range of each other. She checked off other items on my utility belt, brushed at my Kevlar vest as if she saw lint on it, pinched my cheek, said, "Well, you look as invincible as you are cute," and I felt as if I should be a brave boy and go out to the street to wait for the school bus all by myself.

I had gone only a few steps when she softly called my name. She hurried to me and said, "The vest won't puncture, so let me pin this to the sleeve of your sweater."

"Pin what?"

"My little diamond-and-ruby exclamation point. For good luck. It doesn't mean what I told the waitress it meant."

"It doesn't really mean 'Sister, what a hoot it is to be me'?"

"No, and it doesn't mean 'Seize the day' or 'Live life to the fullest,' either."

"What does it mean, then?"

"Never you mind what it means."

I said, "Maybe it means 'We might as well eat.'"

"Sometimes you make no sense, child. This brooch will bring you through alive. Now scoot before I start crying."

I scooted out to the state route, crossed the pavement, and walked south along the farther shoulder of the road, toward the private lane that I believed would lead me to the cowboy and the children, ready to take cover in the brush and trees at the first sound of an approaching engine.

As a man of action, I leave something to be desired. This had been a long and eventful day, but I hadn't yet blown up anything or busted anyone in the chops. If I had been James Bond, I would have killed at least two by now and blown up at least one thing, and if I had been Jack Reacher, I would have left a trail of blood and mayhem more than three hundred miles long. At least I was alive, so there remained a chance that I could find something to blow up before the night was done.

# Twenty-four

BECAUSE THE RANCH-STYLE GATE DIDN'T connect to a fence, its only purpose was to prevent unauthorized vehicles from entering the lane. A call box atop a steel post provided communication with the house, but it was strictly an audio link, with no camera attached.

The simple nature of the barrier and the lack of a posted guard might mean that whoever lived here didn't feel the need for more than minimal security. That would seem to argue that this wasn't a place where seventeen kidnapped children were being held to be killed for sport or art, or whatever.

On the other hand, the lack of security might be only apparent, not real. At this entry point, these people could have chosen not to draw attention to themselves with more security than their neighbors thought necessary, but could have prepared some unpleasant surprises for any intruder who dared to venture deeper into the property on foot.

As I stepped around the gate and entered the lane, I plucked a small canister from one of the Mace holders on my utility belt. Mrs. Fischer had specified not chemical Mace but instead a pressure-stream sedative, which was a highly classified military item supposedly not available to civilians—but which in fact was evidently as available as a can of Coca-Cola. In the limo, she had told me that the stream had a range of fifteen to twenty feet. If the stream splattered the mouth and nose and eyes of the target, he would drop before reaching me. Generally, he would remain unconscious for between one and two hours, depending on the amount of the drug absorbed, which was even a more effective sedative than watching a congressional debate on C-SPAN. Each of my two canisters contained ten shots of a two-second duration, but Mrs. Fischer suggested that I not trust it to provide more than eight.

Every once in a while, not often enough, you see a story on the TV news about some young mugger or home invader having drawn down on an eighty-year-old lady only to discover that she was trained in martial arts and armed with a concealed pistol, whereupon she whupped his butt and taught him something about Jesus, in the tradition of Tyler Perry in drag as Madea. I figured that it would be a mistake for an entire *crew* of young muggers to draw down on Mrs. Fischer, and I felt comfortable leaving her alone in the limousine.

Tall pines crowded along both sides of the lane. Their boughs, which began about twelve feet up their trunks, overhung the pavement. This tunnel, green in daylight but black now, could have harbored a score of assassins crouched and watchful, but animal instinct told me *Not here, not yet.*

As the sole alternative to a direct approach, I could have made my way through the woods, parallel to the lane. Under that canopy of branches, during the day, too little sunlight penetrated to grow much brush, and at this altitude the air was at the moment too cold for even the most motivated, fry-cook-hating snakes to be licking their fangs in anticipation of a bite. But a little brush could make a lot of noise if I blundered blindly through it, and in the dark a low-hanging branch might knock me flat or put out an eye.

After about fifty yards, the driveway arced gradually to the left, and as I fully rounded the bend, I saw light ahead, maybe a hundred yards farther. This section of the pine passageway reminded me of the tunnel reported by people who go through a near-death experience, the long dark tunnel with the welcoming light at the end, except that the radiance ahead of me looked about as welcoming as the glow of a crematorium.

There seemed to be a big house out there, a football field away, with lights in a number of its windows.

But there were also points of flame, like great torches, that for some reason gave me the peculiar feeling that what lay ahead of me was less a modern residence than a medieval village.

Nearing the end of the driveway, I finally eased into the woods on the right. I cautiously proceeded the final twenty feet to the point at which the trees gave way to mown grass. Sheltering under an immense pine, I surveyed all that lay before me.

The most surprising element of the scene was the lake. On this moonless and starless night, I might not have recognized it for what it was if the dancing flames of the torches had not been reflected in the water near the shore. Otherwise the placid surface lay ink-black, not even vaguely mirroring the faint blush of distant Vegas neon that colored the low cloud cover. The painted sky provided barely enough contrast to silhouette the rising land and trees that embraced the water, but I could see enough to estimate that the lake must have been between seven and twelve acres, not vast but larger than a pond. Not a single point of light glimmered along the farther reaches of its shoreline, which I took to mean that the lake and all the land immediately surrounding it were part of this property.

The torches spaced evenly along the nearer shore seemed to have been adapted from those heaters many restaurants use to warm their patios. A propane tank formed the base of each, supporting an eight- or nine-foot pole that, in the original configuration, rose to a large mushroom-shaped cap that distributed heat down and to all sides. The cap had been removed, and the heating element at the top of the pole had been reworked in such a fashion as to encourage the stream of burning gas to separate into lapping tongues of blue-and-orange flame.

Between the lake and the central building of the property, on a broad stone terrace, stood four more propane torches. The house seemed too large to be a single-family residence and might once have been a corporate retreat accommodating a double score of executives for one of those long weekends when they learned to trust one another and bond before they returned to their offices and to the paranoid and cutthroat behavior that they had pretended to put behind them here at the lake. The architecture, a not entirely successful combination of Frank Lloyd Wright's prairie style with classic log construction, featured a deep cantilevered deck on the second floor, overhanging part of the terrace, but no deck on the third floor.

Beyond some of the first- and second-floor windows, people were in conversations, while others bustled through those rooms with evident purpose, engaged in one task or another. At this distance, I couldn't see them well enough to identify anyone, but the gathering included women as well as men. My simmering anxiety might have heated my imagination, but judging by their energy and body language, I had the impression that they were in a state of pleasant expectation, which troubled me. I didn't think they were delightedly anticipating anything as innocent as the next round of hors d'oeuvres.

To the left of the driveway, about thirty vehicles were parked in two rows, and beyond them stood the rhinestone cowboy's fancy ProStar+ that I'd last seen in the garage of the industrial building in a Los Angeles suburb but also in that creepy other place that I called Elsewhere.

Acutely aware of how close I had come to being neutered and left to bleed to death in the supermarket parking lot, I crossed the end of the driveway and, staying close to the tree line, slunk past the cars and SUVs. I gave an especially wide berth to the eighteen-wheeler, moving toward the back of the property.

Every window and door in the sprawling house must have been closed, because in spite of the number of people, no noise escaped those walls. Although the air wasn't cold enough to crystallize my exhalations, the chill kept dormant the insects and toads that usually sang in the night. I heard the distant shrill cry of a bird that I didn't recognize and the closer communications of two owls no doubt complaining that the weather kept too many tasty rodents in nests and burrows.

At the back of the property, fifty or sixty yards from the house, were two buildings. A rectangular single-story structure, painted white, with barn doors, looked like a stable. The other was a stone-and-timber structure approximately sixty by forty feet, with a steeply sloped roof that beetled over deep eaves, and a forbidding quality. Staying close to the tree line, I cautiously approached the stable.

The night bird shrieking out of the depths of the forest, like a disembodied soul in torment, and the soft hooting of the nearby owls did not mask the sudden rush of some beast sprinting across the yard, panting with exertion and eagerness. I halted, turned, saw a swift low shape, blacker than the night. I thrust out my right arm and pressed the button on the top of the little pressurized can. A stream of sedative, which I couldn't see, must have hit the target exactly as Mrs. Fischer had advised. I heard a stifled squeal, canine in character, followed by a snarl that quickly diminished to a tired grumble, the sound of four legs stumbling, a heavy body slumping to the grass, and a sigh almost of contentment.

Even as the sigh withered away, a second beast came fast, paws thumping the ground louder than those of the first, suggesting it was a larger specimen. I fired the canister, and the attacker abruptly changed course. But maybe I didn't score a perfect hit, because the dog, if dog it was, seemed to lumber away, didn't collapse, but instead sneezed, sneezed, and sneezed again.

I was about to follow the creature and try to administer a more direct dose, but the third beast, close behind the second, launched itself even as I became aware of it. Flashing teeth went for my throat, missed by a few inches, chomped instead on my Kevlar vest, and were foiled more entirely than a bullet would have been. Seventy pounds of coal-black Doberman bowled me over and tumbled past me, snarling in frustration.

Certain that I didn't have time to get to my feet, I rolled off my back, onto my side, and triggered the canister as the fallen dog whipped cat-quick onto its feet. I missed, the Doberman issued a short guttural sound that probably meant *Die, fry cook, die,* and it came at me, so close that I saw the drug stream enter its open mouth, as if I were dispensing a breath freshener. Although none of the sedative appeared to splatter the nostrils, the taste alone proved effective, because this trained attack dog halted just short of its prey, which was canine-loving me. It gagged in disgust, shook its head violently, gagged again, and collapsed, face-to-face with me, inches away. Eclipsing its shining gaze, its eyelids lowered like stage curtains.

Before I might breathe any of the fumes issuing from the dog's mouth and spend the next couple of hours sleeping the stuff off with my sharp-toothed fellow druggies, I scrambled to my feet and turned in a circle, expecting a fourth attacker. Apparently the security detail consisted of just three.

Although I was breathing loud enough to silence the two owls in the neighborhood, I could hear the second dog still sneezing, and I went after the poor pup. He was sitting with his head hung, his front legs splayed wide for balance. He raised his head to look at me, and between sneezes and jaw-cracking yawns, he made a miserable little sound that, to my ear, seemed to be in part accusatory. I told him that it hadn't been *me* who wanted to tear out someone's throat, that I understood he had once been a good dog, as all dogs are good, that he had the misfortune to fall in with a crowd of bad people who had taught him to behave in ways that would have disappointed his mother, that I sympathized with him, I really did, but nevertheless, I would have to squirt him directly on the snout. He collapsed when the stuff touched him. I was happy to be alive and unbitten, but I didn't feel particularly good about myself.

I moved a few steps away and studied the house and the surrounding territory. No one inside could have been aware of my encounter with the pack, but if anyone had been outside, he might have heard something. Guard dogs bark to warn off intruders, but attack dogs give no warning and are trained to conduct the entire assault with a minimum of noise. The discretion shown by these three Dobermans worked to my advantage, because judging by the continued stillness of the night, no one knew that I was here.

Evidently, the dogs had been given the opportunity to sniff all of those people on arrival, and therefore knew not to target any of them. Or maybe you could turn off their aggression with a memorable command word—like *frankfurter*.

A snarl caused me to jump so far off the ground

that if I'd had a flaming sword, I could have passed it under my feet with ease, like they do in those athletic Cossack dances. I figured that I had at least three shots in the canister, maybe five, but as it turned out, I didn't need them. The snarl that I had heard was in fact a snore. Then came another. A moment later, all three dogs were vigorously sawing wood in counterpoint.

I was concerned that if anyone came out of the house to any of the vehicles in the parking area, they might hear this doggy symphony and might investigate. I grabbed the nearest Doberman by his four feet, two in each hand, and dragged him about twelve yards farther toward the stable and to the very edge of the tree line. In the short grass damp with evening dew, because of his tight smooth coat, he could be pulled almost as easily as a sled on ice. By the time that I had moved all of them, however, I was sweating and short of breath, and utterly disenchanted with dog-dragging as a hobby.

The Dobies were at rest one beside the other, facing the same direction, back legs crossed at the ankles, forelegs crossed at the wrists, their positions synchronized but their snoring contrapuntal. I have always been a neatness freak, which is a good trait in a fry cook who wants to poison as few people as possible, but I probably have the potential to succumb to obsessive-compulsive disorder. All the scene needed to make a perfect illustration for a children's book were three blankets, three red-and-white-striped nightcaps, and a night-light shaped like a running cat.

If someone came out from the house to the car park—nervously chanting "Frankfurter, frankfurter, frankfurter"—he probably would not hear the snoring. But if he did hear it, he would take it for the grumbling and gnarling of a single wild beast lurking at the edge of the forest and in the mood for a snack. His imagination would conjure up everything from a bear to Bigfoot, and he wouldn't be inclined to get a closer look to satisfy his curiosity.

At a minimum, I had an hour before the Dobies woke, remembered what had happened to them, sniffed one another's butts to confirm their identities, pledged eternal commitment to total vengeance, and came looking for me. Long before then, I would be gone with the seventeen children. If I were still here an hour from now, the dogs would be the least of my concerns, because I'd be either imprisoned or dead.

# Twenty-five

I NO LONGER HELD THE RHINESTONE COW-
boy's image in my mind's eye. He was on this property, very close. If I sought him out with psychic
magnetism, I risked drawing him to me instead of
being drawn to him, as when I had been in the Ford
Explorer and he had run me off the highway.

Instead, I thought of the Payton kids—Jessie,
Jasmine, Jordan—and hoped that I would be drawn
to them sooner than later. Wherever the Paytons
were, the other kids would likely be there, too. Right
now, I couldn't feel them pulling at me.

My strange talent is reliable but not 100 percent
so, any more than the amazing Magic Johnson, at
his peak, could lay the ball in the basket every time
he tried. More often than not, yes, and some of the
misses were breathtakingly close. But no matter
what gifts we're given, we can never apply them to

perfection because we're human, after all, and given to error.

The stable door was held shut by a hinged steel strap and a swivel bolt. I turned the bolt and, loath to make a sound, eased the strap back on its hinge.

I doubted that the children were kept in this building. If they were here, a guard would be stationed outside. But I had to check.

The door creaked slightly as it opened, and I slipped inside, leaving it ajar behind me. The darkness smelled of straw and mold and dust.

The smooth casing of the small flashlight lacked any features that would snag on the stretchy tube that secured it to my utility belt. It came out as easily as a sword from a sheath, and the on-off button, recessed in the handle, brought forth a blade of soft white light, around which I cupped my hand to restrict it largely to the floor, so that it might not fall directly on the windows and be too visible outside.

Although this was a stable, with stalls to either side of the central aisle, no animals had been housed here in years. The only evidence that the place had *ever* accommodated horses were the few horseshoe prints embedded like fossils in the once impressional but now hard dry floor of compacted earth. In some corners were bristling wads of pale straw, like spiny sea creatures from a distant era when these mountains had been the bed of an ocean. Dust filmed everything, and the only livestock were the spiders that hung in still expectancy or crawled their silken architectures.

I walked the length of the aisle. Although there seemed to be nothing for me here, intuition told me that the appearance of the place was not the entire reality of it.

At the end of the building were two rooms opposite each other, doors standing open. One might have been a tack room. The other contained empty feed bins. Neither offered me anything of interest.

I had never been here before, but something about the stable seemed familiar.

For a moment, I stood listening, convinced that if I cocked my head at just the right angle, I would hear something essential to my—and the children's—survival. The silence held.

Keeping the cupped light directed down, I returned along the aisle. As I was about to push open the painted plank door by which I had entered, I realized that the dirt floor had undergone a metamorphosis. It appeared to be concrete now.

Overhead, chain-hung lamps with conical shades cast down a sour light, and I saw that the board walls were also concretelike now, that same too-pristine material that composed the interior surfaces of buildings in Elsewhere. When I put a hand to the wall, it felt smooth, flawless, cool. But when I thought about the rustic walls that had been here a moment earlier, I could feel the rough texture of the lumber and the uneven joints between boards, as if my reality must be submerged and somehow accessible just below the surface of this stable in Elsewhere.

Turning, switching off the flashlight, I found that the stalls and the two rooms at the farther end were gone, the building now just one long, wide space. A series of breakfronts from different design periods stood along both walls, as though stored here by an antiques dealer. No bristling wads of straw, no dust, no spiders or their webs. At the windows, where they weren't blocked by the display cabinets, the night beyond seemed darker than the night in Nevada, the blinding black in which I had struggled with the Other Odd on the roof of that industrial building.

They used Elsewhere to hide things where the best detectives and the most diligent searchers could never find them, and to meet others of their kind to discuss their dark business where no one in this world could hear them.

Because of my paranormal abilities, when I entered these way stations, I perceived the other world that, at these specific points only, was connected to mine. But if I had entered with a friend, he would have seen only the dust-mantled long-unused stable, and when I moved into Elsewhere, I would have become invisible and inaudible to him.

Shower 5 and the basement room at Star Truck, the abandoned industrial building near Los Angeles, and this place did not phase randomly back and forth between worlds, as until now I had thought might be the case. I could neither be kept out of Elsewhere nor be trapped in it. These places existed in both worlds at all times. Unconsciously I had opened this other realm—and closed it away—with an act of will.

Interesting.

And what were they hiding here other than antique furniture?

The lamps dangled along the center of the building, their light pooling on the gray floor between swaths of shadow. Against the long walls, the polished mahogany and pecan and walnut and cherry of the hulking breakfronts glimmered here and there, but I couldn't see what, if anything, the cabinets contained behind their wood-framed glass doors. I had no reason to suppose that anything was on display in them, yet even as dread seemed to shrink my heart within my chest, I felt compelled to take a closer look.

I chose the array of cabinets on the left. The first two were empty, and my flashlight revealed that the shelves and back walls were upholstered in dark-blue velvet, the better to present select pieces of the finest china—Limoges, Dresden, Minton, Royal Doulton, Pickard—as if they were works of art.

Approaching the third cabinet, I saw that it was likewise darkly lined, but neither empty nor laden with china. I opened a pair of doors and found that the shelves held a series of wide, thick glass jars, almost crocks, with lids that had been fused in place with an annealing torch. The jars were filled with clear liquid, no doubt a preservative. Submerged in each jar waited a severed human head.

The nature of my life is such that I have discovered on several occasions various abominations hidden away by collectors who would not be satisfied with rare coins or postage stamps, or butterflies pinned to boards. They say that familiarity breeds contempt, but familiarity with the death trophies of demented sociopaths breeds not apathy, not an absence of feeling, but instead a composure that is feeling without agitation. To an extent, I could regard these heads as evidence, in the calm way that a police officer can study the most terrible aftermath of violence at a crime scene. I could soberly assess the threat of which these trophies warned me, for anyone who could harvest such a cruel collection would require from me absolute ruthlessness if I were to defeat them and safely shepherd the children out of this place.

I moved to the next breakfront and found more heads, eyes fixed open in every case except for three, where one or both eyes had been gouged out. A few other faces bore the marks of torture, which I will not describe, because the dead deserve their dignity no less than do the living. Most of the specimens bore no wounds except for where the necks had been severed, and if they, too, had been tortured, their suffering had involved violence to the body.

On the forehead of each trophy were hieroglyphics apparently drawn with an indelible felt-tip pen, still black in spite of being submerged in a preservative liquid. The script, written horizontally instead of vertically as the ancients would have done, looked like Egyptian to me but might not have been. Although the language was pictographic, I couldn't guess what many of the symbols represented, though in each instance they included the stylized silhouette of one animal, most often one kind of bird or another, or groups of birds in strange arrangements, but also cats, rabbits, goats, bulls, snakes, lizards, scarabs, and centipedes. I couldn't guess the reason for these pictographs, but they seemed to confirm that the murders were ritualistic.

The collection included more women than men, although the male sex was well represented. More of them were white than black, each about in proportion to the percentage in the population, but there were Asians and Hispanics well represented. These collectors—for this could not be the work of one maniac—were equal-opportunity killers. The fat and the thin, the beautiful and the unattractive, twenty-somethings and retirees had met their end on this isolated property and been preserved so that the murderers might stroll this grisly gallery, admiring their acquisitions and waxing nostalgic over glasses of fine Cabernet Sauvignon.

The hair of the dead floated freely in the preservative, and in some cases formed veils across portions of their faces. Sometimes the fright-wide eyes peering through those cloaking tresses seemed to turn to follow me as I moved along, but I knew that I imagined their interest in me, and I could not fear these dead as I feared those who had murdered them.

Suddenly I realized that the most extraordinary thing about the scene was the absence of lingering spirits wanting justice for their murderers. Had I imagined such a place before finding it, I would have expected it to be crowded with ghosts tormented by what had been done to them in the last hours of their lives, haunted and haunting.

With a growing sense of urgency, I toured what remained of the display, and though some faces might have been those of teenagers, none were those of children. I could only assume that this murderous cult, whatever its nature, must be methodical in its depravity, adhering to a policy of progressive outrages, only this night at last arriving at its most extreme transgression to date: the abuse, torture, and murder of the most innocent of victims.

In the last cabinet that contained trophies, the faces were to one degree or another charred, blistered, melted, and I knew beyond doubt that this was the recent work of the rhinestone cowboy. Judging by the size of the skulls, these people had all been adults, but soon he would turn his flamethrower on more diminutive targets.

In the presence of such unspeakable horror, I couldn't any longer maintain my composure, that "feeling without agitation" that I previously described. Even the most experienced policeman and the battle-hardened soldier, courageously and of necessity repressing their anguish at the human condition, can sometimes repress it no longer, and the emotional pain threatens for a while to break them, before they suppress it once more.

Among the nations of Earth in all its history, ours is one of the precious few that has not brought forth its Hitler, its Stalin, its Pol Pot, its Mao Tse-tung, its Vlad the Impaler, the one who is never satisfied to have every knee bend to him but wants also to be the architect of a new world by destroying the existing one. But something is afoot. Atrocities like this, once rare but ever more frequent, would have at one time shocked the country but now seem to titillate as many people as they shock. My vision on the freeway in Los Angeles, others that have come in dreams, and things like this collection lead me to fear that our turn on the rack and wheel is coming. In this age when innocence is ever more mocked, when truth is aggressively denied if not actively hated, when so many people *despise* those with whom they disagree, when priests and teachers molest those whom they should protect, when power and fame are celebrated but true law and modesty are disparaged, what fire wall remains between the people and the forces that would devour them?

I am just one fry cook with a special talent, not David certain to bring down Goliath, one mortal man trying to make his way through a storm in which swarm uncountable leviathans. I am only you, like you, born of man and woman, but with this gift or burden. In that stable in Elsewhere, I felt as you would have felt, overwhelmed and terrified of failing.

At the door, I almost crossed the threshold before I realized that I would be stepping not into the Nevada night where three dogs slept and snored, but into the blind-black wasteland that surrounded buildings in Elsewhere. And waiting in that blighted place was the Other Odd who had wanted to kiss me, who'd said *Give me your breath, piglet, your breath, and the sweet fruit at the end of it.*

# Twenty-six

HESITATING AT THE DOOR, I HAD NO WAY of knowing how long I might have to wait for this dust-free and lifeless stable in Elsewhere to become again the dirty and spider-ruled building in my reality. A minute or two? An hour? Until all the children were dead?

Should the fabled Headless Horseman come here seeking to repair himself, he would have scores of heads to choose from, and if I again encountered the Other Odd, my head also might be available for the horseman's consideration.

Thinking about the Other might quickly draw him to me, but he remained a figure of such dark fascination that I couldn't banish him from my mind. I remembered the disgusting tone and texture of his cold, flaccid flesh, like that of a corpse after rigor mortis had come and gone, when the minions of Death were busy within. Yet he had been strong, unstoppable, and ten rounds of 9-mm ammunition had done no damage to him. Now I had two pistols with fifteen-round magazines, plus four spare magazines, nine times the ammo that I'd had before; but considering that ten shots had zero effect, nine times zero wasn't a calculation worth making.

In that industrial building in Elsewhere, back in that suburb of Los Angeles, there had been a moment when I stared at one of the chain-hung lamps, questioning its existence—whereupon it began to lose substance and to dim. I was certain now that, by an act of will alone, I could cause Elsewhere to wane and my world to emerge once more around me.

Previously this door had been made of vertical planks with a Z of cross braces on the inside, knot-holes visible through the white paint, here and there raw wood revealed where a splinter had been gouged out. The evenly white door before me looked and felt smooth, flawless, like a plastic panel, the half-formed *idea* of a door.

When I pressed the palm of my left hand against that surface and thought hard about its previous appearance, I began to feel the planks, the screw heads, the knotholes partly swollen out of the wood around them.

The lamps hanging from the ceiling went out, and I was left with only the frosty beam of the LED flashlight, which revealed the planks as they should have been, the floor of hard-packed earth, the empty stalls, the spiders poised in their gossamer traps, but nothing of the collection of heads.

I stepped into a night that was not a lightless wasteland, in which the heavens were not as black as the ceiling of a coal mine. Indeed, the storm, which I had assumed would catch up with us once more, must have been so drained by the thirsty desert to the west that it had nothing more to offer. The clouds were tattering and lifting, as though within the hour they might, at least in places, peel away like bandages and reveal a healed and vibrant sky.

I put away the canister of pressurized sedative and drew one of the two Glocks. That seemed the wise thing to do.

*Jessie, Jasmine, Jordan . . .*

Remaining close to the tree line, I approached the stone-and-timber building that had a steep and beetling roof. From the moment I first glimpsed it, even from a distance and in the dark, it had seemed to be an ominous structure. Now as I circled it, on closer inspection, that first impression ripened, grew darker, and I felt that herein I would find corruption and depravity that explained the collection of heads.

The sixty-by-forty-foot block stood like a fortress, forbidding and windowless. Even a medieval castle would have featured arrow loops, narrow openings from which archers could defend against the barbarians, or high clerestory windows to admit natural light. But I sensed that nothing natural was wanted within, that this building had been constructed to *cel-*

*ebrate* barbarism, that its builders felt no need for arrow loops or gun ports, for they knew that civilization, in its current and foreseeable state, would have no interest in mounting an assault against them.

Three broad and shallow steps led up to the only door, which was at what seemed to be the back of the building, out of sight from the main house. I dared the flashlight and saw a bronze slab, green with time, featuring a pattern of scores of little arrowheads in many lines radiating out from a central hub, on which was a word in raised bronze letters— CONTUMAX.

I had no idea what the word *contumax* might mean. It sounded like an over-the-counter laxative or a drug to treat cold sores, although it was certainly neither. Whatever the word meant, the pattern of arrowheads suggested militant hostility to something.

Perhaps the door was most often locked, although not on this night of celebration. When it eased inward, I discovered a shadowy vestibule. Opposite this first door, a second stood a quarter open to a more well-lighted chamber.

I did not want to go inside, to risk being trapped in a place that had one exit, but I sensed that what waited to be learned here was something I must know if I were to be of any use to the children. I stepped inside and eased the outer door shut behind me.

After crossing quietly to the inner door, I stood listening, but heard nothing. I held my breath, the better to hear, but the silence remained absolute.

When I inhaled, a peculiar bitter smell, faint but unpleasant, caused me to grimace. It registered as a taste, too, even fainter than the scent. The flavor reminded me of ipecac, the syrup that doctors use to induce vomiting when someone has been poisoned, but in this case disguised—inadequately—by mint.

I pushed open the inner door, crossed the threshold, and was halted by the drama of the space.

Stone-and-timber walls as outside, cobblestone floor, without a piece of furniture, the room must have been forty feet wide and fifty end to end, the raftered ceiling forty feet overhead. Along the wall to the left and along the wall to the right stood seven concrete pedestals, fourteen in all, each perhaps seven feet high. Mounted atop every pedestal, lit from above by pin spots, angled to peer down imperiously, were the bleached-white skulls of what might have been Rocky Mountain bighorn rams, identifiable by their enormous, curved, and deeply grooved horns.

The cobblestones were flat, without rounded edges, with minimal grout lines, set in a circular pattern that swirled around the room, ring after diminishing ring, leading to a large round stone at the center. With growing alarm, I walked to that medallion and read the word carved into it: POTESTAS. Here was another test of my knowledge—and additional proof of my ignorance.

I looked left and right at the totems on the fourteen pedestals. Set on the sides of those narrow heads, twenty-eight eye sockets, though empty, though black and hollow, seemed to watch and menace me. The builders of this house of the profane did not mean for the skulls to be seen simply as what they were, did not intend for them to be thought of as mere rams' heads, but placed them here as symbols of the great horned serpent who was the prince of this world. Fourteen goatish mouths were fixed open, perhaps to express the insatiable appetite that the prince encouraged and that he promised to feed generously.

I proceeded no farther, but I saw at the front of the room a large slab of what might have been black granite elevated on thick black-granite legs. On the wall directly behind the slab, hanging from two points on a rafter, a long loop of glossy red beads, each as large as a plum, had been threaded through five evenly spaced human skulls that I knew must be as real as those of the bighorn rams.

A miniature version of this macabre construction had hung from the citizens-band radio in the cab of the cowboy's eighteen-wheeler.

From the first encounter that had led me here and in many other moments of the day, I had been given clear clues to the nature of my adversaries. On some level, I noted all those jigsaw pieces, fitted them together—and then refused to acknowledge the picture that they formed.

Patterns exist in our seemingly patternless lives,

and the most common pattern is the circle. Like a dog pursuing its tail, we go around and around all our lives, through the circles of the seasons, repeating our mistakes and pursuing our redemption. From birth to death we explore and seek, and in the end we arrive where we started, the past having made one great slow turn on a carousel to become our future, and if we have learned anything worth learning, the carousel will bring us to the one place we most need to be.

My journey had so far taken almost twenty-two years, but it had become a far more profound voyage nineteen months ago than it had been previously. I have often said that in a quest for the purpose of my life, I learn by going where I have to go. And I *do* learn. But I realized here, only now, that learning had not been my primary motivation, that since the mall shootings in Pico Mundo, I had been on a pilgrimage to seek the sacrament of penance, in search of forgiveness for a failure that I refused to believe could ever be mitigated by ordinary confession and contrition. And I had come now full circle to the same adversary that I had not entirely defeated back then, the same implacable adversary from which I had perhaps saved many people, but not all, not nineteen who died, including she whose heart was one with mine.

The killers at the Green Moon Mall had been members of a satanic cult. And so were the cowboy trucker and the people gathered in this place, this night. Different people, different cult, same enemy. I'd known the truth hours earlier but had striven to repress it.

Denial couldn't be maintained. The skulls of fourteen bighorn rams were positioned, mockingly, where in a Catholic church the fourteen stations of the cross would be. The red beads and the five human skulls insulted the rosary and its five joyful, five sorrowful, and five glorious mysteries.

The enemy was the same, but I was in a darker and far more desperate place now than I had been on that day in Pico Mundo.

The men in that cult nineteen months earlier had made a *game* of evil, committing murder primarily for the excitement of it, playing at satanic faith the way that boys might play at being vampires, with wax fangs and with capes made from blankets. The cultists in Pico Mundo never committed entirely to their faith, not intellectually or emotionally. When the confrontation came between me and them, they had their boldness and their viciousness, but they did not have any genuine power beyond that of other sociopaths. In the end, though deadly, they had been nothing more than thrill killers.

But the pilot of the ProStar+ and the congregation to which he belonged were true believers, so diligent and so passionate in the practice of their faith that they were rewarded with the ability to open doors to Elsewhere. They enjoyed the capacity to blind others to their actions, as the cowboy blinded the people in the supermarket to the fact that he had fired a pistol and threatened to kill innocent shoppers if I didn't come with him quietly.

In this new and pending confrontation, these darksiders greatly outnumbered me. And although my paranormal gifts usually gave me an advantage, their gifts made them at least my equals.

My eyes had adjusted to the lighting, and now I saw that on the black-granite table at the front of the room lay what might have been a thick black book. I was loath to approach that altar, but I knew that I must do so.

Bound in black leather, the volume contained a thousand numbered pages, which must have been blank when it was bound. On the top of the first page someone had printed these words: *This coven of the demon Meridian, founded to glorify his name, on the 7th day of October, in the year 1580, in Oxford, Oxfordshire, England.*

Each of the next 433 pages was dedicated to one year in the coven's existence. The heading of the page featured the year, a name followed by the words *high priest,* and the location. Each page also contained a handwritten meditation on the beauty and the necessity of evil, apparently composed by the priest. As I paged through, I saw that some priests served decades, others a few years. I didn't have time to examine the book carefully enough to determine when they had moved their little cult to America. On page 433 was the current year and the name of the high priest, Lyle Hetland; otherwise that page was blank, for he had not yet written his meditation.

Over four hundred years and numerous generations of madness and murder. They were not the first of their kind and would not be the last. Accounts of such groups dated back to the earliest fragments of written history. If the world survived long enough, accounts of the activities of their latest iterations would be reported on the Internet or by whatever medium might one day replace it. The human heart may choose truth or lies, light or darkness, and even if the world were to become a universally prosperous, totally materialist sphere where everyone claimed to be scientific rationalists, some would secretly worship evil—and commit it—even if none were left who believed in the existence of absolute good. Good people are from time to time exhausted by the relentless nature of the enemy and need some period of peace, but those who worship darkness thrive on the battle, on violence and hatred, and have no taste for peace.

I'd gone where I had to go, and I'd learned what I resisted learning. And now there was only one place left for me: the house, where the children were being held, where the killing would soon begin.

The rams' skulls were only that to me, no matter what they might be to others here, and I turned my back on them.

# Twenty-seven

OUTSIDE, THE NIGHT LAY AS STILL AS IF the world had lost its atmosphere. A wind must have been ripping along at a higher altitude, because the clouds continued to tatter, unravel, and disintegrate before my eyes.

I rounded the church and stood looking at the house, wondering if security would be any better there than at the entrance to this property. I didn't think it would be.

They knew that their fellow citizens, in this brave new century, chose to be unaware of them, to consign their master *and them* to the realm of myth. No one would come looking for them because no one believed in their existence. Who arms himself and goes hunting for the frumious Bandersnatch or leads an expedition to the North Pole with the serious intention of interviewing Santa Claus?

In addition, the cult might have cast a simple spell

upon this property, a spell to blind people to its existence, as the shoppers in the produce section of the supermarket had been unable to see the silencered pistol with which the cowboy shot the cantaloupe. No self-respecting modern person would believe in the effectiveness of such a spell, but it worked just the same without *their* belief.

The Dobermans might be the extent of their precautions. And perhaps those creatures had been trained to patrol and kill less for security than for the pleasure that their trainer took in corrupting three dogs. Dogs are innocent by nature, and people such as these prized nothing more than the corruption— and destruction—of the innocent.

If the rhinestone cowboy thought I might be alive, perhaps guards would have been posted. But he believed that he had killed me in the Elsewhere version of Shower 5. I, too, thought he had killed me. It had sure felt like death, but then everything since had felt like life.

At the front of the house, lights had glowed behind uncurtained windows on all three floors. Back here, the third-floor rooms were dark. Even on the lower levels, fewer people were evident here than had been on the lake side of the building. In fact, on the ground floor, I could see no one anywhere but in the kitchen.

Pistol ready, I crossed the lawn. I sensed that I didn't have time for excessive stealth, but I stayed away from the house until I was past the kitchen windows, through which I could see four people toiling.

*Jessie, Jasmine, Jordan . . .*

I passed French doors with lights beyond, went to a solid door, hesitated, tried it, opened it. Beyond lay a lighted mudroom: pegs on which to hang coats, benches on which to sit to take off or put on boots.

The mudroom offered two interior doors. I heard voices beyond one of them and figured it opened into the kitchen. The other door presented me with a set of softly lighted back stairs, one flight leading up to a landing, another flight leading down, no sound of footsteps above or below.

I felt drawn to the basement both by psychic magnetism and logic. If you've kidnapped seventeen children and are holding them for a series of human sacrifices that would give an Aztec priest second thoughts, the basement seemed the best place to lock away the little ones.

I descended two flights to a door, listened at the crack along the jamb, and liked what I heard, which was exactly nothing. Beyond lay a wide corridor leading the length of the building. On both sides were more doors, none of them open.

None of the doors was marked, either, not even with the universal language of clever symbols that, the world over, identify men's and women's bathrooms, first-aid stations, mail drops, and many other things. Most likely no symbol sign exists that means *kidnapped children here.*

Twenty feet ahead of me, a man stepped into the corridor from a room on the left, pulling the door shut behind him. He was reading a sheet of paper that he held in his right hand, and he didn't at first register my presence.

I had nowhere to hide, no cloak of invisibility, only the pistol that I held down at my side, muzzle toward the floor, and for some reason I didn't at once bring it on target. The Judeo-Christian ethic isn't as easily cast off as we believe it is. *Thou shalt not kill* is a deeply programmed directive; if it were not, normal life would be virtually impossible, every trip to the 7-Eleven even more dangerous than it is now, and no one would survive a season as a judge on *American Idol*. Although self-defense allows an exception, we tend to hesitate nonetheless, especially when the guy we think will kill us appears to be unarmed.

He took two steps, laughed, became aware of me, and looked up from the item that he had been reading. He was florid-faced, with amusingly unruly white hair and sparkling blue eyes and a crooked smile that, as a package, made him one of those people who, upon first sight, you think you'd enjoy knowing.

If he found my two holsters, bulletproof vest, utility belt, and the weapon in my hand alarming, he concealed his concern quite well. Still smiling, he raised his right fist and said, *"Contumax,"* which was the word on the bronze door to their temple. He said it not as a challenge but as one member of a men's club might have called out a greeting to another member, using a secret word that helped them tell the difference between themselves and the Odd Fellows or the Freemasons.

I was somewhat surprised to hear myself answer him with the word in the center of the temple floor: *"Potestas."*

Evidently I pronounced it correctly and it was the right thing to say, because he didn't frown with suspicion. "I'm Rob Burkett."

"Scottie Ferguson," I replied, not sure why I took the name of the lead character in *Vertigo*.

Rob appeared to be delighted with me, perhaps somewhat envious, when he indicated my weaponized appearance and said, "So you're all dressed for the stage. Be hard as nails, man, make it memorable. Which have you been assigned, a little bitch or a little bastard?"

I popped him twice in the chest. The sound suppressor proved to be of high quality, producing only one *whifff* and then another, which echoed quietly along the corridor like a pair of heavily muffled kitten sneezes that couldn't have been heard through a closed door.

Even an unsentimental head-collecting child-murdering fanatic with big-time hoodoo tricks and a friend in the hierarchy of Hell can make a serious mistake. But only one.

In this place infested with human cockroaches, one mistake would be the end of me, too. I dared not leave a corpse sprawled in plain sight, and not just because the state of Nevada had anti-littering laws. I cautiously opened the door through which Rob had stepped less than a minute earlier. A small office with one desk, a computer, two chairs, no people. I holstered the Glock, gripped the dead man by his wrists, dragged him out of the corridor.

In books and movies, at moments like this, the good guy—a title that I'm taking the liberty of attaching to myself—goes through the pockets and the wallet of the thug he had to kill, searching for and discovering clues that tell him who his enemies are. I already knew *what* these people were, and I didn't care *who*. I tucked him into the knee space under the desk.

I'm not sure what I expected the office of a hard-working devil-worshipper to look like. Maybe a lamp with a shade made of human skin, a baby's skull used as a pencil holder, wallpaper after a design by the Marquis de Sade, and a desk calendar with 365 pages featuring the wit and wisdom of Hitler. The reality included a poster headlined THE 12 RULES OF SUCCESSFUL MANAGEMENT and another poster made from a photo of a house cat cornered by a crocodile above the words SHIT HAPPENS. On the desk were a bank statement and spreadsheet. Stuck here and there, Post-its provided neatly printed reminders: SHERRY'S BIRTHDAY GIFT, the culinarily specific HOT SAUCE, GREEN AND RED, and an almost desperate PAPER CLIPS!

I snatched a box of Kleenex from beside the computer, returned to the corridor, and quickly wiped up the blood on the gray vinyl-tile floor. There wasn't much of it. One of the rounds had stopped his heart.

When I picked up the sheet of paper that he had been reading, it proved to be a joke going around the Internet. It concerned two dogs, a famous newspaper, Valentine's Day, and urination. I couldn't imagine why he'd found it funny enough to laugh out loud.

In the office again, I dropped the tissues and the paper in the waste can. I drew the Glock that now held thirteen rounds, turned off the lights, and stood in the dark, taking slow, deep breaths.

There is a keen distinction between the words *murder* and *kill*. Because of envy or greed, jealousy or rage, ideology or sheer blind hatred, the murderer takes the precious life of another. To prevent the murderer from doing so or to deal justice, or to save myself, I may kill him. He murders, I kill. Funny, then, that killers tend to be the ones who have to overcome nausea in the immediate aftermath and who struggle with guilt in the long run, while the murderers go from slaughter to celebration without a hiccup.

I returned to the hallway, pulled the door shut behind me, and almost shot Mr. Hitchcock, which would have been regrettable even if he was a spirit who couldn't be harmed. He stood farther along the corridor, waving at me as if I might be so preoccupied that I wouldn't notice him.

As I approached the director, he turned to his left, giving me his famous profile, and walked through a door. I almost sang the tune from his old TV show: *Dunt-da-da-da-da-dunt-da-da, dunt-da-da-da-da-dunt-da-da.*

When I opened the door through which he had passed, I found him waiting for me in a room about twenty feet square. Deep, sturdy metal shelving units lined all four walls from floor to ceiling. They were packed full of just two items: thousands of rolls of toilet paper and paper towels. It was such a strange hoard that I couldn't help but marvel at it for a moment.

In that singular voice and precise diction, Mr. Hitchcock said, "They must have reason to believe the world will end by diarrhea."

I don't recall my reply. I know I said something, but my own words were forever knocked out of my memory by the sudden realization that he had *talked*.

# Twenty-eight

THE DEAD DON'T TALK. I DON'T KNOW WHY. I've always thought that they are denied speech because, if they possessed it, they would be likely to reveal something about death that the living are not meant to know.

Mr. Hitchcock had died thirty-two years earlier. There had never been any crazy rumors about him having faked his death, as there had been about Elvis. Besides, he chose to manifest as about fifty years of age, when he'd been in his prime as a filmmaker; but if this was the real Mr. Hitchcock, he would be far past the century mark, having been born in 1899.

I stared at him, aware that my mouth hung open but unable to close it.

"Mr. Thomas," he said, "the hour is late, the clock is ticking, and this scenario requires James Stewart, not Tab Hunter."

"Sir . . . you're talking."

"Your powers of observation are impressive. But they alone will not ensure the safety of seventeen children. There are things—"

"But the spirits of the lingering dead don't talk."

"I died, as you know. But I have never lingered in my entire existence, either before death or after. One always has too much to do to linger anywhere. Now there are things I need to tell you, Mr. Thomas, but the telling will be pointless if you are not prepared to listen."

"Call me Odd, sir. Or Oddie. That would be cool. I mean, since I'm such a fan. Your work was brilliant."

"Thank you, Mr. Thomas. Some of it was quite good, some just all right, some unfortunate. Where you may have *serious* complaints, I imagine they should be addressed to the producer with whom I had to work on occasion, Mr. David O. Selznick— wherever he may be. Now shall we get to the matter of the children?"

"Wait a minute," I said, thunderstruck by a sudden realization. "You can't just— We've got to— If you're talking— I mean, then what are you, sir? Are you my . . . my guardian angel?"

"I am touched by your high opinion of me, Mr. Thomas."

"Call me Odd."

"That's very kind of you. But angels, Mr. Thomas, are born angels and are never anything else, except of course when they disguise themselves, when visiting

Earth, as people or dogs, or whatever. I assure you that during my many years on Earth, I was not an angel pretending to be human, and I am not an angel now."

"Then what are you?"

"The hierarchy of spirits and the assignment of various tasks and responsibilities after death are issues more complicated than Hollywood has portrayed them. No surprise there. But if you insist on my spelling out all of that, I assure you that by the time I finish, the children will be dead."

He pushed out his lower lip, raised his eyebrows, and regarded me expectantly, as if to say, *Shall we let them die, then, so your curiosity can be satisfied?*

In defense of my temporary inability to focus on the children, I can only plead that I had recently fended off three attack dogs, toured a collection of severed heads, visited a satanic temple, just killed a man—killed, not murdered—was afraid that I would have to kill many more, had heard a spirit speak for the first time ever, and he was *Alfred Hitchcock.*

But his raised eyebrows and his pout of disapproval, subtle as they were, brought me to my senses, as I imagine that expression and others equally well-practiced had brought errant actors back to the script and to the intended tone of a production with little or no argument. I thought of him turning the same look on Gregory Peck or Rod Taylor—surely never on Cary Grant or James Stewart—and I couldn't help but grin.

As soon as I saw his reaction to my delight, of course, I wiped the grin off my face. "Where are the children, sir?"

"They are under guard on the third floor, Mr. Thomas. Getting them down from there and out of this house will test your wits and courage."

"But I thought they were here in the basement. Jessie, Jasmine, Jordan, and the others. When I thought about them, I was drawn down here to the basement."

"You were drawn here by me. Had you gone to the third floor without certain knowledge that you must have, you would by now be stone dead."

He had my attention. "What knowledge?"

"The people here tonight have come from four states in the West. Most of them know one another, but to some of them, there are new faces."

"I already figured that out by how the guy reacted to me in the hallway."

"Good for you. One likes to have a leading man who is credibly clever."

With some embarrassment, I said, "I don't think of myself as a leading man, sir."

"Frankly, Mr. Thomas, neither do I. Now, chances are, if you holster your guns and go to the third floor openly, as though you belong in this place, you will be met with no suspicion."

"Except for the cowboy guy."

"Yes. Except for him."

"He thinks I'm dead."

"I'm sure that he does."

"What if I run into him?"

"Don't."

"Was I dead in Shower 5, sir?"

"That is not for me to say."

"Did you . . . bring me back from . . . from the dead?"

Instead of answering, he winked. "Pay attention, Mr. Thomas. Now if someone greets you with a raised fist and the word *contumax*—"

"Even though I feel like an idiot, I raise my fist back at them and say *potestas*. But what does that mean?"

"The first is Latin for 'defiant' or 'disobedient.' The second is Latin for 'power.' They are a predictable bunch."

"Except I would have predicted more security."

Mr. Hitchcock shrugged. "They believe themselves to be charmed, given protection by the prince of this world, and untouchable."

"Why do they believe that?"

"Because they are."

"Oh."

"They have nothing to fear from most people. But because of their worldview, they are incapable of imagining or preparing for someone as different as you, Mr. Thomas."

"You mean my gift."

"That is the last thing I mean."

"Then what's different about me?"

"Everything."

"I'm just a fry cook."

"Exactly."

He smiled, and I had the strangest feeling that, like Mrs. Fischer, he was going to pinch my cheek. He didn't. And he didn't tell me what amused him.

Instead, he said, "Because you're so intriguingly geared-up, people will think you're one of the evening's murderers of children. If they ask who's your patron, say Zebulun, and they will especially respect you."

"Who's Zebulun?"

"One of the more powerful demons."

"I almost want to laugh, sir."

"Did you want to laugh when you saw the collection of heads?"

"No, sir. All right. My patron is Zebulun."

"Just try not to say the name too often."

"Why not?"

"It is never wise."

"Okay, all right. Whatever you say."

He pointed at me, which for him seemed to be as forceful a gesture as he might ever employ. In a confrontational business known for temperamental personalities, he had been famous for *never* losing his temper and for walking away rather than participate in an argument. "You must avoid the senoculus."

"What's the senoculus?"

"A lesser demon. Its usual form is a bull's head on a man's body, and it has six eyes, a cluster of three on each side of its face."

"I'm sure I'll recognize it."

"The last time you met the senoculus, it didn't look that way."

A chill quivered along my spine. "The thing on that roof in all the blackness?"

"When you cross into what you call Elsewhere, you are known at once by those in the wasteland, Mr. Thomas. Known and hated. Hated because you are the antithesis of what they are. And because they can enter Elsewhere, one of them will always come for you. The senoculus chooses to look like you now. It will try to suck your life and your soul out of you."

" 'Give me your breath . . . and the sweet fruit at the end of it.' "

"Avoid the senoculus at all costs."

"If it shows up, how do I avoid it?"

"Run, Mr. Thomas. Run."

Doubting my ability to handle this, I said, "Maybe I should just call the police, tell them the missing kids are all here. Maybe I can convince them. Maybe they'll think they have to come take a look."

He regarded me with sadness, as if I were pitiably naive. "Mr. Thomas, the county sheriff is among the guests downstairs."

"Oh."

"Yes. Oh."

The director began to rise off the floor, as though he would leave through the ceiling, as he had done in the elevator at Star Truck.

I said, "Wait, wait, wait."

He drifted back to the floor. "Time is short, Mr. Thómas."

I said, "Why can't you just take the kids under your wing and get them safely out of here?"

"This world isn't run by miracles. This world is run by free will, and I can't interfere with yours or the children's."

"But you stepped in to give me all this advice."

"I was a film director, Mr. Thomas. I don't give advice. I give instructions. And you have the free will to ignore them."

When he started to rise again, like a Macy's-parade balloon, I grabbed his arm to hold him down. "Why didn't you talk to me right from the start, why all the pantomime until now?"

He smiled and shook his head as if to say that I had much to learn regarding the construction of a drama. "One does not reveal such a twist a moment sooner than the end of the second act." His expression grew serious, and he searched my eyes as if taking the measure of my mettle. "Children, Mr. Thomas. Innocent children."

"I'll do my best, sir."

"Do better than your best."

His usual droll demeanor gave way to more emotion than he had allowed himself in public, during his days of fame. "This world can be hard on children."

Later, I would learn that he and his wife, Alma, had had one child, a daughter named Patricia, on whom he doted. There are many charming pictures of portly Mr. Hitchcock and tiny Pat on vacation with Alma in exotic places like Paris and Africa and Switzerland. His smile, though ironic when calculated for publicity, could be sweet, and never sweeter than in photographs with Pat or with her children. At play with the grandchildren, he had been like a child himself, Hitchcockian dignity discarded in favor of participating fully in the game of the moment.

Perhaps his regard for children and their happiness had its roots in his own lonely childhood. At the age of nine, he was sent off to a Catholic boarding school. Until he was fourteen, he was raised by Jesuits who believed most strongly in severe corporal punishment, and before he was fifteen, he quit school and took his first job. He was remembered by others as a sensitive and retiring boy, and he called himself "a particularly unattractive youth," though rare photos from those days don't really support such a harsh self-assessment. One of his earliest vivid memories was of waking late on Christmas Eve, when he was only five, to discover his mother sneaking two toys from his Christmas stocking, putting them in the stockings of his older siblings, and replacing them with a couple of oranges.

"This world can be hard on children," he repeated. "Now, these seventeen think they're being held for ransom. They don't know what's going to be done to them, although a few might suspect something. The cultists want to surprise them, the better to savor their terror as the full horror of their fate dawns on them."

"I'll remember everything you told me, sir. I feel better now that you're on my side. Everything's sure to be all right now."

He raised one eyebrow. "Is it sure to be, Mr. Thomas? Are you really certain that you've seen my films?"

I thought of the end of *Vertigo,* and wished I hadn't.

Again he rose off the floor.

This time I didn't try to stop him, though I did say, "Please call me Odd, sir."

Halfway to the ceiling, he said, "That's very kind of you, Mr. Thomas. Please call me Hitch."

"Yes, sir. Will I see you again, Mr. Hitchcock?"

"I would count on it, Mr. Thomas, whether or not you survive the next half hour."

He disappeared through the ceiling.

The time had come to kill or die. Or both.

# Twenty-nine

NOT BEING A QUICK-DRAW ARTIST, I WAS reluctant to leave both pistols in their shoulder rigs, as Mr. Hitchcock had suggested. I understood that I would be more likely to arouse suspicion if I went everywhere with one of the Glocks drawn and ready for action, but I had to work up the nerve to do as he had instructed.

I turned out the lights in that room of paper towels and toilet paper. I took a deep breath and let it out slowly. I stepped into the basement corridor.

As I moved toward the farther end of the hallway and the back stairs by which I'd come here, a door opened on my right, and a woman came out of the office of the man whom I had killed.

In her twenties, pretty even under enough Goth makeup to supply Alice Cooper through a national nostalgia tour, she wore high-heeled shoes, tight and wonderfully supple black-leather pants, and a sort of half jacket of matching leather that bared her midriff. As most belly dancers have a jewel in their navels, this woman had a carved-bone skull.

She didn't appear to be alarmed, which surely she would have been if she'd discovered a corpse, unless these people found so many corpses with such regularity that all the shock value had gone out of the experience. She smiled at me, and she had the whitest teeth I'd ever seen, though the upper cuspids seemed to have been filed into sharper points than nature would have given them.

I raised my fist and said *"Contumax,"* but I felt like a satanic geek when instead of replying with *"Potestas,"* she said, "Hey, look at you, boy toy."

"Hey," I said.

Being called a boy toy might have been flattering if she hadn't been festooned with knives. At each hip, two loaded sheaths were fixed to her belt. In a scabbard against her back hung a full-length sword, which she could draw by reaching over her left shoulder. From each wrist dangled a straight razor, and though the blades were at the moment safely folded into the polished-ivory handles, I suspected that with a flick of her hands, she could bring both razors out, up, and into service. Whatever all she might want to do to a boy toy, I didn't think I could assume that sex would be part of it.

"You know Rob Burkett, honey?" she asked.

I said, "The twelve rules of successful management."

The sound she made was half laugh and half snort. "Yeah, he's kind of an asshole. Where'd he get that stupid shit-happens poster with the cat and the crocodile?"

"Wherever, it wasn't a Hallmark store."

"You seen him? He said he'd be down here in his office."

Evidently, she hadn't gone around behind the desk and looked in the knee space, where Rob was in the fetal position as if being born into death.

She came close and looked me over from crotch to lips to eyes. "You part of the show tonight?"

"Yeah. Are you?"

"Can't wait. They're givin' me a juicy little boy."

With a flick of her wrist, she brought the dangling ivory handle into her hand and released the straight razor, which appeared to be sharp enough to divide a human hair from end to end.

"Excellent," I said, pretending to admire her dexterity and style. "You ever cut one before?"

"A juicy little boy? Nah. Youngest ones I've cut are like eighteen, they come on to me, thinkin' they're so hot, but they're pussies. Only thing hot about 'em is their blood. My name's Jinx."

*Yes,* I thought, *I suppose it would be.*

But I said, "I'm Lucius."

"I think you're *luscious,*" she said, and she stroked the flat of the razor blade slowly along my left cheek, as if she were giving me a shave.

The steel was cold.

Her eyes were the jaundice yellow of a very sick man's urine.

"Your eyes are amazing," I said.

"They're really blue. I'm wearin' contacts that make 'em this way. Wild-animal eyes. I want my little boy so scared the second he sees me, he pisses himself right then."

"I think he will."

"You think he will?"

"I *know* he will."

Jinx said, "I'm from Reno."

"I'm from Arizona."

"Where in Arizona?" she asked, flicking open the straight razor in her left hand and drawing the flat of the blade along my right cheek.

"Little town you never heard of."

"Maybe I have."

"Lonely Possum, Arizona."

"Sounds like the ass end of nowhere."

"You can get a lot of land cheap. Keep neighbors at a distance."

She said, "Nobody hears nothin' you're doin', huh?"

"None of their business, anyway."

With a quick gesture of each hand, she flipped the blades back into the handles and let them dangle from her wrists again.

I didn't feel any safer.

Jinx said, "What're they givin' you for the show?"

"This girl. They say she's eight."

"Who's your patron?"

"Zebulun."

She was impressed. "I want to see her, the girl."

"What, now?"

"Yeah. Don't you want to see my juicy little boy?"

"Yeah. Sure."

"Maybe in the show, when I'm almost done with him, you can step in and help me finish."

"And you could step in and help me finish mine."

Smiling, she put one finger to my mouth. Her nails were long and glossy-black. Slowly she traced the outline of my lips.

I couldn't decide whether she wanted to kiss them or cut them off.

She said, "Later, should we get it on, really rock it hard?"

This didn't seem to be the kind of woman to whom I could explain that there was only one girl for me, Stormy Llewellyn, and that I was faithful to her.

I said, "The way it looks to me, that decision is entirely up to you."

My response pleased her, and her smile widened. "You got that right, boy toy."

Just when I thought I knew what she would do, she surprised me by pressing close and licking my chin.

Although I had never before had my chin licked by anything other than a dog, I felt pretty sure that this lick would proceed to a kiss either directly or after she licked other facial features that she found appealing. I can fake a lot of things convincingly, but I knew I couldn't fake the rough and hungry kiss that she would expect from me, and in that moment her suspicion would soar.

When she had come out of Rob Burkett's office and had seen me, Jinx had left the door ajar.

I lifted my wet chin and cocked my head and said, "Rob?"

Puzzled, she said, "Who, what?"

"Did you just hear that?"

"Hear what?"

"That was Rob's voice."

I separated myself from her. Although I would rather have turned my back on a crazy man with a chain saw than turn my back on Jinx, I did it anyway. I went to the office door, pushed it open, and turned on the light.

"Rob?" I said.

"I told you, he's not there."

"No. I heard something."

I went into the office and thought that she followed me at least to the threshold. Pretending to be perplexed, looking this way and that, I crossed the room, rounded the desk, registered peripherally that Jinx was just this side of the threshold, glanced down, and said, "Rob, no. What the hell?" As I spoke, I dropped to my knees, hunching my head and shoulders, out of Jinx's line of sight, and I drew one of the Glocks.

"Lucius?" she said.

I heard her coming, and when she rounded the desk, she had a straight razor in each hand, too smart for me, rushing in fast and mean, slashing at me. She hadn't known Rob's body was here, but I had done something to make her suspicious. The first round from the Glock knocked her back just far enough that the razor sliced the air about an inch from my eyes, the blade having been stropped so thin that it seemed to disappear for part of its arc. That was as close as she got, because the next two rounds kicked her off balance and sent her sprawling.

For a terrible moment, she lay there on her back, arms at her sides, the straight razors no longer in her hands but still tethered to her wrists, the blades rattling against the vinyl-tile floor while she spasmed as though trying to hold on to life and stave off death.

And then silence.

Jumpy, half convinced that Rob was reaching for me, I twitched toward him. He was still dead.

No lingering spirit had risen from either Rob or Jinx. They had been collected without delay.

I didn't want to look in Jinx's face. When you're forced to kill people, however, you've got to look at them afterward, at what you've done. It's like an acknowledgment that you owe the dead, no matter who he or she might have been, an acknowledgment that, in this case, she was potentially your sister even if she had fallen farther than you, a recognition that you have brought an end to someone who, no matter how unlikely a candidate for redemption, might nevertheless have been redeemed if she had lived. You've got to look at them for your own good, too, so that it never becomes too easy, so that you never begin to think of your adversaries as animals, even if they think of themselves that way.

I crawled to Jinx and looked at her face. One of the contact lenses had popped out when she fell. Her left eye was sour yellow, but her right was cornflower blue, as innocent a blue gaze as it would have been when, as a newborn, she first opened her eyes. She had been somebody's daughter, and maybe eventually they had abused her or been indifferent to her, but they must have had hopes for her at some point, must have loved at least the *idea* of her, because they hadn't aborted her. For however short a time, she had been loved—until somebody turned her into an engine of hate.

If I had a time machine that would take me back through Jinx's life, so that I could find who twisted her mind with an ideology or sick philosophy . . . Well, no, I wouldn't kill them to spare her from what she became. That way lies madness.

The wisdom of the most sagacious ancient Greeks, the wisdom of the most perceptive rabbis of ancient Canaan, and all the parables of Christ teach us to believe not in justice, but in truth. In a world of rampant lying, where so many lies are used to inflame passions and justify false grievances, the indiscriminate pursuit of justice leads sooner or later to insanity, mass murder, and the ruin of entire civilizations. Therefore, those who wish to punish the current and future generations for the inequities of a generation long gone, and who equate justice with revenge, are the most dangerous people in the world.

I got to my feet, crossed the room, and turned off the lights. In the hallway, I holstered the pistol and pulled shut the door.

There were now ten rounds in one Glock, fifteen in the other. I hoped I would need none of them, but I knew otherwise.

Returning to the back stairs, I started to climb the six flights of steps to the third floor.

*Jessie, Jasmine, Jordan . . .*

# Thirty

PASSING THE SECOND FLOOR, I HEARD THE excited voices of partiers beyond the stairwell door. The action seemed to be centered now on that level, and I sensed an acceleration of the crowd's mood toward some much-desired condition of dark ecstasy.

My impression that this building had once been a lodge or perhaps a corporate retreat seemed to be confirmed when I stepped into the third-floor hallway. Numbered doors, as in a hotel, served evenly spaced rooms on both sides.

Although deserted, the third-floor hall wasn't quiet. Laughter and the muffled roar of fevered conversation rose from below.

*Jessie, Jasmine, Jordan* brought me to Room 4 on the left, where I stood for a long moment with my hand on the doorknob.

I knew beyond doubt that the children were being

kept in there, but intuition told me that I still lacked some information essential to ensure their rescue. As the energy of the crowd grew and as the party noise seemed increasingly to come from the lake side of the house, I needed to see what might be happening out there in the torchlit night.

Although Mr. Hitchcock had said that the clock was ticking, and although no one would know more about ticking clocks than the Master of Suspense, I went to the next door on the left, Room 6. It wasn't locked.

They tortured people for pleasure and to win the favor of their malevolent god, and they made a sacrament of murder, but they trusted one another not to steal. Maybe that was because they also brutally executed their own—like the two men in the basement of the former Black & Buckle Manufacturing building in Barstow—for any behavior that might put the cult at risk or harm any of its members. I suppose the prospect of having your fingers amputated one by one with a bolt cutter and being set afire would make you think twice about sneaking into someone's room and stealing his iPad.

The wall switch just inside the door brought light to the pair of bedside lamps in Room 6. The bedding had not been disturbed. On the dresser, someone had left a newspaper, a set of keys, and pocket change. A few paperback books were stacked on one of the nightstands.

At the wide window, the draperies were open.

The flames of the propane torches, below my line of sight on the ground-floor terrace, made this higher night quiver with sinuous light.

To be sure I was alone, I checked the bathroom. Separate sets of personal-care products beside the two sinks indicated that a couple occupied this unit, a man and a woman. They were on a late-winter getaway: fresh mountain air, an entertaining novel or two, perhaps a little boating on the lake, the ritualistic murder of seventeen children to unwind taut nerves and ensure a good night's sleep. . . .

Satisfied that for the moment I had the room to myself, I went to the window.

Immediately below, at the second floor, on the twenty-foot-wide cantilevered deck that extended the length of the building, more than twenty people were gathered, enjoying cocktails and wine, men and women in about equal numbers. They all wore sweaters, though not only or even primarily for comfort in the cool night air. Perhaps as an act of mockery, every sweater had a Christmas motif featuring Santa Claus or reindeer, snowmen or elves, holiday trees or snowflakes, and some featured words of the holiday like NOEL, FELIZ NAVIDAD, HO HO HO, and JOY TO THE WORLD. They were colorful, festive, and—out of season, under these circumstances—deeply sinister.

I didn't know what the county sheriff looked like, but I saw a well-known film actor, a United States senator, and a couple of other faces that were familiar but that I couldn't identify. The rhinestone cowboy wasn't among them.

In this age of smartphones that can be used surreptitiously as cameras and recorders, for such prominent and recognizable people to attend this abomination seemed reckless in the extreme. But Mr. Hitchcock had said they were protected by their master, the rebel angel who was the prince of this world, to whom they had pledged everything. He said that they were untouchable. And perhaps they trusted one another not to steal and not to betray them with video on the Internet because when they had joined the darksiders, they had surrendered their free will and no longer had the capacity to change their minds and betray the cult. A satanic society, after all, would operate as the ultimate totalitarianism.

Beyond the deck, on the terrace below, in the center of a space defined by four of the tall propane torches, the round steel stage waited for the night's performances. I had seen this same platform when I touched the cowboy in the supermarket parking lot. The three children had been seated on it when he set them afire.

Just past the farther end of the terrace, on the shore, between two torches stood a man with spiky white hair. He wore a blood-red suit, black shirt, and harlequin mask. The cowboy. He held a censer that was suspended by three chains from a handle, and as he turned, swinging it toward all four points of the compass, I could see the pale fumes of incense escaping from the holes in the filigreed lid of the gold thurible.

Only as I looked past the people in their Christmas sweaters and the stage below them, past the cowboy, did I realize that the night had undergone a frightening change. Directly overhead, stars winked between the tattered clouds, the edges of which were aglow with a reflection of an otherwise still-shrouded moon. But beyond the evenly spaced line of tall propane torches that defined the curving shoreline, the lake had been transformed.

Previously, the placid surface had been inky, and only the torches, reflected in the water, had revealed the presence of a lake. Now the pale soil of the shore seemed to flutter in firelight, as if it were alive and trembling with expectation, but the water did not mirror the flames, as though it had drained away. Earlier, across the portion of the sky above the lake, the clouds had been faintly luminous with the refracted lights of distant Las Vegas, providing just enough contrast to see the rising land along the farther shores. Unlike the heavens directly above this property, those looming over the lake were now so perfectly black that looking at them strained the eyes. The farther land and the lake that it had defined were now invisible.

The line of torches no longer marked the edge of the lake but defined the boundary between this reality and that wasteland I had seen through the windows— and from the roof—of the old industrial building in

Elsewhere. Here, that vast cold hateful darkness met our world without the bridge of Elsewhere.

On the second-floor deck, more people were gathering, at least forty now, more colorful Christmas sweaters, and their conversation grew increasingly excited but at the same time quieter, as though they were anticipating the arrival of some special guest immeasurably more prestigious than the senator with the leonine mane of salt-and-pepper hair, far more glamorous than the movie star. Their attention focused now less on one another than on the absolute blackness where the lake had been.

A chill traveled through me, and it seemed that my blood had turned cold and thick. My heart pumped not just faster but also with much greater force, as though higher pressure was required to drive the syrup of life through the arteries to every extremity. I could feel the hard strokes of my heart not merely in my chest and throbbing temples, but as well in my eyes, my vision pulsing, and in the thyroid cartilage of my Adam's apple, my larynx vibrating with each beat, and in the deep pit of my stomach, which might have been my aorta swelling with each surge of blood. The fear that rose in me was unlike any that I'd known before, raw, primal, like a hibernating lodger that all my life had slept in my bones, that I had not known was part of me, until now it came awake.

Within that oppressive gloom where the lake had

been, a presence slightly less black moved, and then more than one. I could discern no shapes, no features. I became aware of things roiling, writhing, creatures that, in their biological convolutions, by far exceeded in strangeness the strangest living things upon the earth. It seemed to me the darkness through which they moved, out of which they came, was without end, that they were many and yet somehow one, that rising toward the shore was something vast beyond measuring and grotesque beyond human comprehension.

The cowboy turned his back upon the blackness. Slowly and without apparent fear, carrying the censer, he started toward the house.

I turned away from the window.

The nightstand lamps brightened and dimmed rhythmically, and because they were not in time with my racing heart, I thought their throbbing must be real, not merely the consequence of my pulsating vision.

I drew both pistols but then holstered them. Such fear as this could inspire irrational action, which might lead me to fail not just one or two of the children, but all of them.

Whatever gate had been opened to whatever realm, whatever presence or legion had come out of the wasteland to the shore behind the house, it was not here to find me and carry me away. It was here to witness the extreme atrocities that these people intended to offer in gratitude for the power and the wealth that they had been given, for the success in their careers that came from the dark grace of their patron. *They* were the real threat to me.

My palms were damp with sweat.

I blotted them on my jeans.

I held my hands before my face, watching them tremble—until they didn't.

Whatever might be out there in the night didn't matter. The world was proving far more mysterious than even I had heretofore imagined, but that didn't matter, either.

The task that I needed to perform was the same task that I had needed to perform since I first saw that vision of burning children earlier in the day. The thing to understand is that you have to do what you have to do, always and without complaint.

That's the way.

# Thirty-one

IN THE THIRD-FLOOR HALLWAY, THE CEILING lights were cycling brighter, dimmer, brighter, but there wasn't another pretty, yellow-eyed chin-licking Goth-girl maniac or the equivalent waiting for me. That seemed to be a good sign. *Stay positive.*

I returned to Room 4, opened the door this time, and walked boldly into the temporary prison where the seventeen children were being watched over by two men.

When I saw that a felt-tip pen had been used to draw a line of hieroglyphics across the brow of each child, I recalled the severed heads in the breakfronts, and had to remind myself to stay positive. But the abhorrence, the hatred of corruption and the detestation of those who ate at the trough of corruption, which I would need if I were to lead the captives safely out of here, did not need to be ginned up; I was almost wild with a righteous hatred and knew that I must get a leash and muzzle on it to avoid reckless action that would ensure the children's death and mine. I dared not let a trace of contempt color my voice or a shadow of loathing darken my face.

The two guards were absurdly handsome, coiffed as if they had a fetish for hair. They looked like Ken dolls that had been infused with life by a malevolent force, had dismembered Barbie, and had come here to take vengeance on these children for having spent years, as dolls, being dressed up in outfits that humiliated them.

The only pieces of furniture in the room were two straight-backed chairs. There were two floor lamps with pleated-silk shades, one in each half of the room, and they throbbed like the lights in the hallway and in Room 6. One of the Kens, a blond hunk with chiseled features, sat in a chair, holding a cattle prod across his lap. He wore a sweater that depicted Kermit the Frog in a Santa hat, overlaid with a shoulder holster and pistol.

*"Contumax,"* I said, pumping my fist in the air.

The other Ken, who wore a Rudolph sweater and also had a gun in a shoulder rig, stood at the window, on the farther side of the large room, watching the preparations for the festivities. He resembled the actor Hugh Grant if Hugh Grant were like three times better-looking than he'd been in his prime. If the two Kens had been close together, I would have been sure of dropping them without taking return fire, but this situation made me nervous. Besides, I didn't want to shoot at a guy standing by the window, in case I blew out one of the panes and alerted the people on the deck below.

Ken #2 answered my *"Contumax"* with *"Potestas"* and a lame fist pump, but Ken #1 just wanted to know when the fornicating action was going to fornicating begin, though the word he used wasn't *fornicating*. I said that my name was Lucius and I was from Arizona. Indicating my weaponry, I said that I was part of the show tonight, that I was a friend of Jinx's, and that we were looking for her, because the action couldn't begin without her. Ken #2 said that Jinx was probably outside somewhere, getting it on with one of the Dobermans, and Ken #1 said he couldn't wait to see the show that witchy bitch was going to put on, she was always over the top, whereupon Ken #2 said Jinx had superdelicious mammaries, with megabounce, though he didn't use the word *mammaries*. Ken #1 said that he liked her mammaries *and* her cool black fingernails but that the yellow contact lenses were just vampire-movie stupid, and Ken #2 agreed that the contacts were stupid and said that the only mammaries more superdelicious than Jinx's were Nedra's, to which Ken #1 replied that he shouldn't have eaten those fornicating wasabi shrimp because now he had fornicating heartburn, by which time I realized that even head-collecting satanists who performed human sacrifices and who lived without rules could be dull conversationalists.

The captives sat on the floor, in a large semicircle, the three Payton children among them, all ten years old or younger, eight boys and nine girls. Some were numb with terror, some twitchy, and others appeared to be emotionally drained, exhausted. They must have cried themselves dry. Two had a sullen and defiant attitude; they might have resisted or tried to flee and been badly hurt, except that each of the seventeen was firmly linked to the next, wrist to wrist, with eighteen-inch lengths of tightly knotted red-satin ribbon, and this chain-gang arrangement hampered them.

The lights stopped pulsing. Whatever presence had disturbed the night by its approach had fully arrived, and the night had adjusted to it.

Annoyed with me even though I had been entirely cordial, Ken #1 said, "Listen, man, I'll tell you what I told the others who've come sniffing around. We can't let you take one of these [fornicating] little muffins into the [fornicating] bathroom for a taste. They have to be pure . . . for later. Besides, they've all just had a piss before we tied them, and now we can't untie any 'cause soon, when we hear the gong, we have to lead them out to the [fornicating] stage."

"Her or him," Ken #2 said.

Ken #1 said, "What?"

"Her or him," Ken #2 repeated. "We can't let Lucius here get it on with one of the girls *or* one of the boys."

"Man, that's exactly just what I said," Ken #1 declared, further annoyed.

"No, what you told him was that we can't let him take *her* into the bathroom for a taste."

After a few words of blasphemy, Ken #1 said, "*Him* was implied when I said *her*."

"Maybe you implied it, but maybe he didn't infer it."

"What the hell's that mean?" Ken #1 asked. "When I said 'taste,' I didn't mean taste, either, but Lucius knew what I was implying." He looked up at me. "Didn't you [fornicating] know what I was implying?"

"Absolutely. But that's not what I came here for."

Ken #1's sneer was sharp enough to peel an apple. "Yeah, right."

"No, really. Rob sent me up here to do something."

"Rob who? There's ninety people here tonight, and I know like three Robs. There's at least twenty people I haven't met before, and for all I know every [fornicating] one of them is Rob."

Ken #2 said, "Except Rob Cornell is actually Robert, but he just doesn't like Bob, so he calls himself Rob."

Before Ken #1 could employ his profane vocabulary even more colorfully than before, I said to the Ken at the window, "I'll need your help with this."

"With what?"

"With what Rob Burkett sent me up here to do."

Stepping away from the window, Ken #2 said, "Why didn't you say Rob Burkett in the first place?"

Getting up from his chair, cattle prod in his right hand, Ken #1 said, "Shit, Lucius, you know how Rob is. He's an office guy, not a field guy. He wouldn't have known what to do if he'd been there in Vegas last night. So it got messy. But we still got those four kids."

I remembered what Chet, the customer in the diner, told us: The kidnappers in Vegas murdered the parents to get their four children.

Looking concerned as he joined us, Ken #2 said, "Who would've thought a milksop Baptist minister and his wife would be carrying concealed weapons?"

Ken #1 sought my sympathy: "Hey, man, the TV news said that [fornicating] preacher and that bitch wife of his had *permits* to carry. What kind of crazy government bureaucrat asshole licenses [fornicating] preachers to walk around with [fornicating] pistols under their suit coats?"

"Good thing," said Ken #2, "the preacher didn't realize there were two of us."

"Good thing," Ken #1 agreed. "A preacher ought to know the Bible says 'Thou shalt not kill.'"

"Actually," I corrected, "if you go back to the root language of the original commandments, it said 'Thou shalt not murder,' but over the millennia and through a lot of translations, it ended up saying 'kill.'"

Puzzled, Ken #2 said, "Murder or kill, kill or murder, what the hell's the difference?"

"Anyway," I said, "Rob is cool with Vegas. It turned out all right, and we have four juicy preacher kids raised pure, the way we need them to be. He sent me up here to do this thing with the little darlings."

"What thing?" both Kens asked.

Winking at them, I said, "You're going to like this."

Inside of me there seemed to be a butterfly farm where two thousand wings fluttered out of a thousand split cocoons all at once.

These kids would have to live with this trauma all the days of their lives, and I didn't want to do anything that would leave them with even darker memories of these events.

Turning to the captives, I remembered that Mr. Hitchcock had said they didn't know what was going to happen to them, that the cultists wanted to surprise the remaining sixteen when the first of them was slashed or chopped, or hammered. "Listen up, kids. It's going to take another day or two for the ransom to be paid, and we can't let you go until then."

One of the two that had an openly defiant attitude, a girl of nine or ten, with a blond ponytail and celadon eyes, said, "That's a crock of horseshit."

"Well, personally, I don't use that kind of language," I told her, "though I can understand why you might feel the way you do. But the truth is, we know you're bored, and since there are a few people here who're magicians, we're going to put on a show for you kids in a little while."

"That's more horseshit," the girl said.

Because I was standing a step in front of the Kens, I was able to wink at her without them seeing what I did. She frowned, not sure what to make of the wink.

I said, "We need one of you to be on stage to assist one of the magicians with a few totally amazing tricks. It'll be really cool."

One sweet-faced boy of about six raised his hand and said, "I'll do it."

"I'm sorry, son, but I'm not asking for a volunteer. We're going to play a fun game, and the winner gets to help the magician. First I need all of you to close your eyes. Come on, now. Close them. Close them tight. You, too. That's right, that's good. You have to keep them closed through the whole game, until I tell you to open them."

I drew one of the Glocks, turned, and shot Ken #1 in the head. His eyes weren't closed, of course, but they didn't even have time to widen in recognition of what was happening.

Ken #2 must have been thinking about superdelicious mammaries, because he was slower on the draw than I expected, and I shot him point-blank in the face and throat before he could get his piece out of his shoulder rig. Just to be sure about Ken #1, I leaned down to where he'd fallen and popped him again.

Every shot was a *whifff,* but the bodies made some hard sounds when they hit the carpet, so I said, "Keep your eyes closed, kids. Keep them closed really tight."

The butterflies in my stomach were snakes now, slippery masses of serpents squirming over one another.

I knelt beside the first Ken, looked into his eyes, and then pulled his Kermit the Frog sweater over his face like a shroud, to conceal his wounds. I looked in the second Ken's eyes and drew his Rudolph sweater over his face, as well.

I thought that I heard a noise in the hallway. I froze, stared at the door, waiting for a knock or for the knob to turn. Nothing happened.

In the farther half of the room, there might be chunks of skull and worse. I turned to the kids to be sure that they had their eyes shut, and they all did, except for the girl with the ponytail. Her stare was wide and gray-green and bright.

"Keep your eyes closed," I told the others. "We're almost ready to begin the game."

I went to the lamp that cast light into that part of the room where debris had fallen. I yanked its plug from the wall receptacle.

Returning to the kids, I said, "When you open your eyes, try not to look too close at things. There's no reason to look close. Okay, you can open them."

They stared at the dead men. Some of them—but not most—looked away. A few started to cry, but I gently shushed them.

"I'm going to take you out of here and home again," I told them. "But you have to be quiet, very quiet, and do exactly what I say."

The girl with the ponytail stared intensely at me, as if she were a living polygraph. She nodded. To the others, she said, "Do what he tells you. If he has to, he'll die for us."

The crying children wiped at their eyes, choked back their sobs.

I smiled at the girl. "No horseshit, huh?"

"Zero," she said.

# Thirty-two

INITIALLY, I THOUGHT THAT THE CHILDREN should be untied or the ribbons cut, but I quickly realized the advantage of leaving them tethered to those on both sides of them, wrist to wrist. If suddenly they were spooked by something, they could not scatter in a panic. I was more likely to be able to protect them if they remained together, less likely to lose one who, in unthinking terror, might run and hide.

I went once more to the window, to assess quickly the state of things.

Directly overhead, the architecture of the now-parched storm continued to come apart. Through holes in the roof of clouds, more stars appeared moment by moment, as if those distant suns were just now being born by the thousands.

Over the lake or where the lake had been, that *other* sky, awful and without one flicker, concealed beneath it what had come from some malignant shore to this one. Dark forms, moving and threatening within a deeper darkness, defied the eye and would not be defined.

As I have explained in previous volumes of this memoir, there are other spirits that I sometimes see in addition to those of the lingering dead, though they might never have been human at any stage of their existence. I call them bodachs because, when visiting Pico Mundo many years earlier, an English boy who apparently had talents akin to mine and who could also see these spirits called them bodachs just before he was crushed to death by a runaway truck. They are as insubstantial as fumes but not transparent, instead soot-black and without features, sinuous. Although they can't pass through walls as ghosts can, they are able to slip through any crevice or crack, or keyhole. Their silhouettes suggest wolf and human both. They slink and slouch, glide and slither, and they have an interest in certain people, especially in those who will soon die by violence and also in those who will murder them.

I've long believed that bodachs feed on human misery, which is why they appear at sites of forthcoming mass murders, where deadly fires will burn, where earthquakes will shake down buildings on our heads. I imagine that they swarm in frenzied multitudes across hard-contested battlefields. They do not appear for single deaths or even for two or three that occur in, say, a car wreck. They are attracted to great slaughters and catastrophes, incapable of harming anyone, as far as I know, just psychic vampires hungry not for our blood but for our pain.

The prospect of seventeen tortured and murdered children should have drawn bodachs to this place, but I hadn't yet seen one. If a horde of them gathered in the churning blackness just offshore, some other entity abided there as well, some greater power than they, to which they were subservient, some power that could inflict enormous suffering rather than merely feed off it.

Unlike that industrial building in Elsewhere, this place wasn't surrounded by the lightless wasteland, but only adjoined it for the coming homicidal performances. Leaving by the back of the building, staying away from the lake, we ought to be able to find our way to Mrs. Fischer.

At the stainless-steel stage on the terrace, the cowboy shook an aspergillum, one of those bulbed and pierced hollow wands with which a Catholic priest sprinkled holy water. Whatever he might have been dispensing, it wasn't holy.

On the second-floor terrace immediately below the window, more members of the cult than ever gathered, seventy or eighty. The senator spoke animatedly with a famous female singer that I had not seen here earlier.

Thus far, I had used one Glock exclusively. Six of fifteen rounds remained. I swapped that magazine for one of the fresh ones on my utility belt.

The children were standing, ready to leave, each of

them linked to two others, except a boy at one end and the ponytailed girl at the other end, who each had a hand free. None of them appeared to be as frightened as I felt.

"I'll lead the way," I told them. "Stay close, two-by-two to keep the line shorter, unless you have to go single file on the stairs to avoid stumbling over one another."

Some of them nodded solemnly, while others stared at me with eyes full of lamplight and determination, all of them past tears.

Our culture sentimentalizes children, and we forget one of the things that we should most remember from that time of our lives: Children *know* that this world can be hard on them, harder than it is on adults. They are physically weaker than adults, financially dependent, and in times of danger, nothing clarifies our thinking more than an awareness of our extreme vulnerability. The power of imagination is at its peak in childhood, and in a crisis like this, it allows no illusions, conjures in the mind a thousand ways that death might come, and thereby makes even the most vulnerable perhaps equal to the moment.

"You might see frightening things and scary people," I warned them. And the next words I spoke were so spontaneous that it seemed they had not been spoken by me, but instead *through* me. "If you do see anything scary, then just say very quietly, 'I am not yours, you may not touch me.' Can you remember that?"

They nodded, some of them softly repeated what I'd told them, and then all of them recited it in a whisper. Some ineffable quality of that quiet chorus so moved me that my heart, having grown as heavy as iron, grew lighter again, and I allowed myself more hope than I'd been willing to entertain since discovering the collection of heads.

As I turned to lead them from the room, a snow-white German-shepherd mix passed through the closed door. My ghost dog, Boo, had once been the companion of the monks at St. Bartholomew's Abbey, and he had been with me since I left that place less than three months earlier.

He came to me, and I lowered my left arm to let him nuzzle and lick that hand. He feels as real to me as do human spirits, as did Mr. Hitchcock, whatever the director might be in his current incarnation.

Boo was one of only two animal spirits that I have ever seen lingering in this world. The reasons that inhibit some dead people from crossing to the Other Side do not apply to animals, which are blameless. Since Boo left St. Bartholomew's with me, I have suspected that he had stayed in this world after death so that I would find him, that he hung out with me not for companionship but because eventually I would need him in a crisis.

Perhaps eventually was now.

The sudden appearance of the dog, the sight of which usually comforted me, alarmed me this time. I thought at once that someone might be in the third-floor hallway, approaching this room, perhaps an entire contingent of cultists, though the Kens had implied that they would be conveying the seventeen sacrifices to the terrace at the appropriate time.

Pistol in hand, I went to the door, which was the only exit from the room, because going out the window would put us in the hands of those apostles of evil on the second-floor deck. I listened, heard nothing over the excited babble of the crowd below, opened the door, stuck my head out, and found the hall deserted.

When I turned, the girl with the ponytail beckoned me. Her brow was furrowed, and she shifted weight back and forth from one foot to the other, as if something excited her.

Leaving the door ajar, I said, "Come on, come on, let's go."

Because she was at an end of the line, she led the other kids across the room. But just short of me, she stopped and reached back as far as she could with her left arm, to keep the maximum distance between her and the second child in the procession.

She whispered, "I have to tell you something."

Ken #1 had said a gong would sound, summoning them to escort the sacrifices to the terrace. I expected to hear it at any moment.

"Tell me later," I said.

"No," the girl said adamantly, although still whispering. "It's really important. I can see him, too."

"See who?"

She craned her head forward, and I lowered mine, and in an even fainter whisper that those behind her could not hear, she said, "The others don't see him, but I do. The dog. I see the dog and how you let him lick your hand."

# Thirty-three

IN MY ALMOST TWENTY-TWO YEARS, I HAD encountered only one other who could see spirits, the English boy whom I mentioned earlier. I had known him less than a day before he had been crushed to death between a stone wall and a runaway truck.

Risking the gong, certain now that the moment for which Boo lingered in this world would soon come, I closed the door, dropped on one knee before the girl, and matched her whisper.

"What's your name, sweetheart?"

"Verena. Verena Stanhope."

"You see people, too, people no one else sees."

Her eyes searched mine, and it seemed to me that the gray-green shade of them darkened just before she said, "Dead people, you mean."

"I see them, too, Verena."

Her eyes were celadon saucers but bottomless, of such great depth that she could take in the knowledge of whole worlds and have room in that gaze for still more.

I said, "You're not afraid of the dead people."

"No. They're just . . . sad mostly."

"You're a strong girl, I know. It's made you stronger."

She looked away from me, as though praise embarrassed her, but then she met my eyes again. "Mister, I sure have a lot of stuff to ask you."

"That will have to wait, Verena."

She nodded and glanced at Boo, who had joined our huddle. "I've never seen an animal ghost before."

"I suspect he's been hanging around me these past few months just for this night. What this means, I think, is that something will happen to keep me from leading you out of this place, and the dog will be your guide."

My words alarmed her. "No, we *need* you."

"Maybe not if you have Boo. That's his name."

"No, you," she said, and clutched my arm with her free hand.

"You've been given a gift, Verena, and it will never fail you. You can fail the gift, but not the other way around. You understand?"

After a hesitation, she nodded.

I said, "You have to do what you have to do, always and without complaint. I know you can. I know you will."

Boo licked the hand with which she gripped me.

"We have to go," I said. "Lead the other kids behind me. And if something happens . . . follow the dog. Wherever he takes you, don't be afraid. He won't fail you."

The girl let go of my arm and quickly kissed my cheek before I could stand up.

I knew what she must be thinking, the very thing that she had earlier said to the others to calm them: *If he has to, he'll die for us.*

"I will, if it comes to that," I assured her, and saw that she understood the promise.

Into the hall, Boo first, then me, and then the seventeen with Verena in the lead. I turned right, toward the back stairs that I had climbed earlier.

From the crowd gathered on the cantilevered deck outside, cries of excitement rose, a swelling wave of sound that was partly a shriek of cold, savage delight and partly a wail of adulation, of *veneration*. Never before had I heard human voices devoted to such an expression, and in spite of its source, the roar was so *in*human that I shuddered as if I were as boneless as a sea medusa.

With a backward glance, I saw that several of the children were all but paralyzed by the deranged chorus. But Verena encouraged them, and pulled them, and with the urging of some of the more stalwart, the reluctant ones came along.

Before I was halfway to the stairs, the volume of the demented crowd subsided but swelled again, louder, louder and markedly more belligerent, more infernal, and more eerily ecstatic than it had been the first time.

The pandemonium inspired in me two feelings that I didn't recall having previously been afflicted by simultaneously, stark terror and sorrow, terror at the prospect of falling into the hands of such people, sorrow at the realization of what they had lost—or thrown away—in their enthusiasm for the thrill of license, for the rewards of absolute corruption, and for the comfort of being in bondage to a master who would, for all their days in this world, provide for them anything they wanted, without admonition or rebuke.

As Boo passed through the stairwell door and as I opened it after him, the cacophony briefly subsided only to increase a third time, crescendoing to a Bedlam pitch. But then, as if an orchestra conductor had slashed his baton down to command a full stop, the roar abruptly became a silence.

Two seconds later, when Verena reached me at the stairwell door, the gong was struck. I could not conceive of its size, because the note was so low and so powerful that it echoed *bong-ong-ong-ong-ong* through my bones as if it would disjoint me, and the building around me rattled and shimmied as it would have done in an earthquake.

At the farther end of the third-floor hallway, one of the modern ceiling lights morphed into a chain-hung lamp with a conical shade. Over there, too, a smooth gray blandness spread across the plastered ceiling, across the wallpaper, across the wooden floor and carpet runner, creeping toward us.

Boo waited on the landing. I urged Verena to follow the dog, and promised to provide protection at the end of the procession. "Hurry, girl. *Hurry!*"

As the children hustled past me into the stairwell, I watched what they could not see behind them: another of the nine low-profile ceiling fixtures transforming into a crude hanging lamp, and then a third, the grayness seeping rapidly toward me.

The last of the children entered the stairs as the sixth hanging lamp appeared, and I would have followed them if a door hadn't opened at the farther end of the hallway, perhaps the door to another set of stairs. The figure who stepped through that door was at too great a distance for me to see his face in fine detail, but by his height and weight and body type, by the way that he moved, I at once recognized myself, the Other Odd. When he drew nearer, I would surely see that he was my twin but for one detail: If Mr. Hitchcock could be believed, the lesser demon known as a senoculus would have three eyes clustered on each side of its head.

Although the cultists wanted the seventeen captives for the cruel sacrifices they had gathered here to celebrate, the senoculus wanted only me. If I followed the children, I would draw this thing to them; and I couldn't guess what would happen then. I couldn't risk that instead of providing them with protection, I would bring upon them their destruction with mine.

I stood my ground in the open stairwell door, watching the hallway in my world morph into a hallway in Elsewhere, the senoculus approaching just behind the transformation.

By the power of its will, the demon was causing that in-between realm to emerge and my reality to recede. In the stable in Elsewhere with its collection of heads, when I wanted to leave, I had brought my world to the fore and caused this one to submerge by a similar act of will.

In spite of my gift and the weird life that I live, I am not an expert in the occult. I have always thought it wise not to study that subject, for the same reason that it isn't wise to make a party game of a Ouija board. Don't knock on a door if you don't know what might open it.

Nevertheless, I thought I understood enough about the way of such things to safely assume that the senoculus was native to the lightless wasteland and could also prowl the in-between world that I named Elsewhere. But it could not come at will into the world of the living, my world, unless conjured either by true believers and kept restrained in a pentagram by proper rituals, or unless it was drawn to take residence in one of the living by whatever action or weakness might be an invitation to possession.

Likewise, I was native to this world of ours and could, when I encountered a way station, move about in Elsewhere. But I could not go from Elsewhere into the wasteland. I was not Orpheus, the figure of Greek legend, who was able to enter Hell to try to rescue his beloved wife, Eurydice. Anyway, Stormy Llewellyn was not in Hell; I had no need to rescue her.

And so this entire residence was a way station. With acts of will, both I and the senoculus could make it emerge from beneath—or submerge below—the world of the living, to which I currently belonged, though perhaps not for much longer. In a contest between me and this creature, I suspected that its ability to summon Elsewhere around us was much more powerful than my ability to make that realm recede. We fry cooks can be a stubborn bunch, but demons have a reputation for obstinacy that way exceeds ours.

The seventh ceiling light remade itself into a chain-hung lamp, and my pursuer drew close enough in the sullen light for me to see his wealth of eyes, my face grotesquely ornamented, and I recalled both the cold, soft feel of this thing and its inhuman strength.

The only advice that Mr. Hitchcock had had for me regarding the senoculus was *Run, Mr. Thomas. Run.* Even if he was not my guardian angel, which he had denied being, he was playing for the right team, and his advice should no doubt be heeded.

I intended to delay as long as necessary before stepping out of the hall and slamming the door. I hoped that good Boo would have led Verena and the other captives all the way down to the mudroom before I followed them. Although the senoculus apparently wanted me above all others, there was every reason to suppose that if it saw the children or smelled them—all that delicious innocence—it would be compelled to fall upon them.

In our previous encounter, this thing had not passed through walls as a spirit could, and it had not floated along swiftly above the floor as Mr. Hitchcock had done. I assumed that in Elsewhere, if not in its native wasteland, its means of getting from Point A to Point B were no more sophisticated than mine, an assumption that, if wrong, might lead to a hideous, cold kiss and to something worse than possession.

The eighth of nine ceiling lights metamorphosed into a lamp on a chain, the gray of faux concrete crawled closer, and the senoculus spoke in my voice as he strode forward. "Give me your breath, piglet. I want it *now*."

I crossed the threshold, slammed the door, and descended only ten steps, two at a time, before I heard the door crash into the upper-landing wall behind me.

Even if the kids were out of the stairwell, they surely had not already left the mudroom. If I managed to plunge to the bottom of the stairs without being snared by the senoculus, I would bring it with me, and it would be upon those innocents before all of them could escape the house, where—according to my theory—it could not pursue them.

I hit the landing and flew pell-mell off it as the

walls turned gray around me. The stairs were treacherous at high speed, my balance never that of a circus aerialist, and I caromed off the walls as I dove into that waterless well.

From behind me, with an intimacy that made the skin crawl on the nape of my neck, the thing said, "Let me suck your tongue, piglet."

# Thirty-four

QUICK THROUGH THE DOOR AT THE LANDing, out of the stairwell, onto the second floor, I heeded the advice of baseball great Satchel Paige, who said about life in general, "Don't look back. Something may be gaining on you." I ran as I had never run while on my high-school baseball team, because in baseball, happily, no rule allows the opposing team to bring in a supernatural soul-stealer to chase down the runner between bases.

A short hall led to a pair of open French doors and a wider hall beyond. There were rooms behind closed doors to the right and open archways to the left, beyond which lay an enormous chamber lined with leatherbound books and furnished as a grand drawing room that offered numerous elegant seating areas on richly patterned Persian carpets. In the farther wall were sets of French doors standing open to the deep deck on which the crowd of cultists, their backs to me, waited for the Kens to appear with the children on the terrace below.

Ahead of me, on the right, elevator doors opened. A man sporting Oscar the Grouch eyebrows and a Snidely Whiplash mustache, with a chin beard unsuitable for *any* cartoon character or Muppet, appeared with a bottle of champagne in each hand, the wire coiffes having already been removed and the corks popped, a thin vapor rising from the open necks. His expression told me that six-eyed death was on my heels, that Satchel Paige was a man of deep insight, as usual.

I threw myself against the wall on my right, gracelessly slid-dropped-rolled-scrambled past the guy with all the facial hair, who found himself in the direct path of the senoculus. In that instant, my theory that the demon must be interested only in me proved to be woefully wrong. The thing leaped upon him, driving him to the floor, champagne bottles rolling away in gouts of foam and sparkling pale-gold wine. With savage violence, the senoculus slammed a knee into its victim's crotch, then a second time even more violently, which seemed to be bad sportsmanship even for a demon. It seized the man's throat and pressed down upon him, lowering its face toward his.

Having slid-dropped-rolled-scrambled to the elevator just as the senoculus took down the party guy, I was alarmed to see the doors already sliding shut. The demon probably wouldn't be distracted more than a few seconds by this appetizer, not long enough for me to get out of sight into a stairwell. I thrust one arm between the doors and had the disturbing thought that it would be amputated below the elbow when they proved to be as sharp as guillotine blades. I knew I should never have watched that Wes Craven movie. Instead, the electric eye triggered the safety mechanism, the doors glided open. I rolled into the elevator, thrust to my feet, pressed the 1 on the floor-selection panel, then pressed the CLOSE DOOR button.

On the floor beyond the doors, the guy on his back was trying to scream, probably not because of the spilled champagne, but the hand of the demon at his throat choked off his cry, so that he was able to make, inappropriate to the moment, a sound more like Donald Duck in a fit of pique. In addition to having six eyes in clusters of three, the senoculus proved to be somewhat less than my identical twin when it opened its mouth and a long forked tongue fluttered out. It licked teasingly at the lips of the luckless guy who had only wanted to have a little bubbly while he watched children being tortured and murdered.

Making urgent sounds as if I needed to go to the bathroom, which fortunately I did not, I pressed the CLOSE DOOR button again. Again.

Past the struggling pair, beyond the open archways, everything changed in the grand drawing room, carpets and furniture and books vanishing left to right as a bland gray wave remade the building in my world into a building in Elsewhere. The chamber wasn't entirely empty. I saw pallets on which were stacked what appeared to be gold bars, hundreds of them, which suggested that the cult used that room in Elsewhere as a secret vault and that they knew something about the future of the U.S. monetary system that might be of interest to *The Wall Street Journal*. The crowd on the deck, waiting impatiently for the spectacle on the terrace, had vanished, apparently remaining on the deck in the world they shared with me. Mr. Champagne, already in the clutches of the senoculus, had the misfortune to be trapped here, which suddenly made me wonder why *I* was still trapped in this realm, why I had not remained in the building in my world when the senoculus willed us into Elsewhere.

The demon forced its mouth onto the open mouth of Mr. Champagne, which must have been an unpleasant kiss for both of them, complicated as it was by the forked tongue and the elaborate and now disarranged mustache.

Although I had done nothing—*nothing*—to the elevator, it seemed to be holding a grudge against me, like a really pissed-off machine in one of those movies about killer cars, which I had mocked earlier but now regretted mocking.

CLOSE DOOR, CLOSE DOOR, CLOSE DOOR, CLOSE DOOR.

My thumb was wearing out.

The dying man thrashed helplessly under his assailant. His eyes bulged in their sockets. His meaty face flushed red, and then purple, and then began to fade to gray as his thrashing subsided. Throughout this good-bye kiss, the senoculus made a series of greedy, disgusting noises that might have been like the groans of pleasure issuing from a ménage à trois that included Hannibal Lecter, the nest queen from *Aliens,* and Gumby.

I drew one Glock. Bullets didn't faze this thing. I drew the other Glock. Forget Clint Eastwood. Two-Gun Odd is in town. Yeah, right. I holstered both weapons.

The doors began to close, and I was so grateful that I wanted to kiss them, except that the very idea of a kiss had been rendered icky for the foreseeable future.

Crouched atop its victim, the senoculus raised its mouth from the dead man's face. A little cloud of vapor, reminiscent of that which had been wafting from the open champagne bottles, floated in its open mouth, enwrapping its hideous tongue. When thin ribbons of that mist began to slip away between the demon's lips, it abruptly sucked them back, closed its mouth, and swallowed. As it looked at me through the gap between the closing doors, its six eyes were clouded, perhaps with ecstasy, but suddenly they cleared, and the thing threw itself at the doors—too late.

With a sigh and hiss indicating that it was moved from below by a hydraulic ram rather than by hoist cables and counterweights, the elevator started down.

Relieved, I closed my eyes, savoring the motion and the sound of descent.

Elisha Graves Otis, who had built the first fully safe elevator in the United States, in a five-story department store in New York City, had probably not lingered in our world when he died in 1861. But if one day his spirit came around to seek my assistance, I would knock myself out to help him cross over to the Other Side.

Maybe the car traveled half the way to the ground floor before coming to a halt.

When I opened my eyes, I stood in the center of a smooth gray cube. The position indicator, now just a flat gray shape above the doors, lacked numbers. The car-station panel beside the doors still offered floor-selection buttons, but none of them had a number on it. I was not in an elevator any longer, but in the half-formed *idea* of an elevator, in Elsewhere.

Nevertheless, I pressed what had been the ground-floor button. Pressed and pressed it. But it had no give to it, no action. None of the other buttons functioned, either.

The *idea* of stairs is a lot more useful than the *idea* of an elevator. As I had proved more than once, you can get from here to there on the idea of stairs, but the idea of an elevator is about as useful as the *idea* of an ice-cream sundae.

Overhead, the light-diffuser panels were gone, as were the fluorescent tubes that had once been behind them. The ceiling was smooth and gray, unmarked even by the outline of the top-exit door that had once been in the center of that space.

A kind of claustrophobia overcame me, made worse by worry for the children. Boo would guide them, yes, but Boo's bite had no effect on living people, and the dead do not bark any more than they talk. I had left the kids with no protection other than words—*I am not yours, you may not touch me*—words that had seemed to mean something when I'd said them, but which I realized now were no more useful to them than was a would-be protector of the innocent who allowed himself to be trapped in the idea of an elevator.

At that moment, I knew one of the seventeen would die, perhaps more than one, perhaps all of them. If I succeeded to any degree this night, it would be but a partial success—with an intolerable element of failure, as on that awful day at the mall in Pico Mundo. The more certain I became of this, the smaller the elevator seemed to be and the more intensely claustrophobia wrapped its suffocating fabric around me.

I pressed on the walls and pried at the doors, to no avail. I almost shouted, though if anyone remained in this particular piece of Elsewhere, it would be the senoculus, which already knew where I was and which would not answer my shout with kind assistance. When I realized that I was circling the gray cube as if I were a frightened rat in a cage, I halted, leaned against a wall, clasped my head in my hands and tried to deny the claustrophobia and the fear for the children that exacerbated it, tried to clear my mind and *think*.

Three realities. The world into which I was born. The blasted black wasteland. Elsewhere.

*Think*.

Our world, a material realm, allowed us to apply the laws of physics and thermodynamics and other knowledge to shape tools, build machines, and use all the riches of nature to provide ourselves with the comforts of civilization, one of which was the leisure to ponder the meaning of our existence. I knew the systems and rules of our world, more or less how it worked and mostly why.

The world of the wasteland, a spiritual realm, call it Hell or what you will, was dark and mean, without grace, populated by spirits that thrived on hatred and pain, that were denied meaning—or had denied it to themselves—that wanted nothing but the destruction of our world, which they might one day achieve through their surrogates among us, and the destruction of themselves, which they would never achieve. If I thought about all of this long enough, I would be able to imagine in pretty accurate detail the systems and rules of *their* world, how it worked and mostly why.

There is, of course, yet another world than these three, the one to which Stormy Llewellyn had gone, but I didn't need to know the systems and rules of that place, because visionaries and theologians have spent millennia pondering them, and I'd probably be given an orientation booklet when and if I ever arrived there.

So then, Elsewhere . . .

Elsewhere was neither largely material nor largely spiritual, but an in-between emptiness, not a world in full, merely an unmapped archipelago of reefs, atolls, and islands of which certain people in our world could make wicked use, into which denizens of the wasteland could venture. In this realm, willpower could shape reality to some extent, but at the same time, both those from my world and those from the wasteland had to move about as if walls and doors and stairways mattered. I did not think that *any* amount of time would be long enough for me to imagine the systems and rules of this eerie place, because it was . . . essentially so formless. No, not that. Because it was . . .

A hard metallic shriek and a cracking-buckling noise drew my attention to the ceiling. Even if I had wanted to live in denial, I couldn't have done so, because as the clamor grew louder, a top-exit panel appeared in the smooth gray ceiling. The *idea* of an exit. It had been thought into existence not by me but by the senoculus, which was even now, on the second floor, prying open the sliding doors to the shaft, intending to descend by a service ladder. This square on the car ceiling wasn't the idea of an exit, really, but the idea of an entrance, a trapdoor by which the demon could get at me.

For a moment, I couldn't understand why it would come after me so indirectly if, with its stronger willpower, it could disable the elevator and halt me between floors. But then I understood that the elevator was at this impasse because our conflicted wills had come to a draw. I wanted the elevator car to descend to the ground floor, from which I might escape into my world, where my enemy could not follow me, and the senoculus wanted the car to return to the second floor, where it could steal everything from me with a kiss, as it had taken life and soul from Mr. Champagne. Its willpower and mine were equally matched.

The senoculus could not *will* the shaft doors above to open because I was willing them to remain closed, which required it to resort to physical effort. My head hurt.

Suddenly I realized that although this plain-gray cube had none of the fluorescent tubes of the car in the real elevator, in the real building, in my world, it nonetheless had light. The *idea* of light, all around, without source. The car should be dark. And it would be black as night just as soon as the demon wanted it that way.

With a last bang and clatter, the busy senoculus apparently succeeded in tearing open the shaft doors on the second floor, because bits of debris ticked against the roof of the car.

Darkness enveloped me. The claustrophobia, having abated slightly, surged back full force.

In the elevator in my world, the rungs of the service ladder would be set in the concrete wall of the shaft. Here in Elsewhere, the *idea* of rungs existed in the *idea* of a concrete shaft. But the senoculus could climb down to the roof of the car as easily on the idea as on the reality.

# Thirty-five

EARLIER I ADMITTED THAT, WHEN I WAS IN high school, lingering spirits distracted me from science studies and math, for which I had no great talent, anyway. English and writing were my strengths, and baseball, and frying anything that might taste good, though that last came naturally and didn't require me to take a class.

The rules of Elsewhere might not have been either a problem of science or math, but figuring them out seemed as daunting to me as mastering trigonometry. I guess that's what froze my mind there in the idea of an elevator, that and anguish at the thought of the kids not making it out of that building alive. Although I'm pretty much a positive guy, especially considering that I'm always slogging through one crap storm or another, I must admit that my anguish almost segued into despair when darkness fell around me and I knew that the Other Odd, with its look-how-scary-I-am six eyes and its stupid forked tongue, was about to descend the service ladder to pop open this can and spoon me out of it.

Then enlightenment. Suddenly I understood that the idea of light in the car had been *my* idea, not a kindness extended to me by the senoculus. And the light had gone out because I had realized that the car should be dark.

The instant I reconsidered that hasty thought, the idea of light returned, all around me, issuing from no discernible source.

If the senoculus and I were equally matched in willpower, with the demon insisting that the elevator return to the second floor and me insisting that it continue down to the ground floor, the stalemate did not necessarily mean that the issue must be decided by a physical confrontation. I had no illusions that I would win in hand-to-hand combat against an undying adversary with supernatural strength. Not even Mr. Schwarzenegger could have hoped to win such a battle in the days before he became a governor and went to seed.

I had supposed that the rules of Elsewhere were impossible to imagine because the place was so formless, independent of the laws of physics and thermodynamics and other systems of my material world. Now, however, my anguish over the children brought me not to despair but to desperation, which is *energized* despair that compels vigorous action. In my desperation, I grasped a most important possibility:

If the senoculus and I were equally matched in will-power, the contest might be decided by which of us was more clever.

Cleverness requires imagination. Evil is not imaginative. It inspires the same transgressions over and over again, with such infinitesimal variation that only the weak-minded are not quickly bored by that way of living. It seeks to destroy, and destruction takes no imagination. *Creation* takes true imagination, the making of something new and wondrous, whether it's a song or an iPad, a novel or a new cooking surface more durable than Teflon, a new flavor of ice cream or spacecraft that can travel to the moon. The vibrant imagination of a fry cook with free will should easily trump the weak imagination of a demon anytime, anywhere.

Instead of willing the elevator car to descend the shaft and being resisted by the senoculus willing it to return to the second floor, I imagined the hydraulic ram that raised and lowered the car in the shaft, and once the idea of the ram was clearly in mind, I imagined it suddenly failing, dropping the car in an instant to the ground floor.

*Wham!* It is a good thing that the fall was only half a story, for otherwise I might have been knocked unconscious or badly injured. But I was only thrown off my feet, and I sprang up at once. The doors flew open before me, as I had imagined they would, and I stepped out of the car, into a hallway.

I remained in Elsewhere, in a smooth gray empty

building, but the layout should be the same as in the real building in my world. I was well aware that the senoculus, that kissing fool, would already be sprinting madly for the entrance to the stairs on the second floor; therefore, I ran faster than I had ever run before. I sought the vacant dining room and found it, sought the vacant kitchen and found it, raced to one of the French doors that faced onto the rear terrace, and opened it. I saw that my reasoning had been correct: My world lay beyond the back door; the building still shared a boundary with the wasteland only on the lake side, where sorcery of some kind had invited the one whom they venerated.

Discovering the true and hidden nature of the world had nearly broken me. I hoped with all my heart that whatever more there might be for me to learn, further lessons could be postponed until I had gotten that dinner of cheese meatloaf, steak fries, and coleslaw, and until I felt confident that I had completed this first semester with my sanity intact.

I hurried across the terrace and about twenty feet into the yard before stopping and turning to look back at the house, lodge, witch's cradle, whatever. Through the windows, I saw not the grayness of Elsewhere, but the warmly lighted house as it had been when I first approached it. Nobody was in the kitchen or visible in other rooms, so they must all be out on the second-floor deck, still waiting for the two Kens to appear with the seventeen sacrifices, although the gong had rung minutes earlier.

Boo and the kids were nowhere to be seen, which must mean they were in the process of making good their escape, if not already off the property.

I resorted to psychic magnetism, picturing Verena Stanhope in my mind's eye, her ponytail and celadon eyes, and at first I felt nothing, nothing. Nothing. Before I could panic, I realized that perhaps my gift might be failing me because I was *demanding* to feel something. As crazy as most of us Californians are, it's nevertheless sometimes true that you have to switch off the motor and go with the flow.

Although the shredding clouds were on the move, it seemed to be the moon that glided into sight, a great round silver ship on a dark but sparkling sea. The moon is very calming, except perhaps for werewolves, and I basked in its light as I took three deep breaths and slowly blew them out.

Suddenly I began to move in the direction that I felt the children might have gone—which turned out to be toward the satanic church where the fourteen ram skulls peered down from high pedestals. I halted after fifty feet, stunned by the prospect that Boo might have led them into that place.

A fourth deep breath, drawn rapidly and blown out hard, cleared my perception, and I realized that they must have followed a route past the church and into the woods beyond. I should stop worrying. In countless true stories, dogs that were lost while on vacation with their families, or that were stolen and taken great distances, found their way home across hundreds of miles of unfamiliar territory. A ghost dog probably had bags and bags of tricks that even the best of living dogs didn't know. Boo must be aware of Mrs. Edie Fischer, because he had been there at the Salvation Army thrift shop when she had been parked at the curb, waiting for me to return. And if Boo had known where to find me precisely when I needed him to lead the children safely away, he would surely know where to find Mrs. Fischer in her superstretch limousine. If for any reason my ghost dog became lost, Mr. Alfred Hitchcock would probably drop in and show him the way.

If I'm insane, a Freudian psychiatrist will be of no help to me whatsoever. By the time we were halfway through analysis, *he* would be in an asylum.

Because I had not passed through this part of the yard on my approach to the house, I hadn't until now seen the circular gazebo, which stood about ten yards to my left. I hurried to it, plucking the Talkabout from my utility belt.

All white, about twelve feet in diameter, graced by elaborate latticework, and with gingerbread around the eaves of the fanciful scalloped roof, it seemed almost to be a mirage, a glimpse of a magical place in Fairyland. Occasionally, with so much to corrupt and destroy, being a committed satanist must get overwhelming, must start to feel, you know, like a *job,* and not an easy one. Some days, they probably want to take a break from the killing and conjuring and endless scheming against the forces of good, take a break and chill out in a less dour atmosphere. Nothing will lighten the spirit more than to spend some time in a whimsical gazebo on a sunny day, with the scent of spring lilacs in the air, birds chirruping all around, while you compose an amusing hate poem and nibble on human sweetbreads.

In the shelter of the gazebo, crouched below the railing that capped its lattice wall, I switched on the Talkabout, made sure the volume was turned low, and said, "Are you there, Mrs. Fischer? Over."

After a mild crackle of static, she said, "Where else would I want to be, dear? Over."

"I was just afraid maybe you were out of range. Be ready, the kids are on their way to you. Over."

"I moved the car out of that funky fire road and closer to your position. Over."

"Good. That's good. They're being led to you by a dog, ma'am, though you won't see it because it's a ghost dog. You'll see *them* sure enough. Over."

"You're such fun, child. It's good to know you're alive. Over."

"Thank you, ma'am. You're fun, too. Over and out."

As I returned the Talkabout to my utility belt and stepped out of the gazebo, clouds claimed the moon once more.

Before I could continue on the kids' trail, I heard voices. When I looked back, a few people were exiting the house, onto the patio. I could see them because they were backlighted, but I didn't think they would see me in the dark of the moon. Three other people appeared around the north end of the house, and more voices arose to the south.

Somebody had been sent to the third floor to see why the Kens hadn't answered the gong. The two were found dead with their sweaters pulled over their heads; and now there would be hell to pay, perhaps literally.

# Thirty-six

NO ONE SHOUTED "GET HIM" OR ANYTHING similar, which seemed to indicate that they had not yet seen me.

The woods were a long way off, nothing but open yard between here and there. The moon would soon emerge once more. Although I wore dark clothes, they would see me when the lunar lamp returned, and I didn't want to lead them in the direction that Boo and the kids had gone.

Between the gazebo and the stable, isolated trees stood here and there, as well as a few shrubs. I drew a Glock and headed that way, as more voices enlivened the night.

They would have guns. They would have knives. God alone knew what all they might have. My swift execution, however, was not what they intended. If they took me alive, I would end up on that steel stage, either here or at another of their secure locations.

They would peel me alive, head to foot, until I spilled every secret that I possessed, which would probably occur even as they were laying out their skinning instruments and sharing with one another fond memories of previous flayings they had conducted together.

I felt like Frodo in Mordor, but without good Samwise to fight alongside me, alone and with no idea where I'd put the damn ring. When Gollum showed up, he would bite off my finger anyway, ring or not, just for the hell of it. If you've never read *The Lord of the Rings*, my apologies for alluding to it at such length.

Huddled under the first tree along my planned route, I scoped the way ahead and couldn't detect any cultists in my path. When I looked back the way I'd come, past the gazebo, I saw three people with flashlights, the beams sweeping the ground ahead of them as they hurried toward their church. The search had begun in earnest.

Before the clouds stopped conspiring with me and the moon became a traitor, I ran in a crouch to a tall pine and sheltered against its trunk long enough to scan the night. I almost bolted for the next bit of cover, but three men appeared, hurrying up the gentle slope from the house, carving away the darkness with their flashlights. I pulled back, putting the pine between us a moment before one of the beams painted the curve of the trunk where I had just been standing.

Because I didn't have a ghost dog to lead me, I

didn't want to make my way through the woods to the road where Mrs. Fischer waited. Psychic magnetism would reliably pull me to her, and there were most likely deer trails that I could follow rather than blunder noisily through the brush, but I would have to use my flashlight, which was out of the question.

I intended to leave via the long driveway by which I'd entered earlier. A crew of cultists would already have taken up position there, guarding the exit. To leave by that route, I would have to be reckless, and I would have to kill everyone I encountered before any of them might go out to the end of the private lane and discover the limo parked along the state route. No doubt Mrs. Fischer was expert with a handgun, smoothed out and fully blue, but she couldn't hold off an army while she loaded the kids in the superstretch.

As the three men continued toward the stable, I saw more flashlights past that building, probing along the tree line. They would soon find the sleeping Dobermans.

The night was a box of dynamite. The fuse had been lit.

Ever since fleeing the house, I'd operated under the assumption that they knew who they were looking for; but that wasn't necessarily true. Rob Burkett, Jinx, and the two Kens were too dead to describe me to anyone. The senoculus knew my face, which was exactly like its face with a more reasonable number of eyes, but just because that demon and all of these devil-worshippers were on the same team didn't mean that they were constantly text messaging one another.

Anyway, in the dark, probing here and there with a light, I might be just another bad guy looking for the intruding bigot who had violated the sanctity of our religious service. Pistol in my right hand, flashlight in my left, I walked boldly away from the pine tree, toward the parking area, beyond which lay the driveway that led out to the state route.

So many flashlights were sweeping this way and that across the large property that I was reminded of the scene in *E.T.* when Peter Coyote and the other feds are searching the woods and fields for any indication of where the little visitor from another planet might have gone. I was E.T. and I really did just want to go home, but these searchers had crossed over from a different movie, *Rosemary's Baby*.

As I walked past the back of the ProStar+, someone came around the side of it and shone a flashlight in my face just as I shone mine in his, and thus began an encounter as choreographed as any Rockettes number. The rhinestone cowboy. High priest of the cult. He wore the suit from the vision in which he had torched three children. He was probably more startled than I was, because he thought that I was dead but I knew that he wasn't. He had a pistol with a silencer, and I had a pistol with a silencer. Simultaneously, we said, "You." We pointed our weapons at each other, but neither of us fired immediately. I hesitated because I suddenly thought there was something I needed to know that only he could tell me. I think he hesitated because, even though I'd taken out the Kens and freed the children, he still felt invulnerable. He said, "Where are they?" I said, "Where are who?" He said, "Listen, pussy boy, I need those kids. I have a commitment, and I'm damn sure gonna keep it." He looked a little fearful, like maybe, if he failed to sacrifice the seventeen, he would spend eternity in Hell, eating toe jam and boogers, and none of it fried. I realized what I needed to ask him, but first I said, "I think everything's now coming full circle for me." With some fury, he said, *"Where are those snot-nosed little bastards?"* I said, "I think soon I've got to go back home." He said, *"You [fornicating] little [fornicating] [fornicator], WHERE ARE THOSE KIDS!"* I asked what I needed to ask: "You people, you or others like you, have something planned for Pico Mundo?" His eyes widened, and I had my answer. He shot me in the chest at the same moment that I shot him in the chest. *Whifff, whifff.* Because he wasn't wearing a Kevlar vest, he collapsed. I *was* wearing one, but I also collapsed, because although the bullet flattened against the bulletproof fabric and didn't penetrate, I felt as though I'd been hit in the breastbone by a hard-pitched baseball. He dropped his pistol. I dropped my flashlight. I knocked his weapon beyond his reach. He tried to kick my gun hand, but with a bullet lodged in the torso, he lacked the strength to follow through. He coughed up some blood, and I spit out a little blood because

I'd bitten my tongue. He was weak and going fast. He called me a disgusting name that suggested I had committed incest, and as I got my wind back, I called him a nutjob. I took the flashlight from his hand and switched it off.

My flashlight, lying on the ground and aimed at me, drew his attention to something, and in a thin, quavering voice, he said, "Why are you wearing *that*, where did you get *that*?" The object of his astonishment proved to be the diamond-and-ruby exclamation point, the brooch that Mrs. Fischer had pinned to the sleeve of my sweater for good luck. The cowboy's gaze shifted from the pin to my eyes. He said, "Who *are* you? Who are you to be wearing *that*?" Instead of answering him, I said, "I'm done with you, Lyle Hetland," and I put him out of his misery with another shot, this time to the throat.

Gagging but trying to be quiet about it, I got to my feet and leaned against the back of the eighteen-wheeler. A quick survey of the night confirmed that our encounter had attracted no attention. The various clusters of flashlights were fanning the night elsewhere, with increasing urgency.

Being a positive thinker, at least overall, I thought that putting an end to the cowboy must be a good omen, a sign that, with my primary enemy dead, I would walk off this property unscathed. That was when the night *really* got nuts.

# Thirty-seven

AFTER SWITCHING OFF MY FLASHLIGHT, I dragged the cowboy from the back of his truck to the side of it and rolled him under the vehicle, sort of tucking him in for the night, though in this case an endless night. I didn't want to waste time on the task, but leaving the body in the open, where someone might stumble across it, seemed likely to complicate my situation.

No sooner was the dead man safely out of sight than a loud thump issued from the trailer. Back in Los Angeles, when I'd looked inside, I'd found nothing behind the rear doors except that ornate stainless-steel gate worked through with all manner of symbols from a Celtic cross to swastikas, to an ankh, and beyond it an empty trailer painted black with arresting patterns of symbols in bright yellow. A quick series of heavy thumps and a rat-a-tat-tat of rapid knocks convinced me that the cargo space was no longer without freight.

Considering that I'd just freed seventeen kidnapped children from these people, I assumed that the cowboy might have stowed a few more captives in this vehicle between L.A. and here. I should search the dead man for his keys, open the rear doors, and—

"Curiosity is not always well-advised," Mr. Hitchcock said, startling me so badly that I let out the thin little *yeep* that a dog will make if you accidentally step on its tail but offend more than hurt it.

In the milky moonlight, the director had a decidedly spooky-dude quality, not merely because he was Alfred Hitchcock and had been dead for more than thirty years, but also because, I think, he *wanted* to be spooky, the better to impress me with the importance of his words.

"Sir, I'm thinking maybe this guy's got captives stashed in—"

"He has one captive in the truck, Mr. Thomas, but it is not one you would be wise to release."

"But—"

Interrupting me with a raised hand, Mr. Hitchcock said, "I stress again that I am *not* your guardian angel, which I suspect might be a thankless task. But after all you've been through this evening, I would be most disappointed if at the very end you did something so stupid that you got yourself violently dismembered."

"That would disappoint me, too."

"The gentleman who owned this truck used an ancient ritual to call forth an entity and to imprison it herein."

I said, "Hmmm. Call forth. Entity."

"As long as he kept it in his control, he shared in its power."

"What entity?"

"Let's just leave it at that, Mr. Thomas. A demonic entity. Now that the gentleman is dead, the aforementioned entity will not be long contained."

"But—"

Something inside the trailer slammed into the sidewall in front of me, and the sheet-metal skin bulged out toward my face.

I did that *yeep* thing again, and Mr. Hitchcock said, "We had best adjourn to more hospitable territory."

Abruptly something of disturbing power and vehemence began to ricochet around the interior of the trailer, slamming into the walls and ceiling, rocking the entire truck, rattling the trailer against the tractor's frame rail and fifth wheel, making the leaf springs twang like poorly tuned bass fiddles, causing the tires to stutter against the pavement. The entire trailer torqued, and the marker lights in the lower side-rail burst from stress.

As I backed away from the ProStar+, the cultists searching the property grew aware of the ruckus and came running. A multitude of flashlight beams found the truck from all sides, seeming to tie it to the ground as if it were giant Gulliver in Lilliput restrained by the fragile ropes of a legion of tiny natives. As though the eighteen-wheeler took offense at their interest, it began bouncing and rocking so violently that I expected the trailer would uncouple from the tractor and crash onto its side.

Everyone appeared to understand the meaning of this furious display. After a moment of stunned disbelief, they erupted into curses and wordless cries, and sprinted to the cars and SUVs parked just to the east of the big rig.

The funny thing about fear is that after so much of it jammed into a short period of time, you become exhausted, you think you're numb to it, you're drained, you're done with it, nothing can scare you anymore, to hell with everything, you're fearless now. And then some little thing happens, like seeing all these satanic murderers in a state of terror, and your fear is instantly refreshed, your terror tank is full to the brim, and you're cranking away with all cylinders once more.

I thought the smartest thing that I could do might be to take one of those cars from its owner at gunpoint and get out of Dodge with the rest of them.

Mr. Hitchcock seemed to follow my train of thought, because he raised his voice above the din and said, "One would be well-advised to stay as far away as possible from anything belonging to these people, Mr. Thomas. On foot. Hurry now."

I ran past the parked vehicles toward the drive-

way, but before I had reached the place where the
overhanging pines formed a tunnel that continued
all the way out to the state route, a colossal noise
brought me to a halt. I turned to see the ProStar+
whipping around and around, as though it were
caught in a tornado, the trailer torn open as if it
were no sturdier than a juice box, the entire vehicle
casting off parts of itself—until abruptly it collapsed
and lay in ruin, as though a giant invisible child had
grown tired of playing with it.

Mr. Hitchcock appeared at my side. "Mr. Thomas,
this might be difficult for you to believe, considering
my movies, but I was always squeamish in life and
remain so to a lesser extent even now. This is not a
place I wish to be."

A couple of SUVs were pulling out of the parking
area, but they didn't get far. Both tumbled away as if
they had been hit hard by the shock waves of a powerful explosion, though no explosion had occurred.
The other vehicles began to rock back and forth,
shuddering together into a tighter and tighter space,
as if they were inside a circular car-compacting machine similar to those that reduce a full-size sedan into
a cube of metal no bigger than an armchair, although
this one would be a disc or a ball of many vehicles.
Windshields burst, metal squealed and crackled—
and the people trapped in the cars screamed.

I smelled something familiar. That scent as sweet
as incense yet suggestive of decomposition. I had experienced this malodor only once before, when it

came to me from the empty black-and-yellow trailer, through the steel filigree of the elaborate gate of symbols. And again I felt the chill draft that came with the smell, not like a breath as before but a full breeze that prickled my face as though with tiny bits of sleet.

When I glanced toward the lake, I saw torchlight reflected on water. The link between this place and the wasteland had been broken. But the thing that Lyle Hetland had conjured and contained in his eighteen-wheeler was loose now and intent on kicking butt.

A cultist appeared on foot, running for the driveway. Spun off his feet, flailing at nothing I could see, he suddenly came apart in midair in such a spectacular fashion that I recalled Mr. Hitchcock's warning about dismemberment, and I ran for my life.

As I raced along the tunnel formed by the pines that overhung the private lane, the racket behind me increased, and I expected to be suddenly flung into the air, but I passed the halfway point with my head still on my neck and all limbs functioning. I saw the portly director standing on the farther side of the low ranch-style gate, where he had fled in his magical way. He waved at me as I approached, pleased that I had finally gotten the message and acted on it.

The moment that I stepped around the gate, the escalating tumult behind me instantly ceased. Startled by the sudden hush, I stopped, turned, and peered back. The house and grounds were at too great a distance for me to see much, but I could discern that chaos still reigned there.

Mr. Hitchcock said, "They are quite loath to be overheard by neighbors even though none are close, so a certain spell was laid down around the perimeter of their property."

When I stepped behind the gatepost, setting foot in the tree-canopied lane once more, the thunderous noise might have been that of the celestial foundry where entire worlds were cast and set spinning. I preferred the silence where the director stood, and I returned to him.

The night was cool, the mountain bathed in silver light. The moon no longer seemed like a ship on a dark sea. It made me think of a cataracted eye that might suddenly open to stare out from the rotted burial wrappings that swaddled a mummy's face.

"Sir," I asked worriedly, "when does it stop—the destruction, the revenge?"

"Never fear, Mr. Thomas. The entity's rage will be restricted to this property."

"Entity." I let the word have its rhythm, pronouncing the three syllables distinctly, perhaps hoping that it would make more sense to me. I knew its definition. It just didn't make sense. "Entity."

"It doesn't belong in this world, you see. Now that it has been released from its bonds, it will settle scores, so to speak, and then depart."

"You're sure?"

"Very."

"Entity," I said.

"This is all new to you, Mr. Thomas. Now that you've learned a bit more about the true nature of the world, you're worried that from here on, it'll be one damn thing after another."

"Yes, sir. My very thought."

"Take heart. It's unlikely that anything this spectacular will ever happen to you again."

"How unlikely?"

"Highly."

"Entity," I said again.

"Give it time, son. To settle in."

"I'll give it a little time to settle in."

"There you go."

From two hundred feet uphill, where she was parked on the shoulder of the state route, Mrs. Fischer switched on the headlights of the limousine, flashed them at me a couple of times, and then switched them off.

"She has the children safely gathered, Mr. Thomas. Not a one was lost or even injured."

"Good old Boo."

"Dogs," he said with evident fondness. "I have always had dogs. As will you, Mr. Thomas."

"You can call me Odd. I'd like that. Or Oddie."

"Yes, Mr. Thomas. And you may call me Hitch."

"Yes, sir. Thank you, sir."

Mr. Hitchcock chose neither to dematerialize like an ordinary spirit nor to float swiftly ahead of me, feet off the ground. He walked at my side, one hand on my shoulder.

"When I was alive in the material sense," he said, "I had many faults, as everyone does. At times I could be something of a glutton as regards both food and drink."

I had no idea where this was leading.

"I remember once at the Chelsea Arts Ball at the Albert Hall, in London, I had much too much to drink and everything suddenly seemed to be receding from me—people, walls, everything. I'm afraid I embarrassed dear Alma."

"Sir, it's hard to imagine you reeling around, out of control." As a director he was known as a perfectionist and a control freak.

"Oh, I didn't embarrass my patient wife in that way. I simply clammed up and found it impossible to engage in conversation, which made me appear to be bored and rude."

We walked a few steps in silence.

He said, "I was raised by Jesuits, you know. They were fierce disciplinarians. I lived in horror of the prior and his punishments, so much so that, as a boy, I developed a morbid revulsion from any behavior that might be considered bad. I came to fear my own capacity for evil and error, which developed into a dread of authority that was almost phobic."

Perhaps it was best that I not ask what capacity for evil the director of *Psycho* had worried about in himself. But then it turned out to be less than I might have imagined.

"As an adult, I loved to drive, to be behind the wheel with open road ahead. But I so dreaded being stopped by a traffic cop—dreaded it like death, Mr. Thomas—that I hardly ever drove. I left all the driving to Alma or hired drivers even before I could afford to hire them. Always questioning your motivations is a healthy thing, but *fearing* your capacity for doing the wrong thing, so that you retreat from many aspects of life, is a terrible error in itself."

If I'd had a father capable of wisdom and interested in passing it along to a son, this might have been what it would have felt like.

I said, "My girl, Stormy Llewellyn, she was the best person I've ever known. She was amazing, sir. She believed that this life is not the first of two but the first of three."

"Quite the philosopher for a young lady who worked in an ice-cream shop," he said sincerely, not with a wry edge.

After the scene that I had just witnessed, nothing more could surprise me that night.

I said, "Stormy called this life boot camp. She said we have to persevere through all this world's obstacles and all the wounds that it inflicts if we want to earn a second life. We're in training, see. After boot camp, there's what she called service. Our life of service will be full of tremendous adventure, as if you had rolled all the adventure novels ever written into one."

"And the third life, Mr. Thomas?"

"She thought that after we finish service, then we receive our eternal life."

I stopped, withdrew my wallet from a hip pocket, and opened it to the plastic window in which I kept the card. I could read it in the moonlight. In fact, I could have read it in the dark: YOU ARE DESTINED TO BE TOGETHER FOREVER.

"We got it from a fortune-telling machine in an arcade at a carnival when we were just sixteen."

"Gypsy Mummy," he said, naming the machine. "Quite a colorful device. I might have used it in a movie if I'd made a few more."

I looked up from the card and met his stare. The kindness in his eyes reminded me of my closest friends in Pico Mundo.

An owl hooted nearby, and a more distant owl responded. Two ordinary owls in an ordinary night.

"I believe this card, sir. I trust it totally. I'm sure it's the truest thing I've ever known."

He smiled and nodded.

"What do you think, sir? I'd really like to know. What do you think about the card?"

"You're not ready to leave this world yet, Mr. Thomas."

"I don't think it'll be much longer. It's all coming around to how it started in Pico Mundo nineteen months ago."

"What must be *will* be."

I smiled. "You sound like Annamaria now."

"And why wouldn't I?" he asked, which gave me something to think about.

Putting away my wallet, I said, "Boot camp. Sometimes, sir, the training seems unnecessarily hard."

"In retrospect, it won't," he assured me.

Mr. Hitchcock walked with me all the way to the car. He pointed not to the front door on the starboard side but to the door behind it, which served the long passenger compartment, and the power window purred down.

I leaned into the window and saw the children crammed into the back of the limousine, a couple of them sitting on the floor. None of them appeared to be uncomfortable. They looked tired but awake, wide awake.

They were silent, but they were not afraid. Neither I nor they needed to say anything just then.

Boo was lying on the floor at Verena Stanhope's feet. The girl gave me two thumbs up.

I withdrew my head, and the window purred shut.

"I'm not sure how we handle it from here," I said.

"Mrs. Fischer will know exactly."

"Yeah," I said, as I began to take off my shoulder holsters. "I guess I'd be surprised if she didn't."

He pointed to the moon. Although the night sky appeared to be clear around that sphere, there must

have been thin mist or dust at some altitude to dif-
fract its light, for the moon had developed a corona,
concentric circles changing color outward from pale
blue to purple-red.

"Quite a visual," he said. "Nicely moody. You
could do it as a trick shot, of course, but the real
thing is prettier."

"I still can't get used to you talking." I turned my
back to him, and he unbuckled the bulletproof vest.
"I sure wish we had time to discuss your movies. I
have at least a thousand questions."

"I'm not about movies anymore, Mr. Thomas."

Turning to him, I said, "Will I be seeing you
again, sir?"

"One cannot say."

"Cannot or will not?"

He put a forefinger to his lips, as if to say that we
must not discuss such things.

As he began to rise off the ground, he said, by
way of good-bye, "Oddie."

"Hitch."

He didn't merely ascend straight up, but also
moved away from me laterally as he rose into the
darkness, fast and then faster, until he vanished behind a remaining patch of clouds.

What a wonderful ham he was.

An owl hooted and another owl returned the call.
Two ordinary owls in an extraordinary night, in a
world unfathomed and perhaps unfathomable by
the living.

# Thirty-eight

ALTHOUGH THIS SHOULD HAVE BEEN A TAXing day for a woman of Mrs. Fischer's age, she appeared to be fresh and alert as she piloted the Mercedes limousine down from the forested heights toward the flats where cactus and mesquite flourished.

Glancing at me, she said, "How are you, child?"

After a long moment of silence while I considered my condition, I said, "It's getting easier, and that scares me."

"You mean the killing."

The guns, the Kevlar vest, and the utility belt were piled on the floor in front of my seat. My feet straddled all that gear.

"Yes, ma'am. The killing."

"How many."

"Five."

I thought of Jinx. How blue the eye beneath the

yellow contact lens. I wondered how much different she would have looked without the Goth makeup and the attitude.

Mrs. Fischer said, "You know what they were— those people. You know what they had done and would have done."

"Yes, ma'am. And I only did what I had to do. But it was still too easy."

"Maybe that was because they were such worse people than you've had to deal with before."

"Maybe."

We reached the flats, passed Jeb's Trading Post, the clusters of modest houses, and then the sprawling complex of large buildings that might have been warehouses. At the interstate, Mrs. Fischer headed east toward Las Vegas.

Four of the children had been snatched from Vegas, but not the others. "Where are we going, ma'am?"

"Exactly where we need to go. You'll see."

After a while, we left the interstate for Las Vegas Boulevard South, where the night was splashed with neon pulsing-rippling-spiraling in different rhythms that somehow all seemed to suggest the thrust and throb of sex, where fountains gushed and waterfalls foamed, where the architecture promised elegance or wild delight, or both, where every nuance of design said that money was bliss and that godlike power could be bought or at least rented, where marquees announced the royalty of entertainment, where multitudes surged along the sidewalks, going to or from a show, moving from one casino to another.

I suppose those tourists might have been portraits of gaiety, rejoicing, sweet contentment, and happiness in all its shades. But where I saw those expressions, they seemed to be masks, and often I saw faces shaped by disquiet, misgiving, trepidation, confusion, and doubt, with body language that translated as anxiety and impatience. Perhaps it was my mood, the head collection and other atrocities still so fresh in my mind, but these people seemed like refugees from places that had gone drab and lusterless for reasons that they could not fully understand. They had come here to find the fun that had been lost elsewhere, fun and brightness and freedom and hope, but they were beginning to suspect, still on some unconscious level, that this hundred-billion-dollar biggest carnival in the history of the world was not an oasis, after all, but just another version of the desert from which they'd fled.

At that moment, there wasn't a party anywhere in the world that I couldn't have brought down in five minutes flat.

Mrs. Fischer drove off the famous Strip, zigzagged from one long, flat street to another, found some hills, and at last pulled into the driveway of a substantial but welcoming house with warm light aglow in all its windows. A friendly couple in their fifties at once came out of the residence to welcome us and to assist with the children, all of whom were escorted inside. No names were offered, and I was not asked for mine, but they greeted me as if we had long known one another—as was true of everyone I would later encounter here.

I sensed by the way that Boo remained faithfully at Verena's side, he might not be my ghost dog anymore, but might have attached himself to a new companion.

This expansive residence, on two levels, was a place where books were honored, as almost every room contained shelves of them. These people had built a shrine to family and to friendship, with clusters of framed photographs of loved ones on tables and mantels and in wall arrangements. Every space seemed to be designed for celebration, with numerous carefully considered groupings of furniture, cozy nooks, and window seats to accommodate easy conversation. Although the place was clean and neat and tastefully appointed, you felt that you could put your feet up on anything, as you might in your own home.

I can describe what happened in that house over the next few hours, but I cannot explain it. No experience of my life has been so radiant, other than my time with Stormy in our years together, and yet so mysterious.

We were brought into the living room, where three dogs awaited us: a golden retriever, a Bernese mountain dog, and a Bouvier des Flandres, all of which at once began to circulate, like huge stuffed toys come to life, among the children.

On the kitchen island, on the dining-room table, on a side table in the living room were trays of cookies and little cakes, and the children were offered drinks, though most of them at first declined. They were still stressed, if not in some degree of shock. At least four of these knew that their parents had been killed. And the limousine ride here, to an unknown destination, had provided no decompression.

After perhaps ten minutes, nine children joined our group, not all of them the sons and daughters of our hosts, because the nine seemed to range in age from seven to ten. I will not say that they were all beautiful by the standards of our culture, which is obsessed with models and airbrushed celebrities, but they *were* beautiful to me, fresh-faced and glowing with good health.

The nine were the most socially adept group of kids that I had ever seen. They were neither hesitant nor forward, and certainly not territorial as most kids are, but spread out at once among our seventeen rescuees, welcoming them, asking about them, touching them affectionately in that unself-conscious way that childhood friends of some duration can be with one another.

At first the seventeen were awkward, uncertain, confused, but sooner than I would have thought possible, they were drawn out of their shells. The twenty-six of them separated into groups of three and four, always with at least one of these new children included, and they wandered off to corners all over the house.

I approached Mrs. Fischer and said, "What's all this? What's happening here?"

"What needs to happen, dear. Just watch. You'll see."

"Who are these other children?"

"Watch and see," she repeated, and pinched my cheek.

I wandered the house, upstairs and down and up again, in a state of wonder as events progressed. Soon our traumatized seventeen were engaged in conversations with the nine and with each other, and now and then I saw tears and trembling and despair that somehow didn't last. I stood listening to many of these conversations, and they all made sense to me and seemed in fact beautiful at the time, but as soon as I walked away from any one of them, I couldn't quite recall what had been said.

The three dogs circulated ceaselessly. Often I came upon one of our seventeen clinging almost desperately to the golden retriever or the Bernese or the Bouvier. Later, their anxious looks and pained expressions had given way to smiles, some tentative but nonetheless smiles.

Cookies appeared in small hands, and mugs of hot chocolate or cold milk, glasses of Coca-Cola. Conversations became more animated, sometimes almost intense, and though I eavesdropped everywhere, and understood, I at once seemed to forget, as if the things they said were truths and consolations that only a child's mind could retain.

For most of those three hours, I felt as if I were in a dream, though every minute of it was as real as any experience of my life. I ate cookies, traveled continuously through the house, and felt at peace as I had not felt in a long time. I knew that whatever might be happening to our seventeen—guidance or therapy, or something utterly different from either—it was a thing of great goodness.

The most dreamlike moment came at the start of the third hour, when five new adults appeared, though the doorbell had not rung. I wondered at once if they were parents of the nine, not because they particularly resembled those children, but because they shared that glow of health and quiet beauty that so distinguished the youngsters, and they were in their late twenties or thirties, the right age to be the parents. No names were offered, none were asked, and the five newcomers spread out through the house, each sitting down to converse with a group of children.

I remembered no more of these new conversations than I did of the previous ones, but I often found myself smiling. None of these five adults made an effort to speak to me. They changed groups from time to time, as if all of them wanted to be sure to speak with all of our seventeen, and when I passed one of them in a room or hallway, I felt the urge to introduce myself, to ask about them. But though I am not by nature shy, I found myself reluctant to intrude. Strangest of all, when I made eye contact with one of them, I looked away, and felt that I shouldn't ask them to see what my eyes had seen, whatever that might mean.

Later in the evening, I noticed that the hiero-glyphics had been removed from the brows of the seventeen. I hadn't seen it being done.

As I made that realization, Verena Stanhope came to me to say that the questions she'd had for me had been answered. She thanked me, and I thanked her for being so brave when it counted the most. She took my hand, and on contact I smiled at what I saw of her in the years to come. "You'll have a beautiful life," I told her.

Still later, I found myself sitting on a sofa, my wallet open in my hands to the card from Gypsy Mummy. I didn't know how long I had been sitting there, but when I raised my head, the mysterious five adults and nine children seemed to have gone. Our hosts and Mrs. Fischer were ushering the children from the living room to the foyer.

I asked, "What's happening?"

Mrs. Fischer said, "They're taking the children home."

"Home where?"

"Each to his or her own home—except for the four who lost their parents. Those will be taken to their grandparents."

The husband of our hostess opened the door, and

his wife led the three Payton kids down the front walk to a car parked at the curb.

I stepped onto the front porch to watch a young couple, whose car it must have been, as they greeted Jessie, Jasmine, and Jordan, and got them aboard.

As Mrs. Fischer joined me on the porch, I said, "You mean they will be driven back to Barstow."

"Yes, dear. They'll be let off at their front walk and watched until their parents open the door to them."

"Do the parents know they're coming?"

"They'll all go home by surprise. Let off at the street but watched until they're safe, so no one will know who delivered them."

The couple with the car were not among the five adults whose eyes I had been unable to meet for longer than two seconds. I asked who they were.

"Good people," Mrs. Fischer said.

That car pulled away, and a moment later another arrived. Our hostess had by then returned to escort a little boy to his ride.

Soon all seventeen were gone, Verena Stanhope in the company of Boo. The ghost dog gave my hand one last lick before departing. Now there were only Mrs. Fischer and the couple whose house this was, and the three dogs, who seemed remarkably bright-eyed considering all the petting they had received and all the comfort they had given.

Our host and hostess wanted to hug Mrs. Fischer, and then they wanted to hug me, and I found I wanted to hug them, though if I had known their names, I had forgotten them.

As we drove away in the limousine, I asked, "What about the police?"

"Tomorrow," Mrs. Fischer said, "the authorities in the various jurisdictions will receive phone calls regarding the location of the property where that foul group of people held their sick games. What they find there will no doubt astonish them."

"What will the children say?"

"That they were driven somewhere and then held in a room for a while, after which some nice people came and untied them and took them home."

"Your limousine is very identifiable, ma'am. And my face was once in the newspapers a lot."

"The children won't remember you or me, Oddie. They won't recall things that might have been said to them by their disgusting captors or what terrible things they were afraid might happen to them. They have been given the gift of forgetfulness."

"Was it in the cookies, the hot chocolate?"

"Good heavens, dear, nothing as crude as drugs. And before you say hypnosis, not that either."

"Then what, how?"

She flashed that irresistible dimpled smile, patted my shoulder, and said, "You know what happened back there, sweetie."

"But I don't. I'm mystified. Who were those nine children and then those five older people?"

"Sleep on it, Oddie. Then you'll wake up knowing."

"What if I don't wake up knowing?"

"Then ask your Mr. Hitchcock if he knows them."

I brooded on that awhile. Then I said, "With all your resources, why didn't you put together a rescue for those children?"

"For heaven's sake, sweetie, *you* are part of my resources."

"Oh."

As she took the westbound entrance ramp to the I-15, I said, "Where are we going now, ma'am?"

"I'm taking you home."

"That's a long drive, ma'am. We're both too tired for it."

"Oh, I never sleep anymore. I don't have time for sleeping, too much to do."

"Well, I'm wiped out."

"You sleep, my dear chauffeur. I'll wake you when we get there."

I closed my eyes, almost drifted off, then opened them and said, "Problem, ma'am. You picked me up along the highway. You don't know where I live."

"I'll figure it out, child. Don't you worry yourself."

Vegas rapidly fell away behind us, and the Mojave night lay vast and starry.

"The people who owned the house where we took the kids," I said.

"I thought you were asleep."

"Did they just happen to be near enough that you drove there? Or if this had happened in Oklahoma or New Hampshire, or Georgia, would there be other people like them, in other houses that feel so . . . good as that one felt?"

"Some places I might have had to drive farther, but people like them are out there, sweetie. They're out there everywhere."

Later, driving with one hand, Mrs. Fischer shook me half awake, worried because I had been crying in my sleep.

"It's all right, ma'am," I assured her. "I was crying because it was so wonderful."

And because it was so wonderful, I slipped back down into that dream of dogs and children and beautiful people who met my eyes and knew me in full, knew me and did not reject me.

# Thirty-nine

HALF AN HOUR AFTER DAWN, I WOKE AND found that we were cruising the street on which I lived, for the time being, with Annamaria and Tim, the boy we had rescued from the creepy estate named Roseland, in Montecito. Mrs. Fischer parked at the curb in front of the picturesque cottage with the roof draped in yellow bougainvillea.

I sat up straighter in my seat, stretched and yawned.

As she switched off the engine, Mrs. Fischer said, "How do you feel, Oddie?"

"Starved. I need a big pile of breakfast."

"First you need a shower, dear, so the rest of us will have the stomach to take breakfast at the same table with you."

"Sorry, ma'am. Excess sweating is one of the negatives about being a man of action."

We got out of the Mercedes, and looked up at the

power lines from which the fitful wind raised an
eerie but not unpleasant sound.

I escorted Mrs. Fischer away from the front door
and along the brick walkway at the side of the cottage. I wanted to see the ocean and then enter the
house by way of the back porch.

As we stood on the beach, the sky far to the east
might have been by Tiffany, lemon light as clear as
colored lamp glass, but most of the heavens were lost
to an overcast. Steel-wool clouds scoured northward.
With no western sky to lend it color, the sea churned
deep gray. Wind swept the whitecaps off the waves
and, by contrast with that sparkling foam, gray water
became black.

"'When the wind blows the water white and
black,'" I quoted.

As Mrs. Fischer surveyed the vast Pacific, the
singing of the power lines sounded like the serenade
of mermaids, not the sirens whose songs lured sailors
to their death on rocks, but the voices of mermaids
who loved the sea and loved the land and yearned for
one when they had only the other.

Under my sweater, the tiny silver bell that I wore
around my neck rang softly, though I stood quite
still.

Annamaria must have seen us arrive. She appeared beside Mrs. Fischer, and each of them at
once put an arm around the other's waist. The three
of us enjoyed the wind for a while, the sound and

motion of the water, the timeless face of the enduring sea.

Then Annamaria said, "Thanks for bringing him home, Edie."

"For a little while," Mrs. Fischer said.

I wondered if I would ever fully understand the true and hidden nature of the world. Perhaps it didn't matter. I had learned enough about it that, for this sweet moment at least, I knew true joy for the first time in more than nineteen months.

YOU ARE DESTINED
TO BE TOGETHER
FOREVER.

# About the Author

DEAN KOONTZ, the author of many #1 *New York Times* bestsellers, lives in Southern California with his wife, Gerda, their golden retriever, Anna, and the enduring spirit of their golden, Trixie.

www.deankoontz.com

Correspondence for the author should be addressed to:

Dean Koontz
P.O. Box 9529
Newport Beach, California 92658

#1 *New York Times* bestselling author
Dean Koontz is at the peak of his acclaimed
powers with his major new novel

# THE CITY

A rich, multi-layered story that moves
back and forth across decades and generations
as a gifted musician relates the "terrible and
wonderful" events that began in his city in 1967,
when he was ten.

Coming Soon from Bantam Books

Turn the page for a special advance preview

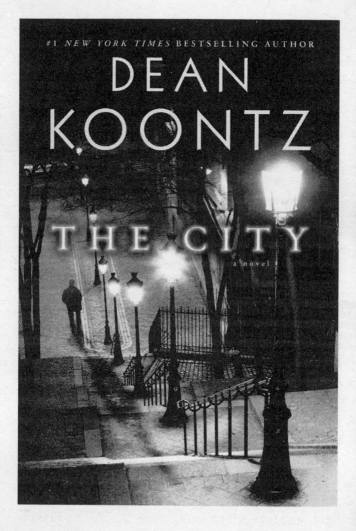

# DEAN KOONTZ

## THE CITY

*a novel*

MY NAME IS JONAH ELLINGTON BASIE HINES Eldridge Wilson Hampton Armstrong Kirk. From as young as I can remember, I loved the city. Mine is a story of love reciprocated. It is the story of loss and hope, and of the strangeness that lies just beneath the surface tension of daily life, a strangeness infinite fathoms in depth.

The streets of the city weren't paved with gold, as some immigrants were told before they traveled half the world to come there. Not all the young singers, or actors, or authors, became stars soon after leaving their small towns for the bright lights, as perhaps they thought they would. Death dwelt in the metropolis, as it dwelt everywhere, and there were more murders there than in a quiet hamlet, much tragedy, and moments of terror. But the city was as well a place of wonder, of magic dark and light, magic of which in my eventful life I had much experience, including one night when I died and woke and lived again.

WHEN I WAS EIGHT, I WOULD MEET THE woman who claimed she *was* the city, though she wouldn't make that assertion for two more years. She said that more than anything, cities are people. Sure, you need to have the office buildings and the parks and the nightclubs and the museums and all the rest of it, but in the end it's the people—and the kind of people they are—who make a city great or not. And if a city is great, it has a soul of its own, one spun up from the threads of the millions of souls who have lived there in the past and live there now.

The woman said this city had an especially sensitive soul and that for a long time it had wondered what life must be like for the people who lived in it. The city worried that in spite of all it had to offer its citizens, it might be failing too many of them. The city knew itself better than any person could know himself, knew all of its sights and smells and sounds and textures and secrets, but it didn't know what it felt like to be human and live in those thousands of miles of streets. And so, the woman said, the soul of the city took human form to live among its people, and the form it took was her.

The woman who was the city changed my life and showed me that the world is a more mysterious place than you would imagine if your understanding of it was formed only or even largely by newspapers and magazines and TV—or now the Internet. I need to tell you about her and some terrible things and wonderful things and amazing things that happened, related to her, and how I am still haunted by them.

But I'm getting ahead of myself. I tend to do that. Any life isn't just one story; it's thousands of them. So when I try to tell one of my own, I sometimes go down an alleyway when I should take the main street, or if the story is fourteen blocks long, I sometimes start on block four and have to backtrack to make sense.

Also, I'm not tapping this out on a keyboard, and I tend to ramble when I talk, like now into this recorder. My friend Malcolm says not to call it rambling, to call it oral history. That sounds pretentious, considering I've never achieved anything that would ensure I'll go down in history. Nevertheless, maybe that's the best term. Oral history. As long as you understand it just means I'm sitting here shooting off my mouth. When someone types it out from the tapes, then I'll edit to spare the reader all the you knows and uhs and dead-end sentences, also to make myself sound smarter than I really am. Anyway, I must talk instead of type, because I have the start of arthritis in my fingers, nothing serious yet, but since I'm a piano man, I have to save my knuckles for music.

Malcolm says I must be a closet pessimist, the way I so often say, "Nothing serious yet." If I wake up with a bad cramp in one calf and walk it out, but there's still pain lingering hours later, and if then Malcolm asks why I'm limping, I'll say, "Just this weird pain in my calf, nothing serious yet." He thinks I'm convinced it's a deepvein blood clot that'll break loose and blow out my lungs or brain later in the day, though that never crossed my mind. I just say those three words to reassure my friends, those people *I* worry about when they have the flu or a dizzy spell or a pain in the calf, because I'd feel relieved if they reassured *me* by saying, "Nothing serious yet."

The last thing I am is a closet pessimist. I'm an optimist and always have been. Life's given me no reason to expect the worst. As long as I've loved the city, which is as long as I can remember, I have been an optimist.

I was already an optimist when all this happened that I'm telling you about. Although I'll reverse myself now and then to give you some background, this particular story really starts rolling in 1967, when I was ten, the year the woman said she was the city. By June of that year, I had moved with my morn into Grandpa's house. My mother, whose name was Sylvia, was a singer. Grandpa's name was Teddy Bledsoe, never just Ted, rarely Theodore. Grandpa Teddy was a piano man, my inspiration.

The house was a good place, with four rooms downstairs and four up, one and a half baths. The piano stood in the big front room, and Grandpa played it every day, even though he performed six nights a week at the hotel and did background music three afternoons at the department store, in their fanciest couture department, where a dress might cost as much as he earned in a month at both jobs and a fur coat might be priced as much as a new Chevy. He said he always took pleasure in playing, but when he played at home, it was *only* for pleasure.

"If you're going to keep the music in you, Jonah, you've got to play a little bit every day purely for pleasure. Otherwise, you'll lose the joy of it, and if you lose the joy, you won't sound good to those who know piano—or to yourself."

Outside, behind the house, a concrete patio bordered a small yard, and in the front, a porch overlooked a smaller yard, where this enormous maple tree turned as red as fire in the autumn. And when the leaves fell, they were like enormous glowing embers on the grass. You might say it was a lower-middle-class neighborhood, I guess, although I never thought in such terms back then and still don't. Grandpa Teddy didn't believe in categorizing, in labeling, in dividing people with words, and neither do I.

The world was changing in 1967, though of course it always does. Once the neighborhood was Jewish, and then it started to go Polish Catholic. Mr. and Mrs. Stein, who had moved from the house but still owned it, rented to my grandparents in 1963, when I was six. They were the first black people to live in that neighborhood. He said there were some problems at the start, of the kind you might expect, but it never got so bad they wanted to move.

Grandpa attributed their staying power to three things. First, they kept to themselves unless invited. Second, he played piano free for some events at St. Stanislaus Hall, next to the church where many in the neighborhood attended Mass. Third, my grandma, Anita, was secretary to Monsignor McCarthy.

Grandpa was modest, but I won't be modest on his behalf. He and Grandma didn't have much trouble also because they had about them an air of royalty. She was tall, and he was taller, and they carried themselves with quiet pride. I used to like to watch them, how they walked, how they moved with such grace, how he helped her into her coat and opened doors for her and how she always thanked him. They dressed well, too. Even at home, Grandpa wore suit pants and a white shirt and suspenders, and when he played the piano or sat down for dinner, he always wore a tie. When I was with them, they were as warm and amusing and loving as any grandparents ever, but I was at all times aware, with each of them, that I was in a *Presence*.

In April 1967, my grandma fell dead at work from a cerebral embolism. She was just fifty-two. She was so vibrant, I never imagined that she could die. I don't think anyone else did, either. When she passed away suddenly, those who knew her were grief-stricken but also shocked. They harbored unexpressed anxiety, as if the sun had risen in the west and set in the east, suggesting a potential apocalypse if anyone dared to make reference to that development, as if the world would go on safely turning only if everyone conspired not to remark upon its revolutionary change.

At the time, my mom and I were living in an apartment downtown, a fourth-floor walk-up with two street-facing windows in the living room; in the kitchen and my little bedroom, there were views only of the sooty brick wall of the adjacent building, crowding close. She had a gig singing three nights a week in a blues club and worked the lunch counter at Woolworth's five days, waiting for her big break. I was ten and not without some street smarts, but I must admit that for a time, I thought that she would be equally happy if things broke either way—a gig singing in bigger and better joints or a job as a waitress in a high-end steakhouse, whichever came first.

We went to stay with Grandpa for the funeral

and a few days after, so he wouldn't be alone. Until then, I'd never seen him cry. He took off work for a week, and he kept mostly to his bedroom. But I sometimes found him sitting in the window seat at the end of the second-floor hallway, just staring out at the street, or in his armchair in the living room, an unread newspaper folded on the lamp table beside him.

When I tried to talk to him, he would lift me into his lap and say, "Let's just be quiet now, Jonah. We'll have years to talk over everything."

I was small for my age and thin, and he was a big man, but I felt greatly gentled in those moments. The quiet was different from other silences, deep and sweet and peaceful even if sad. A few times, with my head resting against his broad chest, listening to his heart, I fell asleep, though I was past the age for regular naps.

He wept that week only when he played the piano in the front room. He didn't make any sounds in his weeping; I guess he was too dignified for sobbing, but the tears started with the first notes and kept coming as long as he played, whether ten minutes or an hour.

While I'm still giving you background here, I should tell you about his musicianship. He played with good taste and distinction, and he had a tremendous left hand, the best I've ever heard. In the hotel where he worked, there were two dining rooms. One was French and formal and featured a harpist, and the decor either made you feel elegant or made you ill. The second was an Art Deco jewel in shades of blue and silver with lots of glossy-black granite and black lacquer, more of a supper club, where the food was solidly American. Grandpa played the Deco room, providing background piano between seven and nine o'clock, mostly American-standard ballads and some friskier Cole Porter numbers; between nine and midnight, three side-men joined him, and the combo pumped it up to dance music from the 1930s and '40s. Grandpa Teddy sure could swing the keyboard.

Those days right after his Anita died, he played music I'd never heard before, and to this day I don't know the names of any of those numbers. They made me cry, and I went to other rooms and tried not to listen, but you couldn't *stop* listening because those melodies were so mesmerizing, melancholy but irresistible.

After a week, Grandpa returned to work, and my mom and I went home to the downtown walk-up. Two months later, in June, when my mom's life blew up, we went to live with Grandpa Teddy full-time.

SYLVIA KIRK, MY MOTHER, WAS TWENTY-
nine when her life blew up, and it wasn't the first
time. Back then, I could see that she was pretty, but
I didn't realize how young she was. Only ten myself,
I felt anyone over twenty must be ancient, I guess,
or I just didn't think about it at all. To have your life
blow up four times before you're thirty would take
something out of anyone, and I think it drained
from my mom just enough hope that she never quite
built her confidence back to what it once had been.

When it happened, school had been out for
weeks. Sunday was the only day that the community center didn't have summer programs for kids,
and I was staying with Mrs. Lorenzo that late afternoon and evening. Mrs. Lorenzo, once thin, was
now a merry tub of a woman and a fabulous cook.
She lived on the second floor and accepted a little
money to look after me when there were no other
options, primarily when my mom sang at Slinky's,
the blues joint, three nights a week. Sunday wasn't

one of those three, but Mom had gone to a big-money neighborhood for a celebration dinner, where she was going to sign a contract to sing five nights a week at what she described as "a major venue," a swanky nightclub that no one would ever have called a joint. The club owner, William Murkett, had contacts in the recording industry, too, and there was talk about putting together a three-girl backup group to work with her on some numbers at the club and to cut a demo or two at a studio. It looked like the big break wouldn't be a steak-house waitress job.

We expected her to come for me after eleven o'clock, but it was only seven when she rang Mrs. Lorenzo's bell. I could tell right off that something must be wrong, and Mrs. Lorenzo could, too. But my mom always said she didn't wash her laundry in public, and she was dead serious about that. When I was little, I didn't understand what she meant, because she did, too, wash her laundry in the communal laundry room in the basement, which had to be as public as you could wash it, except maybe right out in the street. That night, she said a migraine had just about knocked her flat, though I'd never heard of her having one before. She said that she hadn't been able to stay for the dinner with her new boss. While she paid Mrs. Lorenzo, her lips were pressed tight, and there was an intensity, a power, in her eyes, so that I thought she might set anything ablaze just by staring at it too long.

When we got up to our apartment and she closed the door to the public hall, she said, "We're going to pack up all our things, our clothes and things. Daddy's coming for us, and we're going to live with him from now on. Won't you like living with your grandpa?"

His house was nicer than our apartment, and I said so. At ten, I had no control of my tongue, and I also said, "Why're we moving? Is Grandpa too sad to be alone? Do you really have a migraine?"

Instead of answering me, she said, "Come on, honey, I'll help you pack your things, make sure nothing's left behind."

I had my own bright green pressboard suitcase that pretty much held all my clothes, though we needed to use a plastic department-store shopping bag for the overflow.

As we were packing, she said, "Don't be half a man when you grow up, Jonah. Be a good man like your grandpa."

"Well, that's who I want to be. Who else would I want to be like but Grandpa?"

Not daring to put it more directly, what I meant was that I had no desire to grow up to be like my father. He walked out on us when I was eight months old, and he came back when I was eight years old, but then he walked out on us again before my ninth birthday. The man didn't have a commitment problem; the word wasn't in his vocabulary. In those days, I worried he might come back again, which would have been a calamity, considering all his problems. Among other things, he wasn't able to love anyone but himself.

Still, Mom had a weak spot for him. If he showed up, she might go with him again, which is why I didn't say what was in my heart.

"You've met Harmon Jessup," she said. "You remember?"

"Sure. He owns Slinky's, where you sing."

"You know I quit there for this other job. But I don't want you thinking your mother's flaky."

"Well, you're not, so how could I think it?"

Folding my T-shirts into the shopping bag, she said, "I want you to know I quit for another reason, too, and a good one. Harmon just kept getting . . . way too close. He wanted more from me than just my singing." She put away the last T-shirt and looked at me. "You know what I mean, Jonah?"

"I think I know."

"I think you do, and I'm sorry you do. Anyway, if he didn't get what he wanted, I wasn't going to have a job there anymore."

Never in my life, child or man, have I been hotheaded. I think I have more of my mother's genes than my father's, probably because he was too incomplete a person to have enough to give. But that night in my room, I got very angry, very fast, and I said, "I hate Harmon. If I was bigger, I'd go hurt him."

"No, you wouldn't."

"I darn sure would."

"Hush yourself, sweetie."

"I'd shoot him dead."

"Don't say such a thing."

"I'd cut his damn throat and shoot him dead."

She came to me and stood looking down, and I figured she must be deciding on my punishment for talking such trash. The Bledsoes didn't tolerate street talk or jive talk, or trash talk. Grandpa Teddy often said, "In the beginning was the word. Before all else, the word. So we speak as if words matter, because they do." Anyway, my mom stood there, frowning down at me, but then her expression changed and all the hard edges sort of melted from her face. She dropped to her knees and put her arms around me and held me tight.

I felt awkward and embarrassed that I had been talking tough when we both knew that if skinny little me went gunning for Harmon Jessup, he'd blow me off my feet just by laughing in my face. I felt embarrassed for her, too, because she didn't have anyone better than me to watch over her.

She looked me in the eye and said, "What would the sisters think of all this talk about cutting throats and shooting?"

Because Grandma worked in Monsignor McCarthy's office, I was fortunate to be able to attend Saint Scholastica School for a third the usual tuition, and the nuns who ran it were tough ladies. If anyone could teach Harmon a lesson he'd never forget, it was Sister Agnes or Sister Catherine.

I said, "You won't tell them, will you?"

"Well, I really should. And I should tell your grandpa."

Grandpa's father had been a barber, and Grandpa's mother had been a beautician, and they had run their house according to a long set of rules. When their children occasionally decided that those rules were really nothing more than suggestions, my great-grandfather demonstrated a second use for the strap of leather that he used to strop his straight razors. Grandpa Teddy didn't resort to corporal punishment, as his father did, but his look of extreme disappointment stung bad enough.

"I won't tell them," my mother said, "because you're such a good kid. You've built up a lot of credit at the First Bank of Mom."

After she kissed my forehead and got up, we went into her room to continue packing. The apartment came furnished, and it included a bedroom vanity with a three-part mirror. She trusted me to take everything out of the many little drawers and put all of it in this small square carrier that she called a train case, while she packed her clothes in two large suitcases and three shopping bags.

She wasn't finished explaining why we had to move. I realized many years later that she always felt she had to justify herself to me. She never did need to do that, because I always knew her heart, how good it was, and I loved her so much that sometimes it hurt when I'd lie awake at night worrying about her.

Anyway, she said, "Honey, don't you ever get to thinking that one kind of people is better than another kind. Harmon Jessup is rich compared to me, but he's poor compared to William Murkett."

In addition to owning the glitzy nightclub where she'd been offered five nights a week, Murkett had several other enterprises.

"Harmon is black," she continued. "Murkett is white. Harmon had nearly no school. Murkett went to some upper-crust university. Harmon is a dirty old tomcat and proud of it. Murkett, he's married with kids of his own and he's got a good reputation. But under all those differences, there's no difference. They're the same. Each of them is just half a man. Don't you ever be just half a man, Jonah."

"No, ma'am. I won't be."

"You be true to people."

"I will."

"You'll be tempted."

"I won't."

"You will. Everyone is."

"You aren't," I said.

"I was. I am."

She finished packing, and I said, "I guess then you don't have a job, that's why we're going to Grandpa's."

"I've still got Woolworth's, baby."

I knew there were times when she cried, but she never did in front of me. Right then, her eyes were as clear and direct and as certain as Sister Agnes's eye. She was a lot like Sister Agnes in fact, except that Sister Agnes couldn't sing a note and my mom was way prettier.

She said, "I've got Woolworth's and a good voice and time. And I've got you. I've got everything I need."

I thought of my father then, how he kept leaving us, how we wouldn't have been in that fix if he'd kept even half his promises, but I couldn't vent. My mom had never dealt out as much punishment as the one time I said that I hated him, and though I didn't think I should be ashamed for having said it, I was ashamed just the same.

The day would come when despising him would be the least of it, when he would flat-out terrify me.

We had no sooner finished packing than the doorbell rang, and it was Grandpa Teddy, come to take us home with him.

4

THE *FIRST* TIME MY MOTHER'S LIFE FELL apart was when she found out that she was pregnant with me. She'd been accepted into the music program at Oberlin, and she had nearly a full scholarship, but before she could even start her first year, she learned I was on the way. She said she really didn't want to go to Oberlin, that it was her parents' idea, that she wanted to fly on what talent she had, not on a lot of music theory that might stifle her. She wanted instead to work her way from one dinky club to another less dinky and steadily up, up, up, getting *experience*. She claimed I came long just in time to save her from Oberlin, and maybe I believed that when I was a kid.

She'd taken a year off between high school and college, and her father had used a connection to get her an age exemption and a gig in a piano bar, because she was a piano man, too. In fact, she was good on saxophone, primo on clarinet, and learning guitar fast. When God ladled out talent, He spilled the whole bucket on Sylvia Bledsoe. The bar was also a restaurant, and the cook—not the chef, the cook—was Tilton Kirk. He was twenty-four, six years her senior, and each time she took a break, he was right there with the charm, which as far as I'm concerned, he got from a different source than the one that gave my mom her talent.

He was a handsome man and articulate, and as sure as he knew his name, he knew that he was going places in this world. All you had to do was say hello, and he'd tell you where he was going: first from cook to chef, and then into a restaurant of his own by thirty, and then two or three restaurants by the time he was forty, however many he wanted. He was a gifted cook, and he gave young Sylvia Bledsoe all kinds of tasty dishes refined to what he called the Kirk style. He gave her me, too, though it turned out that taking care of children wasn't part of the Kirk style.

To be fair, he knew she'd have the baby, that the Bledsoes would not tolerate anything else, and he never once put any pressure on her about that. He did the right thing, he married her, and after that he pretty reliably did the wrong thing.

I was born on June 15, 1957, which was when the Count Basie band became the first Negro band ever to perform in the Starlight Room of the Waldorf-Astoria Hotel in New York City. *Negro* was the word in those days. On July 6, tennis star Althea Gibson, another Negro, won the All-England title at Wimbledon, also a first. And on August 29, the Civil Rights Act, proposed by President Eisenhower the previous year, was finally voted into law by Congress; soon thereafter, Ike would start using the national guard to desegregate schools. By comparison, my entrance into the world wasn't big news, except to my mom and me.

Trying to ingratiate himself with Sylvia's parents, well aware of Grandpa Teddy's musical heroes, my father chose to name me Jonah Ellington Basie Hines Eldridge Wilson Hampton Armstrong Kirk. Even all these years later, almost everyone has heard of Duke Ellington, Count Basie, Earl "Fatha" Hines, Lionel Hampton, and Louis Armstrong. Time doesn't treat all talent equally, however, and Roy Eldridge is known these days pretty much only to aficionados of big band music. He was one of the greatest trumpeters of all time. Electrifying. He played with Gene Krupa's legendary band from the late 1930s through the early war years, when Anita O'Day was changing what everyone thought a girl singer ought to be. The Wilson in my name is for Teddy Wilson, whom Benny Goodman called the greatest musician in dance music of the day. He played with Goodman, then started his own band, which didn't last long, and then he played largely in a sextet. If you can find any of the twenty sides that he recorded with his band, you'll hear a piano man of incomparable elegance.

With all those names to live up to, I sometimes

wished I'd been born just Jonah Kirk. But I guess because I was half Bledsoe, anyone who ever admired my grandpa—which was everyone who knew him—would have looked at me with some doubt that I could ever shape myself into a man like him.

The day I was born, Grandpa Teddy and Grandma Anita came to the hospital to see me, first through a window in the nursery and then in my mother's arms when I was brought to her room. My father was there as well, and eager to tell Grandpa my full name. Although I was the center of attention, I have no memory of the moment, maybe because I was impatient to start piano lessons.

According to my mom, the revelation of my many names didn't go quite like my father intended. Grandpa Teddy stood bedside, nodding in recognition each time Tilton—who was cautious enough to keep the bed between them—revealed a name. But when the final name had been spoken, Grandpa traded glances with Grandma, and then he frowned and stared at the floor as if he noticed something offensive down there that didn't belong in a hospital.

Now, you should know Grandpa had a smile that could melt an ice block and leave the water steaming. And even when he wasn't smiling, his face was so pleasant that the shyest of children often grinned on first sight of him and walked right up to him, a stranger, to say hello to this friendly giant. But when he frowned and you knew that you might be the reason he frowned, his face made you think of judgment day and of whatever pathetic good deeds you might be able to cite to balance the offenses you had committed. He didn't look furious, didn't even scowl, merely frowned, and at once an uneasy silence fell upon the room. No one feared Grandpa Teddy's anger, because few people if any had ever seen it. If you evoked that frown, what you feared was his disapproval, and when you learned that you had disappointed him, you realized that you *needed* his approval no less than you needed air, water, and food.

Although Grandpa never put it in words for me, one thing I learned from him was that being admired gives you more power than being feared.

Anyway, there in the hospital room, Grandpa Teddy frowned at the floor so long, my father reached out for my mother's hand, and she let him hold it while she cradled me in one arm.

Finally Grandpa looked up, considered his son-in-law, and said quietly, "There were so many big bands, swing bands, scores of them, maybe hundreds, no two alike. So much energy, so much great music. Some people might say it was swing music as much as anything that kept this country in a winning mood during the war. You know, back then I played with a couple of the biggest and best, also with a couple not as big but good. So many memories, so many people, quite a time. I did admire all those names between Jonah and Kirk, I did very much admire them. I loved them. But Benny Goodwin, he was as good as any and a stand-up guy. Charlie Barnet, Woody Herman, Harry James, Glenn Miller. Artie Shaw, for heaven's sake. *The* Artie Shaw. 'Begin the Beguine,' 'Indian Love Call,' 'Back Bay Shuffle.' There are so many names to reckon with from those days, this poor child would need the entire sheet of stationery just for his letterhead."

My mom got the point, but my father didn't. "But, Teddy, sir, all those names—they aren't our kind."

"Well, yes," Grandpa said, "they're not *directly* in the bar and restaurant business, like you are, but their work has put so many people in the mood to celebrate that they've had an impact on your trade. And they most surely are my kind and Sylvia's kind, aren't they, Anita?"

Grandma said, "Oh, yes. They're my kind, too. I love musicians. I married one. I gave birth to one. And, dear, you forgot the Dorsey brothers."

"I didn't forget them," Grandpa said. "My mouth just went dry from naming all those names. Freddy Martin, too."

"That tenor sax of his, the sweetest tone ever," Grandma said. "Claude Thornhill."

"The best of the best bands," she declared. "And he was one *funny* man, Claude was."

By then, my father got the message, but he didn't want to hear it. He had a big chip on his shoulder about race, and he probably had good reason, probably a list of good reasons. Nevertheless, for the sake of family harmony, maybe he should at least have added Thornhill and Goodman to my name, but he couldn't bring himself to do that.

He said, "Hey, look at the time. Gotta get to the restaurant." After he kissed my mom and kissed me, he hugged Anita, nodded at Grandpa Teddy, said, "Sir," and skedaddled.

So that was my first family gathering on my first day in the world. A little tense.

The *second* time that my mother's life fell apart was eight months later, when my father walked out on us. He said that he needed to focus on his career. He couldn't sleep with a crying baby in the next room. He claimed to have a potential backer for a restaurant, so he might be able to go from cook to chef in his own place, and even if it would be a hole in the wall, he would be moving up faster than originally planned. He really needed to stay focused, do his work at the restaurant, and pursue this new opportunity. He promised he'd be back. He didn't say when. He told her he loved us. It was always surprisingly easy for him to say that. He promised to send money every week. He kept that promise for four weeks. By then, my mom had gotten the job at Woolworth's lunch counter *and* her first singing gig at a dump called the Jazz Cave, so it was a difficult time, but only difficult, nothing serious yet.

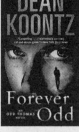

Watch for

the unforgettable conclusion to

#1 *New York Times* bestselling author

# DEAN KOONTZ's

Odd Thomas series

---

# Saint
# Odd

---

Coming December 2014

Visit
# DeanKoontz.com
Sign up for
**Dean's newsletter**
for news, previews,
and more!

**Join Dean on Facebook:**
Facebook.com/DeanKoontzOfficial

**Follow Dean on Twitter:**
@DeanKoontz